PYRAMID GAME

Pixel Dust Book Two

D. PETRIE

MOUNTAINDALE
PRESS

ACKNOWLEDGMENTS

I started this series because I wanted to tell a story. A story of friends saving a game that they loved. I wrote it for myself because, well, it was fun.

To my surprise people liked its quirky characters and ridiculous action. Now, with all of your support, I get to do more, and the world of Noctem gets to grow. For that I am grateful. So thank you to everyone who picked up a copy, left a review, told a friend, or commented on a post. It's because of all of you that I get to do this.

In addition, thank you to my betas Andy, Tara, Kevin, Sean, and Caitlin, as well as my amazing wife Sam and everyone at Mountaindale Press who keep me motivated.

PROLOGUE

Light swept across the night sky in a cascade of shimmering particles as the barrier surrounding the Palace of the Six Wolves failed. The released energy fell like snow across the city of Torn. The roar of engines shook the heavens as two hundred heavy transport ships circled like vultures.

The imperial fleet of the House of Serpents had arrived.

Doors of each craft slid open with enthusiasm—a thousand mercenaries ready to dive into action. They rained down upon the palace like hailstones, each throwing a glass bottle at the ground before landing. Most timed it right, landing with a shockwave of sparks and wind as the item bled away the kinetic energy of their fall. Some were not so lucky. Bodies hit the ground. An acceptable loss, as the rest pushed forward.

The small force of palace guards that stood in their way put up no resistance. Instead, they turned tail and ran, only stopping when they were safe inside the main gates. Laughs and taunts were heard among the attackers as they flooded onto the palace grounds.

It was going to be easier than they thought.

Then a lone figure stepped out onto the main dome of the

palace. The dark gothic robes of a *Cauldron* mage drifted behind him as he walked. His stride was slow but purposeful to match his class, its high damage potential equal only to the care that each spell took to brew. Silver chains coiled through the handful of braids in his long, black hair. They gleamed in the cold light of the moon as his presence darkened the scene.

He ran a hand down his closely-cropped beard and took a moment to survey the oncoming force. Then he snapped open the caster on his wrist, a crimson circle materializing above the crystal that sat at the bracelet's center. He pulled a white velvet pouch from his robe and emptied its contents into the glowing ring. The small selection of items vanished, swallowed up by the void inside to be shaped into something more.

With a stern expression, he waited until the circle shrank into a single point of glowing power. He reached forward as a sigil appeared in the air before him and slapped his hand flat against it. The pattern in the air shined brighter for every second he remained in contact until concentric layers of power appeared around it.

Then he spoke.

His voice boomed, so loud that even the incoming army on the ground could hear him over the distance and the noise of the engines above.

"In the name of Lady Amelia of House Winter Moon, you shall not pass!"

He closed his fist the instant the last word left his lips, and a bolt of lightning slammed into the ground. On contact, it shot out in all directions. The attack ripped through the mercenaries below, killing everyone within fifty feet of the palace gates. A mist of sparkling glitter drifted through the air in their place.

To the other fighters on the ground, the sheer destructive power of the display should have given reason to run. They didn't. They were getting paid, after all. Instead, they ran past those who were unlucky enough to be caught in the devastation without looking back.

The dark mage raised his sights from the chaos below as one

of the transport ships banked toward him, its pilot determined to earn a bit of extra hard. The mage could have run or dodged, but the fight was already over for him. His single attack had drained all of his mana.

A grin crept across his face.

He had bought enough time, and really, that was all he had to do. Throwing his arms out wide, he stood his ground in defiance as the ship slammed into the dome.

◆ ◆

Deep within the palace, a distant rumble sent a trickle of dust falling from the ceiling of the library where Lady Amelia pored over several books. She scratched in lines of text with a heavy pen, faster than she had ever worked before. Chips of stone landed on her shoulder as the name of one of her party members vanished from the tattooed readout on her wrist. Her Archmage was dead. She suppressed an annoyed eye twitch and continued to work. There wasn't time to be irritated. She had to finish. The fate of her city, no, the fate of all Noctem depended on it.

Finally, she slammed a book shut and stood, knocking over her chair in the process. She didn't pick it up. It didn't matter. It wouldn't be her chair much longer anyway. She snatched up the long, curved saber leaning against the door frame, taking a brief moment to feel its weight in her hand. It was a strange sword for a *Blade* class, its hilt lacking a cross guard or tsuba, but then again, she was not an average swordswoman. Amelia tightened her grip around the beloved saber and licked at her teeth in preparation, then burst into the hallway.

Her Knight, an enormous faunus covered in thick muscle, stepped forward from a small party of guards. The horns of a ram curled around the woman's head like a helmet. Her hand bore the emblem of a *Rage* class. It was an unorthodox choice for the First Knight of their house with its focus on offense over defense, but like Amelia herself, Winter Moon was an unorthodox house.

"Kashka, how many are there?" Lady Amelia looked up at the massive woman.

"Hundreds, with more landing every second." The *Rage* rested her rusty claymore on her shoulder.

Amelia stared down the hall as the long, furry ears of a reynard twitched atop her head, her tail wagging lazily behind her. "And Klaxon?" She gestured to the space on her wrist where his name had been listed as part of her party. "Was he able to slow them down?"

"The Archmage has fallen," Kashka tightened her grip on the handle of her claymore, "but he took plenty of the Serpent's men with him."

"Heh, that sounds like a good way to die." Amelia bowed her head. "It wasn't in vain. We may lose our claim on Torn tonight, but I'll be damned if I let the House of Serpents take all of Noctem."

"Damn right." The *Rage* readied her sword as the sound of combat reached them from down the hall.

"Still glad you signed on as my First Knight?" Amelia patted the back of her hand against Kashka's worn, leather armor. The *Rage* nodded, getting a warm smile from Amelia in return. "Okay, you're with me. The rest of you," she turned to the small party, "make them work for every inch they take."

"It will be our pleasure." The leader of the party bowed his head before leading the others toward the sounds of violence.

Amelia watched them go before drawing her saber, Corpse Maker, from its narrow sheath. A faint mist drifted from its edge. "Let's go." The *Rage* fell in line behind her, and they sprinted in the other direction.

The palace was under siege as the Serpent's mercenaries pushed forward with relentless fervor, stepping over their dead as they did. Amelia didn't hold back either when she came upon a party of six finishing off a few of her men.

Their leader stumbled when he saw her like he'd expected

her to have evacuated long ago. Surprise was on her side. She laughed as the edge of her blade slipped past his defenses.

Amelia wasn't one to flee.

Using the length of the Corpse Maker to her advantage, she pulled the saber from the man's throat and spun back on the enemies behind her. In almost the same motion, her blade sliced through the group. One scratch was all she needed as the dark mist flowed into each of their wounds. Crimson light streaked across their skin before fading away, leaving dark veins of color that spread through their flesh. They fell one by one, and she wasn't even winded.

The two remaining combatants, a *Shield* and *Cauldron* stood before her, hesitating, clearly startled by the speed at which she dispatched their cohorts.

Her long hair fell across her eyes in a mass of flaming red curls as she glared daggers at them. Her ears flipped back at the sound of a bowstring from behind. She didn't turn. She didn't have to. Amelia knew Kashka had her back. That was what a having a Knight was for.

Flipping her sword back, she held it downward with both hands in preparation for her next strike. The enemy *Shield* brought up his gauntlet, activating the barrier of energy it generated. The *Cauldron* behind him tossed a few ingredients into the glowing circle that hovered above his caster.

Amelia darted forward, low to the ground. The *Shield* responded well, adjusting his stance to block. Instead of attacking, she rolled past him, hopping back to her feet behind. She swept her blade through the *Cauldron's* throat before they could activate their spell.

With the momentum of the strike, Amelia continued toward the opposite wall where she kicked off with one foot to redirect her attack. Confusion struck the *Shield* as the tip of her blade punctured his breastplate. She didn't stop there, shoving her prey back until the hilt of her saber was buried in his chest.

"You good over there, Kashka?" Amelia turned, pulling her saber free as the man fell to his knees and vanished.

The burly *Rage* gave her a simple nod as she withdrew her rusty claymore from the chest of the last remaining enemy.

From there, they tore their way straight to the heart of the palace in a marathon of carnage and death. Amelia exploded into the throne room, finding it empty. Kashka moved fast to secure the large doors of the great hall with a thick cross beam.

"What now?" The *Rage* gave an awkward shrug.

"We wait." Amelia ascended to the throne for what she knew would be the last time.

The pelts of various monsters lay draped over the arms and back of the chair, covering its ornate carvings beneath a layer of fur. It was a little crude, but the pelts made the stone chair far more comfortable. The furs were an addition of her own, which Amelia thought appropriate, considering she had murdered her way to the seat of power to begin with.

Though nothing lasts forever.

She lay her blade across her lap unsheathed, letting its mist drift across her legs. *Soon*, she thought. Her tail swished beside her as silence set in.

Just when Kashka began to relax, the sound of footsteps bled through the door, continuing for a few minutes. Then they stopped.

"You should probably take cover." Amelia leaned back in her throne.

The eyes of the huge *Rage* widened as she ducked behind her sword. An instant later, the massive doors exploded inward with a burst of flame and smoke, sending a shower of debris into Kashka's weapon.

Amelia remained seated as splinters of wood fell at her feet. She wasn't one to flinch. Her gaze settled on the smoldering hole.

Suddenly, a dozen *Blades* flooded into the hall, their swords drawn before the dust had time to settle. They were followed by twice as many *Leaf* class players, arrows already nocked to their bows. Mages were next, a few *Cauldrons* followed by a lone *Venom*, his caster open and ready to inflict debuffs at the first sign of trouble. Several *Breath Mages* brought up the rear, hiding behind the others to heal from relative safety. Amelia's lone protector, Kashka, First Knight of House Winter Moon, stood before the horde, her pledge of loyalty staying true.

Finally, a *Shield* class entered, followed by a *Coin* in a long, green coat. The *Shield* was a monster of a man, gruff and clad in black armor. He wore an unsettling grin on his roguish face that made him look a little too excited to be at war. The *Coin* was short in comparison but far more elegant. Near perfect cheekbones and youthful face reminded Amelia of a model from a clothing catalog. He wore a smile as well, almost seeming friendly, though his eyes were dangerous. A crown of gold wrapped around his head, splitting in the front into two points of curling filigree. It looked as if it had always belonged there below his stylishly tousled brown hair. Strangely, he carried no dagger or grappling hook, the standard equipment of his class. It was as if he simply didn't need them.

His eyes locked on the throne. "I'm so glad to finally meet you, Lady Amelia."

"Yes, Lord Berwyn." Amelia forced a smile. "I hope you'll forgive me if I don't get up."

Berwyn laughed and pushed his coat back so that he could slip his hands into his pockets. "Oh, don't worry about it. I just wish we could have met sooner. You never come to my parties. I have invited you, you know."

"True, true." She leaned her chin on one hand. "I must admit that I have spent far too little time indulging in the frivolities of life in Noctem, like you. My attentions have been elsewhere." She ran one hand across one of her pelts, making sure the act was as overdramatic as possible.

"Fair enough." He shrugged and took a step closer toward her Knight. "Although, I must say, I wish we had gotten better acquainted, after seeing you in person. I can tell that you're a woman of considerable beauty, and I do enjoy spending time with your kind. I have always found reynard women," he gave her a toothy grin, "exotic." He bowed, keeping his eyes trained on her throat.

Amelia grimaced as if she'd bit into a piece of rotting meat. "I prefer not to offer my company to snakes." She was done with the play-acting. "Now, if you have a valid reason for defiling my territory with your house's presence, I would have to request that you leave. You're too late anyway. I no longer have what you want. I spent it." She grinned back at him, spacing her next few words out. "All. Of. It. Active farming territories for my people and bounties on everything, including you. I bought everything available. So, you'll get no spoils here. The treasury of Torn is gone."

Berwyn's face fell, leaving just his dangerous stare resting on her throat. "Alright, I can be patient for another week." He motioned to his *Shield* in black armor and stepped aside. "Kill them please, Mr. Ripper."

Amelia stood with saber in hand as Kashka moved forward to defend.

The dark *Shield*, Ripper, activated his gauntlet, but instead of producing an energy barrier, its clawed fingers began to glow an angry red. Amelia's attention fell on the gauntlet; she had only heard rumors of it.

That was when a pair of women, one reynard and one faunus, dropped from the ceiling's rafters to either side of Kashka. The faunus, another *Coin*, slipped a grappling line around the *Rage's* neck before retracting it back into her wrist launcher. The wire tightened around Kashka's throat. Being significantly smaller, the *Coin* shot back up toward the ceiling where she had looped the line over a beam. She caught a wall sconce with her free hand to stop her accent, and Kashka's feet lifted off the ground. Her rusty claymore clattered to the floor as panic filled her eyes.

Hanging wasn't enough to kill in Noctem, but still, the psychological effect must have been devastating. At least she didn't have to endure it for long. The other woman who had leaped from the rafters drew a pistol and fired three rounds, holstering it again within the space of a heartbeat. Kashka's body hit the floor in a crumpled heap.

Amelia was stunned by the savagery of the attack, so much that she almost forgot to fight back. Then it was too late. As soon as she started to move, the twenty archers lining the room fired.

The force of the arrows threw Amelia back into her throne, where a few more pinned her down, sending a sensation of pain prickling through her entire body. It faded to a dull throb. She glanced at the readout tattooed on her wrist, finding a third of her health remaining. Somehow, she hadn't taken enough damage to die. It was as if the arrows were fired with the intent of incapacitating, rather than killing.

She glared at Berwyn with as much intensity as she could muster. Then she laughed, her voice tinged with an unsettling rage. "You think this will stop me?" She fought against the arrows that held her back. "You may take my city but—"

"Okay, okay, I get it. You're tough," Berwyn interrupted her threats as he ascended to her immobilized body, "but you see, that's the point. It wouldn't be fun if you weren't." He leaned closer, his face only inches from hers as he touched her chin with one hand. Her flesh crawled as his fingertips slithered across her cheek. "It's all about the struggle. About the chase."

Suddenly, his fingers were pushed away by the cold energy of her cage as the barrier swept over her skin on reflex, forbidding him from touching her further.

Amelia gasped.

She had never needed to call on the ability before. She never thought she would. It had no purpose in combat. The cage was a failsafe that everyone had, meant to protect those younger and far more innocent than herself. In that moment, though, she was glad it was there. She didn't want him touching her.

"Okay." Berwyn laughed and clapped his hands, as if forcing her to use the ability gave him some kind of satisfaction.

"I think we're done here." He turned and stepped back down from the throne, gesturing back at her. "Have at her."

Two dozen bows fired as Amelia thought about what had happened. She was prepared to die but not to lose. The sickening sound of arrows hitting her body was the last thing she heard before the world of Noctem fell away.

Emily woke only ten minutes later, safe in her apartment in Salem, Massachusetts. She pulled off the slender headpiece that was her gateway to the game, Carpe Noctem, and tossed it aside. Apparently, it was late enough for her Somno to wake her up rather than respawning her back into Noctem.

She rolled over, pulling her comforter up around her head and groaned as she looked at the clock. It was already seven in the morning, and she had work in an hour. She groaned again, then sat up.

"I'll have to plot my revenge on my lunch break."

CHAPTER ONE

NIGHT ONE: THE PITCH

Clouds passed by as MaxDamage24 struggled to keep his focus on the cockpit window in front of him, his hands gripping the stick of his transport shuttle.

"Hey, Max?" Kirabell leaned on her hands, sitting like a child in the cushioned seat beside him. There was an excited sparkle in her eyes that didn't match her tone, which was level. Almost too level.

Max suppressed his eyebrow to keep it from climbing up his forehead. She was acting suspiciously. The last thing he wanted was to give her anything that she might interpret as a response.

"Hey?" she tried again, her tone still a little too even.

He continued to ignore her and focused on piloting the ship. Landing still wasn't his strongest skill. In the past, he'd sold off transports online for some quick money, so there wasn't a need to learn to fly. They usually teleported everywhere anyway, but since the ship had been a part of his payment from Checkpoint Systems after completing that insane mission last year, he was uncomfortable selling it. Plus, it was cool, and he liked it.

The craft was well armored, with a comfortable cockpit surrounded by wide panes of rectangular glass that made for some impressive views. Wings tilted up from the back like a bird's, each with an engine built in. Along with two additional engines attached below, that Kira had insisted were unnecessary, it was one of the fastest ships available.

The only thing he hated was the color. He'd wanted black, but his pint-sized partner had guilted him into letting her customize the outside, which was now a bright white. Like a happy cloud. At least he got to name it, sort of. He'd wanted to call the ship the Wind Breaker, but the consensus was that no one wanted to ride in something named after a fart joke. Thus, the Cloudbreaker took to the skies.

"Hey?" Kira leaned closer.

"No," Max grumbled as he decreased the power to the levitation plate that ran the length of the ship's underside.

"Hey, Max?"

"NO!"

Kira sunk back into her seat, pouting as Max cut the power.

He cringed as the craft dropped the last few feet before coming to a stop. Apparently, the ground wasn't as close as he thought it was, but the maneuver still passed for a landing in his book.

The hum of the engines faded, leaving them in silence. Kira wasted no time in filling it with another, "Hey, Max?"

"What!" he shouted, knowing that it was exactly what she wanted him to do.

Kira smiled from ear to ear, her violet eyes sparkling. "Do you think I could raise my leather craft skill enough to make a belt out of wrist watches?"

Max sighed as heavy as he could, hunched over, placing his forehead on the console of toggle switches before him. "No, I don't."

For a moment, her smile faded. "Yeah, you're probably right, it would probably be a waist of time." With that, she looked straight at him with her mouth wide open, as if to ask, get it?

"Let's go. It's almost time." Max ignored her joke and shifted in his chair to stand, causing the vinyl cushion to squeak in a way that was easily mistaken for something else.

Kira snorted at the sound.

"It was the chair!" Max defended, despite there being no other possibility since there was no need for a body to release gas in a virtual world. He wiggled back and forth anyway, unable to repeat the noise.

"It's still funny." Kira giggled as she turned to stand, producing an even more authentic squeak from her cushion.

"Nice, I should call you Kirasmell."

"No way. I smell amazing." She flipped her hair in his direction to give him an opportunity to see for himself.

Max ignored her and climbed out of his chair, leaving the fairy alone to smell herself. Of course, Noctem's system didn't process things like scents unless there was a sensory profile to load, like there was for some food items. Understanding that, whatever Kira smelled like, would depend on how Max's mind perceived her. He sped up as he walked toward the door. He wasn't about to admit that she smelled like freshly laundered sheets.

That would be awkward.

He stepped out onto the ground in the outskirts of Thrift, one of Noctem's six major cities. Stone dragons decorated its walls, and the towers of Castle Garant peeked over in the distance. It would have been nice to have landed on the airship docks inside the city since they had a better view, but that meant a docking fee of one hundred credits. Sure, it wasn't real money, but still, Max would rather spend it on bullets. Being a *Fury* class wasn't cheap, after all. As a tradeoff, they could walk through the city's moon flower gardens on the way in.

He passed under the wall's circular entrance, its carved dragons watching as Kirabell jogged to catch up, taking her place at his side. "It's odd, right?"

"What is?" Max pulled out a leather-bound journal and flipped to its map page, where a line inked itself from their location toward a waypoint located in the city.

Kira leaned over to see. "Like, why would Alastair suddenly invite everyone from the quest last year out together? We haven't heard from him in weeks. Why now? And why did he ask Farn to invite us for him instead of messaging us himself? And why would he pick karaoke of all things?"

"Well damn, Kira, when you say it like that, it sounds fishy as hell." Max considered it as he stared off down the garden path. "He's a busy guy though. Maybe he just wants to celebrate. It's been almost a year since we all met. That seems like something he would want to make note of."

"True." Kira hopped ahead of him and looked back. "I'm just glad he didn't pick a place in Torn. I don't want to get anywhere near that mess." She fell silent for a moment. "You ever been?"

Max snapped his journal shut and shoved it back into the item bag on his belt. "Been to where? To Torn? You know I have. We went there a week ago."

Kira brushed his answer away with her hand. "No, not Torn. I meant to karaoke."

"Nah. Not really my thing."

"Oh." Kira turned away to look at the iridescent flowers that lined their path.

Max raised an eyebrow. "Are you nervous?"

"No," she spouted before betraying her answer with a, "Maybe."

Max jumped on the opportunity, taking a few long strides to get ahead of her. "Ha! Is my snarky little fairy nervous about singing in front of people?"

Kira rolled her eyes. "Yeah, so what? In the real world, I have a goofy voice. I couldn't carry a tune, even if you gave me a bucket."

Max stared at her in silence before finally letting out a sigh. "As much as I hate to make you feel better, considering the twenty minutes of dad jokes I had to endure on the way here, I will put your mind at ease. None of us care what you sound like."

"Oh, thanks, you're so helpful," Kira forced through a layer of sarcasm.

Max kept walking. "It will be good to see everyone together again, though."

Kira perked up noticeably at the mention of the others. They had seen everyone pretty often over the year, especially Farnsworth, who had joined them on most nights and had taken over Max's farming duties, but they hadn't gotten everyone together all at once for months.

"I can't believe it's been almost a year already since Carver's whole apocalypse thing." Kira added air quotes on the word, apocalypse, which was what the group had been calling the mission that had brought them together. It seemed appropriate, after fighting the Four Horsemen.

"I can't believe it either." Max nudged her in the arm with his elbow. "Speaking of which, I know Ginger has been looking forward to seeing you."

"Ugh." Kira dropped her shoulders and folded her arms. "That's just because she wants to organize a beach day and won't go without me."

"That sounds fun. You should go. You could get yourself a cute, little swimsuit." Max gave her his most irritating grin.

"Yeah, no thanks. I do love swimming, but I'm not big on the idea of frolicking around in public without the rest of my gear on."

"I guess I can see that." Max stared off into the trees.

Kira glowered at him. "You're picturing it now, aren't you?"

"I plead the fifth." He held up one hand.

"At least you're honest."

Max shrugged. "I saw everything you got to offer last year anyway."

Kira covered her face with her hand. "Come on, man, you gotta stop reminding me of that."

Max laughed. He'd noticed that his partner had been dressing a little more feminine lately. He assumed it had something to do with the fact that she'd had to save the world in a frilly, white gown the year before. In the months since, she'd stopped wearing pants altogether in favor of a sleeveless dress with a hood and a window cut out in the back for her wings. According to her, it was easier to move in than her old gear.

Although, judging from the pair of tight shorts that she wore underneath, she was still worried about an uncooperative wind blowing in. It must have been her way of maintaining some of her real-world counterpart's masculinity, an effort that was undone by her next statement of, "Aww, cute," as they entered the street beyond the city's garden.

Kira bounced over to a small bakery to the side where she smooshed her face into the glass. She leaned in to look at the goods on display, inadvertently putting her own goods on display as she bent over with her rear in Max's direction. He ignored it—with a relative degree of success.

"No time for snacks. Besides, I'm sure there'll be plenty at the bar." He crossed his arms and kept walking.

"But they look so fluffy." She pointed at a row of small buns, baked into the shape of a lagopin, the crust on top suggesting the shape of long ears and a pair of wings.

"We're still not stopping."

Kira blew out a huff. "Fine, but we're coming back on the way out."

"Whatever."

Kira nodded before throwing in another, "Hey, Max?" under his radar.

"Yeah?" he responded, realizing the trap just as the words left his mouth.

Kira gave him a bright smile. "Do you think they have other pastries? I cannoli imagine the possibilities."

Max let out yet another a heavy sigh. "Why are you like this?"

CHAPTER TWO

Max arrived under a sign featuring a vertical line of letters in another language that he didn't recognize. He glanced down to Kira, who gave him a shrug, then checked the waypoint in his journal. They were in the right place. He plucked his inspector out of the back cover of the book and held the rectangle of glass in front of the sign. The word karaoke appeared, using the item's translator. He returned Kira's shrug and stepped inside.

Max expected to find a dim bar with a small stage, like what he'd seen on TV, but instead, they were greeted at a well-lit front desk by a polite reynard woman with fluffy, white ears. He leaned one elbow on the counter. "Hey, we're here to meet Alastair Coldblood."

The woman checked a page in a book in front of her for the ridiculous name of Checkpoint's CEO. "Sorry, I don't have any reservations under that name." She closed the book with a smile, then ran her eyes over him, letting them travel to his partner beside him. "I do have one for a Farnsworth, though."

Max jerked his arm off the counter and took a step back. He had thought that the woman had been an NPC. Most of the desk clerks in Noctem were, but from the knowing smile that she gave him, he was certain she was real. His mind began processing the situation. If she was real, then she was probably a Checkpoint Systems employee posing as an NPC.

What the hell did we walk into?

Max couldn't help but flash back to that night a year ago when he and Kira had walked blindly into a tavern's back room after receiving an anonymous message.

Kira took a step closer to his side.

Max hesitated. The smart thing to do was to turn and walk right back out the way they came. He didn't. Instead, he offered a weak, "Oh, that must be it," at the suggestion of Farnsworth's reservation.

The woman smiled back at him. "Great, she hasn't arrived yet, but a couple members of your party are already waiting in box sixteen. It's down the end on the right."

Max took a breath and started walking down the hall. "Something's up."

"Yup," Kira offered with little enthusiasm.

"It can't be anything too bad, right?" Max tried not to let his imagination get the better of him as he put his hand on the handle of a door marked with a silver sixteen. "I mean, Alastair's not a bad guy."

"True," Kira leaned her head to one side, "but we should probably stop trusting him so easily. We're pretty easy to trick, as it turns out."

Max entered into a small room lined with somewhat comfortable looking couches on three walls, the kind of furniture that you wouldn't sink into too far, making it easy to get up and down, and a large pane of glass hovered on one wall near the door above a single chair. They weren't the first to arrive.

Taking up the seats closest to one corner, were a *Leaf* and a *Blade*.

The *Leaf*, Kegan, sat so casually that it seemed to take effort. The well-tanned elf had his feet up with his hands behind his head, looking pretty much the same as usual. His black hair was still streaked with maroon and spiked up on the side like a character from an old JRPG. His sleeveless tunic and loose pants seemed comfortable, even with the large number of sashes wrapped around his waist. The only thing missing was his bow, which he must have stored in his inventory to save space in the small room.

Corvin, on the other hand, had done nothing but change through the year. He'd been climbing levels so fast after starting over as a *Blade* class that Max could hardly believe he had been the same timid player that they'd slain Nightmares with the year before. Hell, he'd had a new set of gear almost every time Max had seen him.

Corvin had also updated his avatar to represent his age closer. He was almost twenty after all, and he'd only been sixteen back when he created the character. The result was a mid-level reynard, far more badass than before. His black pants were reinforced with leather plates, while a matching hooded vest lined with white fur covered a plain gray tunic. Instead of the fabric wrap that he'd used to cover his basilisk eye, he now wore a small, leather eye patch at an angle. Black scales peeked out from underneath. Even his hair was longer, tied back loosely with leather cord. The only things that he'd left alone were his tall black fox ears and fluffy tail.

"What level are you now?" Kira looked him over, clearly impressed.

"I, ah," he stammered before answering, ruining his new image, "seventy-seven."

"Nice, you're halfway to catching up to us. We'll be able to play together in no time."

"Hope so." He nodded just before they were interrupted by a blur rushing through the door. It streaked across the room at record speed, leaping over Kegan's outstretched legs and capturing Kira in a tight embrace.

"Hi, Ginger, I missed you too." Kira let her body relax as if there was no use in resisting the woman.

"I love the new dress." The *Coin* released the annoyed fairy.

"Yes, I'm adorable. We have covered this fact." Kira straightened her clothing.

Ginger gave Max him a wink. "Don't worry, you're cute too."

He shrugged, trying to take the compliment from the beautiful *Coin* as nonchalant as possible. She was probably just being nice anyway. He hadn't upgraded his gear much, so he still resembled the same tactical, gunslinging pirate he always did.

He was about to pay the *Coin* a compliment in return but stopped as a couple players he didn't recognize entered the room behind her. "You brought friends?"

The pair stood in the door, awkwardly waiting to be introduced. Each wore the starting gear for their class, making it clear that they were new or at least still below level ten. The girl on the right was a reynard like Corvin, but carried the pistol of a *Fury* class like Max. The other was a deru with a pair of orange crystals poking out from his hair like horns.

Ginger motioned to the pair. "You remember my kids, Wren and Toby." She rolled her eyes. "Or should I say, Piper and Drakenstein."

"Hey." Piper glanced around the room before snapping her eyes back to Max. She looked young, which made sense since she was only sixteen. A single braid hung in her hair, most likely done forcefully by her mother. Max stepped out of the way so she could get by.

"Wait a sec." Kira stepped toward the boy. "Did you just mush Dracula and Frankenstein together for your name?"

"Maybe…" He stared down at the small woman. His avatar was tall and looked a couple years older than he actually was, maybe closer to eighteen. "And didn't you just mush the names of two popular fairies together to get yours, Kirabell?"

"Oh yeah, I definitely did that." Kira tilted her head and placed a hand to her chin, then snapped her fingers. "I'm just gonna call ya Drake. Cool? It's shorter and sounds better."

"I guess," responded Drake as if he had a choice.

Ginger and her family took the couch on the end, with

Piper sitting in the corner closest to Corvin. Kira and Max dropped into the middle of the remaining couch and conversed a few more minutes until the door opened again, this time for Alastair.

The CEO of Checkpoint Systems had come through the events of last year looking pretty good. Mostly because his ex-partner, Carver, had pissed off a lot of players after luring hundreds of them to their virtual doom. Since the man never resurfaced after causing all that trouble, he never got the opportunity to defend himself. In the wake of everything that went down, public opinion had swung in Alastair's favor, allowing him to set foot outside the Citadel in Valain without fear of being recognized. Which was why it took Max by surprise to find the man wearing mid-level *Cauldron* robes with a large hood that hid his face rather than his usual gear. It had been his standard outfit for trying to go unnoticed.

Something was definitely up.

Alastair pushed back his hood just as Farnsworth entered behind him. As usual, her gear made her look like a Viking raider, her curly hair tied back with a pair of braids hanging down to frame her face. A spattering of dark freckles adorned the brown skin of her cheeks. She smiled as soon as she saw Kira.

During the ordeal a year ago, the *Shield* had grown close with the fairy. Hell, Kira probably wouldn't have survived the quest without Farn. Though sometimes, after a life or death situation is over, people drift apart after realizing that they weren't as close as they thought. Kira and Farn had done the opposite. In the months that followed, the two had become annoyingly close, both of them always laughing and constantly talking about their favorite shows like a couple nerds.

As a result, their friendship also brought Farn and Max closer. Things had started a little awkward between them, but as time went on, he started to feel more comfortable around her. Like she was one of the guys. Not to mention, she was the best *Shield* he'd ever partied with. They pushed each other to new levels of badassery with every quest. Despite that, he was caught off guard when she passed over her BFF Kira and squished herself in beside him in the corner, her hip pressed against his, and he tried his best to act casual, catching Ginger's eye as he looked around the room. The *Coin* gave him a smug smile as Farn settled in next to him.

Alastair claimed the chair near the door and got situated. "Wow, I haven't been getting out much lately. I feel like it's been forever since I've seen all of you." He looked to Kira. "How've you been feeling? It's been a while since your last vacation, right?"

Max could feel the fairy's body tense at the question. "Oh, I'm fine."

Kira had been in and out of 'vacation' every few months, which was really just a nice way of saying quarantine. It wasn't a subject she talked about much. She wasn't sick or anything, but after being used as a guinea pig for Carver's experiments, she'd never fully returned to normal. The whole adventure had left her with the ability to connect to Noctem's servers without the use of a Somno system. The vacations were a way to counteract what Craver had done to her, keeping her away from any form of internet connection that her rewired brain might try to access.

Her first quarantine last year was spent in a literal cabin in the woods without even electricity. It had not been fun for her, nor did it actually fix the issue. Sure, her brain did return to normal for a time, but it wasn't permanent. Since then she had been forced to take three more vacations in a special electronically shielded apartment in one of Checkpoint's Florida offices. The small studio had been built special just for her, and it blocked all wifi and cellular networks to ensure she could sleep normally. It hadn't been proven that connecting without a Somno was harmful or not, but it didn't seem wise to take chances.

Max didn't think her vacations seemed so bad; the room was kept stocked with comics, and she got a week off work every now and then. Still, her brain being a part-time Somno emulator was obviously not something she wanted, but thanks to Carver, it had become a fact of her life. It wasn't hard to see why she didn't talk about it much.

Alastair gave her a warm smile. "I'm glad to hear you doing well. Just let me know if you need some time off."

"I will." Kira nodded.

Alastair turned back to the rest of the group. "Anyway, I know you're all probably excited about an evening of karaoke, but sadly, that will have to wait for another day."

"And here it comes." Max's jaw tightened as his suspicions were confirmed.

"Indeed, it does." Alastair's face grew serious. "We have things to discuss."

CHAPTER THREE

Ginger jumped a good foot in the air as the room erupted into chaos. The hairs on the back of her neck stood up, her mind flipping between fight and flight. Both of her children looked to her with confusion as Max leaped up from his chair.

The *Fury* stabbed an accusatory finger in Alastair's direction. "I knew it! Inviting us out at random, putting the reservation under Farn's name, and seriously, karaoke of all things?"

Ginger's mouth went dry as he listed off the reasons to be suspicious of the meeting. She couldn't believe she hadn't noticed anything strange about it until now. She probably would have figured it out sooner if she hadn't been distracted, but no, she had been too busy contemplating what Farn snuggling in so close next to Max a moment ago might mean. *Honestly, I could really spend less time thinking about other people's relationships.* Then again, what did it mean? Max and Farn would make a nice couple. She shook her head, shoving the question to the back of her mind for later.

Kegan's feet fell off the coffee table, clearly just as surprised by Max's outburst as she was.

"What is it?" Corvin glanced to Kira then back to Alastair. "Is Carver back?"

Farn jumped in, eyeing Alastair before he could answer, "Wait a sec, you used my name for this reservation?"

"What kind of mission is it this time?" Max jumped to the point.

Ginger leaned back and folded her arms in resignation. It was too late. She was already there, and her daughter would never let it go if they left now.

"Woah now, let's everyone just stay calm." Alastair held up his hands in front of him, deflecting questions from all sides. "I assure you all, I am absolutely not here to hire you for another ridiculous quest, and Carver is still missing. I'm just here to talk."

Ginger relaxed, sinking back down into the couch. *Maybe there isn't anything to worry about.*

Then Alastair cracked a villainous smile. "And I totally did not lure you all into a clandestine meeting where I used Farn's name as a cover and showed up in disguise so that it couldn't be traced back to me." Sarcasm flooded into his tone, cranking the tension in the room back up to eleven.

"Like I said, what's the job?" Max folded his arms, matching Ginger and creating a united front, like a pair of parents questioning their child. With that, the group quieted down.

Alastair leaned back in his chair. "I meant the part about not being here to hire you for a mission, mostly because the situation at hand has left me contractually unable to interfere. So that option is out. All I can do now is talk. What you all decide to do after, that is up to you."

Ginger arched an eyebrow, letting her curiosity get the better of her. She tugged it back down again before anyone noticed.

Max scoffed. "So, talk."

Alastair took a moment as if he wasn't sure how to start. "Okay, I assume you all know about the fall of Torn last night."

"Yeah, it got taken by the one-eyed snakes," Kegan commented, referring to the House of Serpents.

Ginger shot him an annoyed look and flicked her head toward her kids, who she had been trying to act mature in front of. It was a shame, considering she usually enjoyed that sort of humor.

Alastair sighed. "Yes, it was conquered by the Serpents. Thank you for making a dick joke, Kegan."

"No problem, that's what I'm here for."

"Anyway, the fall of Torn marked a point of no return for everyone in Noctem."

At that, Max and Kira looked at each other, clearly not following the conversation. Honestly, it had always surprised Ginger how out of touch the pair were with world events. *I guess that's what happens when you spend all your time in dungeons and only head into the cities to resupply.* In fact, both of them almost seemed to avoid player conflicts, like they just didn't care to get involved.

Ginger, however, didn't have a choice but to keep her thumb on the pulse of current affairs. It was part of her job at the Everleigh Club, which happened to be a brothel, or at least it was before she'd taken a leave of absence to spend time with her kids online. Prior to that, she'd spent time with clients belonging to houses all over Noctem and, in the process, heard all the gossip. The most interesting of which had always been about the game's kingdoms.

Noctem had taken a new approach to how its world operated. In such, only one city was actually controlled by Checkpoint Systems, while the other kingdoms and their territories were governed by the players. At any time, a well-organized house could seize control of any city. All they had to do was get their Lord or Lady to the throne and have them take a seat.

Well, maybe claiming a kingdom wasn't that easy. The throne was usually occupied by someone else, and they would have to surrender or abandon their city first, and that almost never happened. Most of the time, the previous ruler had been executed or assassinated. It was par for the course, really.

Years back, when the game had launched, cities changed hands more often than most people changed their sheets. Eventually, as the houses got more organized and rulers understood their positions more, they got better holding their thrones. The stronger houses even recruited contract users to defend their kingdoms. After that, Noctem's ruling structure gave the players a different kind of game to play. While users like Max and Kira were out fighting Nightmares, a select few were waging war and hatching plots of intrigue and espionage.

The only question was why. Why do all that just to sit in a fancy chair and call yourself king? Well, fame for one. Ginger had spent the night with more than a few Lords with their eyes set on the spotlight. With millions of users pledging loyalty to the territories, it wasn't hard to see why. Some rulers went public with their real-world identities, gaining endorsement deals, even making talk show appearances. Though, for those that kept their identities secret, such as Lord Berwyn of the House of Serpents, there were still plenty of perks. Getting their own palace to use however they wanted could make for some truly epic parties. Though, that was the icing on the cake.

What really made ruling a city worth it was the significant quantity of hard mercury, awarded to their treasury. Often referred to simply as hard, the substance was technically a crafting item, just plates of mercury held in solid form through an enchantment. What made it special was that it could be exchanged through Checkpoint for real-world currency. By giving it out to the ruling houses, it encouraged rulers to up the ante.

A kingdom with a coffer full of hard could resupply farming zones and offer one-time bounties for difficult monsters to keep their loyal subjects engaged in the game. Not to mention, there were always a few mercenaries or assassins willing to take on a task for a bit of hard. Of course, there were strict rules in how much a ruler could send to a single user at a time, and there was no way to transfer it to themselves, so they weren't going to get rich off the stuff. Still, even in Noctem, money was power. Ginger had learned that well enough during her years at the club.

Alastair rolled his eyes as he continued, probably just as surprised at Max and Kira for their lack of interest in Noctem's royalty. "Torn is the third city to fall under the control of Lord Berwyn and his Serpents. Now, he controls half of the world, and it doesn't seem like he plans to stop. I'm not exactly looking forward to the day that his army marches on Valain. 'Cause technically, he could do it within the rules of the game."

Max waved a hand dismissively. "So why don't you just have your clerics deal with him?"

"Unfortunately, that would also be considered interfering, and since he hasn't done anything to violate the rules so far, we can't really do that without a public backlash."

Farn leaned forward. "Okay, to play devil's advocate. If he takes over Noctem, how bad could that be? I mean, it's not like he's running around using other people's identities to make karaoke reservations or anything." She leveled her eyes at Alastair.

"True, sorry about that. But to answer your question, Carpe Noctem is a game, and people play it because it's fun."

Farn tapped a finger against her chin. "And Berwyn is ruining people's fun?"

"When Berwyn claimed the city of Reliqua as the capital of his empire months ago, he did it by assassinating the previous Lord. If he'd stopped there, it wouldn't have been a big deal, but after that, he used a portion of the city's hard to organize a small force of mercenaries to attack Sierra, which still had over half of its budget left in its treasury."

"Why is their budget important?" Drake chimed in, getting a sharp look from Ginger for participating.

"The budget is important because we give each city all that hard so that they can use it to keep the players in their territories happy and encourage them to play more. The problem is that Berwyn is using it all to fund his conquests instead of maintaining his kingdom. The result is that farming areas are running dry, and people are having trouble getting crafting materials. Which is making it hard to get decent gear. Which is making it hard to level up."

"Well, crap," Max leaned back and threw his feet up on the coffee table. "Didn't realize the hard you gave out had that kind of impact. We never pledged ourselves to a kingdom, so we didn't really notice."

"Yeah, we're kind of free agents." Kira gestured to herself and Max.

Ginger could understand that. After all, she'd maintained her own status as a Ronin too. She liked the freedom it granted, even if it meant she couldn't claim some of the rewards available. Though, now that she thought about it, she was curious. "How much hard do you give out anyway?" Ginger tried her best not to sound too interested.

"A little over twenty thousand bars to each city." Alastair leaned his cheek into one hand as if it wasn't that impressive.

Ginger ran the conversion in her head; then she nearly choked despite not eating anything. "That's like, three million dollars!"

Kegan breathed a quiet, "Damn."

Kira added a slow whistle as Farn's eyes widened.

Max snapped his fingers, pointing one at Alastair. "So if Berwyn just took Torn, how much does that give him on top of what he already had?"

"That's where we got lucky," Alastair dropped one hand to his lap. "He blew most of what he'd gained from Reliqua and Sierra on last night's invasion. But thanks to Lady Amelia, he got almost nothing from Torn. When the invasion started, she used her hard to purchase enough farming resources for months and placed bounties on everything and anyone she could. It was genius on her part. She'd figured out what Berwyn was after and denied him a win. If she hadn't, Berwyn would have gotten enough hard to make a move on Lucem or Thrift."

"So that should be it, right?" Farn crossed her legs and leaned on her armrest. "He can't conquer anything else without paying his army."

"Almost." Alastair held up one finger. "The problem is that the fourth anniversary of Noctem's launch is next week. At which time, the vault in Reliqua will be replenished with all three cities' hard."

Ginger's heart sped up. "That's nine million dollars."

The room fell silent, letting that sink in until Max spoke up, "So why don't the remaining cities attack him now while he's out of money?"

"That would be ideal, but both Lucem and Thrift have always remained neutral during conflicts. And it doesn't look like they will develop much of a military strategy in the next few days." Alastair placed his hands together and smiled before spreading his fingers back out toward the room. "That's why I have decided to share some information with all of you. You saved this world once before, so if anyone can do it again, it's you."

"What, you want us to take him out?" Max made finger guns with one hand and pantomimed shooting himself in the head.

Ginger would have preferred that he not suggest an assassination so casually in front of her children. Although it was a valid option.

"Perfect! That would fix everything," Alastair said through a layer of sarcasm before sinking into his chair a little deeper. "Unfortunately, things won't be that easy, thanks to someone breaking the Nightmare contract system," he looked at Kira before continuing, "Berwyn has gotten his hands on an item that makes assassination impossible."

The rest of the group glowered at the fairy, who had inadvertently altered the game's contract system, causing it to hand out items or abilities created from the players subconscious.

"What?" Kira squirmed under everyone's gaze. "It's not like I meant to."

"Anyway," Alastair let her off the hook. "We know Berwyn has at least one contract item, and we think he has a second. The one we know of is a crown that he never takes off. Its effect stops him from taking any form of damage."

"Well that's just broken." Farn slapped a hand down on the sofa.

"There is a catch." Alastair held up a hand. "It will only work so long as he doesn't draw a weapon or use an ability."

Ginger chewed that over. "Okay, so he can't fight."

Kira leaned in. "But as long as he can get someone else to fight for him, he's un-killable."

Alastair released a heavy sigh. "And he's already paid up with a few of Noctem's nastiest mercenaries."

Max fidgeted like a student sitting through a boring lecture. "So what do you want us to do about it?"

"Well, as I said, I'm just here to talk. It would be irresponsible for me to suggest anything. But…" Alastair flashed a grin worthy of a Bond villain, "he does have a weakness that I don't think anyone has thought of. It's nothing that's a secret, but it's not well known either. And if I were to tell you and you were to come up with an idea to stop him on your own, well, then who would I be to stop you?"

"Go on." Kira eyed him incredulously.

Alastair took a moment to glance at the door as if giving everyone a chance to leave before saying more. No one did. Instead, everyone leaned forward, even Ginger, despite her best efforts to act like a disapproving adult. Even her kids were on the edge of their seats.

Alastair cleared his throat. "There is, let's call it a misconception, on how the cities handle their hard. I'll use Berwyn as an example. When he hires a player as part of his army, the most he can transfer to them is four bars per job. Now, they can still claim bounties or take another job to get more, but the most they can carry in their virtual inventory is ten bars which, if you're doing the math, is about two thousand dollars' worth."

"Go on," Kira repeated, this time in unison with Max.

"Now, no one has really thought of this because it never actually happens since it takes a lot of work to get that much hard, but let's just say, for argument's sake, that a mercenary has maxed out their virtual inventory and has yet to transfer the rest of his hard to Checkpoint for payment. And with all that, he forgets and takes on a bounty. He would have to carry the additional hard in his item bag. Now, let's say he drops a bar from his bag and logs out. Who would that belong to?"

Corvin raised his hand for a second before dropping it back down and speaking without waiting to be called on, "No one, technically."

"Exactly. So when it comes down to it, in Noctem, possession is ten-tenths of the law, since all players have a virtual inventory that's coded to their character data to keep their items safe. Players can also store things in their house vaults or get an additional vault in any city. All of which work the same way, in that they dematerialize an item and store it as data so that there's no way for anyone to steal it."

Ginger's heart raced as she began to see where he was going.

Alastair paused dramatically and swept his eyes over the room. "The misconception is that the royal vaults work the same but with a larger virtual capacity. But in fact, they're really just a secure room in the palace with stacks of hard physically piled up in them. And technically, the only thing that designates ownership of that hard is that it exists within that room."

"Holy crap!" Kegan sprang upright. "You want us to rob him."

Alastair said nothing. Instead, the corner of his mouth curled up. Gasps filled the room as Ginger waited for someone to argue.

No one did.

"What?" Ginger choked out, shocked that she of all people had to be the voice of reason. "You want us to steal nine million dollars' worth of hard. Do you have any idea how insane that sounds?"

Alastair tilted his head from side to side. "Hypothetically speaking, if a group of talented individuals was to gain access to the vault and successfully remove its contents from the city, then all that hard would belong to them."

Conflict erupted within Ginger's mind, the *Coin* versus the mother. "But what if we got caught?"

"My guess is Berwyn would just kill you," Alastair answered matter-of-factly, "but then you would just respawn and go about your night."

"But what about the law? And, and, you know, the cops?" Ginger struggled with her words, fighting against the excitement of her own thieving nature that told her to shut up and get on board. It was almost painful.

"I've had my legal team look into it. It's shady but not technically against any rule. So there wouldn't be a reason for the law to get involved. Instead, it would be up to us at Checkpoint to handle the aftermath, which would give us a perfect excuse to get involved. We could spin it as a group of players standing up for their world in the only way available. People like that kind of story. And since it would essentially bankrupt the three cities under the Serpents' rule, we could bypass Berwyn and replenish all their farming zones to keep the players happy. Then without the money to back him, it would only be a matter of time before he gets overthrown. Most likely, his own people will probably take him down for us." Alastair sat back with his hands in his lap, a smug expression plastered on his face.

Ginger flicked her eyes around the room, searching for other skeptical faces. "Oh come on, it can't just be me. You guys can't actually think this is a good idea." Her gaze fell on Max and Kira, who were uncharacteristically quiet. The pair exchanged a number of looks and gestures without saying a word. Ginger's heart sank. "Oh god, you two are already planning it, aren't you?"

Kira smirked. "Umm, we're weighing our options."

Max turned to Alastair. "Isn't there a limit to how much we can exchange?"

"Nope, that's another misconception. There's only a limit to how much a city can transfer to a player. Stealing it would bypass that."

"Seriously!" Ginger leaped out of her seat. "For the love of god, my kids are here. Can we not plan a heist in front of them?"

"Well I didn't tell you to bring your kids." Alastair stared up at her like he was somehow innocent.

Piper let out a giddy laugh that sounded far too excited.

Ginger shot her a disapproving glare, after which she collapsed back into her seat and buried her face in her hands. "Oh god. I brought my kids to a heist. I'm the worst parent in the world."

There was a long pause where no one said anything. The silence almost crushed her as her nature went to war with her conscience. There was no way she could go through with something so absurd. She had to be strong. She had to put her foot down before things went any further. Still, all that couldn't change the fact that she was covering her face to hide an insane grin that could have gotten her committed. It took everything she had not to burst into fits of mad laughter. She was almost salivating.

Ginger couldn't deny that she loved being a *Coin*. The last four years of unapologetic thieving had become a part of her. In many ways, it made her feel free. Ultimately, she couldn't stop herself from doing the math.

Ginger pulled herself together, making sure to at least stop drooling before she raised her head. "Wait a sec, if we can only exchange so much at once, how long would it take to process it all?"

"Oh, so now you're on board?" Max raised an eyebrow along with Kira.

"Of course I'm on board." Ginger blew out an exasperated breath. "It's nine million dollars. I'd be an idiot if I wasn't. But I should at least be conflicted about it before I lead my kids into a life of crime."

"That's very responsible of you," Alastair sounded both sincere and sarcastic at the same time, "and to answer your question, it would take a few weeks to get everything into your bank accounts, so you would need to stash it somewhere."

"Um." Corvin patted his knees awkwardly with his hands. Apparently, he still had a long way to go before his attitude matched his appearance. "If all we have to do is get in the vault and take its contents, won't that be really easy since we have Kira with us, I mean?" He glanced at the pendant chained around the fairy's neck, its amethyst stone matching the sparkle of her violet eyes.

"Oh, yeah." Kegan pointed an excited finger in her direction. "You're still basically a god, right? Can't you just..." He didn't finish his question. Rather, he acted it out by raising both arms in front of himself, then folding them and blinking *I Dream of Genie* style. Only Ginger got the reference, leaving her feeling old.

Kira shrank back into her seat at the mention of the ability she had picked up the previous year—the ability to take control of the game's system and bend it to her will.

Fortunately, Alastair answered for her so that she didn't have to talk about it, "While it is true that Kira is still linked with the system that runs Noctem and can still influence it if she tries to, she has been advised by our medical team not to activate that link since it could be potentially harmful." He looked at her briefly as if asking if she wanted to add anything.

She shook her head.

He continued, "Besides, it would tamper with the vault's data, which would look like hacking. And that would bad. If you were to steal that much hard using some kind of cheat, it would close the loophole that you need and make your actions quite illegal. If that were the case, there would be consequences that I couldn't stop."

Max folded his arms and nodded. "Okay, godlike powers are out. Sorry, Kira."

She let out a humpf and turned up her nose. "Didn't want

to use them anyways," she added, clearly forcing herself to joke about the subject. It would have been successful if there hadn't been a touch of fear in her voice.

"So what's this vault like?" Max moved off the subject.

"Oh, you're going to have to figure that part out on your own," Alastair shrugged and held out his hands empty as if offering them nothing, "but I can tell you that Berwyn will be holding a celebration at the palace in Reliqua tomorrow night. And if any of you were to secure an invitation to an event like that… Well, I'm sure you could make good use of your time there."

"So we should case the place?" Max assumed.

"Oh, lord no. I would never suggest that you do something like that." Alastair made a point of nodding in the affirmative as he spoke. "In fact, I've said too much as it is. I should probably get out of here before any of you say something that I don't want to hear. You know, plausible deniability and all." He stood up. "Oh, and Farn paid for the room for the next hour, so if there was a gang of hoodlums looking to do some planning, they could get started as soon as I leave." He grinned as he backed out of the door, adding one last, "Hypothetically speaking," before vanishing from the room.

Farn pulled out her journal and flipped to her transactions page. "What the hell? He did use my account for this. That's literally a crime. It's not even a gray area."

Kira laughed. "I'm sure he'll pay you back."

Farn settled down. "Yeah, he did hire me, so I guess there's that."

Max surveyed the room, settling on Ginger. "So, is everyone in?"

She failed to suppress a wry smile that felt right on her face.

"Good, then it's settled." He grinned back at her. "We're going to rob the Imperial Treasury of the House of Serpents."

CHAPTER FOUR

After some discussion, Max came to one conclusion. With less than a week before Noctem's anniversary, time was going to be in short supply.

"We're going to have to divide and conquer." Max stood and stepped to the door. Kira hopped up as well, staying close by his side, only to be stopped short by Ginger.

"Sorry, but I'm going to need this one." The *Coin* claimed his partner by the back of her dress and dragged the fairy back to her side of the room. Kira fidgeted with her item bag, her separation anxiety almost palpable in the space between her and Max. He would have felt sorry for her, but she perked back up when Ginger beckoned to Farn as well. "I'll need all the ladies for the night for what I have planned."

Farn rolled her eyes but acquiesced to join the women on the other side of the room, leaving Max with Corvin by the door. Kegan wasted no time in throwing his arms over both their shoulders to complete their half of the team.

Max sighed. "At least Corvin's cool."

"Hey, I'm cool." Kegan gripped his shoulder and steered

Max out the door. "Besides, when was the last time we had a guy's night out."

"Fine, let's get this done." Max sighed again and took the lead.

For the guys, their job for the night seemed easy—just find out what they could about the vault. Considering how fast Alastair had made his exit, they weren't going to be getting anything else out of him. The next best thing was to find someone who had recently had access to a similar vault. As luck would have it, someone fitting that description had just been overthrown. Hopefully, that might also give them motive to help. The tricky part was going to be finding them. After all, Lady Amelia had all of Noctem to hide in.

With Ginger absconding with his partner and Corvin's class change to a *Blade*, Max was left without a teleporter. That meant that hoofing it back to where he'd landed the Cloudbreaker was his only option, not that he had any idea of where to go once they got on board.

Max threw himself into the pilot's chair and took out his journal. Flipping to his inspector, he used the small screen to navigate to Noctem's message boards. Corvin and Kegan reached for their journals as well, checking in with every trusted contact they had for information.

Max hoped that between the three of them, they could track down the recently dethroned Lady of the Winter Moon. Amelia had earned a bit of fame during her rise to power a few months back, as well as a level of infamy from the number of players she'd taken out in the process. It was safe to say that it would be hard for her to stay off the radar for long. Despite that, they found nothing.

Max let out a frustrated growl. "There has to be a better way. This is taking forever."

Kegan sat up from where he lay in the floor of the cabin. "It's only been fifteen minutes."

"Yeah?" Max considered the time, then shook his head.

"No, that's still too long. Let's think about this a bit. How could she not show up anywhere?"

"She might not be logged in." Corvin gestured with his journal held open. "It's only been a night since Torn fell, so she might be taking some time off after that."

"Nah, I wouldn't take a night off," Max stood up and paced in a little circle, ducking so that he didn't bump his head on the low ceiling, "but I suppose I wouldn't want people bothering me either if I was still pissed off about losing my throne."

Corvin raised his head. "Okay, so if you were her, where would you go?"

Max sat down on the floor for a moment tapping his hand on one leg. Then he hopped back up and took the pilot's seat again, firing up the engines. "You're a genius, Corvin. I know exactly where she is." With that, the Cloudbreaker ascended into the sky.

In Noctem, if a player wanted to get somewhere off the map, where people wouldn't bother you, then there was really only one place—Tartarus. Being entirely built by the players, it literally did not appear on any map. If Amelia was there, it would make sense that no one had posted about her. It wasn't a place you wanted to bother people, lest you receive a stabbing.

Max set the Cloudbreaker down at the edge of the canyon that held the hodgepodge of a city on its walls. There was no real leader or organization in Tartarus, just a bunch of independent groups that had laid claim to different structures or built their own when they'd run out of room. The city wasn't exactly well constructed either since most players didn't know much about safety codes or proper building techniques. The result was a collection of oversized tree houses fastened to the walls of both sides of the canyon from mostly farmed materials.

Structures ranged from crudely formed decks joined by rickety pathways to larger, more stable buildings with complex support systems that actually looked like they might hold a decent number of players. Max hoped Amelia was in one of those.

Between the canyon's walls, a spiderweb of bridges stretched across the gap. Some were only made up of a few ropes weaved together into a footpath with excessively wobbly handrails. Others used heavy chains and wood to create stable footing. Arbitrarily placed torches attempted to chase away the shadows, never quite succeeding.

Max stood looking down into the city from the top of the canyon wall while a few monsters roamed the landscape behind him. "We should get down there before something spots us. Don't want to get stuck fighting a basilisk again. Ain't nobody got time for that."

Kegan kicked at the ground. "I don't know. It would be kinda neat to see which is stronger, a real basilisk's eyes or Corvin's."

"Mine is," Corvin declared, seeming pretty sure of himself.

Max shot him a questioning look.

"What? I had to test it." Corvin flipped his eye patch up to show his yellow eye. "Although, I would have thought that it would be the other way around since they have two and I only have the one."

Kegan shielded his eyes from the *Blade's* uncovered gaze to avoid its paralyzing effect. "Maybe being part of a contract makes it stronger. Pretty cool either way though."

"Heh, yeah, plus the eye patch makes me look tough." Corvin cracked a confident smile.

As surprising as it was, considering the odd pairing, Corvin and Kegan had become regular partners in the last year. The *Leaf* had even traveled to the fallen city of Rend to see a witch about having himself cursed. The result had tied his progress to Corvin's for a few months, dropping his level to match the new *Blade's* before reverting back to normal. It had stunted Kegan's progress, but he was able to play with Corvin without ruining the experience gains. If it wasn't for Kegan, Corvin wouldn't have made it so far in just a year.

Not to mention that the *Leaf's* special brand of irresponsibility and lack of proper judgment helped balance out Corvin's polite nature. They complimented each other almost as well as Max and Kira. The pair even had a pair of matching bracelets since Farn had loaned them the Shift Beads that she'd gotten as part of a contract the year before. It was a little unorthodox to lend such a valuable item, but she and the others had made a point of supporting him. Besides, the defense boost that came with the bracelet's basic enchantment was pretty strong at mid-level.

"Anyway, let's get going." Max stepped down onto a rope ladder, beckoning for the pair to follow.

Moments later, boards creaked underfoot as he hurried down into the flickering light of the city to search for clues. Asking around earned him several dirty looks, but it didn't take long to find evidence of Amelia's presence in the canyon. Especially since she'd already started a couple fights throughout the night, creating a trail that lead them to one of the larger establishments. It was a tavern, though it didn't have a sign in front. Instead, there was just a crude carving of a mug on the door.

Max spotted Amelia as soon as they entered. It would have been hard not to, considering she posed prominently in a large chair seated on a raised section of the room like a throne. Max glanced around the room, noting a large number of players in the space. Probably all members of Amelia's house, Winter Moon.

"Eep." Kegan pulled at his collar with one finger. "I'm starting to wish we brought our healer with us."

Max felt the same way but for a different reason. Kira was a hard person to get mad at, which would be good to have when dealing with a player known for stabbing first and asking questions later. A couple brief flashes went through his mind of how the situation would have played out with Kira present. First, a joke to lighten the mood, followed by a cut to her violet eyes capturing their hearts. Cut to her buying everyone food. Maybe a choreographed musical number. Then finally, everyone toasting drinks while she sat on the table, looking at the camera and laughing as everything worked out.

Max's mind snapped back to reality as a tall man in a midnight black robe stumbled off a bench, spilling a drink and knocking over a nearby table. The man's long dark hair, which featured silver chains braided through it, was spread out on the floor. He didn't get up.

"Okay, I live here now. Ple, please have my mail delivered to my new address." He reached out for his mug and poured the last few drops into his mouth.

Kegan leaned to Max's side, holding a hand up in front of his face as if to tell a secret but canceling the gesture by speaking a little too loud.

"That guy's trashed."

Fortunately, nobody noticed them. Yet. Though, if they kept standing there like a bunch of idiots, they would probably start gaining someone's attention.

"Follow my lead." Max started toward Amelia.

The others fell in line at his sides a little behind him, which helped to make him look important. He stopped in front of the raised space where the Lady of House Winter Moon sat looking bored.

"Umm, excuse me." His stomach did a quick somersault as he tried to sound confident. "You're Lady Amelia, right?"

Amelia's long ears pricked up as she leveled her gaze on him.

"I am."

She appeared steadier than the rest of her house, like she hadn't been drinking as much. The reynard set her mug down on a small table to the side. Then she placed her hand on the arm of her chair, close to the handle of a long sword that leaned against it. A little too close.

Max flicked his eyes from the grip of her weapon back to her.

Amelia ran her tongue across her elongated canines in a predatory manner.

A lump rose in Max's throat. He swallowed it back down. "Umm," he started, running out of words almost immediately.

He hadn't thought that far ahead, and things were going south fast. Then he had a thought. *What would Kira do?*

"Did you hear about the guy in the battle yesterday that lost his left arm and leg?" He gave an awkward smile.

Amelia's eyes narrowed.

Max waved a hand aside. "Don't worry, he's all right."

"What?" She tilted her head a little, one of her fluffy ears twitching.

"Well, that didn't work." Kegan lowered his voice so only the three of them could hear.

"Sorry, I thought acting like Kira would lighten the mood," Max whispered back.

Corvin covered his mouth to suppressed a laugh.

Kegan shook his head. "You are nowhere near cute enough to pull that off, man."

"Is there something you want, or should I just kill you now?" Amelia's hand drifted toward her sword.

"This might not be going well." Corvin gave his thigh a nervous pat.

"Okay, new plan." Max fell back into his role as leader. "We fight, then ask questions."

That was when the rest of House Winter Moon started to notice their exchange as well as how annoyed their Lady appeared. Players stood from their tables.

"Oh geez." Corvin placed his hand on his sword's grip.

Amelia sighed and picked up her blade. "I'm getting impatient."

Max braced himself before speaking, "Hi, Getting Impatient. I'm Max."

CHAPTER FIVE

I wonder how Max is doing, Ginger thought as she led Kira and Farn through the city of Lucem, its Grand Archway stretched across the sky overhead.

Ginger shook off the thought and returned her attention to her journal. She'd written a polite, albeit slightly flirty, message to one of the managers at the Everleigh Club where she worked. She read the message over to make sure it sounded right, then scribbled a messy check mark on the corner of the page. The text vanished with an irregular fade, leaving the word 'sent' at its center before it too disappeared.

That was when Kira floated forward to hover beside her, the fairy wings humming as trickles of shining dust drifted to the ground. A few heads turned, slack-jawed. It wasn't a common sight.

Ginger arched an eyebrow. It wasn't like the fairy to go out of her way to draw attention.

Kira's eyes settled on her open journal.

"What do you want?" Ginger snapped the book shut.

"Just, you know, wondering where you're taking us." Kira

clasped her hands behind her back and floated back to the ground.

"Yeah, I'd kind of like to know too," Farn added in a suspicious tone as she trailed behind.

Ginger could feel the *Shield's* stare burning a hole in the back of her head. "I already told you, we're going to see a friend of mine."

Farn sauntered up to Ginger's side. "Well, yeah, but that's what one might call an intentionally vague statement. Am I right, Kira?"

"Yes."

The *Shield* stalked around Ginger's side like a wolf. "And at this point, now that you're clearly leading us toward the red-light district here in Lucem, Kira and I have decided that we would like to be let in on the plan here."

"Yup."

Ginger tucked her journal back into her item bag, stalling while she thought of a good answer. "Oh, you're both being ridiculous. We're just meeting with a guy I know. What's so suspicious about that?"

Kira pushed off the ground and floated over to Farn's side. "Well, you did ditch your kids back in Thrift."

"And you sent them on a literal fetch quest to get bear pelts." Farn tucked her thumbs into the front of her belt. "It's almost as if you didn't want to take them to wherever we're going."

Ginger let out an exasperated breath. "Bears in that area are basic enemies for beginners. They need experience, and the pelts sell well. What's wrong with that? Plus, I can't really have them hanging out while we plan a heist here."

"True, true." Farn nodded.

"Yes, that all sounds on the up and up," Kira added.

"Thank you." Ginger released the tension in her shoulders.

"But," Farn held out both hands empty, "we just have to ask, are you…"

"…Intending on pimping us out at your old brothel for

information?" Kira finished Farn's question, her eyes narrowing.

Ginger gasped and placed one hand against her chest as she searched their faces for sympathy. She held the pose for a long beat, then dropped her hand back to her side and blew out a sigh.

"Kinda?"

Farn and Kira continued to stare her down with judgment in their eyes.

Ginger threw up her hands. "What? We need an invitation to the palace in Reliqua. And I happen to know one of the higher-ups back at the Everleigh Club that has been invited before."

Kira floated off the ground to hover at eye level. "And that would involve auctioning us off to the highest bidder?"

Ginger brushed the accusation aside, waving her hand back and forth like she was wafting away an odor. "It's not like that. It's just that he's a busy guy and it's hard to get a meeting with him on short notice."

Farn folded her arms across her armored chest. "And bringing us along will get you in the door?"

Ginger gave her a mischievous smile. "I might have told him that I have two friends that were interested in jobs," she hesitated for a few seconds, "and I may have sent him a picture of Kira."

Farn's mouth dropped open. "Not cool."

Ginger shrugged. "What? I would have sent him your picture too, but honestly, you're cute, but you look like you're about to pillage a Norse village." She stepped forward and wrapped her knuckles against Farn's chest plate, which covered anything of interest. "I mean, I've known you for a year, and I still have no idea what you have going on under here."

Farn clicked her teeth and pushed Ginger's hand away with a couple fingers. "I'm pretty sure that leaving my photo out is not the problem here."

"I know, I know, but really, we need an invitation, and this is our best bet. Unless either of you knows anyone else that can get us in."

The pair fell silent. Which wasn't a surprise considering that their social circles consisted mostly of each other and Max.

"That's what I thought." Ginger gave a victorious nod. "Which is why you're lucky that I've spent the last few years sleeping with half the servers to make the connections we need. Besides, this way, when we get our end of the job done faster than the guys, we can rub it in Max's face later."

Kira tilted her head from side to side. "I do like rubbing things in Max's face."

Farn slapped a hand over her eyes and groaned. "I assume we don't actually have to do anything. Right?"

"Great!" Ginger snapped her fingers and spun on her heel. "Knew you'd see it my way. And no, you don't have to do anything. Just stand behind me and try to look sexy." She glanced back over her shoulder at the pair as they stood, looking awkward. "You... might want to practice on the way."

Fifteen minutes and a few more arguments later, Ginger finally reached the entrance to the Everleigh Club. She'd been employed there for years but hadn't set foot inside for over a month after taking time off to spend with her kids. Despite her absence, there was still something welcoming about the place.

The building was pristine, with gold lining its windows and doors, like a stylish art nouveau hotel akin to the Moulin Rouge. It may have been a brothel, but she had always felt safe there, and no one had ever asked her to do anything she didn't want to. Sure, she could see the pity on people's faces whenever she explained what she did to provide for her family, but really, she'd always considered that to be their problem, not hers. After all, sex was nothing to be ashamed of. Nor was being good at it.

Ginger checked on her compatriots one more time before heading in. Then she rolled her eyes. Somehow, Farn looked more intimidating. Even worse, Kira, the one person she thought she could count on to at least be inadvertently sexy, was hiding behind Farn. Ginger buried her face in one hand.

"Well, you work with what you have."

"What was that?" Kira poked her head out from behind Farn's side.

"Nothing. Now get out here." Ginger grabbed the fairy by her belt and dragged the adorable spaz out of hiding.

Farn gave a short wave and started marching back down the street. "Okay, you two have fun in there."

Ginger cleared her throat, stopping the *Shield* mid-step. "Nice try."

"It was worth a shot." Farn's shoulders sank.

"You're both adults. You know that, right?" Ginger glowered at both of them.

"Yeah, I pay bills." Kira poked at the ground with her toes.

"Good, then let's get going." Ginger stomped her way into the club. *Honestly, they're worse than my kids.*

Inside, a tall elf named Butterscotch held down the customer service desk near the brothel's selection kiosks. Her hair was tied in a loose braid that trailed forward over one shoulder and down her chest in a way that drew the eye to her cleavage without being too obvious about it. The woman had always been skilled at flirting, even if all she did was work the desk.

"Hey, Scotch." Ginger gave a warm smile as she approached.

"Hey, I thought you were taking time off to help your kids level." The elf leaned forward on the desk.

"Oh, I am. Just stopping by to introduce a couple friends to Sam. I messaged him earlier, so he should be expecting us."

Scotch leaned to one side to check out the awkward pair standing behind Ginger. Her face went blank for a long pause. "Um, okay. I'll get you a key to one of the open rooms." She turned and reached into a cabinet behind the desk. "How are the kids coming along by the way?"

Ginger rested an elbow on the desk. "They've been catching on quick. I was thinking of taking them up to Rend next week, see how they handle Castle Alderth."

Scotch pulled her hand out of the cabinet with a quick tug and slapped a gold key fob down on the desk. "You monster. Those are your children. That place is terrifying."

Ginger offered her a sarcastic shrug. "I know. I'm not even going to warn them first."

The elf fell silent, then the corner of her mouth tugged upward. She let out a laugh. "I expect those kids will be taking down Nightmares before the end of the year."

"That's the goal. Can't go easy on them now." Ginger gave a slight bow to celebrate her parenting skills.

"I suppose not. Anyway, you can use room two-eleven. It has a nice sitting area."

"Thanks." Ginger snatched up the key.

Scotch winked. "I'll give you fifteen minutes to get your friends ready before I let Sam know you're here."

Ginger cringed and took a look back at her friends. Farn immediately looked to the floor, and Kira gave a dumb little wave. Ginger nodded and pocketed the key.

"Yeah, that might be best."

She thanked Scotch once more before leading her friends over to one of the gold-encrusted elevators. They both glowered at her as the doors sensed the key in her pocket and opened.

"Oh, just get in." Ginger shooed them onto the lift, where they continued to stare at her in silence all the way up.

The room upstairs was similar to the one Ginger had used to take clients before—a large hotel suite, complete with a canopy bed and seating area with a sofa and two chairs that surrounded a low table. The wallpaper was covered with pink and red filigree, and a chair rail of dark wood wrapped the room like a slender belt. The space was lit by a chandelier and a few sconces that made the gold accents that lined the furniture sparkle. It would be a nice place to enjoy a bit of adult fun.

Kira and Farn stood in the doorway as if they couldn't find the courage to enter.

Ginger tapped a dimmer switch on the wall to lower the

light, then turned her attention to the pair. It was time to get to work.

The fairy stepped a little closer to Farn and held up a hand in front of her mouth to whisper, "I'm not sure I like that expression."

Ginger folded her arms and tapped one finger on her side. "Kira, you look…" she paused before finishing the thought, "fine."

"Ahh, thanks." Kira patted the back of her neck. "You look okay too."

Ginger twirled one finger in the air. "Could you turn around." Kira shrugged and complied with a half spin that let the bottom of her dress fan out. Ginger nodded in approval. "I was going tell you to take off the item bag, but it actually draws attention to your butt."

"And that's good?" Kira leaned to one side, still sounding a little worried.

"Of course." Ginger strafed around her. "It's your best feature."

Kira snorted and twisted her body, trying to check out her own ass. The fairy spun around three times before giving up and asking Farn.

"Is it?"

Farn offered a sarcastic, "Sure, it's great."

Kira scoffed. "Oh, come on, you didn't even look."

Ginger ignored her and shifted her focus to Farn, feeling like a weight had just been dropped on her shoulders. "Okay, off with the armor. What else you got?"

"I have this." Farn held her arms out like a child showing their mother an outfit at the store.

"I think she looks cool." Kira bounced on her toes.

"I never said she wasn't cool," Ginger tugged on the *Shield's* baggy pants, "but it's not really the look we're going for right now."

Farn dropped her arms back to her side. "Well, I don't really have anything else. So…"

"Fine, warrior princess it is then." Ginger deflated and dropped into a chair, giving up on the uncooperative pair.

"Great." Kira plopped herself down on the couch, putting an end to the conversation. "Now that that's settled, who is this Sam guy we're meeting? And how can he help us?"

"Down to business then." Ginger kicked her feet up onto the coffee table. "His name's Samhain. He runs the upper floors that cater to the club's wealthier clients. He had offered me a job up there once."

Farn sat down on the couch next to Kira. "But you turned him down?"

"I did. It was more money, but I liked the floor I was on. It was affordable for most clients. And the sad truth in this business is that the more someone pays for you, the worse they treat you. If I'm going to sleep with someone, they need to give me the respect I deserve." Ginger leaned back. "That being said, Sam is a decent guy and does everything he can to keep the girls happy up there. Which is hard when you have to foster good relationships with Noctem's elites."

"And he's been invited to the palace in Reliqua before?" Farn asked.

"Yeah, he went to one of Berwyn's parties to represent Everleigh a few months ago."

Kira stretched out onto the sofa, laying down against the armrest on the other side. "So what should we expect from this meeting? It's like a job interview, right?"

"And how long do we need to play along?" Farn scooted down to give Kira more room to stretch out.

"Not long. I just needed you two to get Sam in the room. I can take things from here; I've known him for a while."

Farn slapped a hand down on the armrest. "Wait a sec, if all we're doing is talking to this guy, why did you want me to change my gear?"

"Oh, that's just because most men, Sam included, like pretty girls. I figured he would give us whatever we wanted if we asked nicely and batted our eyelashes. Provided he's not too angry that I lied about the reason for meeting him."

Kira's eyebrows climbed up her forehead. "That's a little manipulative."

That was when a knock came at the door.

Ginger pulled her feet off the table and got up, stopping as she passed Kira to tell her, "Sit up straight like a grown up."

The fairy groaned and stretched like a cat before cooperating.

Honestly, it really is worse than dealing with children.

Ginger continued to the door, opening it to find herself staring at the burly chest of a massive faunus. He wore a velvet frock coat lined with gold buttons that matched the club's luxurious interior.

"Hi, Sam." She waved politely.

Samhain ducked through the doorway, bumping a pair of thick horns into the frame.

"Damn things," he complained.

He'd once told Ginger that he'd designed the avatar to be intimidating to help him handle the clients upstairs. Rich or not, they still thought twice about messing with someone his size. Though, that was about the only thing about him that could be considered threatening. He wasn't even level ten, not to mention that he was one of the gentlest men she'd ever met.

"How's the break?" He leaned down and gave her a welcoming hug. "We've missed you 'round here." His voice came out deep but soft in her ear.

"I've missed everyone here too." Ginger hugged him back.

He let go and closed the door. "It's good to get away every now and then though, and family is important. So I'm glad you're taking some time off. Just let someone know when you want to come back."

"I will." Ginger nodded.

He patted one hand against his thigh. "I wish I had more time to catch up, but I actually have another interview lined up."

Guilt caught Ginger off guard as it prickled at the base of her neck. "Oh, yes, that's okay. I appreciate you seeing me on short notice."

He walked toward the sitting area. "Anyway, you two must be Farnsworth and Kirabell." He gave a slight bow. "Ginger has a lot of nice things to say about you both. Do you mind if I sit?"

"Ah, sure." Kira gestured toward the open chair, her hand shaking a little.

"Thanks." He took a seat and pulled out a notebook. "Okay, first off, obviously, fairies are in short supply, and we're always looking for more help. So we'd be happy to have both of you join the club. I do have to ask some questions, though, and just a disclaimer, they do get pretty personal. As long as that's okay?"

That was when Ginger sat down opposite him. As much as she'd enjoy watching Kira and Farn squirm while answering a bunch of embarrassing questions about their sexual histories, she couldn't keep the ruse going. Samhain had actually been the one to interview her years ago, and he'd helped her a lot over the years. She felt worse about misleading him than she expected and didn't want to waste any more of his time.

"I have to stop you there." She held up a hand. "As much as I agree that these two would be amazing for the club, I have to admit that getting them jobs is not really why we're here."

"Oh." His eyes widened, and he glanced back at the two sitting together on the couch.

Farn bowed her head while Kira leaned forward and clasped a hand around her pendant, both of them offering a quiet, "Sorry."

Sam dropped his notebook into his lap and leaned back. "Well, I hope you have a good reason for tricking me into meeting on short notice. I really am busy, so I wish you had sent me a message about it."

"I know. I'm sorry." Ginger stared at the floor for a second, guilt stealing her breath away. "But Kira here is in a tough spot, and we really need some information to help her out." She felt even worse at how easily a new lie came to her. She was already building a story about a sick relative when Kira decided to speak up.

"Umm yeah, that's totally true and not in any way a lie."

Ginger's mouth dropped open at the fairy, who was apparently sabotaging her further attempts at deception.

"Is it now?" Sam cracked a grin at Ginger as she started to sweat.

"I'm sorry," she repeated, not sure what to say next. To her surprise, Farn came to her rescue.

"We are all sorry, but you're already here, and we promise this won't take long."

"I guess that's true." He sighed and settled into his chair, despite it being a little too small for his body. "What do you need?"

Ginger took back over, a weight lifting off her chest that she didn't have to continue lying. "We need to get into the palace in Reliqua, and I was hoping you might have an invitation that you wouldn't mind parting with."

Samhain scoffed. "Oh god, you're getting involved in that mess. Now I definitely don't want to help you."

"Yeah, but you will." Ginger made an attempt at a charming smile.

"And why would I do that?" He folded his arms across his enormous chest.

Ginger cringed. "Because you still like me… hopefully."

"Humpf, if you say so." He frowned, as a slight upward curl of his lip betrayed him. "Why do you need to get into the palace?"

Ginger released at the breath that she'd been holding. "We need to learn everything we can about the place. Layout, security, a way back in for later. All of it."

Sam eyed the pair on the couch. "So what are you two? Assassins or something?"

"Something like that." Kira snapped open her casters as a

show of force, clearly forgetting that she was the least threatening thing in the room.

He said nothing for a moment, tapping a finger on his notebook. Then he grimaced. "They call the palace the Jewel of the Sea, and let me tell you, the name fits. It is impressive. The party I went to was to celebrate Berwyn's rise to power as ruler of Reliqua. I didn't get to explore the palace since he had most of the place closed off, but maybe you three can figure something out."

"Does that mean you'll give us the invitation?" Ginger tried to sound hopeful.

Samhain tapped a few options woven into his stat-sleeve, and a green envelope with a gold seal materialized in his hand. He held it out before pulling it back. His face grew serious.

"If you're making a run on Berwyn and his Serpents, I want you to be careful. Don't get me wrong, I had a good time when I was there, and Berwyn treated me well. But I've met men like him before. He's smart, charming, and ruthless. None of that really makes him a bad guy or anything. Though, it's a dangerous combination. Not to mention that his whole conquest thing is hurting the game for other users. I may not get to play it much, but I don't like some of the complaints I'm hearing. So if I give you this invitation, you have to promise that whatever you have planned will bring misfortune upon the House of Serpents." He finished with a warm smile.

"Thank you." Ginger's eyes nearly welled up.

"You're welcome." Samhain inclined his head. "You'll be allowed a plus one and two bodyguards. Though, your guards will have to keep an eye on you from the balcony since they aren't allowed in the ballroom. There are no weapons allowed inside either, so you and your plus one will have to disarm before entering." He held the envelope out to Ginger but pulled it away again before she could touch it. "Wait, you aren't part of a house, are you?"

"No, should I be?"

"Definitely. Where you're going, titles matter. If you're not part of a house, then you're nobody. I'd suggest stopping by the House Registry here in Lucem. You need a minimum of three members, so you should be able to get one started tonight with your current party." He offered her the envelope again, this time placing it in her hands.

"Hmm, Lady Ginger." She took the item. "I like the sound of that."

He laughed. "Yeah, don't let it go to your head. Also, it's a fancy event, so you're going to have to blend in."

Ginger took in a sudden breath. "How fancy?"

"It's a ball in a palace. So, pretty fancy."

She clutched the envelope against her chest and shifted her gaze to Kira.

The fairy leaned away. "Umm, why are you looking at me like that?"

Ginger let a giddy smile have its way with her. "I'm taking you shopping."

Kira responded by flopping back onto the couch and going limp.

"Looks like you have your work cut out for you." Sam gave Ginger's arm a playful nudge, then took out a pen. "I can mark a good clothing shop on your map. It's a little different, but you can buy some custom-crafted garments there. None of that mass-loaded stuff they sell at the basic shops."

Ginger took out her journal so he could mark a point on her map. Afterward, she spent a few long seconds staring up at his face. "Thank you so much. For everything. I really don't know what to say."

"Don't say anything, just don't trick me into meeting again like this." He placed one hand on her shoulder, adding a gentle squeeze as punctuation.

She dropped her eyes to the floor again. "Sorry about that. We have a tight deadline."

"I can understand that." He dropped his hand back to his side. "And speaking of being busy, I should probably get back to work." He stood from his chair and gave a little bow to Kira and Farn. "If either of you ever decides you want a job, I could still find a place for you here."

Kira didn't move from her place spread out across the couch but gave him a thumbs up. Farn opened her mouth to add something, but Ginger stepped in to cut off the awkwardness that was almost certainly coming.

"Don't worry, I'll make sure they come to you if they decide to… try things out here. And thank you again, we'll put this invitation to good use."

"You're welcome, just stay safe with whatever you have planned." Sam paused as he opened the door to leave. "Seriously, Berwyn isn't the kind of enemy that goes down easy."

"Well that's foreboding." Kira sunk further into the couch cushions.

"True, but more importantly," Ginger hugged the envelope against her chest, letting her excitement show, "we have errands to run."

CHAPTER SIX

The pulse spell hit Max like a truck, launching him across the tavern and into the wall. He crashed to the floor near a bench that flipped over on top of him.

"...Ow."

He struggled out of a quasi-embrace with the piece of furniture and glanced at the tattooed display of digital ink on his wrist for his health. He'd lost over ten percent, and his brain did a little fart, trying to work out how. He'd been hit by pulse spells before, usually by Kira in attempt to annoy him. The spell was nothing more than a puff of energy and didn't carry any damage. He shook off the haze in his head. Somehow, this version of the spell was different, stronger, to a point where it could throw him across a room. It was probably the impact with the wall that had caused the drop in his health. He wasn't even sure who had cast the spell.

From his position on the floor, he searched the room for Amelia, finding her still standing on the raised platform where she'd been. She nodded to the tall man in black robes that was no longer resting on the floor. *Well, that explains where the pulse came from.* The mage was a *Cauldron*, which also had the spell.

Still, Max wasn't sure how the guy had packed so much power into something so weak.

Amelia glanced back to Max, her eyebrows creating a diagonal line across her forehead, clearly still wondering who he was. Her confusion didn't last or she just didn't care because she gestured to the mage in the black robes. "Klaxon, kill him please."

The *Cauldron* wobbled on his feet and let out a long, "Hmmm," before snapping his fingers and adding a casual, "M'kay."

Max struggled to get his new, close friend, the bench, in front of him to block whatever was coming. An instant later, a crystal shard burst through the back, lodging itself in the wood and sending a cloud of splinters into Max's face. He spat them out as Klaxon raised a caster and opened his spellcraft menu, a field of glowing glyphs appearing in front of him. Max had seen Kira cast enough pulse spells to recognize the selection, but what happened next was new.

The mage swiped down to cast, but instead of releasing, he held the spell. A strange sigil appeared in the air and Klaxon pressed his hand against it for a few seconds—seconds that Max used to get to his feet and leap behind a table before another pulse erupted into the space where he'd been. The remains of his friend, the bench, popped into the air and smashed into the ceiling. Max scurried under another table and kicked it over for cover. That was when he remembered he hadn't come alone.

Kegan jumped over a bench nearby and loosed a handful of arrows. Half were aimed at the men in the room, and the other half were at Amelia herself. She blocked but took one in the shoulder. The woman pulled it out without flinching and tossed it to the ground.

She looked pissed.

Good. Max smirked. The distraction bought him a little breathing room.

Kegan gave a salute to Max and Corvin, adding a simple,

"Good luck," before running out of the front door of the tavern.

The rest of Amelia's Winter Moons stood awaiting orders.

"Well, go after him!" she growled as if it should have been obvious.

Almost instantly, the room emptied as her house poured out the door after Kegan. As soon as they were gone, she shook her head and blew out a sigh, tapping the bottom of her sword's sheath against the floor. Then she drew the weapon and turned to Corvin, mist drifting from its edge. She smiled.

"I think a duel might be what I need right now."

That's probably not going to go well. Max peeked out of his hiding place.

"It would be my honor." Corvin bowed his head with respect. He sounded calmer than Max would have expected. The mid-level *Blade* took his stance, knees bent with one hand on his sword, ready to draw.

Distracted by the duel, Klaxon seemed to have forgotten he was also in the middle of a fight. It suited Max just fine as he leveled a pistol at the man's head and squeezed the trigger.

In theory, a *Fury* should have no problem dealing with a *Cauldron* mage. Max was faster, but that didn't seem to matter when another pulse knocked Max's hand aside, causing him to put a round into the wall. Another burst of energy punched him in the stomach from the opposite direction. Neither carried the same impact as the first two. *Probably because he'd cast them from his quick-cast queue instead of setting it up with his spellcraft menu. He must not be able to use that charging sigil on stored spells.*

Max tried to get his gun back up, but a crystal shard materialized in the air and flew straight at him. He leaped back into the cover of the tables and kicked another over. Crystal spikes traced a line through the wood in a staccato of splintering thunks.

Max scrambled back on his rear, his brain releasing another squeaky fart as he struggled to understand why he was losing so poorly. Then it hit him. He could go toe to toe with any of

Noctem's Nightmares, but this was PVP. He wasn't fighting an AI. Considering that Klaxon came from a house with a reputation for conflict, the man must have had far more experience fighting players. That much was clear in the way he used nothing but a couple low-level spells to control Max's movement and keep him on the run.

On instinct, Max glanced at his stat-sleeve for his opponent's health bar. It wasn't there. That was when he remembered that the game only gave that information for monsters.

Crap!

Max didn't even know what level the guy was. To find that out, he'd have to look closer at the embellishments around the man's class emblem on the back of his hand. And really, he didn't want to poke his head up long enough to check.

Klaxon set up another round of pulse and crystal shard spells and dropped them into his quick-cast queue for later as Max peaked through a crack in the table. Then the mage snapped open his second caster.

Crap!

Max's eyes widened, the additional equipment telling him that he was up against a high-level mage.

Klaxon held out his wrist, above which a small circle of crimson light appeared. He reached into his robe with his free hand to produce a pouch of red velvet. The circle glowed brighter as he dumped the contents of the bag into the portal. He cast another pulse in Max's direction as he dropped the pouch to the floor.

Thaumaturgy was the ability that set the *Cauldron* class apart from other mages. Max knew at least that much. Sure, they still had access to a spellcraft menu like Kira's, but that was just for basic incantations. The rest consisted of two things —a circle of power, and ingredients to fill it. Depending on the recipe, the results could be far more destructive. Fortunately, the whole process took time to prepare. For most *Cauldron* mages, the time it took to brew left them defenseless. Unfortunately, Klaxon's second caster allowed him to rain down a hail of quick-cast spells to buy time, making him into an offensive powerhouse.

Max ducked as the table behind him was pelted with crystal spikes, forcing him to move from one spot to another for cover. He needed to find an opening. Max swept his eyes over the room, settling on the red pouch that had held the ingredients for whatever spell Klaxon was brewing. Most *Cauldrons* he'd partied with had used colored pouches to differentiate what the resulting spell of their contents would be. Granted, each mage's preferences were different, so the color could mean anything. More likely than not, the mage was probably brewing something fire based. Considering they were indoors, even in such a large room, it would have to be something without much range. *A flamethrower*, Max assumed.

Armed with that knowledge, he started moving. He couldn't just keep jumping from cover to cover. That would give Klaxon too much time to brew. Plus, he would run out of tables eventually.

Max drew his pistols and blind-fired a couple rounds over the top as a distraction. Then dropping to the floor, he leaned out from the side and fired twice more, this time taking the care to aim. The hits almost scored a solid critical, but the *Cauldron* raised an arm faster than Max expected.

In PVP, criticals were everything. Especially for Max, who depended on them to dish out enough damage before having to reload. Of course, he considered unloading both magazines at the guy and hoping for the best. But that would leave him open, and he wasn't sure how much health the Klaxon had. Granted, hiding under tables wasn't working either. He had to tip the scales back in his favor or at least do something unexpected.

Max glanced to the door at the far end of the tavern, Klaxon standing in his path. *I'm not gettin' out that way.* Apparently, expecting a second exit, to comply with proper safety standards, would be asking too much of the tavern's designer.

"Well, time to bring this place up to code," he said to himself as he tried to remember what had been around the building. *What's on the other side of that wall?* He was pretty sure it was a stairway to the level below. Like, seventy percent sure. Of course, that also meant that he was thirty percent sure that there was nothing there but a fall straight into the river below. He nodded, accepting the odds.

Holding one pistol in front of his face, Max whispered the words, "Custom Rounds," followed by the first level of the skill, "Fracture." The resulting bullets wouldn't cause much damage, but they would weaken any structure that he hit. He stood just as Klaxon finished brewing his attack.

Max just hoped he was right about the spell being a flamethrower and not something that would kill him outright. He thumbed the select-fire switch on both pistols down to full-auto. Then all hell broke loose.

Power blazed toward Max from the *Cauldron's* hand in a torrent of orange flames as he backed away and fired half a magazine at the mage. Klaxon threw up his other arm to protect his head, his robe covering his face.

Gotcha! Max fired again until the slide locked back empty, this time at the man's exposed casting hand.

Klaxon whipped his arm back, clearly forgetting that he was still spewing fire from his palm as he set half the room ablaze. He stumbled, struggling to keep up his defense and get his aim back on target.

Max took the moment to unload his Fracture rounds into the nearby wall before the jet of fire swept back toward him. Bullets peppered the surface, throwing jagged fragments of wood into the air as Max ran toward safety. Well, safety might not have been the right word for it. Regardless, he jumped onto one of the few remaining tables and leaped. His shoulder hit the wall with a victorious crack, the fire licking at his back. The wood splintered, and fresh air filled Max's virtual lungs as he soared into the air over… nothing.

"Oh, holy shit, mother—" was all he got out as he flailed his arms in imitation of an injured flamingo being thrown out a window.

As it turned out, he was right about the stairway being outside, but he had been wrong about its position. It was there alright but two levels below and with a gap of empty space before it. The momentum of his leap carried him across before dropping him nearly twenty feet onto the rickety stairs. He landed with a loud crack, as the stairs creaked in protest.

Max let out an embarrassing ompf as the fresh air evacuated his lungs, getting the hell out of there before he got into any more trouble. Then as if on cue, the stairs gave way, dropping their burden down another level to the next flight along with a collection of broken boards.

Max wheezed as he struggled to roll to one side so he could access his item bag. He downed a health vial, watching his hit points fill back up to half on the display inked across the underside of his wrist. Then it stopped and began ticking back down. Max raised an eyebrow at the readout. Then he smelled the smoke wafting up from his boot that was still on fire. He blew out a labored sigh.

"That could have gone better."

CHAPTER SEVEN

Farnsworth pushed against the heavy door of the House Registry in Lucem. Intricate carvings swirled across its surface like the ridges of a fingerprint. It was the same pattern that marked the doors of all of Noctem's house registration offices. Up close, each line was made up of rows of tiny figures, players joining together as one.

Farn probably wouldn't have noticed the suggestion of unity that the door's design implied. Then again, she didn't have a choice as she slammed her face into its surface. She peeled her cheek off the door and turned around, rubbing her nose.

"It's a pull door," the statement fell out of her mouth like a bit of lettuce, embarrassingly dropped whilst eating a salad on a first date.

"I see that," Ginger shifted her hip to one side, "and you're going to be my bodyguard tomorrow night, huh?"

Farn rubbed at the tip of her nose. "You can always have Max."

"I'm not sure which is worse." Ginger reached past her and grabbed the door handle to head inside.

"You're welcome to be my bodyguard." Kira hopped

forward and walked backward through the threshold, her hands tucked behind her back.

"I suppose that would be appropriate. We are still linked here." Farn held up her hand where a black onyx ring hugged her finger, its mate still sitting on Kira's.

"True, but I'm still going to keep taking mine off every time we're in combat." The corners of the fairy's mouth tugged down as she spun to walk forward. "I don't want to see you die for me."

The rings had been a contract item that Farn had stumbled across in a shop the year before. They had the ability to pass one fatal hit from the fairy to Farn in exchange for increased stats, lasting five minutes before killing her. They were a last-ditch option for when things went bad. Kira avoided using them, always taking hers off when things got messy. She didn't seem to hold her own life at the same level of importance.

Farn opened her mouth but shut it again. It would have been easy to call the little hypocrite out, especially since she had almost given her life for real the year before, but that wasn't really something to use as a comeback. Instead, Farn tucked her thumbs into her belt and followed Kira through the door.

Inside, the House Registry was huge, with mahogany filing cabinets lining the walls and paintings of the night sky filling the opulent ceiling. Clouds drifted through the murals despite being made of paint. Below, several jerobin clerks hurried around the marble floor. The little kangaroo-looking NPCs carried ledgers and files, moving them from one cabinet to another. Farn stopped short as one hopped past her, a sheet of paper falling from a folder that it clutched in its rodent-like hands. She dropped to one knee to picked up the paper as the NPC stopped short and turned around. Its movements were quick and jittery.

She held out the sheet, and the thing hopped once toward her, lowering its mousey face. It raised its eyes to make contact as it reached for the paper, uttering a quiet, "Thank you," as it slipped the sheet from her hand. Its voice cracked a little, like a teenager trying not to make a mistake on his first day of work. He hopped away without another word.

Farn smiled. The little guy seemed to be working hard, even if he was just an AI repeating the same tasks to make the place look busy for the players. The NPC probably dropped that piece of paper several times a day.

Farn pushed herself back up to her feet and caught up to the others as they approached a row of service windows, where a bored looking woman filled out some paperwork. She wore a pair of gold-rimmed glasses perched on the tip of her nose and robe that looked like it had been freshly ironed. A severe frown marred her face. Farn decided to let Ginger take things from there.

"Pardon me, but we're here to register a new hous—"

The woman held up one finger without looking away from the paper on the counter.

Farn let out a snort as Ginger flinched back at the sudden rudeness. Only when the NPC had finished the line it had been working on did she place her pen down and look up.

"Yes?" she asked in a sharp tone.

Ginger took a second before responding.

"Well spit it out, dear," the clerk snapped.

"Ah, we're here to register a house."

The NPC clicked her tongue. "And who will be the Lord or Lady in charge of this house?"

Farn took a step backward, leaving Ginger standing at the window, bumping into Kira who did the same. Ginger didn't look back but sighed nonetheless.

"That will be me."

"And you have at least two other members with you, including a mage and melee class?"

"Yes, right here." Ginger pointed over her shoulder.

The NPC reached forward and pulled a few sheets of paper from a bin beside her window. "Please place each of your hands on the forms to swear loyalty."

Farn grimaced. It wasn't as if swearing loyalty actually

meant anything. The oath only gave access to the bounties in Lucem's territories. Still, her heart sank a little as she stepped back up to the window and reached for the sheet of paper.

"Are we sure we have to do this?" Kira's hand hovered above the registration form like it might bite her.

Farn pulled back her hand, leaving Ginger alone lowering her fingers on the paper. The word Lady faded into existence across the top of the page in a decorative script font. It vanished as she lifted her hand back up. "I know. I don't like it much either, but we're in a hurry, and we don't have much of a choice."

"Is there a different city we would rather join?" Farn leaned around Ginger. It wasn't that she disliked Lucem, just that she didn't feel much of a connection with it. "We could probably teleport somewhere else without losing much time."

"I don't know." Kira dropped an elbow to the service counter and sank her cheek into one hand. "I don't really feel close to any of the kingdoms in Noctem. I've spent most of my time in dungeons with Max and you guys."

"Well you can't be loyal to a dungeon, so you'll have to pick something." Ginger crossed her arms and inclined her head at the mopey fairy.

"It's too bad we can't choose somewhere like Rend. I mean, it used to be a city, at least according to Noctem's lore. And we had a pretty epic fight there last year."

"The city of Rend fell decades ago." The NPC shifted in her chair, several wrinkles appearing on her forehead.

Farn's heart skipped a beat as she gasped. As far as she knew, NPC's worked off preset dialogue scripts, keeping things vague so that it didn't seem obvious. If there was a line programmed in about the city of Rend, then that meant something. Farn studied the woman.

"See, you can't pick Rend. It fell years ago." Ginger didn't seem to notice anything unusual, holding out a hand toward the woman.

Kira bobbed her head in a mocking gesture. "It fell years ago—"

Farn slapped her gauntlet down on the counter, making the fairy jump mid-sentence.

"Woah, what was that for?"

"Sorry, but something just hit me." Farn let her excitement show as she held up a finger. "NPCs usually ignore players when they talk amongst themselves."

"And?" Ginger leaned against the side of the counter.

"And, this one just chimed in on your conversation about Rend." Farn let that sink in, then spun on the NPC, leaning into the window. "Is there a way to create a house loyal to Rend?"

The woman sighed and crossed her arms across her chest, making it clear that there was a programmed response to the question. "You are lucky enough to be here in Lucem, and that question is an insult to this Kingdom."

Farn smiled. She was right. There was something there. If there wasn't, the woman would have just skipped back to her earlier dialog. "Sure sure, but that's not an answer. So is there a way to pledge loyalty to the city of Rend or not?"

"Not here there isn't," the woman snapped.

"Then where?"

The clerk stood and jabbed Farn in the breastplate with a finger hard enough to emit a hollow clunk. "The city of Rend fell to the darkness, and it should stay that way. If you would like to join it, you are welcome to take your house there." The NPC ended her declaration by reaching up and slamming the service window's shutter down.

Farn flinched backward, blinking. "What just happened?"

"You just got told off by an AI." Kira let out a snort.

"So much for getting things done fast. I should have known things were going too smoothly." Ginger buried her face in one hand.

"I thought I was onto something." Farn took a shallow breath. "I thought there might be a way to join Rend."

"Well she did say we can go there, so maybe there is." Kira raised her eyebrows, hopefully.

"We don't have time to go all the way to Rend." Ginger shook her head.

"You don't have to," a meek voice said from behind.

Farn glanced around for the source. "Who said that?"

"I did." The voice came from beside one of the mahogany filing cabinets. The same jerobin that had dropped the piece of paper earlier peeked out from one side. He glanced back and forth, then beckoned with one tiny hand.

Farn walked over and took a knee. "What do you mean we don't have to go there?"

"Shhh." The little guy reached up and pressed his fingers to Farn's mouth then shot a worried look to the closed service window. "Not here."

Farn played along, peeking back at the window and lowering her voice to a whisper, "Okay, where can we talk?"

Kira joined in, happily dropping down on all fours. "And what do you know about Rend?"

"Shhh," the jerobin repeated, this time covering both of their mouths. "Go to the alleyway behind the registry. I'll send out my…" His eyes darted around the room as if he wasn't sure what to say. "My brother. Yes, he will meet you there."

Farn and Kira held still, with the rodent's hands pressed against their lips. They both nodded in unison. He pulled his fingers away as soon as they did. Again, he glanced at the window, then gave a shooing motion at the pair on the floor.

Farn stood, Kira following her back to Ginger, who was watching with a smirk. The timid little jerobin scurried off to meet two more of the small clerks at the edge of the room. They seemed to be whispering to each other. Farn couldn't make out what he was saying to the other jerobin, but at one point, he turned and pointed at her.

Farn hesitated as the three NPC's hopped out of the room through a door in the back, grabbing a folder of papers on their way out.

"Well, that was a little weird."

"Yup, but interesting," Kira chirped, her violet eyes sparkling as she started for the door. "Let's go."

Ginger caught the fairy by the back of her belt. "Are you just going to rush off every time someone invites you to meet them in a back alley?"

"Clearly, I am." Kira struggled to drag the *Coin* behind her.

"Okay, why not?" Ginger let go to watch the little mage fall forward, flailing her arms.

"Let's not keep our friends waiting." Farn ignored their antics like a mature adult and pressed her hand against the door, this time remembering which way to push.

The alleyway behind the registry was darker than Farn expected. Lucem was a city of light after all, so it was odd to find a part of it that felt so gloomy. The walls were plain stone without the decorative flair that Noctem's designers seemed to prefer. It was as if the place was meant to be overlooked. A few wooden barrels were stacked along the wall and into the alley, an easy place for someone unsavory to hide.

A form moved from the back of space, too large to be the little jerobin's brother. Farn stepped to the side and threw one arm out in front of Kira on instinct. She gripped her sword just in case.

"Who's there?"

The shape moved closer, becoming more recognizable as a tall man in a heavy cloak. His hood was pulled down to hide his face. He lumbered toward her, staggering as if drunk, his middle swaying with each step.

"You three them? The ones who pissed off the clerk inside asking about Rend." The man's voice came out gruff but labored, like he was putting in effort to sound tough. There was something familiar about it. On top of that, his head seemed... small.

"That's us. Are you the one who can get us set up with a house?" Ginger stepped forward.

"That's me, the name's Finn." He pointed to himself with a

rather short arm for someone of his stature. "My, ah, brother sent me to get things sorted."

"Okay, how do we do this?" Farn raised an eyebrow as Finn's face came into view, the mousey features of a jerobin hiding under the hood.

"Same as inside." The oversized jerobin shifted in an unnatural way, like he was trying to reach a pocket inside the cloak but couldn't quite find it. A quiet squeak came from his stomach; then finally, he pulled out a ratty looking book and dropped it open on top of a barrel. Three pieces of aged paper lay folded inside.

"These forms were salvaged from Rend by my grandfather just after it fell. Each of you got to put your hand on them and say what I say."

Kira wasted no time, snatching a sheet off the barrel slapping it against the wall so she could press her hand against it. The word Archmage stained the paper in a heavy, gothic font that didn't match the forms inside the registry.

Ginger pointed a finger at Finn and swept it up and down. "So are we just going to ignore the fact that this guy is obviously three jerobin in one cloak standing on each other's shoulders?"

Finn winced, then immediately went on the offensive, "I have no idea what you're talking about. I'm a prime physical specimen of jerobin strength. You don't see me accusing you of anything."

"Yeah," a second voice said from around where Finn's knees would be.

Ginger rubbed at the bridge of her nose, then dropped her hand back down to her side limply. "This is not how I envisioned becoming the Lady of my new and glamorous house."

"Too bad, you're one of us, and this is how we do things." Kira wiggled impatiently. "Now get your hand on that paper. I want to be an Archmage."

"Yeah, we're not exactly glamorous," Farn added.

"I should have expected this when I threw in with a bunch

of dungeon rats." Ginger gave in, taking a form from the book and slapping it against Kira's back with her palm.

"Hey!"

"Deal with it. That wall looks filthy."

Farn chuckled at her housemates, a warm feeling filling her chest as she took the last form and pressed it against Ginger's back, the words First Knight appearing across the paper.

"Repeat after me." Finn staggered closer. "I, state your name, will call Rend my home."

Farn felt Ginger take in a breath beneath her hand, and together, the three of them declared their homeland.

The moment the last word left Farn's mouth, her hand tingled, and ink spread across the paper, surrounding her fingers with a pattern of intricate line work. It was beautiful, like lace and embroidery.

"Done." Finn picked up the old book from the barrel and held out his hand. "Give me your forms. I'll file them in with everyone else's inside."

"That's it?" Farn handed hers over.

"Almost. You still need to choose a name and an emblem." Finn fished around within his cloak again until a small wooden box fell out the bottom. His face froze as a small arm reached out from the underneath to pick up the item. The box disappeared again only to reappear poking out of his collar, held up by another rodent-like hand. He took it without acknowledging that there was anything out of the ordinary. "Here, this is your ring box. It will always have a ring inside that you can give to a new member whenever you open it."

"Thanks." Ginger took the item as Lady of the house.

"You all should be able to figure the rest out on your own." Finn started to bow but almost fell over. "Best of luck with your new home in Rend. I'm sure the fallen city will give your house a warm welcome."

"If it doesn't kill them first," a voice mumbled from where Finn's stomach would be, followed by a sudden movement under the cloak. "Ouch, watch where you're kicking."

Finn cleared his throat.

"Yes, anyway. If anyone asks who helped you tonight, I was never here." The tall jerobin stepped away, supporting himself with one hand against the stack of barrels as he went.

Ginger shook her head at the awkward form, then turned her attention to the box in her hand. A second later, her brow furrowed. "It doesn't open."

"Hey, this box doesn't open!" Farn ran a few steps down the alley after the strange NPC.

Finn's shape disappeared around a corner, but his voice traveled back.

"Of course not. I already told you, you need a name first!"

CHAPTER EIGHT

One year.

That was it.

The entirety of Corvin's career as a *Blade* had added up to one year. Actually, it hadn't even been that long. He was still a month shy. He certainly wasn't anywhere near reaching high-level. No, he was level 77. Almost 78.

Nevertheless, here he was, bowing all polite like to Amelia, the Lady of the Winter Moon. Judging from the look in her eyes, she had intent to end him.

She inclined her head, then stepped down off her platform to join him on the floor. She was a reynard like he was, but somehow, the ears and tail made her look more like a wolf than a fox.

His heart raced as he suppressed a shiver that threatened to add a tremble to his hand.

Damn.

Badasses don't shake.

Or sweat.

Yeah, they definitely don't sweat this much.

Corvin wiped his forehead and backed up to give her room.

Behind him, Max kicked over tables. Corvin cringed at the ruckus and decided not to look. Instead, he just assumed that Max had things under control. He hoped the same for Kegan since the *Leaf* had run from the tavern only moments before, with the majority of Amelia's house chasing him out the door.

They'll both be fine, Corvin told himself. *At least their levels are higher than mine.* The thought brought him back to the fight ahead of him.

His palms started to sweat.

Amelia strafed to the side as if sizing him up. Her tail swished back and forth as she moved. She cracked a smile as she drew her sword, throwing its sheath to the floor. A dark mist wafted from its curved edge.

He didn't recognize the weapon. It was longer than most swords, single-edged and lacking a hand guard. The saber was probably a contract item. The mist, some kind of poison or curse. He couldn't let her scratch him.

"I've seen that stance before." She pointed her sword at Corvin's feet. "You've been taking lessons out there in the real. Kendo, if I'm right?" She had a way of forming words that somehow always kept the tips of her canine's visible. Also, she was right.

He swallowed. "Ah, yeah. I started classes a few months back. I thought—"

"You thought it would give you an edge in-game?" she interrupted.

Corvin offered a weak nod, to which Amelia flicked her furry ears forward and clicked her tongue. "Can I give you some advice?" She didn't wait for him to answer. "Training out there with an instructor is all well and good, but for most of us in here, we learned by doing." She swiped her sword through the air between them. "The result is pretty much chaos. So discipline and form don't mean much here." She punctuated the statement with a wink. Then she lunged.

A blur of purple mist came at him, too fast to dodge. He thrust his sword forward, drawing it a few inches so that the steel peeked out from its sheath, enough to block. Impact radiated through his palms as a rush of wind blew past his face. The air crackled, and his feet slid back a few inches. Whatever damage bonus she was getting from her stats must have been massive. He glanced at his wrist. She hadn't even hit him, and he'd still taken a bit of damage from the impact to his hands.

She forced him back another foot, metal scraping against metal. Amelia's eye shifted to the three inches of steel sticking out of his sheath that held her at bay.

"Nice block. You improvised." She sounded surprised.

"So this is a lesson then?" Corvin grunted, partly to sound tough but also because it took everything he had to stay standing.

"I'd feel bad killing you without at least teaching you something first." She shrugged, releasing some of the pressure held against him.

There it was. The moment he'd been waiting for. Corvin cracked a smile, a fang poking out the corner of his mouth.

"My turn." He slammed his katana back into its sheath, trapping the edge of her saber in between as he twisted his weapon in an attempt to wrench hers out of her hands. She fumbled and jumped backward but didn't lose her grip. He didn't wait for her to recover, tearing his sword free from its scabbard and whipping the empty sheath at her head. Her sword swept up, splitting the black lacquered wood in half as part of it clubbed her in the eye.

Corvin heaved a breath, still hunched over in the follow-through from his throw. Obviously, he was aware that a few kendo classes wouldn't beat someone like Amelia who had developed her own style of fighting through years of improvising. No, that would never work. He needed to fight like the rest of his friends. All instinct and attitude. A hot mess of chaos and skill. Lucky for him, he'd had a helpful *Leaf* to teach him. Well, teach might not have been the right word. Kegan had made a habit of shooting him with arrows every time he had his back turned. It was meant to troll him, but eventually, Corvin had gotten good at finding ways to fight back.

Amelia lowered the tip of her saber to the floor, a blank expression on her face. A crimson glow faded from her eyebrow. The hit hadn't carried any real damage since it wasn't from his sword, but still, it must have been unexpected. She let out a single mad laugh, her face hard to read. Then her mouth turned up into a terrifying smile.

"What level are you?"

His left ear twitched as a couple gunshots went off behind him. Corvin debated on lying to keep her in the dark about what abilities he did or didn't have but settled on the truth. "Seventy-seven."

Amelia flipped her saber down and pushed its tip into the floor so she could rest one hand on the butt of its grip. "And here I was spouting off lessons on improvisation like an ass when you've got that part down." Another few gunshots fired off from the other end of the room. She didn't flinch.

Corvin suppressed the urge to look behind him. "I have strong friends. I had to catch up."

"I see—" Amelia started as the far side of the tavern erupted into a storm of fire and bullets. Max's fight had taken a turn for the worse.

Corvin held his ground, tilting his sword so that he could see the reflection of what was behind him.

Amelia rolled her eyes as her *Cauldron* mage stumbled and lit half the place on fire. "Hey, Klaxon, I liked this place."

The mage ignored her and refocused his spell on Max as the *Fury* threw his weight into a wall, smashing through it. Klaxon's spell ran its course soon after, but not before guaranteeing that the tavern's days as a purveyor of libations was over. The mage glanced at the Max shaped hole in the wall. Then he staggered over to the bar where he grabbed a bottle, uncorked it with his teeth, and took a drink. With his priorities in order, he walked out the door to find Max.

Corvin returned his attention to his opponent, who was

again leaning on her sword as the building began to burn around them. She plucked the saber out of the wood and raised it in his direction.

"Ready for more?"

"Okay, maybe you can teach me something else." Corvin took a shallow breath of smoky air as flames climbed the walls.

"Maybe." Her eyes narrowed.

Corvin raised his katana just in time to deflect what came next. Steel sang as her saber slid to the side of his head close enough to give him a nose full of purple mist. It smelled like lilacs and death. A second later, she planted a foot in his gut. He crashed against the bar, knocking over an empty mug. It hit the floor with a hollow thrum. Amelia hooked the tip of her weapon through its handle mid-bounce and launched the mug in his direction. He ducked as it sailed overhead, smashing a bottle on the shelf behind the bar. She kept coming.

He kicked off the floor and threw his weight against the counter as her saber streaked through the space where he'd been. A few innocent bar stools took the hit, and he landed with his rear sitting on the counter like a ridiculous puppet hiding an arm up his backside. He blocked a blow aimed at his neck. The impact sent him tumbling behind the bar. She followed with a downward strike that split the countertop above as he hit the floor. He sprang up only to duck back down as her saber tore through the air, crashing through the contents of the bar's shelves. Broken glass rained down on him along with a shower of booze. A tiny flame icon appeared on his wrist next to his name to represent a newfound weakness to fire. Corvin's jaw tightened.

That's not good.

He stayed down and searched the floor around him, finding an unbroken bottle. On the other side of the bar, Amelia's footsteps strafed to the side, probably waiting for him to poke his head up so she could cut it off. Corvin focused on the sound, trying to pinpoint where she was. Then he jumped straight up onto the bar and threw the bottle.

She cut the projectile out of the air, shattering the vessel and successfully covering herself in bottom-shelf virtual rum. Corvin didn't waste time, lunging at her with all his strength while she was distracted by her new flammable status. She dodged to the side, and his sword hit the floorboards with a solid thrust, lodging it in place. "Damn," he cursed as he abandoned his weapon, unable to pull it back out without getting bit by her saber.

He scrambled away toward the flames at the other end of the tavern and yanked the remains of a wooden stool out of the fire by an unburnt leg. He lobbed it in Amelia's direction, and it hit the floor with a burst of embers, forcing her back, away from his sword. He dashed for his weapon.

Then things got out of control.

Amelia pressed two fingers against the back of her saber and slid them down its length, adding a current of energy to the weapon. Corvin reached his katana as she wound up and shouted the word, "Shockwave!" Corvin didn't bother pulling his sword free. Instead, he ducked down, bracing himself against his blade and shielding his head with one arm. A blast of power swept out from her in an arc that crashed into him and everything around him. His skin lit up crimson in a hurricane of tiny needles. Tables and chairs flipped behind him as embers exploded into the air.

Corvin didn't have that attack yet. No, he wouldn't unlock that skill for at least another year. A glance at his health told him that he couldn't take another.

Amelia didn't let up, her fingers already swiping down her saber for another. Corvin tore his katana from the floor and ran for cover, expecting another Shockwave only to be surprised when she yelled, "Phantom Strike," instead. He stopped dead in his tracks as an invisible blade streaked past his face like heatwaves through the air. It carved a path through the room until it smashed straight through the wall.

She twirled her saber and spun on her heel, throwing

another three phantom blades as she danced to one side. Corvin dodged two but took the third to his leg. He fell to one knee with a grunt and touched two fingers to the back of his sword. *When in Rome*, he thought, as he whispered, "Phantom Strike." At least it was a skill he had. He swung, sending an invisible force through the air. It destroyed a chair but ran out of power a few feet shy of where Amelia stood, leaving her unharmed and laughing. The skill didn't have the range to compete at her level.

He stabbed his katana into the floor and hoisted himself back to his feet. His chest heaved as he coughed out a lungful of smoke. He hadn't even landed a real hit. Of course, he still had his trump card—the basilisk eye hiding beneath the patch on his face. Though, any way he thought of it, using his eye felt like cheating.

Embers drifted through the air as the fire consumed every-thing, climbing each and every surface but the floor between them. Corvin's health ticked down below twenty percent from the heat. Amelia glanced at her wrist, clearly realizing the danger they both were in. She didn't run, or at least, she didn't run for the door. She wasn't finished with him yet. A wild yell erupted from her throat as she charged.

Corvin pushed off into a labored run to meet her. He drew back his sword, resigned to go down fighting. He had never expected to win, just to slow her down long enough for Max and Kegan to tip things in their favor. Then a loud crack came from above.

Panic flooded Corvin's body as the ceiling's support beam began to fall, its surface consumed by fire. He dropped to one knee and dug his sword into the floor to stop himself before he ran straight under it. Amelia kept running, her ears pinned back while her mouth cried out the same mad scream. Her eyes were trained on his head.

She doesn't see it, he realized. *She's running right into danger.* The beam was going to crush her. Dread bubbled in his chest. He didn't want her dead. They needed information, and dead players didn't talk. With that, he ripped off his eye patch and met her gaze.

Amelia's face blanched white as she froze in mid-step, her body locked in place by Corvin's yellow eye. A pulse of pain hummed through his skull just as the ceiling's beam crashed into the floor in a mass of fire and debris. The sound was deafening. He lost track of Amelia, unsure if he'd been able to stop her in time to keep her from being flattened. Flames crept close as he fell back on his rear. He checked his health. Down to ten percent. The tiny flammable icon still hung above his name, taunting him. Then a saber slammed into the floor beside him.

"Get off your ass. We've overstayed our welcome." Amelia reached her hand down, leaning on her sword. Apparently, she'd reevaluated their relationship.

Corvin grabbed her wrist as she took his and yanked him to his feet. They lowered their weapons and ran for the door, the opening engulfed in flames.

She shrugged off her coat and threw it over both of their heads, pulling him in close to her shoulder. "Try not to die, right?"

Corvin flashed her the status readout on his wrist, the sliver of what was left of his health shrinking as the heat grew.

"I'll try."

CHAPTER NINE

Kirabell stood tall in the middle of one of Lucem's empty side streets. With one hand on her chest, she let the importance of what she was about to say fill her voice with emotion. "How about the House of Pizza?"

"We're not calling it that." Ginger walked past her without even looking, her face buried in her journal, where a new page read 'House Settings'. A line labeled 'Name' remained blank.

Kira spun and ran back to the front of the party. "What about the House of Badass Mother—"

"It won't let you write swear words." Farn walked past her as well, tapping away at her journal with a pen. A grid of shapes filled the page, allowing her to combine and scale them to form something new. "Are you sure you want me to make our house emblem?"

"Of course, you work as a designer at Checkpoint." Ginger ignored Kira as she passed by her a second time. "I have no artistic talent whatsoever. It will be better if you do it."

Kira deflated as both of her friends ignored her, resigning to following in silence. She had been making house name suggestions ever since they left the alley behind the registration building. None had been a winner so far. She pulled out her own journal and opened it to her map. The waypoint that Ginger's friend Samhain had given them stained the page with a red dot. They were almost there.

Supposedly, the waypoint lead to a shop where they could buy custom clothes to blend in during the party tomorrow night. Kira made a face at the point highlighted on the map. She wasn't looking forward to dress shopping. Especially with Ginger, who would probably force her into getting whatever was the most revealing.

Kira sighed and flipped to her house settings page to look at the grid of shapes that Farn had been agonizing over. It reminded her of when she had created her character, back when she had to pick the activation icon for her stat-sleeve that now adorned the underside of her wrist as a tattoo of virtual ink. She turned her forearm over to where the black outline of a keyhole sat below her caster and touched it with one finger. Her stat-sleeve, a delicate pattern of filigree, bloomed from the shape, covering her skin to display her party readout along the underside of her arm. Her main menu options appeared on top, woven into the design. She tapped keyhole again, and it all shrank back into itself as if it was never there. Then she got an idea.

"Hey, what did you guys pick for your stat-sleeve's activation icon?"

Ginger flashed Kira her wrist. "I picked a heart. Figured it was appropriate considering I only started playing to get a job at the club and make ends meet."

"And you picked a Celtic knot." Kira didn't need to ask Farn since she'd seen her icon enough times while hiding behind the woman's shield to remember it well.

"Really? I always liked those." Ginger strafed over to the *Shield*, looking down at her arm. "What does it mean?"

"It's a love knot." Farn lowered her journal and clasped her free hand around her unarmored wrist. "It was the default icon that came with the Celtic sleeve design. I didn't know what it meant when I chose it."

"Then why did you pick it?" Ginger pried.

Kira cringed at the question, having asked it herself before.

Farn shrugged plainly. "Because Noctem doesn't have many sleeve designs that show up well on dark skin. The Celtic one was easiest to see on my arm since it's bolder than most. So yeah, being black doesn't always give you many options."

Ginger gave a sheepish nod. "You should tell Alastair to change that. I mean, you do know the head of the company. Then you could pick a new one. Something you like."

"I don't think I'd change it. I don't dislike the design, and the love knot reminds me that I have people in my life that I care about now." Farn ran the metal fingers of her gauntlet over her wrist.

"Well, that settles it," Kira declared, grabbing both Ginger's and Farn's hands so that their activation icons were visible. "We started this house together; we should use our icons as part of its emblem."

Farn opened her journal again. "Okay, a heart, a keyhole, and a Celtic love knot. Let's see what I can make with that. She didn't take long, tapping the page here and there to move and scale the shapes until she gave a nod and smiled. "How's this?" She turned the book outward to show a heart bordered by Celtic line work, a keyhole at its center.

"That's perfect." Kira bounced on her toes.

"Looks like we have a name." Ginger raised her journal and started writing. "Welcome to House Lockheart."

The moment her pen stopped moving, a system chime sounded in Kira's ears.

Ginger opened the ring box that Finn had given them to find a plain, silver house ring. It rippled and reshaped like liquid to form the emblem of Lockheart. The *Coin* slipped it on her finger, then opened and closed the box to produce two more rings.

Kira admired hers as it resized itself to fit her small finger.

She checked her status page to find that her title of Archmage had become official. On top of which several notifications faded onto the paper below her name.

WELCOME TO HOUSE LOCKHEART!
Loyalty: The City of Rend
Members: Three

HOUSE CHATLINE ENABLED
Activation Instructions: Hold your equipped house ring within three inches of your mouth and speak normally to broadcast your voice to all members

NEW SKILL SLOT UNLOCKED
As one of the three leading members of House Lockheart, you gain a fourth skill slot for your character

NEW ARCHMAGE SKILL, OVERCAST
Description: Allows any mage class to add additional mana to any spell to increase its potency

NEW UNIQUE QUEST, RECLAIMING REND
Objective: Unknown
Reward: Unknown
Part One: Locate a survivor of the fall

Kira's heart fluttered as she read through the pages of her journal. "I didn't know you got skills for starting a house. We should have done this sooner."

Farn flipped a few pages as well. "Yeah, I read that online. You get a new one for being the top three members of a house. It's different depending on your title."

"Even I knew that," Ginger added.

"Okay, I'm out of the loop, apparently. Max is the one who researches things. That's too much work for me." Kira shrugged. "Anyway, what's with this unique quest with all the unknowns? I have to admit, I'm pretty interested."

"Must have something to do with our house being loyal to Rend," Farn assumed.

Ginger's face lit up, and she started writing something in her journal. "What good is being friends with the head of Checkpoint Systems if you can't ask him about a weird quest? He might not answer something like this, but it's worth sending a message." She finished writing, then scribbled the word 'send' across the page, followed by a check mark to confirm.

Kira closed her journal and shoved it back into her pouch. "So what skills did you guys get?"

Farn and Ginger read off their notifications.

LADY OF LOCKHEART SKILL, ROYALTY
Description: Grants a player the power to claim a city for the glory of their house.

FIRST KNIGHT SKILL, SURE-FOOT
Description: Allows any combat class to hold their ground and fight while standing on any surface, ignores gravity.

"Holy crap, I think I can wall-run." Farn grinned from ear to ear. "Max is going to be crazy jealous."

In contrast, Ginger deflated. "Mine kind of sucks. I don't really want to be royalty."

Kira offered nothing more to the conversation. Instead, she kept her face hard to read and snapped open a caster, her spellcraft menu appearing after an upward swipe. A curved grid of glyphs glowed before her as she spun the rows to set up a simple pulse spell. She made sure to add in the new symbol for Overcast. She paused to choose a target, feeling a wicked, little urge guide her hand as she swiped down the activation column.

A circular sigil appeared before her, catching her off guard. Eventually, the system highlighted a hand print at its center when she took a second too long to figure out what to do with it.

She pressed her palm against the sigil, feeling an electric tingle as rings formed around it, drawing lines between them as the shapes glowed brighter. Each circle seemed to represent five percent of her overall mana. At the rate they appeared, she realized how easily she could blow her points. She pulled away, leaving a full quarter of her mana in the spell.

Ginger let out a laugh. "Nice going, what did you intend to cast that on without any targets?" Her face fell as Kira's mouth began to curl upward. "Oh, shi–"

The pulse spell was easily the weakest in the game. It was also Kira's only offensive ability, leaving her capable of little more than throwing an annoying burst of energy that could at best deflect an attack. At least, that was before she had become an Archmage.

A white puff of power exploded into the air in front of Ginger, mid-swear, launching the *Coin* six feet through the air. She hit the ground in an end-over-end tumble that left her sprawled out in the middle of the side street with her rear sticking up toward the sky. Incoherent curse words spilled from her mouth as she shoved her body off the cobblestones.

Kira checked the *Coin's* health, which was still close to full. Even with Overcast, the spell still didn't carry much damage, but man, the force of it was ridiculous.

Ginger stomped her way back to Kira with rage burning in her eyes.

"Wait, wait." Kira held up her hands.

Ginger didn't wait, her hand darting out, fingers spread wide, their tips curled like claws. Luckily, that was when Kira remembered she could fly, and the *Coin* got a handful of air as she shot up just out of arm's reach to hover overhead.

"I regret nothing," Kira declared before weaving to the side to dodge a grappling line that streaked through the space where she'd been. *Damn, forgot Coins can do that.*

"Hold still, damn it!" Ginger retracted the line that she'd fired from the launcher on her wrist. "I'm trying to murder you."

Kira placed her hands on her hips and flew in a little circle. "But aren't we in a hurry to buy fancy ball gowns? You can't dress me up like your personal doll if I'm respawning."

"I'm so going to pick out something you hate now. It's gonna be all high slits and booty."

"But, my Lady," Kira kept her tone polite, "you were going to do that anyway."

"Well, this house fell apart in record time," commented Farn, somehow from directly behind Kira.

She turned to find the *Shield* grinning at her while standing on the wall of the building behind her as if it had been the ground. Kira laughed.

"Hey, Spider-Farn. What happens if you jump like that?"

Farn shrugged, then took an experimental hop, falling as soon as she broke contact with the wall. "Damn!" She reached out for anything to stop her fall, the closest thing being Kira's foot.

"Nice, Farn!" Ginger jumped into the air and pumped a fist. "Now, drag her down. I knew having underlings would come in handy."

Farn clutched her journal in one hand and clung to Kira's ankle with the other. "Umm, I don't really have that kind of control here."

Kira gritted her teeth and pushed mana through the spell-work of her wings as the dangling *Shield* weighed her down. The result left Farn bounding along the ground like an astronaut on the moon before she let go. Ginger caught up soon after, rubbing her hands together like a cartoon villain as Kira settled back to the ground.

"Okay, truce?" Kira cast a light heal to recover the small amount of health the *Coin* had lost.

"Fine. I didn't really want to kill you anyways." Ginger flicked her in the forehead with two fingers.

Farn raised her journal and blew a layer of pixie dust off its cover before turning back to her map. "Good. 'Cause I think we found that dress shop we were looking for."

Kira turned, rubbing at the skin between her eyebrows where she'd been flicked. The shop sat at the end of the side street where a single lamp flickered, its flame struggling to stay lit. "That's it?"

"That is not what I expected." Ginger double checked her map, then looked back up at the shop. Its cracked windows smiled back with a jagged grin.

Kira stepped closer to read the sign that hung next to the door on a pair of rusty chains.

"Fashion Souls?"

CHAPTER TEN

Kegan burst through the tavern door at breakneck speed, only to run smack into a railing. The river below filled his view. Apparently, the walkway outside had been smaller than he remembered. His heart made a run for it, leaping into his throat as the rickety wood cracked and splintered under the strain of his weight. A string of rushed obscenities escaped from his mouth.

Suddenly, the door behind him flew open as the entire fighting force of House Winter Moon erupted from within. Kegan spun, his back against the rail, his gaze meeting the furious stares of his pursuers.

Then he snorted.

He couldn't help it.

Their eyes bulged, and their skin blanched as the look on their faces shifted from determined murder, to 'oh god, must stop now'! The player in front skidded and threw out his arms in an effort to hold back his comrades. His effort went in vain as the rest barreled forward, shoving him toward the edge where a flimsy bit of wood stood between Kegan and the empty canyon.

Well, here we go, Kegan thought before doing the only thing he could, leaning back and flipping over the rail. The world went end-over-end. He reached for an arrow, nocking it as he fell. He glanced at the fletching at the end to make sure he'd grabbed the right one. The silver feathers of a Shift Arrow glinted as he let it fly into a walkway below. It hit the wood with a solid thunk.

Kegan held his breath as his body imploded into a single spark of light, feeling like a beverage being sucked through a straw. A fraction of a second later, he burst into existence just a dozen feet to the side, holding the arrow he'd fired in one hand. He'd landed upside down on the platform, but at least he wasn't falling. That was more than he could say for the Amelia's men.

Wood cracked and snapped above as the lead player flew past him. Their eyes met for a brief second as the man plummeted to his death. Kegan gave him an upside-down wave as four more of his comrades flew past.

Five down, a few dozen to go.

"The *Leaf* is on the lower level!" a voice shouted from somewhere above.

"Oh good, one of their fallen must have told the others where I was over their house chat on the way down." Kegan righted himself and waited. He was trying to keep them busy, so he couldn't have them losing so fast.

He shoved the spent Shift Arrow back into his quiver as its fletching dulled from silver to gray. He grimaced at the fading enchantment. The feathers had cost him more credits than he cared to admit. He cursed Ginger under his breath for extorting him a year ago when she'd sold them to him. He'd been using them sparingly ever since, but now, he was running low.

Damn, only two left.

There wasn't time to worry about it, as a group of unhappy players poured down a stairway nearby.

"There he is!"

Kegan took off at a sprint, an arrow whizzing by his head while bullets pelted the wall nearby. He ducked past a pair of players, who happened to be in the wrong place at the wrong time, just as an arrow struck one in the leg. The following dispute slowed down his pursuers, allowing Kegan to race across a bridge to the other side of the canyon in relative safety.

Or so he thought.

Suddenly, a massive woman crashed through another group of random players ahead of him, pushing two over the edge. Again, wrong place wrong time. Kegan couldn't help but feel a little responsible as their screams faded into the distance below.

The woman was a faunus, judging from the curled horns that wrapped around her head. The leather gear of a *Rage* class covered her body, and a Winter Moon banner hung from her shoulder like a cape.

"I guess there's no chance you're here for someone else?" Kegan hooked a thumb at a player behind him, who backed away out of view in record time.

"Huraaaggggg!" The *Rage* pushed off into a run.

"Why do *Rage* classes always respond like that?" Kegan made a ridiculous pop with his mouth as he blew out a breath. Then he shrugged and started running to meet her. *When in Rome and all that.* "Yarrrrrrr!"

The woman ripped a rusty, two-handed claymore from its sheath with a metallic screech. She swung the weapon out to her side, holding it low so it smashed through each of the posts that held the railing to the walkway as she ran. The wood exploded on contact. A wave of splinters trailed in her wake. Her weapon damage must have been through the roof.

The pounding vibration of her steps shook the boards under Kegan's feet as he closed the gap and leaped to the side. She swung, her blade tearing through the air, missing him by mere inches. He pivoted on one foot and slipped past her, only looking back to laugh. "Ha–yurk," was all he got out before a hand snapped back and grabbed the collar of his shirt. Her claymore clanged to the floor as he was thrust out over the edge of the platform, held by a pair of meaty fists. He scrambled on instinct to get a grip on her wrist and keep from falling.

Kegan's mind slammed into a wall of panicked confusion. The woman shouldn't have been that strong. No, in Noctem, physical strength echoed a player's real-world body, unless they'd done something dumb, like pick the fairy race as a character. Though, that would only make a player weaker. For her to be that strong, she would actually have to be that big in reality as well. He swallowed with an audible gulp.

"Hey now, this isn't the sort of physical relationship I was looking for. I mean, we don't even know each other's names."

"Kashka," the woman grunted right before shaking him like she was trying to evenly distribute pulp in a carton of orange juice. He hated pulp. It made his teeth feel weird.

"Nice. To. Meet. You," Kegan squealed as his head whipped back and forth. His brain took a moment to settle before he remembered he was still clutching his bow and had two more Shift Arrows in his quiver. He smiled and choked out a defiant, "Go ahead, drop me."

Kashka must have seen his little teleport trick earlier because her grip held firm. She was probably planning to hold him there until the rest of the Winter Moon's troops could arrive.

Kegan flailed his legs, half in an attempt to free himself from her grasp and half to get a look around. The rest of Amelia's house rushed across the bridge with clear intent to make him as un-alive as possible. Again, he did the only thing he could. He reached for an arrow and repeatedly stabbed his massive captor in the hand. It worked about as well as he expected.

The *Rage* might not have been much for conversation, but she wasn't dumb enough to drop him. Instead, she simply threw him at a stack of barrels nearby. That was when Kegan learned something new. He was already aware that the *Rage* class had a perk that allowed them to equip anything as a weapon and apply their damage bonus to it. What he didn't know was that the passive ability worked by adding their stats to anything they held. Apparently, the last thing that this particular *Rage* had held was him.

The barrels burst on impact, sending a wave of ale splashing into the canyon wall behind, along with Kegan. He hit hard enough to crack stone. A nearby support pin sprang from the rock, and the entire platform tipped downward. Ale poured down the incline like a waterfall.

Kegan slipped on the wet boards, virtual ale dripping in his face from his hair. His clothes were soaked. He checked his wrist, where a pair of tattooed koi fish swam around his health readout.

Down halfway.

He got back to his feet, then flinched as a roar echoed from behind. Kashka stood, the glowing red marks of where he'd stabbed her in the wrist fading away. The rest of the Winter Moons grouped up behind her. Kegan sighed and made a break for the nearest set of stairs.

An army of shouts and curse words followed.

From there, he led his pursuers on a merry chase up several stairways and across the largest bridge in the city. It was at that point that a second group, almost as large as the first, rushed up the stairs from below to merge into one. Apparently, there were more to Amelia's troops than what had chased him from the tavern, forcing him to wonder if he had enough arrows in his inventory. He shrugged. It was too late to worry about that now.

That was when he caught an explosion out of the corner of his eye from back at the tavern where he'd started. A ball of fire erupted from the side of the building, a slightly crispy Max leaping out of it. Kegan smiled as he climbed another flight of stairs.

"Oh good, looks like he's doing fine."

Behind him, Kashka had fallen behind, being too large to navigate the narrow walkways with ease. The rest of the house rushed past her.

Finally, Kegan turned onto a narrow bridge made of

nothing but boards and rope. It was perfect. He ran halfway across, then spun. It was time he started fighting back.

He let off a handful of arrows, killing the three in the front with a few well-aimed criticals. The others retreated back while a couple *Leaf* class players made their way to the front. The two opposing archers carefully nocked their bows and fired one arrow each. Kegan hooked his foot around one of the ropes attached to the side of the bridge and threw his weight against the opposite handrail. One arrow missed, while the other grazed his shoulder, leaving a glowing strip of crimson across his skin. The rope against his back creaked under the strain of his weight as he fired back.

The hits landed.

Two criticals on each.

Kegan pulled back a fifth arrow, letting its feathers rest against the corner of his mouth. He whispered the words, "Piercing Strike," then let it go. The arrow streaked through the group, penetrating one player after another, followed by a trail of red light. The damage decreased with each consecutive hit, but still, it was enough to let the players in the back know that they weren't safe. In response, several retreated off the bridge, and a couple heal spells went off in the distance.

That was when the hulking *Rage* reappeared. She pushed her way through their numbers to the front of the group with a *Shield* class in front for protection. She'd reclaimed her claymore and carried it resting on her shoulder. The Winter Moon banner billowed off her shoulder as the wind blew through the canyon.

Kegan took that as his cue to get moving again. He spun on one foot, only to stop dead in his tracks while a second group of players filed onto the bridge at the other side. They must have gone around to flank him. They had been smart about it too, putting two *Shields* in front to keep the *Blades* that followed safe. There wasn't much he could do against that.

"Crap." Kegan checked his quiver. He only had five arrows left, including the two Shift Arrows he'd been saving. "Double crap." He grimaced at the thought of blowing another one just to escape. He'd probably get trapped again anyway. *Unless...* he thought as the corner of his mouth tugged up into a crooked grin.

The surrounding players closed in carefully, like he was a wild animal, cornered but still dangerous. Once they got close enough, their *Blades* would overtake him. The *Rage* tightened her grip on her sword and pointed a threatening finger at him. Kegan ignored her, looking past to the rear of the group to wait for the last of them set foot onto the bridge.

The more the merrier.

Kegan whipped his head from one side to the other as if searching for a way out. Then he grabbed three arrows and ran. In a desperate charge, he nocked his bow and sprinted toward the smaller of the groups. A final roar erupted from his throat. He was going to die fighting. At least, that was what he wanted them to think.

One of the *Shields* dropped low while the other guarded high, their gauntlets held steady, ready to stop whatever useless attack he could throw at them.

Kegan suppressed a laugh. They may as well have been holding up a sign saying 'right this way, sir'. He jumped, stepping one foot on the glowing generator of the first *Shield* before hopping up to the second like stairs.

"Thanks for the boost."

He kicked off and leaped over the side, his back arched like a high jump competitor. Then he drew back his bow and shouted one word to activate a skill, "Cutter!"

The air split as two streaks of green shot past the sides of the rope bridge. Then all fell silent. It didn't last long. Fibers snapped one after another, the supports tearing apart with a satisfying crack. Screams and expletives came next as the entirety of House Winter Moon's numbers scrambled back toward the canyon walls.

It was far too late.

Kegan took a moment to admire his handy work, the players, falling like rain, their arms flailing. The sight reminded him that he was in the same boat, running out of time before he hit the water below. He gave one last chuckle, then nocked another arrow. Its silver feathers sparkled as he let it go. Still one Shift Arrow left.

CHAPTER ELEVEN

The shop window squeaked against Kira's face as she struggled to peek inside. At first glance, the store seemed to be closed. The place was dark except for a dim flickering from somewhere near the back. There were silhouettes of small forms, but no matter how hard she pressed her cheek against the glass, she couldn't make out much else. Despite appearances, the 'open' sign hanging on the door left little room for argument.

"I guess we go in." Kira peeled her face off the window.

Farn nodded and took the liberty of going first, probably a habit for a *Shield* like herself.

Kira didn't argue.

A bell chimed from above the door as she opened it. The sound faded away as soon as the door closed behind them, leaving the shop in silence once again. No one came out in greeting. Kira snapped open a caster and activated a low-level light spell to make its crystal glow brighter to brighten the dim space. She immediately wished she hadn't.

Ginger gasped, holding her breath as if not letting it out would somehow keep her hidden.

"I'm not so sure this is the right place after all." A shiver crawled down Kira's spine, and she took a single step back toward her friends. Toward protection.

They were surrounded, eyes staring at them from each of the figures that had sat hidden in the shadows. They lined the shelves from one wall to the other, sitting motionless. Still as death.

"Dolls," Ginger said the word with a quiver in her voice. "Why would a clothing shop be full of dolls?" She took a step toward Kira as if being together would keep her safe.

There were dozens of them. No, hundreds. The dolls covered every available surface except for a sales counter near the back. Each wore a different outfit with their ball-jointed bodies staged in various poses. It was as if someone had put a lot of effort into dressing each one to be unique. Although, that didn't make them any less creepy. Not to mention, there was something familiar about them.

Kira suppressed a shiver, shoving the feeling down until only her thumb tapped against her thigh. "Maybe Samhain was still mad about being tricked into meeting and decided to trick us back."

Farn groaned and walked across the shop to the sales counter where a single doll sat next to a leather-bound book. "They're just a bunch of dolls. What's the big deal?" She opened the book to a cover page that read 'Welcome to Fashion Souls'. Below that, the words 'Request Consultation' appeared on the page. Around the text, a line traced the outline of a handprint. "I guess that's self-explanatory," Farn assumed as she reached for the page.

That was when the doll beside the book moved. Its porcelain face snapped up in a jerky, unnatural motion to gaze at the *Shield*.

"Fashion," the doll said in a voice like tearing paper despite its mouth not moving to form the word.

"Mother shit!" Farn leaped away from the counter.

Kira did the same, nearly jumping out of her skin. She didn't make it far before running into Ginger, who glommed onto her. Kira didn't care, wrapping her arms around the *Coin* right back in panic.

Farn activated her *Shield* gauntlet, its generator snapping out and rotating into place to project a barrier. She pressed her back up to Kira and Ginger as they clung to one another. From all around them, the dolls turned their heads to stare in their direction, neck joints creaking with an awful creak.

A chorus of, "Fashion," erupted from all sides.

Kira threw herself between Ginger and Farn, only peeking around the *Shield's* shoulder for a second.

The doll on the counter readjusted its head to lock eyes with her.

"Request consultation."

No one moved.

"Request consultation… or die."

"Okay, nope." Ginger pushed Kira forward as sacrifice, then started for the door.

Farn did the opposite, inching toward the counter while keeping her shield up and reaching for the book with her free hand.

Kira froze in the middle of the shop. She could either hold her ground with Farn or head for the door.

Again, the dolls spoke, "Fashion." Their high-pitched voices sounded like a whirlwind of broken glass.

Kira made her choice, leaping past Farn and slapping her hand against the book's open page. She held her breath and closed her eyes tight.

Everything went quiet.

Kira cracked open one eye as the shop's lights brightened to a normal level. The dolls remained right where they had been, staring straight ahead, as if they had never moved to begin with. They looked completely different in the light, to a point where they were almost pretty.

Ginger took her hand off the door and stepped back into the center of the shop to rejoin Kira and Farn.

"Glad to know you'd leave us behind when things get scary, M'Lady." Farn nudged Ginger in the arm.

"That's right. I'm Lady of our house. My life takes priority." Ginger held her head high.

"I guess they're just dolls." Kira leaned over to the doll on the counter. "Now I feel kind of dumb."

That was when someone cleared their throat behind them.

"Actually, they would have killed you if you hadn't passed Noctem's level twenty-five cap."

The three members of House Lockheart spun to find a strange man standing in a doorway at one side of the shop. Kira hadn't heard the door open. Come to think of it, she didn't remember there being a door there in the first place. The man leaned one shoulder against the wall, removing a pair of thin-rimmed glasses from his face to clean them with a cloth.

"I may have dressed them up a little with new outfits, but the dolls themselves are technically monsters. Level twelve marionettes, actually." He placed his glasses back on his nose and stuffed the cloth into a vest pocket so that half of it remained hanging out the top. Then he ran a hand over the nearest doll, feeling the fabric of its dress between his fingers. "I picked them up in the orphanage in Rend, actually. Had to trap each in a trunk and drag them back here to have them re-tasked. I find they keep away the normals."

"I knew they looked familiar." Kira relaxed, somehow less scared of them upon hearing that they came from her new home city.

"Yes, well, welcome to Fashion Souls. My name is Larkin." He bowed his head, placing one finger on his glasses so that they didn't slip down his nose. "Now, if you would come with me, we can get this consultation underway." He clapped his hands and faded back through the door as if they were expected to follow.

Kira exchanged looks with the rest of her house, then shrugged, following the strange shopkeep through the door and up the narrow staircase beyond.

The man's character model was human as far as she could tell. He wore a long apron wrapped around his waist with a large pair of scissors tucked into a sheath hanging from the back of his belt. They bounced as he stepped up the stairs, as did the red ribbon that tied back his light blue hair.

A large attic space waited at the top of the stairs, complete with a high ceiling full of exposed beams. Crating materials littered the room—wood, fabric, leather, and metal. Some of it was organized and stored on shelves while the rest had been left lying about as if they were part of an ongoing project. There were even a few buckets filled unceremoniously with gemstones.

Three full-length mirrors occupied one wall, positioned to show multiple angles to the viewer. The other side of the room held dozens of tools hanging from hooks. A headless mannequin sat in the far corner, draped in beautiful white fabric.

Larkin kicked a few things to the side to make some room, then strode over to the table and leaned against it. He snatched up a player journal from its surface and dug a pen out of the slot in its binding. "Now for your consult–"

"Oh, you're a person?" Kira interrupted.

Larkin let his journal fall so he could stare at her properly. "Of course I am. Did you think I was an NPC?"

"Kind of. You run a shop, and you're not wearing any real gear."

He placed his book back on the table and held up a couple fingers. "You are wrong in two ways. First," he pushed off of the table and swept a hand across the room, "this is a custom fashion boutique. I have a deal with Checkpoint Systems to provide and develop this space. And I assure you," he ran his fingers down the buttons of his vest, "while this outfit might not have the stats that some other equipment does, it is not without its advantages." A knowing smile washed across his face before he returned to his place at the table and picked up his journal. "Now, as I was saying. You three are here for a consultation. Yes? May I have your names?"

Ginger stepped forward to answer.

Larkin wrote down a few lines and flipped to the back of his journal to where his inspector sat in the recessed space in its back cover. He tapped at it a few times, bringing up each of their public profiles. They didn't contain much more than their class, level, titles, and house affiliation, but it was probably enough to give him an idea of who they were.

Kira wondered if he would notice their new-found loyalty to Rend listed under their house name. His brow furrowed, looking puzzled.

Guess so.

He hesitated, as if trying to figure out how to proceed. "May I ask how you heard about this place?"

"A friend of mine at the Everleigh Club sent us. His name's Samhain."

"Ah, yes." Larkin slipped back into customer service mode. "And I assume he mentioned my fee?"

Ginger hesitated. "Umm, no."

Larkin's pen stopped moving. "I should inform you that my cost is one thousand dollars each, transferable by payment ledger."

"What?" Kira jumped like a startled cat while Farn let out a sudden, awkward laugh.

"Seriously? We can get dresses anywhere," Ginger argued.

"Dresses?" Larkin's eyebrow twitched up.

"Yes, we need formalwear for an event tomorrow, as well as appropriate gear for two bodyguards."

"Hmm, interesting," he mumbled to himself. "No one asks for that sort of thing. No, mostly, they just want custom armor." He tapped his pen against his lips, then pulled it away in a quick motion. "What event are you attending?"

Farn tucked her thumbs into the sash around her waist. "Some kind of party at the palace in Reliqua."

Larkin scoffed. "The snake's conquest ball? I think not. I'll have no design of mine ingratiating anyone with that crowd. Lord Berwyn and his little power play have practically crippled my ability to get some of the materials I need." He finished the statement by flicking the pair of shears out from the sheath at his back and driving them into the table beside him. The impact splintered wood and shook the room.

Kira flinched at the sudden moment, searching for the class emblem on the back of his hand. Sure enough, it had appeared along with his stat-sleeve as soon as he'd drawn the pair of scissors, the icon of a *Rage*. It was really the only possibility, since the crafting tool now stuck all the way through the thick table; it obviously carried a massive damage bonus from the class perk.

Judging from the embellishments around his class emblem, his level was maxed at the current system cap of 175. Kira took a breath and swallowed. It was thirty levels above her own.

He could probably kill all three of us without breaking a sweat.

Regardless, she stepped closer before the *Rage* had the chance to throw them out altogether. "Umm, would it help if we told you that we don't exactly have good intentions for being there?"

Larkin froze mid-way through an annoyed huff. "Meaning?"

Ginger slinked up behind Kira and placed her hands on her shoulders. "Meaning that Berwyn and his house may not be a problem for you if we're successful."

Larkin held stock-still for a moment. Then he smiled. "Well, why didn't you say so? If that is the case, I'll make sure the three of you turn heads, and if what you say is true, I would even waive my fee." He clicked his tongue. "That is, if what you say is true."

"That's more than reasonable," Ginger's fingers relaxed on Kira's shoulders, "but we're not really looking to stand out. For what we have planned, it would be much better to blend in."

Larkin let out a loud laugh and dropped his journal to the table beside him, its back cover open with his inspector showing a few lines of text.

"I'm not sure that's possible. Honestly, you lost the ability to blend in when you pledged your loyalty to Rend. How that happened, I have no idea." He leaned to the side and glanced at the small glass screen beside him. "Not to mention that your Archmage is a level one-forty-seven fairy *Breath* mage."

"What's wrong with that?" Kira threw her hands to her hips and shifted to one side.

"Nothing. It's just unheard of." He stared down at her. "I've never seen a fairy over level fifty, and the Archmage title almost always goes to a *Cauldron*. Occasionally a *Venom* mage gets it, but never a *Breath*. They're too squishy and have no offense. The Overcast skill that the title comes with is a waste on healers. What are you going to do, pulse something to death?"

"Wanna find out?" Kira snapped open a caster and narrowed her eyes.

"Okay, that's enough of that." Ginger stepped in to push Kira away before she started a fight she couldn't win.

"I'm not complaining." Larkin chuckled to himself. "On the contrary, I don't think I would want it any other way. I craft unique items and gear. It only makes sense that they should be worn by a house that's equally," he clicked his tongue, "unique."

Kira settled down.

"Shall we get started?" Larkin began moving before anyone had a chance to answer, dashing to the wall and pulling several bolts of fabric from the shelves. He dropped them on the table, then walked a circle around Ginger with one hand tapping against his chin. "As Lady of the house, you get to be first."

Ginger shifted uncomfortably for a second but found her bearings, dropping one hand to her waist and arching her back just enough to draw attention to her chest.

Larkin looked her over without lingering on any part of her more than necessary. He let out a long, "Hmm," then snapped his fingers. "You seem like a dangerous woman, beautiful but treacherous. Although there's something else about you. Sort of an air of reluctant responsibility. There's a conflict there. Like someone who wants to take what the world has to offer but holds themselves back."

Ginger's posture faltered. "Umm, I guess that's accurate."

"Of course it is." Larkin picked up the bolts of fabric again and lifted them close to her face without warning. "I read people. It helps me personalize my work."

Ginger took an uncomfortable step back as he stood a little too close.

"No. Nope. Close but no." He dropped the first three bolts of fabric to the floor before settling on one containing a green silk that matched her eyes. Larkin dropped it as well, holding the end of the fabric so that it unraveled to the floor. He tossed it in the air, letting it drape around her shoulders like a shawl. Then he took a step back to admire his choice. "This is silk from the giant spiders that dwell in the Gu Caverns. Have you ever been there?"

Ginger shook her head.

"I don't blame you. It's a terrible place. Everything there is aggressive and inflicts a poison status of one kind or another. The monsters even attack each other. As a result, the spiders, which are at the top of the food chain, have gained what you might call a super venom by consuming the smaller enemies. It causes paralysis, weakens defense, adds a vulnerability to all elements, decreased strength, and obviously adds a particularly deadly poison effect. It doesn't last long, but it's a nasty piece of work."

"And that is important why?" Ginger adjusted the silk on her shoulders, which was starting to slip down on one side.

"It's important because any garment made from this fabric will add the same effect to your weapon damage. You can lock any opponent in place for a couple seconds with the paralysis effect and drop their HP by about a thousand before it wears off. Of course, there is a lengthy cooldown of ten hours before it will activate again, so don't waste it. You'll need that ability to protect the rest of your house after all."

"What about the defense stats?" Ginger asked.

Larkin gave a shrug. "Unfortunately, there is a price to pay for fashion."

Ginger raised an eyebrow. "Meaning?"

"Meaning, don't get hit."

"Oh." Ginger deflated.

"I'm kidding. I have something for that." He spun on his heel and disappeared into a closet, only to reappear dragging a treasure chest behind him. He snatched a strange tool from the wall, some kind of reverse bear trap looking device.

Kira wasn't sure what to expect; then she noticed a telltale detail on the chest's side handle. They were bent slightly. She immediately materialized her wings and shot up a few feet as Larkin unlocked it and threw open the lid.

"Holy shit! A mimic!" Ginger shrieked as two rows of gleaming, silver teeth snapped open, and an enormous, barbed tongue flapped out to search for the man that had disturbed the chest.

Larkin moved in what seemed like a practiced motion, thrusting the bear trap like tool into the creature's mouth and pulling a pin. The device snapped open, lodging itself in the jaws of the wicked chest.

"Well then." Larkin passed underneath Kira to grab a pair of pliers from the wall. He stopped on his way back to the mimic, holding his hand up to let some of the sparkling dust that fell from her wings land on his skin. Rubbing his fingers together, he examined the particles. "Interesting, I didn't know pixie dust was actually real. I've never seen one of your kind with a level high enough to have wings. Do you think you could come by sometime later and let me collect some?"

Kira floated back down. "I guess so, but it fades away after a few seconds."

"I might have a way to preserve it." He stared off at a row of jars on one shelf. "Maybe I could craft some kind of health bomb." He shook off the distraction. "Sorry, where was I? Oh, yes." He marched back over to the snarling chest. "Sorry about this, Joe." He clasped the pair of pliers he carried around one of the thing's teeth and yanked. "I named the mimic Joe, by the way." Then he pulled another few teeth, which was when Kira noticed that the chest was already missing several.

He set the silver teeth down on the table and dragged the angry chest back into the closet. He came back out holding onto the end of a rope, which he promptly yanked. The strange bear trap tool slid out of the closet tied to the other end, and he slammed the door shut. Noise erupted from the other side, like a teenager throwing a tantrum. Larkin pushed away from the door.

"He'll go back to sleep in a minute or so. Mimics are ambush predators, so they tend to settle down if there's nothing within reach. I'll lock him back up later."

"That was probably the most horrifying thing I've seen in a while." Farn let loose a full body shiver.

"Yes, I realize that, but it's easier for me to keep one of those things around rather than to go find and kill one every time I need teeth."

Kira poked at one of the silver fangs on the table. "And why did you need them?"

Larkin swept the gleaming items into one hand. "Mimic teeth can be melted down and formed into or added to almost anything. They're an excellent method of implanting stats and effects to a new piece of equipment. I'll use them to force some defense into some of the detail work of Ginger's dress. You'll still want to be careful about taking damage, but you won't be completely vulnerable."

"Can I take this off now?" Ginger lifted the silk from her shoulders.

"Oh, yes, sure." Larkin waved a hand in her direction, then spun on Kira. He clasped his hands and pointed in her direction with both index fingers. "Now for this little one."

A tingle swept through Kira's body, sending the hairs on her neck standing on end. She wasn't looking forward to her turn.

"Ah, that's interesting." He stepped closer, his gaze dropping to the pendant resting on her collarbone.

"What—" Her voice got stuck in her throat for a second before she started again, "What is?"

"That amethyst matches your eyes perfectly." He stood silently, looking the rest of her over.

To her surprise, Kira relaxed. She knew what it felt like to have someone's eyes all over her, but strangely, Larkin's gaze was different. He wasn't undressing her with his mind, but the opposite. It was like he was mentally trying on every style of dress he could imagine.

Larkin pointed to her neck. "Can we lose the pendant?"

"I wish," Kira muttered before explaining, "It's bound to my character. So no."

He dropped his hand down at his side. "Well, I can't match that color with what I have. But…" He chewed his bottom lip, then shifted his eyes to the mannequin in the corner, draped in white silk. He let out a sigh and crossed the room to pick up the beautiful material. "If I can't match that amethyst, I might as well make it pop."

Larkin returned to her and gently laid the silk over her shoulders, being careful not to cover her pendant as he wrapped it around her chest. The silk was cool against her neck. For a moment, it made her feel confident—and maybe a little sexy. Of course, then her entire face burned red to betray her.

The fashion-obsessed *Rage* stepped back with a peaceful expression. He let out another sigh. "I guess I can't save it forever."

Kira clung to the fabric with both hands. "What is it?"

He laughed. "That is a sheet from the bedchambers of Dorian, the Nightmare of Temptation. I wasn't able to kill the actual boss, but I was able to escape with that stored in my inventory. I've been saving it for the right project."

"What makes it special?" Kira asked.

"Well, it can store mana for one. Which makes it perfect for an Archmage, since the Overcast skill increases consumption. It will give you a reserve supply of at least a thousand. And second, it's the purest white I've found, so it should make your eyes and pendant shine. Not to mention, it's basically the embodiment of temptation. A bedsheet the color of virgin snow that holds the promise of unimaginable pleasure. You do the math."

Kira squirmed as her body warmed.

"But wait, there's more." He ran to one wall and reached for a bucket, dropping it on the table and grabbing a handful of tiny crystals from it. "These are morning stars in their raw form. They're pricey but not uncommon. You're probably already wearing some if you have any accessories that regenerate mana."

Kira raised one hand, where a thick band of platinum wrapped around one thumb. "This gives me one point of MP every three seconds, but there're no crystals on it, just metal."

Larkin took her hand in his and examined the item. "That's where you're wrong. Metals in Noctem don't carry any magical properties on their own. So if you look close here, there are flecks of something reflective in the platinum. Those are morning stars." He released her hand so she could see. "Most crafters will crush the crystals with a mortar and pestle and add the powder to the metal while it's in liquid form."

"Why don't they just set the crystals at the center or something?" Kira examined her thumb ring.

Larkin clicked his tongue. "They're too small, mostly. So just a few won't make for very impressive jewelry, but if I use them as they are in the hundreds as part of a dress, I could max out the game's mana regeneration, maybe close to two MP per second."

Kira's heart skipped a beat. "That's insane. I'd be able to add Overcast to almost every spell I use. I mean, I'd still aggro every monster we face by using that much mana, but man, that would still be pretty cool."

"Plus, you'll sparkle like a shooting star." Larkin let the crystals sprinkle from his hand down the silk surrounding her.

Kira suppressed an excited squeal, opting for a controlled smile instead. "Okay, I'm sold." She didn't bother asking about her defense. Low physical stats were pretty standard for most fairy gear anyway.

"Perfect!" Larkin swept across the room toward Farn, who had been keeping quiet. "Now for your loyal bodyguard."

Farn gave a sudden snort and stepped backward. "I'm just going tomorrow for protection. There's no need for anything special."

"I will have none of that." Larkin threw a hand up in front of her face. "You are the First Knight of House Lockheart. I will have you dress accordingly. Now, which of these two are you in charge of keeping safe?"

Farn paused to release an annoyed growl. It was obvious she wasn't going to make it through the night without a makeover. She pointed unenthusiastically at Kira.

"The little one is mine, I guess."

Kira couldn't help but snicker at her wording.

"Great, you should match her in some way, and think I have just the thing. I made a set for a *Shield* class a few months back, but he ended up not liking the stats, and I've been stuck with it ever since. Honestly, he didn't understand the importance of fashion. It's not enough to be able to take a hit—you have to look good doing it."

He led Farn over to the three mirrors near one wall and touched his fingers to the surface of one. "There's a quick change system here, so you shouldn't need any privacy."

Lines of text appeared on the mirror and he scrolled down to select each part of her new gear. "Now, I originally made this set for a man, but they turned it down on account of it being too pretty. So it should still have a good effect on you." He gestured to the glass. "Whenever you're ready."

Farn glanced over her shoulder at Kira and Ginger then back at her reflection. She gave one last groan in protest and reached her hand to the line of text that read 'Preview'. The second her finger touched the glass, her armor and clothing vanished in a sweep of glowing particles. At the same time, a second wave of light replaced everything seamlessly to keep onlookers from seeing anything they shouldn't.

Kira immediately placed a hand to her mouth.

Gone was the visage of the rough Viking raider that she'd grown accustomed to. In its place was something else.

A white breastplate with a matching waistcoat seemed to fit Farn like a glove. Ornate silver clasps secured it in front, and black accents detailed her sides. A tunic made of metal scales peeked out from underneath like a skirt. Below that, black tights clung to her legs. A pair of matching boots and bracers covered from the knees and elbows down, all a solid matte white. Black fur encircled her shoulders, attached to a medium length cape that tapered to a point down her back. The fabric was white, like the rest, but with a layer of more metal scales between the black fur on top and the rest of the cape.

Larkin stepped back and took a bow. "I call this design, the Shield of Rose and Thorn, and I must say, it suits you well."

"Why rose and thorn?" Kira asked out of curiosity.

"Oh, the gauntlet is called the White Rose, and, um, there used to be a sword with it called Black Thorn. But I sort of sold it separately."

"That's okay. My sword is a contract item, so I wouldn't want to use something else." Farn turned in front of the mirror, checking herself out from all angles.

"What's your sword called?" Larkin tapped a few options on the mirror's quick-change readout.

"Feral Edge." Farn gripped the weapon's handle.

"Okay." Larkin tapped one last command to change the name of the equipment. "From now, this set is called Feral Rose."

"That works." Farn held up her left hand to look at her new gauntlet. It was more compact, with slender silver joints covering her fingers. A round shield generator sat at the back of her hand, much smaller than what she'd had before. The rest of her arm was covered with a black sleeve attached to her waistcoat, her other kept bare to display her party readout. Farn stepped back and spun to face Kira and Ginger.

"Okay, I might like this." She let a goofy grin spread across her face.

"You look like one of those gender-swapped, Disney prince drawings," Ginger fanned herself with one hand, "and I have to say, it's kind of working for me here."

"Very dashing. You can rescue me anytime." Kira gave her a thumbs up.

Farn laughed. "I usually do anyway."

She went back to the mirror and untied the ribbon that held back her hair, running her fingers through to fluff the mass of black curls. She pushed it all to one side so that it cascaded down past her ear. It matched the outfit better. "So what are the stats like?"

Larkin raised one hand and tilted it back and forth. "Eh."

"What do you mean, 'eh'?" Farn let her arms fall limply.

He shrugged. "The overall defense is nothing to write home about—probably the same as what you had on before—but it's lighter and easier to move in. The tunic underneath is made of dragon scales coated in silver, which gives some solid fire resistance. Also, the White Rose's shield generator has no moving parts, so you can deploy your barrier two seconds faster."

Judging from the downward curve of Farn's mouth, she was not impressed. "So what makes it special?"

Larkin grabbed her shoulders and repositioned her to face the mirror. "You look amazing," he coughed, "and it's free."

"Can't beat free." Farn shrugged.

"That's better." Larkin agreed, tapping a line of text displayed on the mirror to release ownership of the set to Farn. "Now, you mentioned you had one other guard?"

Ginger stepped in. "Yes, we have a *Fury*. His name is MaxDamage24, and he'll be protecting me. Can you throw something together for him too? He dresses like a slob, so he could really use something more formal."

"Awesome, he's gonna hate that." Kira squealed with excitement.

Larkin arched his eyebrow at her. "Okay then. I'll throw something together with what I have. Just send him here tomorrow to pick it up, and I'll make sure he's miserable."

"Perfect." Ginger smiled. "That's what I like to hear."

Larkin started picking up the mess he'd made, setting things aside to begin work at the table. "If that is everything, I should probably get to work on all of this. Obviously, there are some shortcuts that I can take with this all being a game, but it is still custom work. It will take some time."

"And you want us to leave so you can get to work?" Kira pulled off the silk fabric that still adorned her shoulders and lay it down on the table.

Larkin snapped his fingers. "Could you?"

"Oh, of course." Ginger beckoned a hand at Farn who was still stealing glances at herself in the mirror. The *Shield* crossed the room with an added bounce in her step as her cape fanned out behind her. Ginger headed for the stairs as well.

"Thank you for lending us your talents." Kira held out her hand to Larkin. It only seemed right to thank him. He was an artist after all. He deserved some gratitude.

He took her hand, accepting her contact information as she passed it along with the gesture. "The only thanks I need is seeing Lord Berwyn thrown out of power. If House Lockheart can do that, then consider us square." He released her hand and bowed to the group.

"And thank you for choosing Fashion Souls."

CHAPTER TWELVE

Klaxon staggered out of the nameless tavern in Tartarus, coughing as smoke billowed from the door behind him. He cringed at the damage he'd caused whilst trying to set that duel-wielding idiot on fire. Even worse, the *Fury* had escaped. He shrugged off the guilt. What was done was done. He couldn't really do much about the damage to the tavern now anyway. Besides, he still had a player to catch.

What was his name? Max? No, that's not right. Maybe Matt? He shook his head. It didn't matter. The guy would be dead in a minute anyway.

Heading down the walkway that clung to the wall of the canyon, Klaxon took a drink from the bottle he'd snagged from the bar before making his fiery exit. He cringed again. *Too sweet.* Some kind of weak coconut rum. In his haste, he hadn't been picky. Again, what was done was done. There was no sense wasting rum. He threw back another mouthful while trying to walk at the same time.

That was a mistake.

Klaxon stumbled, only catching himself on a barrel to keep from falling over the side of the narrow platform. He wasn't completely wasted, but he was that special kind of drunk, the kind where he'd lost the ability to do anything gently. He pushed himself upright, inadvertently shoving the barrel he'd leaned on off the platform at the same time. It smashed through the roof of a small shack a few levels down. *What was that again, about what's done is done?*

Klaxon wiped a few stray drops of rum from his robe with his free hand, then reached into an inner pocket. He pulled out a blue velvet pouch. He groaned and shoved it back in, this time retrieving a dark purple one.

"Ah, there you are." Loosening the bag's drawstring with his teeth, he snapped open his caster to activate his circle of power. The crimson portal opened at an odd angle since he was still holding a bottle of rum and didn't want to spill it. It took him a few tries to get all of his ingredients into the circle. Once that was done, he continued on his way, following the sound of broken stairs and swearing.

The Fury isn't very stealthy now, is he?

Sure enough, he found the player kicking stray boards away and patting at one of his legs. Smoke wafted from the *Fury's* boot. Klaxon snorted. He must have tagged the guy with his flamethrower just before he'd escaped. He tossed back a little more rum and started out across a nearby rope bridge to give himself a good vantage point to cast from.

Little more than a tightrope with handrails, the bridge swayed as soon as Klaxon set foot on it. He immediately regretted that last sip of rum.

The player below reached for a railing to pull himself up.

Can't have that, Klaxon thought as he cast a pulse. The rail burst into splinters, sending the unfortunate *Fury* falling back into the mess of broken boards. He returned fire, faster than Klaxon expected, forcing him to duck to the side. Bullets clipped the rope beneath Klaxon's feet, the bridge swaying but remaining firm.

Klaxon took a moment to get back to a stable position. The *Fury* didn't let the chance to run slip by. He dashed up a flight of stairs, leaping them several at a time until he made it to the landing above. That was when the spell brewing in Klaxon's circle finished.

Tossing his drink to his free hand, he stretched out his fingers to aim. The surface of the wood below the *Fury* glowed as a circular pattern of interlocking purple shapes and glyphs expanded from under his feet. The player fell to one knee as the effects of the Gravity Well spell took hold. It didn't carry any damage, but it did stop the slippery little *Fury* from scurrying around.

Klaxon peered down, leaning on the rope handrail while making sure to look as smug as possible. He took a small sip from his bottle.

"Matt? Was that your name?" He tried to remember what the player had called himself earlier.

"No," he grunted back as the grav spell weighed him down to the platform, "it's Max."

"Oh? Okay." Klaxon began to tip back the bottle again but staggered, the bridge wobbling along with him. The motion forced him to drop the rum in order to hold onto the side. His aim wavered, releasing Max from the spell for a second. Hope flashed across the *Fury's* face just before Klaxon caught him in the spell again, locking him back down.

Max struggled to raise his arm high enough to aim. Klaxon smirked, doing nothing to dodge. He didn't even cast a pulse to disrupt him. The *Fury* fired a few rounds anyway, probably hoping to get lucky. All but one caught nothing but air. The remainder must have hit someone because Klaxon heard a voice yelp from a few bridges over.

"Sorry!" The *Fury* cringed.

In response, the same voice called back an apathetic, "It happens."

Max tilted his head at the response, before collapsing to the platform under the weight of the Gravity Well spell. Klaxon laughed.

"Well, are you just gonna watch?" Max held the muzzle of his gun against the wood floor to support himself.

"Maybe. I'm just waiting for that platform you're stuck on to break so I can drop you into the river." The sound of splintering of wood met his ears. "Shouldn't be long."

The *Fury* lowered his head in defeat, resting his head against the side of one of his pistols. Klaxon lowed his arm to the handrail to hold his spell steady. That was when the Fury started laughing.

Max raised his head, a defiant smile on his face.

"Balls," Klaxon uttered as he realized that the *Fury* hadn't lowered his head to his gun to rest a moment before. No, he had been converting his remaining bullets to custom rounds.

Max fired at the wall of the canyon with what must have been a Fracture shot, destroying the support to his own platform. The whole landing he was on dropped through the area of effect of the Gravity Well. Klaxon tried to readjust his aim but wasn't fast enough. The *Fury* leaped as he fell, just barely making it to the broken stairs where he had started. He fired again.

Klaxon lost count of the shots as the pistol barked at him. He raised his arm to at least avoid a critical hit. If he could survive taking the damage, he could still fight back. Then another surprise hit him.

There was no damage.

He hadn't even been shot. For a second, he thought that Max might have missed. Then he fell, the Fracture rounds having shredded the rope bridge he stood on like paper.

The canyon spun as again Klaxon regretted drinking so much. All he could do was loop a hand through a loose bit of rope that had been a handrail. He hit the stone wall with a crack of damage and a dull pain in his shoulder. "Ouch." He slipped and scraped his feet against the rock, searching for something that could support his weight. Finally, his foot caught a slight crack. He blew out a sigh of relief. Then a board creaked behind him.

"You look like you could use a hand." The *Fury* sat down at the edge of a platform just a couple feet away. His grin stretched from ear to ear as he casually pointed a gun at Klaxon's head.

"Well get on with it," Klaxon grumbled.

Max sucked air in through his teeth, then dropped his pistol to his lap and offered a hand. "Nah. I didn't come here to fight. Truce?"

Klaxon raised an eyebrow. "Fine. But you're buying me another drink."

Amelia burst through the flaming doorway of the tavern, the near-dead *Blade*, Corvin, held close to her side. She tugged her coat down over their faces to shield them. Blind with the heavy fabric covering her head, she almost forgot to stop before running straight off the walkway's edge. Almost. She planted one heel and gripped her burden tighter until they came to a stop, letting out a breath when they were safe.

A lungful of fresh air rushed in, too fast. She had gotten used to taking shallow, smoky breaths. Corvin erupted with a hollow cough beside her as she whipped off her coat and hunched over the handrail with him, hacking in unison.

She drew in air until her virtual lungs adapted, eventually settling down with a few wheezing breaths.

"You alright?"

The mid-level *Blade* cleared his throat and checked his health. Amelia tried to make out the numbers on his wrist, but he flipped his arm back around before she could. "I'll live."

"Well, I'd say that's a wee presumptuous." She shrugged back into her coat.

"Huh?" Corvin's black fox ears twitched.

"You saved me from being crushed by debris, then I saved you from being cooked. That makes us even. If my math is right, that puts us back to square one." Amelia snatched her sword from where she'd left it leaning on a railing and leaped away, leveling the saber at his throat.

Corvin let out a sigh, his shoulders deflating as he picked up his katana from where he had dropped it. "Okay, but I'm not putting my eyepatch back on."

"Sure, I just won't look." Amelia gave him a taunting smile. In truth, she desperately wanted to look at that eye of his. Like a moth to a flame. She knew she shouldn't, but she wanted to all the same. She resisted, staring at his nose instead.

"What is that eye by the way? A contract?"

"Yeah."

Amelia nodded. "Is it like a basilisk's ability?"

"Think so. Hurts when I use it, though."

"That's strange."

Corvin shrugged casually, then lunged forward in the same instant, slapping her sword away with his.

Amelia grinned as she pushed the kid back, having fun for the first time since the previous night. In fact, the duel had been so good that she hadn't even thought about losing her city or her embarrassing death. She almost couldn't believe that a mere mid-level *Blade* could survive this long against her. Of course, he still didn't stand a chance. Judging from the shade of the class emblem on his hand, his health must have been near empty. Even if it wasn't, all she had to do was scratch him.

Corvin deflected a blow that sent him stumbling back onto one of the city's largest bridges. It was a sturdy bit of construction, a rarity for Tartarus. He regained his balance and probed at her with that yellow eye. She watched his weapon instead, avoiding making contact.

Between attacks, Amelia caught the rest of her house in her peripheral. Her men had that *Leaf* cornered a few bridges over. She chuckled and took a swing at Corvin.

"Looks like your friend over there is not long for this world. Serves him right for that cheap shot earlier." She backed off for a moment to gloat and give her opponent time to watch the

Leaf's fate unfold. Corvin paused, then returned his attention to her, unfazed by display.

"I'm not sure what you mean. He seems fine to me." His mouth twitched upward at the corners.

That was when the sound of ropes snapping struck Amelia's ears. She whirled around as the bridge holding the majority of her house snapped. Her men fell like confetti. She searched the scene for the *Leaf*, hoping to at least see him hit the water below. She found him, plummeting along with her house, drawing back an arrow. Her mouth hung slack.

Is he… aiming at me?

As soon as the question passed through her head, the arrow flew into the air, losing momentum a dozen feet above where she stood. Then it began to fall. What came next was impossible.

Silver light flashed as that damn *Leaf* exploded into existence upside down in the air, holding the arrow in his hand. He nocked it and fired. A solid thunk hit the boards of the bridge behind her. A pulse of pain streaked through her left ear before dulling back down to nothing. She slapped a hand to her head in surprise. *He hit me.* Worse, he'd only been a couple inches away from a critical head-shot.

The *Leaf* hit the bridge in an uncoordinated lump but rolled and pushed himself up to one knee. "That was a warning shot, m'lady. How 'bout you leave my pal alone?"

Amelia blinked once and glanced back at Corvin. He was still standing at the ready but not making any motion to attack. She returned her attention to the *Leaf*. He only had one arrow left in his quiver. She cracked a smile, making sure to show a fang. She could still win. "Are you really in a position to be making threats?" Amelia flicked her eyes to his last arrow.

The *Leaf* didn't flinch. "Try me."

Can't argue with that, Amelia thought as she rushed the *Leaf*. *Just one scratch. That's all I need. Kill him, then the other.*

The *Leaf* reached for an arrow as she closed the gap. She drew back her saber and swung with everything she had.

The metallic clang of swords rang through the canyon as Amelia's mind failed to process what had happened. She had been mere inches from killing the *Leaf*, but he was gone. In his place was Corvin, his sword held firm against hers. His yellow eye made contact, locking her in place just as the tip of an arrow gently touched the base of her skull.

Her brain worked things out. She wasn't sure how, but the two had swapped places. She sighed.

"I assume that was some kind of contract ability?"

"You know what happens when you assume," answered the *Leaf* from behind.

Amelia groaned at the response.

"Sorry about him." Corvin held up his wrist where a string of beads dangled. "It's a contract item. A pair of them actually. Kegan has the other one." He gestured to the *Leaf* behind her with his eyes, breaking contact so she could move again.

"Ah, so you got yourselves a pair of friendship bracelets. That's cute."

"That's what I keep telling him." The *Leaf*, apparently Kegan, jabbed her a little with the arrow. "Anyway, think we can call a truce here? Or do I need to ventilate your head?"

"That depends on what you want."

"We want information!" another voice called from a platform above, where that damn *Fury* leaned over a railing. Klaxon stood next to him with a sheepish expression.

Amelia rolled her eyes. "Klaxon, why the hell aren't you trying to murder him?"

"Ahh, we came to an understanding." The mage scratched at the side of his beard.

The *Fury* rested his hands on the butts of his pistols. "Yeah, I decided not to throw him in the river."

"So you just became pals then?" she called back up.

"Well, Max here said he'd buy me a drink if we talked like civilized people," Klaxon gave a shrug, "and I dropped my rum, so... it all worked out for the better."

Amelia sighed and raised her hands. "Okay, I give. What do you want?"

"We're after Berwyn. We need intel that you have," Max explained.

She narrowed her eyes at the mention of the name. "Why?"

Max hesitated. "Let's just say that we don't have his well-being at heart."

Amelia flicked her wolfish ears back. "What if I don't want you to harm him? What if I want to kill Berwyn myself?"

"I'm sure we can work something out. You can still have your way with him when we're done."

"I can agree to those terms." She turned and pushed Kegan's arrow away with a finger.

Max nodded with a satisfied grin, but before he could speak again, his attention seemed to be pulled away to something behind her.

Amelia turned to find a group of angry players marching out onto one of the bridges. A high-level *Venom* mage lead the procession.

Max opened his mouth to speak, but the man gestured toward the canyon around them.

For the first time in the last few minutes, Amelia looked around the city. Players were attempting to help as some of her housemates struggled to climb the ends of a broken bridge. Several more were trapped on a platform where the stairs had been destroyed. She winced as the roof of the tavern she'd left in flames caved in.

The *Venom* mage leading the group of angry players glowered at her.

"He started it." She stabbed a finger up at Max.

Max panicked, pointing to Klaxon. "He threw the first pulse."

Klaxon raised his chin and folded his arms. "Amelia told me to—"

He was cut off as the *Venom* mage in the center of the crowd yelled a furious, "Shut up!" He hunched over a handrail, breathing heavy. Then he threw a hand out to point at the edge of the canyon. "Get the hell out!"

Max patted Klaxon on the back. "Okay, you heard the guy. I'll get you a drink in the next port."

"That's probably best," he agreed.

Corvin stepped aside to let Amelia pass. She held up her house ring to let the rest of her people know where she was going. She also had some choice words for the idiots still clinging to the wall that couldn't even kill a single *Leaf*. Max waited for her on the platform above. Apparently, he had a transport ship waiting. Unfortunately, the path up to where he'd left it took them past the row of angry players who definitely wanted them gone sooner rather than later. They stared daggers at her as she passed.

Granted, the mob could have tried to kill them right there, so in that, Amelia figured she was getting off light. Although, after the fight they had just witnessed, they probably didn't want to risk the rest of their city's buildings being caught in the crossfire.

Max turned sideways to squeeze past the *Venom* mage in the center. "'Scuse me, sorry. I parked up there." He pointed a finger toward the top of the canyon.

"Get out!" the man yelled in his face, spittle flying.

Max wiped his cheek with the back of his hand. "Alright, alright, god."

Amelia squeezed by behind him only to be followed by the same irate *Venom* mage all the way back up. She could feel his death stare on her back. It was as if he wasn't going to be satisfied until he saw them board the ship and fly off. She shoved her hands into her pockets and took one last glance at the city.

Smoke flowed up one side of the canyon.

"I guess I won't be coming back here for a while."

CHAPTER THIRTEEN

Farnsworth marched through the door of the Hanging Frederick Tavern, her cape trailing behind her majestically. The bracers on her legs rattled as she walked, like a drum roll announcing her presence. She had been standing tall ever since they'd left Fashion Souls back in Lucem.

In her new gear, she felt strong, confident, and in a way, beautiful. She was the First Knight of House Lockheart, and she looked the part. With that, she held her head high and strode through the tavern to where the party's usual table sat near the back.

A regular of the establishment, a player named HastleThe-Hoff, sat on a stool in the corner, playing a cover of R.E.M.'s "Losing My Religion" on a ukulele. He paused to wave.

"Lookin' good, Farn."

She responded back at him with a click of her tongue and a quick finger gun before flipping her cape back over her shoulder with a flourish.

"Ack!" Kira squeaked from behind as the fabric swatted her in the face. "Watch where you're flapping that thing."

"Oh god, I'm sorry." Farn spun around, knocking over a chair in the process. "I'm still getting used to it."

Ginger sighed at the display. "Yeah, that's about what I'd expect from this house." She slipped past her subjects and settled into a seat in the corner.

Farn picked up the chair and glanced around to see if anyone had noticed her making a scene. The tavern was empty, save for a couple other groups, like always.

The Frederick was one of Noctem's best-kept secrets, tucked away in the back alleys of the city of Valain. What made it special was that its merchant system worked off in-game credits rather than real-world dollars. This made food and drinks, which were considered luxury items, practically free. Since Max still hadn't checked in, it was as good a place as any for Farn and her cohorts to hang out and wait.

Farn had spent many nights at the Frederick over the past year, either to play cards with Max or help Kira consume the entire menu. The place was dim, dingy, and half the tables wobbled, but in a way, it was home. Even the faces that watched her from the dozen or so portraits that hung on the walls in a plethora of mismatched frames welcomed her.

Kira made her way to the bar while Farn settled in. The Frederick didn't have much of a drink selection, just a massive keg of the darkest stout ever imagined and smaller one of a particularly lovely hard cider. Kira didn't bother taking orders, returning with a few wooden mugs. A beer for Ginger in one hand and two ciders in the other for her and Farn. Her hands shook with effort as she struggled to hold them steady.

Farn jumped up to help her. It was easy to forget how weak the fairy actually was. She gave Farn a delicate smile in thanks. Then the fairy dropped into a chair and slouched down until her head was practically level with the table.

"What's wrong with you?" Ginger gestured at her with her mug, a few drops of dark beer spilling over the side.

"I wish I had stopped at the bakery I saw back in Thrift.

They had some lagopin buns that looked good, but I forgot to go back and buy some with everything going on."

"Oh!" Farn let a wide grin stretch across her face as she scrolled through the inventory tab on her wrist and materialized a box. She turned it to face the fairy and opened the lid. Inside were six of the fluffiest lagopin-shaped buns the world had ever known. "I bought them to have at karaoke, but that didn't end up happening so..." She trailed off as the fairy leaned forward, her eyes locked on the two rows of bread.

"You got six?"

"Yeah, the guys were going to be there too, so I got one for everyone."

"Oh," Kira glanced back over her shoulder and lowered her voice to a whisper, "but they're not here now."

Farn snorted as she followed Kira's line of thinking. "No, I guess they're not."

A gluttonous grin claimed the fairy as she reached out with both hands. "So we each get an extra."

"Really? You're not going to at least save one for Max?" Ginger shook her head. "Isn't he your bro?"

"Food before bros," she explained through a mouth full of sweetened crust.

"Can't argue with that." Farn raised one of the bunny-shaped buns to her mouth and casually bit off its face.

Ginger cringed, prompting Kira to do the same, except slower while making eye contact with the *Coin*.

"You got problems, you know that?"

"Probably." The fairy wiped a crumb off her nose.

Ginger nodded and took a sip from her mug before giving her attention to Farn. "Anyway, I couldn't help but notice that you were sitting quite cozy with Max back in Thrift?"

Farn winced. "Umm, what do you mean?"

"I mean, how are you two not a thing yet? I've been starting to think you didn't like him or something, but there you were, squished into a couch with him instead of your bestie here." Ginger gestured to Kira.

"I, um…" Farn squirmed in place, her eyes seeking out the fairy for help.

Kira shifted her view away toward one wall and sipped her cider, holding it up with both hands.

Traitor, Farn thought as the little mage hid behind her mug from the embodiment of awkwardness that was Farnsworth as a person. She groaned and sank into her chair as low as she could, trying to find someplace where Ginger's curious stare couldn't find her. It was clear the woman had been waiting all night to probe her about the matter.

In all honesty, Farn didn't know what to say. Pretty much any answer she gave would raise more questions. Just saying that she wasn't interested in Max like that wasn't going to fly for Ginger. She settled on a half-truth. "He hasn't asked me out or anything."

Ginger set her drink back on the table hard enough for the near-black liquid within to splash into the air before falling back into the mug. A laugh followed. "So ask him first. I'm pretty sure he'd say yes. After all, the poor guy has been single for as long as I've known him. It's not like your calendar is full either." The *Coin* poked at one of the lagopin buns. "I mean, what do you do on your Saturday nights anyway?"

Farn sunk a little lower. "I don't know. Get Chinese food, watch a season of a show, and go to bed." She left out the part about snuggling with a Japanese body pillow until she fell asleep. No, best to leave Riku-chan out of the conversation.

Ginger sucked air through her teeth. "That's just a little sad."

"I'm aware." Farn blew out a sigh. "I'm not really good at that sort of thing. I kinda had a bad dating experience a while back, so I haven't really gotten out there much." She made a point of not mentioning how long it had actually been.

The *Coin* raised an eyebrow as if picking up on the omission. That was when Kira finally quit minding her own business and weighed in. She cleared her throat and set down her mug. "Ginger's right."

Farn couldn't slouch any further, so she just closed her eyes in defeat. She was really hoping her best friend would back her up a little.

"Sorry, what I meant was Max would definitely say yes, and if you were looking for a great guy, then I can't think of anyone better." She leaned forward, closer to Farn. "But if you don't feel ready to put yourself out there, then that's fine too. So relax, Max isn't going anywhere. That dude can't even ask you out, and you're awesome. So, I hardly think he's gonna get snatched up by someone any time soon."

Ginger laughed. "I don't know. He is kinda cute."

Farn snorted and sat up straight. "Oh, really? Maybe we should be pressuring you into asking him out then."

Ginger waved away the suggestion. "Nah, I'm pretty sure he's not looking for an instant family. That's a deal breaker most of the time when you come with two kids." Ginger shrugged it off. "But that illustrates my point. Life happens, so you may not have as much time as you think. Case in point, me. So don't waste time. After all, your heart is free, you just have to have the courage to follow it." She raised her mug high as if toasting.

Kira arched a silver eyebrow at the *Coin*. "Did you just quote *Braveheart?*"

Ginger gave her a wink. "Maybe."

The fairy scoffed. Then she scoffed again a second later. "I hardly think Mel Gibson is the best person to quote about love."

"True, but it applies." The *Coin* gave her a smug grin and sipped her beer.

Kira tilted her head and raised her mug before adding a quote of her own, "As you wish."

The reference clearly passed over Ginger's head as a simple acknowledgment, but the words warmed Farn's heart. It was a far more appropriate quote, *The Princess Bride* being a favorite movie of Farn's. She and Kira had already discussed the film at length while farming.

The fairy gave her an enchanting smile, then chomped into

her second bun. A look of pure happiness spread across her face. The warmth in Farn's chest grew into an ache.

Stupid, adorable fairy, she thought, immediately feeling guilty for it. Farn tilted her head back to stare at the ceiling. The sight of Kira was more than she could take without blurting out the real reason for her lack of interest in Max.

She was already in love with someone else.

Kira hummed as she ate, piercing Farn's armor without even meaning to. It only made her feel worse. Kira had been her first friend in nearly a decade, so in a way, falling for her felt like a betrayal of that relationship. Farn didn't even know when it had happened.

During the mission last year, the fairy had almost died, and Farn had seen every side of her back then as she went through the trauma. Back then they had only known each other for a day and a half, but Farn had adopted her as a new best friend regardless. Then after nearly sacrificing herself, Kira had been whisked away for quarantine without even a chance to say goodbye. It had only been for two weeks, but as they say, absence makes the heart grow fonder. Farn had built up the memories in her mind, so by the time she set eyes on the fairy again, it was already too late. She was in love.

Farn sighed.

Things were so much easier in the real world. There, she could just carry a gay pride mug around the office, and no one batted an eye. It wasn't like she was in the closet or anything. She had been outed back in high school, after all. It was old news. However, the thing that people don't realize about coming out is that you have to keep doing it every time you meet a new group of people.

During the mission last year, Farn wasn't even sure she would see everyone again afterward. Not to mention that there hadn't been a good time to bring it up. What was she going to do? Gather everyone around to announce her sexuality in the middle of a Nightmare battle? No thanks. Farn was awkward enough as it was.

After that, time went by fast. Too much time for it to be something that she'd simply left out. She started feeling guilty, like she was somehow being dishonest with everyone by not saying anything. Eventually, it grew from being something that she felt anxious about to something she feared. It was like high school all over again; a wall that Farn just couldn't climb.

Kira pushed the box of baked lagopin toward Farn. "You still have a second one."

Farn sat back up and shook off her melancholy. "You can have it if you want."

Kira's glistening, violet eyes widened, but she pushed the box away. "No, it's yours."

"Okay," Farn closed the box and stored it back into her inventory, "I'll save it for later."

"Or you could give it to Max." Ginger waggled her eyebrows, clearly oblivious to the truth running through Farn's mind.

She stared to respond, but Kira spoke first, rescuing her from the conversation.

"So are you gonna be this nosy when Piper discovers boys?" Kira asked, spitting crumbs in Ginger's direction.

This time, it was Ginger's turn to slouch her way into oblivion. "That's already happening. My lovely daughter is actually crushing on a guy pretty hard right now."

"And how are you handling that?" Farn laughed, glad to have a subject to talk about other than her own love life.

"Pretty well, actually." Ginger slung one arm over the back of her chair. "I don't really have to worry about it."

"Why not?" asked Kira.

"Well, mostly because the guy she likes is older and knows damn well that I'd kill him if he touched her. Plus, he's a good guy, and I trust him."

Kira lurched forward, almost spilling her drink. "Oh my god, it's Corvin!"

Ginger laughed in confirmation. "His dorm is a couple towns over from my house. He's an engineering student, so I asked him to help Piper with math. She's always done well, but she started advanced placement classes this year and has needed a little more help than I'm capable of. He's actually a great tutor, and Piper is doing so well now that if she keeps it up, she should be able to get into any school she wants."

"But she's been having trouble getting the attention of the boys at her school. Probably because of her hearing aids." Ginger frowned, her eyes welling up for an instant. "She's at a fragile age, and Corvin is nice to her. Plus he's not that much older when you think about it, just four years. Though, that's still quite illegal last I checked." Ginger sat up straight and folded her arms. "My girl is just growing up so fast, faster than I'm ready for." A bit of sadness crept into her voice.

Suddenly, a system chime sounded in Farn's ear. Then a second one. Kira jumped in her seat as if startled. She must have gotten one too. Farn pulled out her journal, an icon of a feathered quill overlapping a scroll staining the binding to indicate a new message. A third chime sounded as she opened the book to her inbox. Then a fourth and fifth. Messages appeared one after another on the page, each from a different sender.

Ginger received another two while Kira got flooded with seven. Farn scanned over the subject lines. Many were written in all caps.

The *Coin* opened one message and stared at the page. Then one of her eyes twitched. "How am I not surprised?"

CHAPTER FOURTEEN

Max threw open the door of the Hanging Frederick, startling a few players in the process. A version of "Africa," played on a ukulele, stuttered to a stop, several notes plucked out of order. Max ducked his head, not realizing how hard he had pushed on the door. "Sorry, Hoff."

The player with the ukulele gave him an annoyed nod before picking up the song where he left off.

Max glanced to the pair who came in behind him. Corvin closed the door gently while Kegan shoved his hands in his pockets. Max gave them a nod, then continued his strut through the room with a prideful swell in his chest. He had completed the night's mission with overwhelming success, so he deserved to show off a little. He couldn't wait to tell Kira, Farn, and Ginger about everything he'd learned after buying Amelia and her mage a couple rounds. Probably best not to mention getting kicked out of Tartarus, though.

He approached his party's usual table near the back as three pairs of eyes fell upon him, each narrowing to slits.

Uh oh. What do they know? Max gave them a slow wave. "Umm, hey."

"Hey yourself." Ginger held completely still.

"Welp, I'm gonna get a water." Kegan stretched his arms and slithered his way out of the line of fire. Corvin followed, backing away without making a sound.

Max ignored the two deserters as he tried to avoid the *Coin's* accusing stare. "What's with the new getup, Farn?" he asked as a distraction.

Ginger answered for her, "She's a strong and powerful woman. She should have gear to match."

"Cool, cool. Very cool–"

"So we hear you spent some time in Tartarus tonight?" Ginger crossed her arms.

Max ran his fingers along the back of an empty chair. "Yeah, we may have stopped by."

Kira placed her elbows on the table and leaned forward to rest her chin in her hands. "Would you say your visit was— eventful?"

Max groaned. "Okay, clearly, you know already. So yeah, we kind of had an altercation."

"Altercation? You destroyed half the city." Ginger tossed her journal onto the table and jabbed two fingers into its cover. "The three of us have been getting messages for the last half hour about it."

Max waited for her to finish. "Things may have gotten a little out of control. However, it was Amelia and her Winter Moons who started it."

"Yeah, we just finished it." Kegan returned, sipping from a goblet and placing a mug of beer down in front of Max.

"Does that mean you got the information?" Ginger leaned forward.

"I'd say so." Max placed his palms flat on the table and gave her a smug grin. "And how did your end of things go?"

The *Coin* smirked and opened her journal before sliding it across the table to display her status page. "Take a look at my title." She tapped the paper with her finger. A heart-shaped ring on her hand caught his eye.

Max did a double take as he read the words 'Lady of House Lockheart' sitting just below her name. "Holy crap, you started a house."

Ginger spread her hands out toward Farn and Kira. "I'd like to introduce you to my First Knight and Archmage."

"Why Lockheart?" Max leaned to the side. "That's a little, umm, feminine."

"Too bad." Ginger revealed a small box and produced three rings from it, placing them in front of Max.

Kegan reached past him and snatched two up. He tossed one to Corvin, who almost dropped his drink to catch it.

Max examined one before slipping the ring onto his finger. The metal rippled as it resized to fit. "So do we get titles too?"

Ginger seemed to fake a frown. "Sorry. No."

"Well, now I feel left out." Max sat down and tipped back in his chair. "So why did you need to start a house anyway?"

Ginger flashed the corner of a green envelope from under her cloak. "The invite we got is specifically for a lord or lady and their plus one."

"I guess that makes sense." Max flipped through his journal to check his new house affiliation now that he wore its ring, finding House Lockheart listed on his status page. Then he read the line below it. His leg kicked involuntarily in surprise, throwing his chair off balance. He caught the table with his foot just in time to stop himself from crashing to the floor. His journal flew forward as he flailed his arms.

Kira ducked the book.

Finally, he steadied his chair, blurting out the words, "Loyal to Rend? How?"

"You can thank these two and the literal back-alley deal they roped me into." Ginger swept one hand in the direction of Kira and Farn. "They triggered some kind of hidden quest. Something about reclaiming the city."

Max's jaw went slack. "What the hell does that even mean? It's a dungeon. Can Rend even be reclaimed?"

"Beats me. I messaged Alastair about it, but his response was… unhelpful."

Kira jumped in. "Yeah, all he wrote back was a long line of maniacal laughter. Like, mwahahahahahaha."

"You done?"

She took a breath before continuing. "Hahahaha."

Max ignored her and picked up his mug, gesturing it in Ginger's direction. "Anyway, so if you're the Lady of the house, who are you taking to this party as your plus one?"

"Probably Kira. She'll make a good distraction while I case the place."

"I'm very distracting." The fairy held her head high.

"That's not a good thing." Max sipped his drink.

Farn leaned forward on the table. "You and I will be going in as bodyguards. They won't let us in the ballroom, but that's almost better if we can check out other parts of the palace."

"True, I doubt we'll get enough time to find the vault, but at least we might be able to get an idea of what security options Berwyn has the place set up with."

"Speaking of," Ginger steepled her fingers like a crime lord, "what were you able to find about the vault?"

Max started to speak but stopped, taking a moment to scan the tavern for potential witnesses. It was mostly empty, save for a few tables of adventurers wrapped up in their own conversations.

"Okay, the vault will be on a basement level with only one way in. The door itself will be at the end of a long corridor. That much we know for sure, but as far as what that corridor is going to be like, that's a mystery. According to Amelia, it's customizable. She was able to tell us what some of the different options could be, but we'll have no way of knowing what Berwyn has chosen. The only saving grace here is that the corridor is only so long, so there's a limit to how many defenses he can fit in it."

"That doesn't sound good." Farn leaned forward. "What kind of things could we be up against?"

Max shrugged. "Could be almost anything. Guards, weight sensitive floors, traps, puzzle locks, mana fences—"

"What's a mana fence?" Kira interrupted.

"Basically a laser grid but powered by magic," Kegan added before taking a casual sip of his water.

"Seriously?" Kira eyed Max skeptically.

"Yeah, I know, but what kind of heist would this be if there wasn't a hallway of lasers to maneuver through?"

"What about identity scanners, like fingerprints and retinas and what not?" Farn rubbed her fingertips against each other.

"That's where we got lucky. There's no way to verify things like that since the system doesn't always render them consistently. And Checkpoint only lets businesses use the ID system, so we won't have to worry about that either."

"Well that's good, at least we won't have to cut out anyone's eyeball." Ginger ran a finger across the table casually.

Kegan snorted before letting a mouthful of water pour from his mouth back into his cup. "Holy crap, Ginger, weren't you the one trying to stop us from even doing this heist a couple hours ago?"

"Yeah, but that was then. Now, I smell money." She punctuated her sentence with a wink.

"Well that's kinda terrifying." Kira scooted her seat a few inches away from the *Coin*.

Ginger leaned back with her hands behind her head. "Oh, relax, I was kidding. I know the system wouldn't let me cut out a player's eye to begin with."

Max accepted her point with a nod, a little too casual for the subject matter. "Moving on, the invitation will get us in, but only for the night. We'll have to find a way to get back in later."

"Could we fire one of Kegan's Shift Arrows though one of the windows or something?" Farn pointed a finger at the *Leaf*.

Kegan snorted. "Not a chance. I'd never make that shot. Not from outside the wall. Also, I only have one of those arrows left and have no idea where to find the feathers to craft more. Unless you can find Carver and ask him for another mission."

"No thanks." Max shook his head. "That won't work anyway."

"Why not?" Farn let her finger fall back to the table.

"Mostly because the vault won't be the only thing we have to worry about."

"Meaning?" Farn furrowed her brow.

Max let out a sigh. "How much do you guys know about the shield generators that each city's palace has?"

"We know that they can project a shell around the building to keep people out in the event of an attack, not sure how much damage they can take though," Ginger waved her hand, "but Berwyn won't activate the shield without a reason, so I wouldn't think that would be an issue if he doesn't know we're there."

"That's the problem, there's no way in without him knowing. What most players don't know is that the palace shield never actually shuts down all the way. It just goes into a passive defense mode when not active. Even if we can't see it, it's still there. We'll be able to walk through it tomorrow night since we have an invitation, but if we try to go back later on, we'll set off the alarms as soon as we cross it."

"And a Shift Arrow would get picked up by it?" Farn asked.

Kegan nodded. "Probably. Using them feels more like moving really fast rather than actually teleporting. So I think it would still count as passing through the barrier."

"And we don't have access to a teleport point inside the palace to bypass it either," Kira guessed.

"We could use the Shift Beads." Farn gestured at the bracelet that she had loaned Corvin to boost his defense as he leveled. "I'm pretty sure they transfer you from one point to another without actually moving you there. That's kind of like teleporting. If I can find somewhere out of sight while we're inside tomorrow, I could swap places with someone outside to get them in."

"But we would just have to swap again to get you back in. Otherwise, someone might question where you are. That still leaves us unable to stay inside beyond the night of the party," Corvin reminded.

"Not if you two hold hands." Farn grinned.

The fuzzy-eared *Blade* tilted his head to one side. "I'm sorry, what?"

The *Shield* leaned one arm across the back of her chair. "The beads can shift anything you're holding along with you. So if you hold hands, you should appear on the other side together. Then you can just let go and swap back to leave someone inside. Then they can hide somewhere and wait."

Kegan laughed. "Okay, sure, but the bracelets only have a range of a few hundred feet, so we would have to get close enough to the palace for it to work."

"Well, we are guests. Maybe we can land the Cloudbreaker on the palace's private dock. That way we could smuggle you past the outer walls and most of the guards." Max folded his arms and tapped his foot against the leg of the table. "And if we can recruit one more player to swap the shift bracelets around with, we could sneak Corvin and Kegan in together."

"That would mean giving up another cut of the loot." Ginger let out a harrumph.

Max gave her a judgmental stare.

"What? I'm a *Coin*. I'm greedy. Plus, we'd have to find someone else we trust and let them in on the whole plan."

"Maybe not." Max leaned to the side, looking past Ginger at a pair of players that had just sat down at a table behind her. Each wore a low-level cloak with the hood pulled up. Max smirked. They weren't fooling anyone.

"I seem to remember that there are two players that already know what we're planning and would probably help us, even without their own cut."

Ginger scoffed, adding a sarcastic, "Who?"

Max didn't answer, giving her a moment to think about it.

Her eyes widened as she sputtered a response. "Oh no you don't. You're not recruiting my kids for this."

He ran a hand through his hair. "Oh, don't be so dramatic. It's not like we're actually breaking any laws here."

Ginger gasped with indignation, but before she could respond, one the players at the table behind her spun and pulled back their hood.

"We'll do it!"

Ginger cringed with her entire body as soon as she heard the voice, then craned her head back to look over her shoulder.

Her daughter, Piper, greeted her, hanging over the back of a chair. Her foxlike ears stood up straight with excitement. Beside her sat Drake, her brother.

Ginger squinted at them. "How long have you two been there?"

"Long enough," Drake offered as he tipped a little in his chair.

Piper cracked a wicked grin that resembled her mother's. "What was that about cutting out someone's eyeballs?"

Ginger slapped a hand to her face and dragged it downward. "Fine. You can help with this one thing. But that's it. And no more following me while I'm doing shady things. I have a good mind to deactivate my location marker on your maps."

"Sure, scout's honor." Drake held up one hand.

"Toby, you're not a scout," Ginger reminded the young *Rage* class, using his real name as if he was in trouble. "Now, get over here and keep your voices down. We don't want to have to cut in everyone in the tavern."

Piper dragged her chair over to join the party. Drake followed her lead but sat backward in his seat, clearly trying to act cool. They bracketed their mother on both sides.

Ginger groaned and pushed away her beer. "Now, with that settled, how do we get the hard out of the vault?"

"And get it past everyone in the palace without being noticed?" Kira added.

Max glanced at his stat-sleeve. "We'll have to figure that out later. Right now, it's getting late."

"That's right." Ginger smiled. "And we still have to get you some formal gear."

"What's wrong with this?" Max looked down at himself.

"I won't have my personal bodyguard looking like," she gestured in his direction, "that."

Kira snorted. "She has a point."

Max winced. "Why do I feel like I'm not going to like this?"

CHAPTER FIFTEEN

NIGHT TWO: PARTY HARDER

Max tugged at the necktie that practically choked him as he piloted the Cloudbreaker over the ocean toward the city of Reliqua. He hated ties. Even more, he hated formal wear. Why he had to dress nice in a fantasy world, he had no idea. Of course, that didn't stop Ginger from dragging him to some bizarre shop in Lucem full of creepy dolls, where a strange *Rage* class threw a bunch of clothes at him.

Clearly, Larkin had been busy working and wasn't thrilled to have another person showing up for some free gear. From the look of what he got, Larkin had just shoved a bunch of hand-me-downs at him and called it a day. A double-breasted vest, white dress shirt and a pair of slacks. After that, Ginger had branded him with a small banner that hung from his belt to one side that bore their new house crest. Honestly, she was getting a little too into her new position of power.

The outfit's stats were all over the place, including a ten percent boost to his nonexistent mana. At least the vest was lined with some kind of scales that brought his defense up to a reasonable level. It was also light and easy to move in. What really bothered him, though, was the fact that he had to switch his pistols from the drop-leg holsters he was used to over to a shoulder rig. It definitely looked classier, but it made it hard to draw weapons quickly. He felt like he needed to practice in front of a mirror for a few hours.

"Quit tugging at your tie. It's not going to go away no matter how much you fidget with it," Ginger chided Max as Reliqua's coast appeared in the distance. Her face lit up at the view, and she forgot all about him within seconds. Shoving to the front, she leaned over his shoulder for a better look. The excitement in her eyes made him smile. She was right to be excited; the city was breathtaking.

In front, a vast ocean swept across the view while a range of mountains wrapped around the city's rear to form a natural wall. Lush groves of palms and lagoons of crystal blue water littered the tropical paradise.

Most of the buildings were small, but what they lacked in size, they made up for in quantity, practically spilling into the ocean. Some even stood on stilts just offshore. The city's streets weaved this way and that in a casual, almost haphazard manner. It was as if the place didn't care about efficiency, like relaxation was more important.

Max frowned.

Berwyn had certainly chosen the right place to claim as his capital. Atmosphere aside, the city was near impenetrable. Sure, it might have seemed laid back, but between the mountains and the sea, there was no way for an army to approach. Not to mention that the sprawling roadways would slow any progress from the lack of a direct route. Obviously, Berwyn had realized the same thing. Max's tactical thinking was cut short when Kira threw herself against the windshield.

"Oh, wow." She shoved Ginger to the side with her rear, the ship lurching to one side as the *Coin* bumped the controls.

"Back off. We don't want them to think we're drunk." Max elbowed at the two of them.

"Sorry, sorry, sorry…" Kira trailed off. "But check out that palace. I've never seen it from the air before."

The Jewel of the Sea rested near the back of the city, its outer wall surrounding a wide, square palace. Its sides were lined with brightly lit windows and ornately carved stonework covering nearly every inch of the four-story structure. At each corner of the square sat a tower only slightly taller than the rest out of which a crystal obelisk reached toward the sky. They were beautiful, but even more so was the center. Starting at the top of the inner edge of each wall rose a pyramid of crystal, polished to a flawless shine. Its surface glittered in the night like a star.

I guess that's where the Jewel gets its name, Max assumed.

Appearance aside, the palace was far wider than most of the others in Noctem. Getting from one side to the other must have been time-consuming.

What's inside the pyramid? Max wondered, going back into tactical mode. He shrugged and begun the descent toward the royal landing field just inside the wall. He glanced back at his team, noting Kegan and Corvin hiding in the back. *I hope this works.*

Max connected the ship's com-plate to the palace's private channel as instructed by their invitation. "Cloudbreaker to Palace Guard, this is the personal shuttle of Lady Ginger of House Lockheart, invitation number 46294845, requesting permission to land."

Silence answered back.

He held his breath, hoping that Ginger's contact from the brothel had notified someone in charge about the change in recipient. After a tense moment, the response came back.

"Lockheart?"

Max cringed. "Uh, yeah. That's, umm, us. May we land?"

Ginger squinted at him.

"What?" Max whispered back at her.

The com-plate emitted a sound like someone flipping

through pages followed by a low voice clearly not meant to be heard over the transmission.

"Loyal to Rend?"

This time, it was Max's turn to squint at Ginger.

She rolled her eyes while Kira and Farn pretended to be minding their own business, pointing out a window.

Finally, the same voice came back on, "Lockheart, you're clear to land."

"Nice, it work—" Kira got out before both Ginger and Farn grabbed the little mage. The pair each slapped a hand over her mouth as if one wasn't enough. Everyone's eyes fell to the still active com-plate. Silence filled the craft; the only sound was a muffled word from Kira that suggested an apology. Then the com-plate disconnected.

The cabin blew out a collective sigh.

"Nice, it worked," Kira said again, this time quieter.

Max shook his head.

The landing field sat at the end of a long reflecting pool that stretched out in front of the palace. It was quite a walk to get to the palace doors. There were closer places to set up the landing area, but it seemed like Berwyn wanted to give his guests the full view of the palace as they entered. Either that or he wanted to make sure that everyone knew that they were less important. It rubbed Max the wrong way as he set the ship down as gently as he could, which was dramatically better than usual. He didn't want to make them look like amateurs.

Max opened the Cloudbreaker's door and hopped out. Ginger waited inside since it would have been inappropriate for a Lady such as herself to jump the three feet to the ground from the door. Max reached down to pull out the ship's retractable ramp, realizing that he'd never used it before. Why would he? His party wasn't actually important, so things like ramps had never mattered before. There seemed to be some kind of latch, but he couldn't figure out how to disengage it. That was when a pair of armed guards approached to check his invitation. He started to panic, yanking on the handle and trying his best to pretend he knew what he was doing. He stalled by rolling up his sleeves as if he was afraid that they would get dirty. Then a whisper came from the cabin.

Ginger peeked out from the edge of the door, one hand cupped to the side of her mouth. "Push, then pull."

Max grumbled. She was right. The ramp slid out easily just as the guards stopped behind him. He stood back up and offered his hand to his Lady. Ginger rolled her eyes but took it regardless before stepping outside.

The Lady of House Lockheart walked past Max with confidence, her body hugged by the shining, green silk of the dress Larkin had slaved over the night before. It slid around her legs like a second skin as she walked. The front was open down to her navel, with a dark metal ring connecting the fabric in the middle to cover her chest.

Max caught himself noticing a little too much as she turned to the palace guards. Her eyes matched the gown perfectly. With a charming smile, she handed over the invitation. Then she simply turned to wait for her plus one.

The guard looked up from the envelope, then froze.

Kirabell stepped down the ramp, her bare feet touching the stone of the landing platform. White silk clung to her as if it had been poured over her slender frame. It flared out just below her waist, forming delicate folds that fluttered like a flower in the wind. A simple halter top left her shoulders and back exposed. Across the front of her modest bust ran a thin line of tiny crystals that traveled down her body, dispersing into a field of stars. Each caught the light, making her shine as bright as the crystal pyramid beyond. As always, her unwanted pendant rested upon her collarbone, its heavy silver chain encircling her throat. She gave a slight bow to the guards as they stepped aside to let her and Ginger pass, barely looking at their invitation.

"I guess it is better to stand out," Ginger whispered, holding her house ring close enough to her lips so that it carried her voice to the others across the house line.

Farn exited the ship last, allowing one of the guards to

inspect the inside of their transport for any stowaways that might be trying to infiltrate the palace. Fortunately, Corvin and Kegan had already slipped out while their Lady was showing off her dress.

"You guys good?" Max asked across the house line as the guards made a show of doing their job.

Kegan's voice answered back, "Had us sweating for a bit there, but yeah, we're good. Hiding behind the statue to your right. There're plenty of guards about, but they don't seem to be paying much attention."

"The guards are probably just regular players trying to make a little hard. You can't expect a fully trained security force." Max added as he took the lead.

Ginger and Kira fell in behind him with Farn at their back. With so many houses gathered in one place, it was safe to say that not everyone was on the best of terms. In fact, an event like this could be a veritable pit of vipers. They would have to keep their eyes peeled for threats.

Max raised his house ring. "You ready to be the center of attention tonight, Ginger?"

"Ready as I'm going to be. I think I can pass as the leader of a powerful house," she answered back casually.

"Well, you certainly look the part."

Ginger laughed. "What's that supposed to mean?"

Max's mouth dropped open as he hesitated to explain, "Ahh, I, I just mean you look nice. Or, well, all of you do," he added, including Kira and Farn in the complement in an effort not to make things weird.

Kira snickered.

"Aww, thanks," Ginger said, sounding appreciative, "and you're right, we do look good. To be honest, I think I could seduce anyone in this dress, and Kira sure as hell cleans up nice. By the end of the night, I bet she'll have at least a few men wrapped around her little finger."

Kira laughed dryly. "Ha ha, no. I shall not be doing any seducing."

Farn scoffed. "You probably shouldn't have let Larkin dress you then. That guy definitely knows his way around a needle and thread."

"Blah." The fairy let her mouth hang open as if spitting out the word.

"Kira, put your tongue back in your mouth and act like a lady," Ginger urged before returning to the subject at hand. "Actually, I was thinking before logging on tonight about a way we could go about this. Are you familiar with a honey pot?"

Max laughed. "You mean, like, a con where you seduce a target while you rob them blind? Why does that suggestion not surprise me coming from you?"

"First of all, shut up. And second, yes, that's exactly what I mean. Some of what Samhain said got me thinking, so I messaged a couple girls I know from the other clubs in Lucem this afternoon. Apparently, back when Berwyn first rose to power, he used to hire out women from the brothels to stay in the palace for when he had guests. Which was frequent."

"Why doesn't he do this now?" Farn inquired.

"He canceled the arrangement since, at this point, there are always attractive players interested in lounging around his palace."

"So you're thinking you might be able to get an invite to stay."

"Well, considering I look this good, I think it's a possibility. As long as I can make a good impression."

"And what happens if he expects something in return for letting you stay?" Kira sounded skeptical.

Ginger laughed. "I'm not going to sleep with the guy, if that's what you're asking."

"That's good to hear," Farn commented sarcastically.

"Although I could probably lead him on for quite a while," Ginger added.

"Jeez, I feel bad for the guy now." Max shrugged. "Well, not that bad, though. So yeah, do that. Although, I'd like to go on record that I'm not in love with the idea of using you like that."

Ginger let out a sound over the house line that sounded surprised. She followed it with a sigh. "I'm a grown-up. I can handle myself."

"I know." Max glanced back at her. "Just don't do anything I wouldn't do."

"Hey, sorry to interrupt," Kegan's voice came over the line, "but we're ready, just to let you know."

"You're in position?" Max couldn't help but sound surprised. Things were going too smoothly.

"Yeah. I don't know exactly where the palace's barrier is so I don't want to get much closer, but we should be in range to use the Shift Beads depending on where you are in the palace. You see the patch of palms to your left? We're in there."

Max scanned the area. "Umm, I see a bunch of palms. You're going to have to be more specific."

"I don't know. It's like, just to the left," Kegan repeated unhelpfully.

"There's a statue next to it," Corvin clarified.

"Okay, there's more than one statue," Max commented.

Piper's voice cut in, "Guys, I just marked us on the map."

Max glanced at his journal. "Oh, there you are. You guys snuck over there fast."

"Lots of practice. Been crawling around dungeons I shouldn't be in for the last year," Corvin commented, sounding modest.

"Plus, I'm naturally sneaky," Piper added, sounding less so.

Ginger sighed. "Probably not something to brag about, dear."

"Really, then should I forget about you bragging about your ability to seduce anyone in that dress?" Piper's tone was extra snarky.

Ginger slapped a hand to her face, clearly forgetting her daughter had been on the line.

"Hold up." Max stopped in his tracks as the air around him rippled like water, and a strange energy washed over his body. "I think we hit the barrier." He immediately started walking again as if it had been nothing, not wanting to draw attention. "Piper, can you mark our position on the map? I want to know exactly how much room we have to work with inside."

"Already done. I'm tracing the barrier's perimeter around the pyramid, assuming the palace is sitting at the center."

"Thanks." Max lowered his house ring as he approached the main entrance. A wide stairway lined with statues and light posts seemed to invite them in. More guards waited at the top to check their invitation again before showing the party into the entry hall. A young elf dressed in scarlet robes greeted the other guests at the next door. Before going any further, the guards parted ways, gesturing for Max and Farn to follow.

"I guess this is as far as Farn and I go." Max stepped aside to let Ginger and Kira pass.

Farn bowed with respect as they parted.

Kira looked back to Max, a terrified expression on her face. She clearly wasn't interested in rubbing elbows with Noctem's version of high society. *I won't let your sacrifice go in vain.* Max couldn't help but chuckle. Of course, he didn't want to mingle either.

From there, Farn fell in behind him while the guard showed them through a side door and up to where they would be spending the evening.

The room was simple with a balcony that overlooked a ballroom so they could watch over the festivities. The atmosphere was more relaxed upstairs, with the other houses' bodyguards talking amongst each other. Many seemed to know each other, as if they ran in the same circles. Max felt a little out of place. Fortunately, Farn was with him.

"Shall we see how our Lady and her companion are faring down there?" He found a place at the railing and watched over at the scene below.

Farn gave a snort. "We shall."

CHAPTER SIXTEEN

Okay, act normal.

Walk like a lady.

Don't trip on your dress.

Everything will be fine.

Kirabell struggled to keep her nerves in check.

Oh no, who is this guy, and what does he want?

An elf in scarlet robes seemed to glide towards her and Ginger. He glanced at a book in his hands so fast that she almost missed it. "Thank you for coming, Lady GingerSnaps."

The *Coin* took a sharp breath at the sound of her full player name, as if she had been caught off guard. It sounded vaguely stripper-esque, to begin with, but it was even weirder with the added 'Lady' in the front.

Kira let out an involuntary laugh that drew a puzzled glance from the elf. She promptly shut her dumb mouth.

Ginger recovered and took a step forward, placing a hand on his forearm. "And thank you for having us. May I ask your name?"

"Yes, ahh, of course, I should have introduced myself first." The elf smiled and blushed. "My name is Dartmouth, Lord

Berwyn's right hand and Archmage. Let me show you to the gateway ballroom." He spun on his heel and pushed open the door at the end of the hall. The space beyond sparkled with bright gold trim on nearly every surface. It was almost blinding after coming in from the night. Kira shielded her eyes.

"Come along, Kira dear." Ginger thanked Dartmouth with a wink. "We should go find our host and thank him in person."

Kira didn't really know what to say, so she just followed in silence. She gave a slight bow to Dartmouth as she passed. He smiled back before closing the door again.

The room was huge, though Kira wondered why Dartmouth had called it a gateway ballroom. Maybe it was just one of many. *The palace certainly is big enough to have more than one.* She couldn't help but be curious about what might be inside the pyramid.

Crystal chandlers hung at varying heights while alcoves lined the walls. Marble figures stood on pedestals in each, most of which were nude or barely clothed. Kira shuddered, trying not to be reminded of the statue of herself that she'd encountered last year. The image of her own body seated on a grave haunted her. She still didn't know what to make of it, nor did she want to think about it. She let out a sigh and shook her head.

Two massive staircases wound themselves down from both sides, meeting in the middle at a landing. An equally massive door stood at its back. People filled the space from wall to wall, each dressed in opulent clothing that defined their status. They sipped from long-stemmed glasses and held polite conversation. That was when Kira noticed something important. They had food! Hors d'oeuvres from the looks of it.

Kira twirled in place, her eyes scanning the room like Max searching for a target. It didn't take long for her to spot one. There he was. A man in what could pass for a green tuxedo. He held a tray aloft.

The rest was inevitable. She left Ginger's side to stalk her prey.

The man lowered his bounty to her height as she approached. She didn't even try to figure out what they were before reaching out with both hands. That's when she heard her name spoken in a displeased voice. Kira froze, turning to find the Lady of House Lockheart behind her. Ginger's eyebrow twitched.

"One, just take one."

Kira withdrew one hand, resigning to only claim a single item from the tray. It turned out to be a bacon wrapped scallop. Or at least a virtual representation of one.

Kira didn't like scallops. It was a texture thing. She found them squishy. Though, it was wrapped in bacon, so she ate it anyway.

Another server came by with a tray of champagne. Ginger also reached out with both hands, claiming two glasses. She handed one to Kira, probably hoping that she would be less likely to shove food in her face if one hand was holding a drink. Kira took it reluctantly as she began searching for a new prize.

"Oh, that guy has meatballs."

Farn leaned over the balcony railing searching for the fairy and her Lady. She found Ginger almost immediately. It was hard not to. The *Coin* was tall and commanded the space around her with ease. *It must be nice to have that kind of presence*, Farn thought. Ginger seemed right at home, mingling with the leaders of Noctem's most powerful houses.

"I don't see Kira." Max leaned a little further forward in his place next to Farn.

Kira was harder to spot, her short stature keeping her hidden. The crowd just overtook her. That was when Farn started watching the food instead of the people. With that strategy, she found the gluttonous little mage right away. "There she is, stalking the server with," Farn squinted at a tray, "I think they're pigs in a blanket."

"That makes sense. Kira could never pass up meat and bread."

"She's nothing if not consistent." Farn smiled.

They both stopped to watch the fairy patrol the ballroom. She seemed to be mapping the course of one specific server so that she could make sure she was always in his path. Farn should have been doing more to case the palace than watching Kira stalk a tray of food, but it was entertaining, Plus, the dress looked amazing on her.

Farn raised an eyebrow when Kira broke off her single-minded pursuit of food to look at one of the statues. Something had drawn her attention, but Farn couldn't tell what. Whatever it was had Kira examining the figure intently. Then she reached out one hand toward the back of its pedestal.

Max groaned and raised his house ring. "Kira, are you about to dump a handful of used toothpicks behind that statue?"

The fairy froze in place, a panicked expression washing over her. She pulled her hand back as if holding something but doing her best to hide it. Then she glanced around, looking up.

"Yeah, that's right. We see you down there," Max continued.

The mage responded with a shrug before casually reaching behind the statue anyway. She stepped away a moment later with her hand empty, rubbing her fingers together as if they were sticky. For a moment, it looked like she was going to wipe her hand on the pristine fabric of her dress.

Max opened his mouth to stop her, but fortunately, common sense took hold, saving the gown from its wearer and leaving her holding her hand awkwardly at her side. Max raised his ring again. "There's a washroom to your left."

Kira didn't respond, but she did start walking toward it.

Of course, there was no real need for anyone to wash their hands in Noctem. Germs weren't an issue in a virtual world.

Though, in the more luxurious places, it was common to find a washroom nearby. There were no toilets, obviously, but a user could at least freshen up at a sink or use a quick-change panel.

Kira returned moments later, looking more comfortable.

Farn let out a laugh as the fairy resumed her pursuit of food.

Max sighed.

CHAPTER SEVENTEEN

Unlike a certain pint-sized Archmage, Ginger had been hard at work. She spent a half hour putting names to faces and finding out everything she could about Berwyn. The other guests were a mix of Lords and Ladies from all over Noctem, but also, members of the House of Serpents were present. Many had lead raiding parties of mercenaries during the attack on Torn, while others had been part of the force that took the throne room. A few even claimed to have dealt the final blow that finished off Lady Amelia.

Berwyn seemed to treat his people well, allowing them free use of the palace, even upgrading it to suit their recreational needs. Throwing events like this one was another way that he rewarded their service. Surprisingly, the Serpents weren't that large of a house, with only fifty-three members including the top three. Everyone Ginger talked to spoke highly of their Lord. More importantly, they seemed loyal. *This could be more difficult than I thought.* She wasn't expecting Berwyn to be such a good leader.

On the flip side, there was also a fair amount of interest in the new and mysterious House Lockheart that had appeared from nowhere. Ginger had found herself answering more questions than she could ask at times. The most common inquiry being how their allegiance to the fallen city of Rend had come to be. Of course, Ginger made sure to keep things vague. She had to maintain some of their secrets, after all. This only added to the air of mystery that hung around the name Lockheart. It also helped that Ginger performed her role perfectly. She almost always knew exactly what to say to keep the illusion going.

Above all else, though, playing her new role was fun. She enjoyed pretending to be the enigmatic leader of a powerful house. It was like living a fantasy from her younger years. She was Lady Ginger of Lockheart, and she loved it.

The real surprise was that Kira had been gaining a similar reputation without even trying. Actually, it may have been because she wasn't trying. Ginger overheard more than a few guests comment on the enchanting fairy that had been seen wandering the crowd. The fact that she hadn't interacted with anyone had even added to their curiosity. After that, it didn't take long for people to realize she was a high-level *Breath* mage. Someone must have looked up her public profile. Ginger smiled. If that was the case, then they also knew what house she belonged to.

Suddenly, Ginger's thoughts were interrupted as music began to play. The spectacle that followed was like something out of a major award show. Berwyn entered, top left, the music playing him down the stairs until he reached the landing.

Ginger had seen his picture before. It had been posted everywhere during his rise to power, which she had researched during her day offline. She knew he was good looking, but the pictures hadn't done him justice. In person, he carried himself with something extra. Something more than confidence. He simply owned the spotlight.

Despite the high security around the palace, there were no guards near him, as if he had nothing to fear from anyone. It wasn't surprising considering that the golden crown that graced his brow made him nearly immortal. The crowd stopped, turning with all of their attention before he even had to speak.

Ginger noticed Kira, standing on her toes to see past the sea of shoulders ahead.

"Hey!" Berwyn waved in a casual manner that somehow seemed charming. His voice carried through the room as he continued, "First of all, thank you so much for coming to celebrate our acquisition of Torn. It was really an amazing undertaking to be a part of. I can't tell you how rewarding it was to see the house that I started grow into a full-fledged empire. Albeit, I am kind of regretting giving it such an evil sounding name. The Empire of Serpents doesn't exactly sound friendly, am I right?" He laughed with a seemingly intentional awkwardness. It got him several laughs in return from the crowd.

"But hey, at least it's memorable." The crowd laughed again. "Anyway, I gave a lengthy speech last time I invited you all here, so I'll spare you a repeat performance. Instead, let's just get on with the party. I see some new faces that I'd like to get to know, and I'm sure many of you would like to get caught up as well. So without further ado, let's move this thing to the real ballroom." He turned and walked toward the massive doors behind him. They seemed to open on their own in response to his presence so that he didn't need to slow down.

Ginger had assumed that the enormous ballroom that she stood in was as grand as things got. She was wrong. By bod, she could not have been more wrong. The night had only just begun.

The pyramid awaited.

CHAPTER EIGHTEEN

"Holy crap," Max breathed as he picked his jaw up off the floor.

Farn had a similar reaction, blocking the doorway as she froze at the sight of the inside of the pyramid.

Max had obviously realized that the crystalline structure was large. Still, now that he was inside it, the scale of the pyramid was something else entirely. He felt like he was outside. The walls even matched the exterior of the palace to reinforce the illusion, all stonework and brightly lit windows.

The crowd followed Berwyn through a door to an enormous stone patio surrounded by hanging lanterns. Max caught a glimpse of Ginger as she entered. An expression of what could only be described as wonder settled across her face.

Beyond the patio, a strip of sand divided the space, complete with a natural pool that filled the other side. No, pool wasn't the right word; it was more like a private beach. A stone walkway reached across the waves with a massive throne rising out of the artificial sea at its end. Water poured from the upper floors behind it like a curtain at the back of a stage. Moonlight shimmered across the water's surface.

Max raised his head, expecting to find the geometric crystal ceiling he saw from outside. To his surprise, it was as if the ceiling wasn't even there, just a romantic field of stars. An aurora effect danced across the sky as if refracted by the crystalline surface.

Farn let out an awkward laugh from beside him. "Berwyn may have gone overboard with his throne room."

Max stepped up to the railing, finding Ginger and Kira again down below. The *Coin* had composed herself back to the cool and mysterious leader she had been portraying so far. The fairy, on the other hand, was enthralled by the fact that there were new food options inside the pyramid.

The servers had rotated, along with the menu. The men in tuxedos had moved up to the balcony to serve the bodyguards. Below, trays were now carried by women wearing light togas. Amongst them, nearly all of Noctem's races were represented. All except for fairies of course, probably due to their rarity. As far as Max could tell, Kira was the only one of her kind at the party.

The rest of the guests gathered around the perimeter of the patio, which now doubled as a dance floor. Berwyn took his time, casually approaching one of his guests with a hand outstretched. She looked as nervous as she did excited to have been chosen. An orchestra perched on a balcony began to play as Berwyn took her by the hand and spun her onto the floor. The rest of the crowd paired off and joined the couple. From there, the party got started.

Max turned away from the view and snatched a mini egg roll off a tray, along with a glass of champagne.

"Might as well try to blend in."

Farn followed his lead, grabbing a drink of her own. "I'm going to take a walk around the balcony and see if I can find anywhere to invite our stealthy friends in." She shook her wrist to draw attention to the Shift Beads she wore.

"Good plan. I'll hang back here and keep watch on things."

Farn nodded and sauntered off on her own.

Max grabbed another egg roll and resumed his sentry duty, which comprised of watching Kira hide behind Ginger to avoid dancing. He chuckled to himself at his friend's discomfort. That was when a voice startled him from behind.

"Oh wow, do you actually dual wield?"

He dropped half an egg roll off the balcony and turned to find a wide-eyed reynard woman. Her ears stuck up straight with enthusiasm as she examined his pistols. She stood a little too close.

Max instinctively stepped away, the railing behind him pressing into his back. "Ah, yeah…" He tried to pretend that he hadn't just dropped food onto the patio below.

"That's awesome!" She took the space beside him without asking if he wanted company and immediately got comfortable, leaning her elbows on the railing. "I tried dual wielding once, but I could never handle it. I missed too much with my left hand." She mimed finger guns firing in different directions. "So no thanks, I'll just stick with the one." She angled her rear toward him to draw attention to the gun that was holstered at the small of her back next to her tail. She grinned as she proudly displayed her backside. The woman was either oblivious to the effect or didn't care.

Max tried to check out her gun, but the leather flap of her holster kept most of it hidden. Plus he had trouble doing so without it looking like he was checking out her ass. He shook his head, confused by her sudden familiarity. "I'm sorry, who–"

She cut him off before he could finish the question. "Oh, damn, sorry. I'm Nix." She stepped back from the railing and held out one hand for him to shake.

Max responded a little slowly, catching only her fingers as he introduced himself. She adapted by performing a ridiculous curtsy while holding the hem of her skirt. A lock of black hair fell across her smoky, blue eyes. He smirked. It reminded him of something Kira would do.

"Anyways, sorry to bother you. I just don't see many other *Furies*, especially not a dual-wielder. So I had to say hi." She shoved the lock of hair back between her fuzzy ears, giving it a messy but wild quality.

"I don't meet many *Furies* either." He leaned back on the railing, prompting her to join him.

She nodded. "It's a class that has a lot of appeal for beginners, but most seem to find it too challenging since it relies on speed and aim. I stuck with it, but I'm still only mid-level now, so that's not really impressive. How 'bout you?"

"My level's pretty high." He gave her a knowing smile but tried to keep things vague.

"Thought so." She nodded as if congratulating herself. "I didn't recognize your pistols, so I figured they're a set that I haven't come across yet."

"Yeah, they weren't easy to get." He left out the fact that they were contract items.

"So, you're not a fan of ties either?" Her eyes flicked to the loosened knot around his neck.

"What?" Max asked, before realizing what she meant. "Oh, yeah. It was choking me to death. I'm not big on formal wear."

She snorted a laugh. It wasn't as musical as Kira's, but it sounded honest. "I know, right? I'm not exactly wearing this by choice." She motioned down as if her appearance was enough to explain her point.

Her outfit was similar to his. Just a vest and shirt with a loose tie. The only real difference was that where his clothing was black, hers was gray. Well, that and the rather short, pleated skirt that flipped up in the back where her tail connected to her body. It would have been a little too revealing if she hadn't added a pair of leggings underneath to keep things PG.

"Plus, who wants to be wearing a tie if there is a chance of getting in a fight? I mean, it's pretty much a giant vulnerability." She grabbed the piece of fabric and mimed being choked by it with her tongue hanging out.

Max laughed at the display.

"So, which one's yours?" She pointed down at the crowd,

her tone sounding like a proud parent asking another which kid on the playground was theirs.

Max decided not to admit to the fairy below who was currently trying to juggle a glass and a handful of tiny eclairs. Instead, he pointed out Ginger.

"I'm here with House Lockheart. That one down there in the green dress is our Lady."

Nix followed the line of his finger to the floor. "Oooo, she's pretty."

"Yeah, she turns a few heads." Max shrugged, then hooked a thumb down at the guests. "Which one are you saddled with?"

"I guess that one." She poked a finger in the direction of Lord Berwyn.

Her words hit Max like a truck. The reynard wasn't wearing a house ring, so he hadn't considered the possibility that she was one of Berwyn's Serpents. The simple acknowledgment marked her as an enemy, and here he was making conversation like an idiot. He couldn't afford to let his guard down.

"Oh, so you're part of Berwyn's house?" he fished for information.

"Nah. I'm just here to make some hard." Nix waved a hand then snatched a stuffed mushroom off a passing tray with the other. She took a small bite then spit it out over the railing. "Ack, crab."

Max ignored the act. "So you're a mercenary then?"

She tossed the remainder of the offending mushroom over to join the rest. "Yeah, I guess." She brushed a few crumbs from her hand. "My partner and I took out Amelia's First Knight during the attack on Torn. That's her over there. Her name's Aawil." Nix pointed toward a female faunus leaning up against one wall, a *Coin* from the look of the wire launcher on her wrist. She stood with her arms crossed like they were a barrier to keep others away.

Nix shrugged. "Aawil's no fun at parties, though. That's why I have to go chat up random *Furies*."

"So you've been to parties here before?" Max probed.

"I should hope so. I kind of live here. Well, obviously, I don't live here. I live in Philly, but I have a room in the palace that I have set as my home point."

"Oh, so Berwyn just lets his mercs hang out here? That's a nice perk."

"Not all of them, just the ones he keeps on retainer," Nix grinned, "and yeah, the perks are amazing. This place has everything. There's the beach, a movie theater, a bowling alley, and a tavern with pretty much every food item in the world available for free." She listed everything off on her fingers.

Jeez, it's like Kira's paradise, Max thought. "Sounds like a good deal. I wouldn't expect a guy bent on world domination to treat his people so well."

Her tall ears twitched at the comment. "He's gentle as a kitten. I mean, I wouldn't cross him, but he does right by us. I think he's a bored rich guy or something out in the real world. Just doing this for fun."

"So he's conquering Noctem, as what, a hobby?"

Nix shrugged. "That and dancing, I guess. He loves showing off on the floor."

Max shifted his view to watch the Lord of Serpents. The man looked at home as he twirled an elf away before pulling her back into a dip. "I guess he knows his way around a ballroom."

Nix leaned forward. "That's nothing. I've seen him do more out there. I think he's holding back to keep pace with his partner."

"I don't really know much about dancing."

"You should try sometime. Take that gorgeous Lady of yours out for a night on the town."

Max couldn't help but laugh at the suggestion of him and Ginger together.

"Or you could give your partner here a spin." Nix leaned to look past his shoulder and gestured with her head to where Farn now stood.

Max froze for a second, unsure how Nix knew who Farn

was without an introduction. He pushed off the railing and tried to act natural. "Oh, hey, how was the walk? This is Nix. She works for Berwyn," he tried to inform his housemate that the over-friendly reynard might be an enemy without making it obvious.

Farn stopped short, glancing between the two. "Ah good, good." She extended a hand to the woman and gave her name. "The pyramid is really something. Especially over by the water-falls in the back. You can actually walk behind them."

"I know, right? That's one of my favorite spots." Nix looked back at her partner and let out a sigh. "I should probably go back and hang out with Aawil over there before she withdraws any further, but hey, it was awesome meeting you two. You should talk to your Lady about allying with us. I want to see you dual wield, and I'd prefer to be on the same side when that happens." She gave Max a wide smile, then stalked back to her partner.

"She seems... nice. For a bad guy," Farn commented.

Max tapped one finger on the railing. "Maybe."

"Why maybe?"

"How did she know we were housemates? I don't think she could see your ring."

"Maybe she saw us together earlier." Farn furrowed her brow.

"Yeah, maybe. Or maybe she's keeping tabs on us since we're new. I can't shake the feeling that there was more to that exchange." Max folded his arms. "I don't know, maybe not. She doesn't seem that organized. Anyway, did you find a way to sneak the guys in?"

Farn sighed. "Nope. Every door on this balcony is either locked or has a pair of guards positioned at it. Even behind the waterfalls. I can't tell if they're players or NPC guards. They're all wearing the same gear sets so they could be either or a mix."

"Damn, we have to think of something." Max leaned back on the railing.

That was when Farn grinned. "I think I have an idea."

"And that is?" Max arched an eyebrow.

Farn began to walk backward. "Sometimes, the best solution is just to be yourself. And I... am embarrassing." As soon as the last word left her mouth, she collided with a server.

Max winced as Farn fell, taking a tray of champagne with her. The resulting crash was louder than one might have expected.

"I'm okay, I'm okay." Farn pushed herself off the ground, empty stemware falling off her as she did. Champagne ran down her vest. Droplets of liquid peppered the fur that lined her cape.

"Oh, I'm terribly sorry!" The server helped her up, clearly worried about complaints. "Let's get you to a washroom to refresh your armor."

Farn shot Max a wink.

"No need to apologize. I wasn't watching where I was going," Farn bowed her head, "but yeah, I should probably refresh my gear. Don't want to end up sticky all night."

Max shook his head as Farn was escorted out into the hall.

"House Lockheart. We may not have style, but we get the job done."

CHAPTER NINETEEN

Corvin lay prone next to Kegan and Piper. The sound of music reached his tall, fuzzy ears, muffled by the walls of the palace. It helped fill the awkward silence that hung over them. A stick was digging into his thigh. He held in a sigh.

Suddenly, Farn's voice came over the house line in a whisper, "Grab onto each other, 'cause I'm shifting you in."

Corvin's eyes locked with Kegan's, then fell to Piper.

She grabbed each of them by the shoulder and yanked Corvin toward her so she could reach her house ring without letting go. "Ready."

"Okay, I made it to a washroom. Try to keep quiet. There's a guard just outside the door," Farn warned.

Then the familiar darkness of the void between spaces claimed them. It was immediately followed by a blinding light, taking a few seconds for Corvin's eyes to adjust. At least the stick digging into his thigh was gone.

A few stalls made of dark wood lined one side of the opulent room. The other wall contained a row of sinks set into the surface of a floor to ceiling mirror. Small chandeliers hung from above.

Piper took in the room, her eyes growing wider with every second. "This is the most beautiful bathroom I have ever seen."

"Not quite." Kegan pushed open a stall, revealing an empty space with a quick-change panel attached to one wall. "No toilets."

"Oh, that makes sense—" Piper only got out a few words before vanishing.

Farn appeared, standing in her place almost instantly. She wasted no time, pulling the string of beads from her wrist as one faded from black to red. She slipped the bracelet over Corvin's hand.

Her vest looked wet, like something had spilled down her front. She pushed into one of the stalls only to emerge a second later, dry as a bone. "Okay, there's a guard outside waiting to take me back to the party, so I can't stay, but here's what I know so far. There are guards positioned throughout the palace. I don't know how many, but at least some are players. I think the rest are NPCs. They all wear the same gear, so it's hard to tell which is which."

"That's it?" Kegan threw up is arms.

"Sorry, I've only been outside the ballroom for five minutes. I didn't have time to see much. The rest is up to you." Farn opened one of the stalls. "Hide in here, just in case the guard looks in the washroom."

Corvin stepped inside. Kegan shoved in behind him.

Farn whispered a last, "Good luck," then closed the stall. Her footsteps headed for the door.

"You dry now?" a masculine voice came from outside.

Farn gave an awkward laugh. "Yes, much better. Thank you for letting me freshen—" The door cut off the rest of her words, leaving only muffled voices coming from the hall. Eventually, silence took over.

Corvin waited another uncomfortable minute with Kegan's elbow jabbing him in his side. It was just as bad as the stick from before.

"You know, we could have hidden in different stalls."

Kegan nodded. "This is true."

"Okay, I think we can get out now."

The pair shoved each other out of the cramped space.

"Hey, have you ever been inside a lady's room?" Kegan fixed his hair in the enormous mirror.

"No. Have you?"

"Once or twice. Kinda like this actually. Very clean. Just stalls and sinks."

"Good to know." Corvin ignored the subject altogether. "Let's check out the hall."

They poked their heads out from the doorway. Thankfully, the lighting was dimmer than in the washroom, no doubt to add to the relaxed atmosphere of the palace.

A row of thick pillars ran down the center of the hallway, supporting a vaulted ceiling. The marble floor was polished to a perfect shine. Corvin could almost see himself in it, even in the low lighting.

A pair of guards patrolled the hallway further down.

"You think they're players or bots?" Kegan kept his voice low.

Corvin watched as they walked away. "They're bots."

"What makes you so sure?"

"Their stride is too even." He took a breath and snuck over to the nearest pillar. Kegan followed.

Unlike the *Leaf* class, which was designed to move from one sniper's perch to another, *Blades* were not known for their stealth abilities. No, they were more of a frontline class. All damage and speed. Fortunately, between the shadows and the sound of the orchestra, Corvin had little trouble staying hidden.

Kegan placed a finger to his forehead and whispered the words, "Light Foot," to reduce the sound of his movement. Then he slipped ahead to the next pillar and beckoned to say the coast was clear.

Corvin shifted his weight and moved in a low crouch, making sure to hold his sword with one hand to keep its sheath from tapping against the floor. From there, they followed the pair of guards, moving from pillar to pillar, until they approached a large stairway protected by another set of Berwyn's bots.

Each flight of stairs wrapped around a formation of white crystal. A gentle glow came from within.

"We must be at the south corner of the palace," Corvin whispered from the shadow of a pillar. "I think that's the base of one of the obelisks that we saw from outside."

Kegan mouthed the word 'wow'. "It must go all the way down to the ground before rising through up through the roof."

Corvin pointed one finger up. "Speaking of the roof, I think it might be our best bet at finding a place to hide. Provided we can get past those guards."

The sentries faced outward almost unflinching, both *Blade* classes from the look of it. Pretty standard for basic melee enemies.

"We could just kill them," Kegan suggested.

Of course, they would have to hide the bodies since the corpses of guard type enemies didn't turn to bones like monsters did. As long as they could hide the evidence before another patrol came by, the guards should just respawn a little later with no memory of having been killed.

Corvin shook his head. "No, this is a palace, not a dungeon. Killing them might trigger some kind of alert. Best not to take chances." He examined the two men. "Okay, most enemies have a cone of vision, right? So if we hug the wall, we might be able to get behind them and onto the stairs without them noticing."

"That's not a great plan, but it's a plan." Kegan shrugged and began to creep forward.

That was when one of the guards reached into his pouch and pulled out a player journal.

Corvin's eyes widened, and his fuzzy black ears flipped back. He ducked his head on instinct.

Kegan turned with panic in his eyes, crouching only ten feet away from a completely human guard that they had assumed had been an NPC like rest. The *Leaf* mouthed the words 'holy freaking crap.' All it would take was for one of the guards to glance in his direction.

At least with NPCs, they might have had the option of taking them out, but players would probably remember getting killed when they logged back in. Corvin resisted the urge to scramble back behind the pillar, and instead, crept in reverse as quietly as he could.

Kegan did the same, finding safety back in the shadows.

Then right on cue, another patrol entered the hallway back where they had started.

Corvin took in a sharp breath that froze in his throat. They couldn't go forward or backward, and in just a moment, the patrol would be on top of them.

Kegan slinked up against the nearest pillar, glancing around. He stabbed a finger up at the ceiling, then dropped his hands and interlocked his fingers.

Corvin looked up to where the top of the pillar connected to the vaulted ceiling. A ridge of decorative stonework ran along every edge, almost like handholds. He nodded and placed his foot in the *Leaf's* hands. It wasn't easy, but a few seconds later, he had all four limbs hooked to the carved ceiling.

Kegan reapplied his Light Foot skill and climbed up behind him. He hugged the top of the pillar while resting his weight on a small ridge. Corvin held his breath as he waited for the patrol to pass underneath, only letting it out when the guards reached the stairs.

As the pair of NPCs passed the nearly identical human sentries, one of the players turned to the other. "Do you find it creepy that those guys are fake and we're real, but we're all dressed the same?"

"I guess," the other player replied, sounding uninterested as he flipped to the inspector embedded in the back cover of his journal. "Hey, that girl I met last night sent a pic. Check it out." He angled the book to the other guard.

"Dude, don't just go around showing people that."

"What? If she didn't want people to see, she shouldn't have sent it."

The other player rubbed his temples. "I know, but did you think for a second that there was a chance that she only meant for you to see it? There's trust in that, man. Have some class."

"Thanks, now I feel like a dick."

"That's probably because you are a dick, Steve."

Corvin's eye began to twitch. The entire exchange was irritating. Then he felt a puff of air against his tail. He glanced down to find Kegan attempting to blow it away from his face.

"Sorry." Corvin pulled it away, leaving the *Leaf* twitching his nose back and forth and making a face like he was about to sneeze. Corvin's eyes bulged. *Oh no you don't. This isn't a cartoon. You hold that in.*

Kegan made a series of intense expressions but finally settled down.

Corvin let out a relieved breath. "Any ideas? My arms are getting tired." It was only a matter of time before he lost his grip. Not to mention another patrol would be by any minute.

If they had been in a normal dungeon, Corvin would just throw an echo stone down the stairs to distract the guards. He had his doubts that a living player would be so easily manipulated. *If only I had a cardboard box to hide under.*

That was when he noticed Kegan rummaging around in his item bag to produce a shiny, new echo stone.

Corvin couldn't get a word out fast enough to stop the *Leaf* from throwing it.

The small, enchanted stone sailed over the two guards, bouncing off the flight of stairs before falling. From the sound of the impact echoing back up, it must have dropped straight down to the first floor.

"Seriously?" Corvin gave Kegan a firm stare.

Then to his surprise, the pair of players actually took the bait. One walked two flights down while the other followed part way.

"Good enough." Kegan immediately dropped down and scampered his way up the stairs while their backs were turned.

Corvin's heart almost leaped out of his chest at the realization that this was happening whether he was ready or not. He wrapped his legs around the pillar and shimmied to the floor as quietly as he could. He really wished he had Kegan's Light Foot skill.

Heavy footsteps began coming back up the stairs.

"There's nothin' down here," said one guard.

"Don't you dare say it must have been the wind," responded the other. "Check the hall down there. I'll look up here."

Corvin scrambled on all fours like one of those lizards racing across the sand in a nature documentary. He probably watched too many documentaries, but that wasn't important now.

He reached the stairs just as the sound of boots reached the landing behind him. It took every ounce of self-control he had not to leapfrog several steps at once. That would have been too loud. Instead, he kept low and distributed his weight as even as possible.

Footsteps kept coming. They were almost on top of him.

Don't screw this up. The words passed through his head again and again. He couldn't bear the thought of letting the team down.

Corvin gritted his teeth and gave one last, desperate push.

The guard placed his hand on the railing, then stopped to stare off into the glowing crystal obelisk for a moment. He shook his head and scanned the stairs for anything out of place.

Corvin lay pressed flat against the half wall of the banister, his jaw almost tense enough to crack a tooth. Kegan lay half underneath him. The guard's hand rested just above their terrified forms. All the man had to do was look down.

Finally, the player turned back. "Steve, I hate to say it, but maybe it was the wind."

The other guard laughed as they returned to their positions.

Corvin let out the breath that had been lodged in his throat.

He may not have had any stealth abilities of his own, but as it turned out he hadn't needed any. Well, provided he dove on top of a conveniently placed *Leaf* with an active Light Foot skill to act as an elven sound dampener.

Corvin expected a complaint. Instead, he found Kegan batting his eyelashes seductively as they lay face to face. Corvin rolled his eyes and crawled off the *Leaf* toward the next floor.

There weren't any guards stationed on the stairs above. In fact, other than the patrols that circled each floor, there weren't any other guards at all. It wasn't convenient, but as long as they kept their distance, they could safely move around the palace undetected.

After making a full loop of the top floor, Corvin stopped short. "Hey, do you notice anything strange?"

"No, but I take it you do." Kegan slipped almost casually between the pillars.

"From outside, there were windowed gables on the roof."

"And?"

"If there's a window, there must be a room. But I don't see any more stairs going up." Corvin gestured toward the ceiling. "I think there might be a space outside the map, like the last boss in Doom II."

Kegan shook his head. "Didn't play that one. To busy having a social life back then."

Corvin ignored the jab without skipping a beat. "The last boss in Doom was a giant goat skull with a weak point in its forehead."

"Sounds cute."

"Not so much, but the whole thing was actually just a picture on a wall. The weak point was a window into a secret room where the real boss was hidden. There was no way in without cheating, so the only way to kill it was to fire rockets through the window and hope the splash damage would hit it."

Kegan raised an eyebrow. "That just sounds lazy. What was the hidden boss?"

Corvin searched the gaming encyclopedia in his head. "It

was one of the game developer's head on a stake. John Romero, I think."

"Yikes."

"It's actually really interesting. It was put there as an Easter Egg. I think the photo they used of him was from *Business Week* magazine—"

"More guards," Kegan interrupted the history lesson and pointed down the hall.

"Oh." Corvin canned the rest of the explanation and ducked into the nearest unlocked room to find a guest suite. It must not have been claimed by anyone.

If he had been invited, Corvin could have registered the lavish room as his home point. Unfortunately, they were far from welcomed guests. *Berwyn probably has a couple guards to check the empty rooms every now and then.* That's what Corvin would have done if he had been the Lord of the palace.

He ignored the room and stepped out onto its private balcony. The decorative stonework made for an easy climb. Although, he still made it a point not to look down, letting out a breath once he had pulled himself up onto the Spanish colonial tile above.

The roof was steep but not so steep to make it difficult to walk on. It wasn't long before they reached the nearest gable. Its arched window welcomed them as they stepped through.

As expected, the hidden space was empty and undefined. It wasn't even that big, just a narrow hallway that connected the inner and outer windows. That being said, it was perfect. There was no easy way to get to it, so there was little chance of being discovered.

"And now we play the waiting game." Kegan slid up to the window facing the crystal pyramid and rested his arm on the sill.

Corvin lay down on the floor. "Get comfortable. We're going to be waiting for a while." The sound of the orchestra below just barely met his ears now.

He reached into his bag and pulled out the emulator he

always carried. The third-party app was skinned to look like a small book and housed almost every retro game that a bored reynard could ask for. He set the volume so that it was only audible to him and flipped on the screen within, selecting a title with an embedded d-pad. A logo appeared along with a rather dated graphic of a T-rex peaking up from the bottom. It moved its jaws with a roar that spoke the word, "SEGA."

He got comfortable. "Let's just hope everything else goes well downstairs."

CHAPTER TWENTY

"You must be Lady Ginger."

Ginger nearly snorted a mouthful of champagne as a familiar voice came from behind. She spun to greet the last person she expected to run into, making sure to act as if they didn't already know each other.

"Mister Coldblood, it's so nice to meet you."

"Please, call me Alastair. Mr. Coldblood is my fathe… Well, no, my name is made up, so that's not true, now is it? Anyway," Alastair played along, speaking loud enough for those around her to overhear, "I'm sorry, but I just had to stop by and meet the Lady of the only house loyal to Rend. That sure was an exciting development."

Ginger gave a polite laugh. "Yes, I can understand why you would take an interest in something so rare, but I have to admit, I am flattered that someone like you knows my name."

"Nonsense. I keep my thumb on the pulse of Noctem. I couldn't miss a player as enchanting as yourself." He stepped closer. "Would it be unreasonable for me to ask for your company on the floor?"

Ginger froze for a moment before giving an uncomfortable nod and handing her drink to Kira.

"Perfect." He took her by the hand and led her onto the dance floor where they could speak without being overheard. He smiled as if he was just out enjoying the night as he pulled her close and waited for the music to start up again. "I wasn't going to come tonight, but after your message about Rend, I felt the need to check in to see what you had gotten yourself into."

"I assure you we have everything under control." Ginger wobbled as she stepped back in an attempt to perform a simple box step.

"Everything but dancing I see– Ouch."

Ginger stepped on his foot.

"Sorry, but you're going to have to pretend that I'm good at this for the sake of appearances. I am quite terrible."

"No problem. Appearances are important." Alastair's eye twitched as she stepped on his foot a second time. He pushed on without complaint. "I take it the plan is going smoothly?"

"Corvin and Kegan are already hidden in the palace, and Berwyn has been stealing glances our way for the last few dances. So I should have him just where I want him before the night is done." Ginger smiled. "So we don't need you checking up on us."

"I suppose not." His tone fell, but his face remained enthusiastic. "I see Kira is having a good time."

Ginger turned, whilst narrowly missing Alastair's toes. Kira was near the edge of the floor, attempting to eat while holding two glasses. "Yes, she's been a very… helpful plus one so far. At least her gown has made the right impression."

"Yes, that is quite the dress."

"Speaking of plus ones, where is your special someone tonight?"

"Right there." Alastair lead her in a circle so she could face the other side of the room.

Ginger suppressed a laugh as she found Alastair's assistant, Jeff-with-a-three, over by a statue, clearly putting in effort to act

nonchalant. "That is unexpected. I wouldn't think this was
J3ff's scene."

"Actually, he insisted on coming to check up on you."

"Really?" Ginger arched an eyebrow.

"Of course, this whole heist was his idea from the start. I
hadn't even thought of it."

"I think I like him a little better now." Ginger smiled, realizing that the uptight assistant might have a wild side that she
hadn't seen before.

"Indeed, I was surprised, too when he suggested it." Alastair
dodged her foot again. "He really is full of surprises."

"Speaking of surprises, what is this reclaiming Rend quest
about?"

"I wouldn't want to spoil it." Alastair chuckled, giving her
an annoying grin. "I told you all last year that we had plans for
that place. I'm just glad that someone has set them into motion.
And honestly, I can't think of a house that I'd rather see take on
the task."

"That's unhelpful." Ginger frowned as the orchestra
finished their piece. She took that as her cue to spare Alastair
any more injury. Apparently, he wasn't going to give her a
straight answer anyway. "Well, if that is all, we should probably
part ways before people start to question how well we know
each other."

Alastair's body relaxed. "Oh thank god. I wasn't sure how
much more my feet could take."

"I'm not that bad." Ginger forced a smile for appearances
but squeezed his hand a little too hard. "Would you rather
dance with Kira?"

"Umm... no." Alastair lead Ginger off the floor. "Kira
would probably blow her cover immediately."

"I don't know." Ginger returned to the fairy. "She can keep
it together when it counts."

"Who can keep it together?" Kira handed over a glass of
champagne as soon as she was off the dance floor. Ginger held

it up, finding a couple toothpicks floating in the glass. She glowered at the fairy.

"Oh, sorry." Kira took it back and handed her the other one, sans toothpicks.

"Well, it has been lovely meeting you, and I wish you the best of luck in Rend," Alastair said a little louder than necessary.

With that, he took his leave, greeting one of the other Lords just as politely as he had greeted her.

That was when Max's voice came across the house line, "Heads up, Ginger, you got incoming. Berwyn is making a beeline to your position."

Ginger suppressed a grin, pretending to take a sip of her champagne. "It's about time."

With everything that she had been doing all night to build House Lockheart's mysterious reputation, Ginger would have been surprised if the man hadn't taken an interest.

There was, however, still one problem. She was a worse dancer than she thought. Sure, Ginger had plenty of... rhythm when it came to other activities, but after using Alastair as a test subject, her confidence was shot. She would never make the right impression with Berwyn if she stomped all over his feet as well. She had to come up with another way. Fortunately, she had other options. Ginger might not have been able to dance, but what she did have was the devious mind of a *Coin*.

"You ready to make a good first impression?" She turned to Kira who was trying to sip from her glass without swallowing a toothpick.

The fairy gave an expressionless nod along with a simple, "Nope." Then she spun on her heel and attempted to exit the situation before it began.

"Oh, no you don't." Ginger expected the reaction, cutting off the mage's escape with an outstretched hand. "You're just as much a part of this house as I am."

"Nah, I'll just get in the way," Kira brushed the argument aside.

"I wouldn't be so sure." Ginger slinked toward her with a predatory smile. "I think I can find a use for you."

Kira took a sharp breath and held it in a way that inadvertently improved her posture.

"Perfect." Ginger gave her a wink then laughed as if the fairy had just said something funny. She didn't want to seem like she had been expecting anyone as Berwyn appeared beside her.

"Oh!" She pretended to be surprised.

"Hi there." Berwyn gave a friendly wave then shoved his hands into his pockets. He wore a casual smile that was downright charming on his handsome face. It made him seem less intimidating, as if he was genuinely having fun. "You must be the Lady of House Lockheart that I've been hearing so much about tonight."

Ginger returned the smile. "Thank you for not adding an infamous before that."

He let out a laugh. "Well yes, I will say, I wasn't expecting to meet anyone tonight with a house affiliation with Rend." He jumped right to the point. "I have to admit, I wasn't sure what to expect when Samhain messaged me to say he was sending some interesting guests in his place."

Ginger gave him a knowing smile. "Yeah, we don't exactly conform to the norms." She stepped to the side. "That reminds me, let me introduce my Archmage, Kirabell."

Kira let out a squeak followed by an unintentionally pretty laugh. Berwyn's face lit up.

"I'd say we need more players in Noctem that stray from the norm. I don't think I've had a fairy in the palace before. Especially not a *Breath* Archmage. Color me impressed."

"I have some good housemates. They do their best to keep me alive." Kira stared at the ground for a second before finding the courage to look him in the eyes. Her violet irises sparkled.

"And I'm sure you must do the same for them." He shifted his view back to Ginger as if to confirm.

"That she does. She may even be one of the game's

strongest healers when it comes to raw stats. At least, that's how we planned it."

"I should probably be careful of you then. Any house with that much forethought must be a force to be reckoned with."

Ginger placed a hand on his arm. "Well, as long as you don't go marching your army on Rend, you shouldn't have anything to worry about." She took a sip of her champagne. "Oh, and keep throwing parties like this. The palace is absolutely beautiful by the way."

"Thank you. It made the chore of choosing a capital easy. There's something to be said for having your own private beach. You both will have to come by sometime when it's not so busy."

"We would love to," Ginger chortled polity at his invitation. Though, in reality, it took everything she had to keep from full-on cackling.

Excellent! My plan is unfolding perfectly. Now to seal the deal.

"You're quite the dancer by the way." She gave him her most charming smile.

"I can't take all the credit." Berwyn took a slight bow. "Dancing is all about teamwork. It's a partnership. One that I happen to enjoy." He held out one hand to her. "Would you care to give it a try?"

"I would be honored, but," she withdrew her hand and placed it on her chest, "unfortunately, while I may excel at many things, dancing is not one of them."

Berwyn's hand dropped a few inches as his smile fell a little. With that, Ginger acted fast. So fast that Kira didn't have time to react when she snatched the fairy's hand and placed it firmly in Berwyn's.

"But Kirabell here is quite light on her feet."

The little mage froze as a shade of bright pink consumed her. She might as well have had a sign on her forehead saying, 'Please be gentle with me.'

The Lord of Serpents lit up like the sun. "I would be absolutely thrilled. That is, if you don't mind, Kirabell?"

"Umm, no." She gave him a shy smile. "Of course I don't mind."

It wasn't like she actually had a choice.

Ginger was going to catch hell about it later, but that was later. Right now, there was just the mission and the waiting at the end.

That was when a man with long, blond hair cut in. "Excuse me, Lord Berwyn, sorry to interrupt, but I was hoping that we could talk before the night's over." He was pale and seemed to be sweating.

Ginger nearly throttled the man. *Damn it! Go away, you freaking jackass. Can't you see we almost had him?*

From the look of it, Berwyn may have wanted to throttle the man as well. A flash of anger streaked across his face, then settled into an expression of general annoyance. Finally, he sighed and let his friendly smile return. His eyes fell to Kira as he pulled back his outstretched hand. "I'm so sorry."

"It's okay. I understand." Kira's shoulders relaxed.

Berwyn turned to the nervous looking man. "Yes, Mr. Holiday, it's good to see you. You're right, we do have things to discuss, but this is a party, and as such, it's not a place to talk business. Plus, I have just asked this lovely lady to the floor. There will be plenty of time to talk afterward." He offered Kira his hand again and shot her a wink.

She glanced to Ginger for a split second then reached out and gave him her hand.

Berwyn bowed to her in return, raising her hand at the same time as if to place a kiss on it. Kira immediately turned several shades of red at once. He stopped, just inches from her skin, his mouth close enough to activate the house ring on his finger. "Mr. Dartmouth, would you mind coming down to the door and showing Mr. Holiday up to my study while I get in one last dance for the night?" He finished with a gesture to the man that told him to go and wait elsewhere.

Holiday winced, then nodded to Kira and Ginger as if it was an apology before heading back toward the entrance.

Berwyn gave his attention back to Ginger. "Sorry about that. I will bring back your Archmage as soon as she tires of me." A goofy grin took over his face again as his gaze fell to the trembling fairy. "And Kirabell, I am now in your debt for giving me an excuse to ditch that guy for a few minutes. I know you just met him, but trust me, he's super annoying." He rolled his eyes as he spoke, giving her a glimpse of a more casual side that was clearly meant to put her at ease. "Now, what say you and I go make everybody jealous?"

Without another word, he led her off onto the dance floor. Kira's panicked face was only visible for a moment before disappearing into the crowd. Though, in that last second, she made sure to stare daggers at Ginger.

"Yeah, I'm definitely gonna hear about this later." Ginger accepted just as Max's voice came over the house line again.

"Did you just throw Kira to the wolves? Or I guess the Serpents, in this situation."

Ginger looked up to make eye contact with her guard. "I stand by my actions." Then a wry smile crept across her face. "Besides, Berwyn has been stealing glances over at us all night. And I'll tell you this, he wasn't looking at me."

CHAPTER TWENTY-ONE

Kira clenched her jaw as the house line erupted with chatter. Several voices overlapped and talked over each other.

"What's happening?" Kegan asked.

"Ginger just gave Kira to Berwyn as a dance partner to save herself," Max answered.

"Oh, she'll be fine," the *Coin* insisted. "Quit making me out to be a monster."

Kegan laughed. "Oh my god, I can't believe we're going to miss this, being stuck up here."

"Quit nudging me," Corvin complained.

Finally, Farn drowned them all out, "Everybody quiet down. Hearing all of you laughing can't be helping her." Silence returned for a second before Farn spoke again, "Now, Kira, I know you can't answer me right now, but just try to relax. You can do this."

Kira smiled; at least someone was looking out for her.

"And you're too light to hurt him if you step on his feet," Ginger added.

Berwyn walked a slow pace through the crowd as if he was making sure not to rush her. He even held her hand gently.

Kira's heart raced as people surrounded her. Her dress flowed around her as her bare feet padded across the floor. Of course, that was the moment that she realized that it wasn't a good idea to go dancing without shoes.

Berwyn lead her to a space near the center of the floor just as the orchestra paused before starting a new piece. "You know, I've never danced with a fairy before. Honestly, I'm kind of nervous."

"Me too," she admitted as he turned to face her.

His chest took up her view. "Okay, then let's just take a moment and breathe."

Kira laughed.

"I'm serious. It helps when I'm nervous." He held her hands as he took a few deep breaths. The guy looked ridiculous.

She gave in and joined him, inhaling like an idiot. She sighed when she realized it was working. "Okay, I'll give you that one, and my best advice for dancing with a fairy is don't step on my feet. I only have fifty HP, so a few missteps could actually kill me."

"Thanks for the added pressure." Berwyn cringed. "Good thing I know what I'm doing." He looked down at her feet. "So it must be true then that fairies can't equip footwear?"

Kira nodded as he raised her hand in his and held it out to the side. He placed his other on her back, prompting her to rest hers on his shoulder. "I'll be honest, I don't know much about fairies. Just that it's a tough race to play. So I have to respect you for sticking with it." He said gesturing to her second caster with his head. "Your house must be pretty lucky to have a healer like you."

To her surprise, he spoke as if she made her house stronger. Most of the other guests that she and Ginger had spoken to had assumed she had only gotten that far through the protection of others. She let out a quiet, "Thanks," just as the orchestra got ready to start again.

Right on cue, she felt his hold shift from a loose to firm,

ready to lead her. It wasn't too tight, but it locked her into position and forced their eyes to meet.

Farn's voice whispered over the house line one final supportive, "Good luck. Just try not to trip or bump into the other couples, and it will be over in a—"

Her voice fell silent as Berwyn stepped forward.

Farn must have been imagining her tripping over her partner and knocking over every couple on the floor like a set of dominos. Kira smiled. That would have been funny, but that wasn't what happened. Instead, Kira simply stepped back, then to the side and so on, executing the same simple box step that Ginger had struggled with. Not only did she not trip, but she performed it flawlessly, transferring what little weight she had from one foot to the other with each step.

Berwyn tilted his head to the side as a smile registered on his face.

Farn's voice came again, this time sounding shocked, "What the hell? Since when do you know how to dance?"

Ginger was next. "What!"

Kira caught the *Coin* in her peripheral climbing the stairs by the door for a better view.

Suddenly, Berwyn shifted his stance, pulling her closer. Then instead of stepping forward into the space where her foot would be, he stepped diagonally into her.

Kira adapted, mirroring the move in the opposite. The space between them vanished until their thighs almost touched with each step.

With less room to move, Berwyn also drastically reduced their margin for error. It was as if he was testing her.

He smiled.

She was passing.

Max chimed in from above with three words, "Kira, show off."

Kira let a grin find its way to her face. She could only imagine how smug Max must have been right about now.

Berwyn raised an eyebrow. "It looks like Lockheart was hiding something. You can dance, can't you?"

The question was also a test. He was obviously checking to see if talking would disrupt her concentration.

It didn't.

"Yeah, I can play the harp too," Kira joked, feeling more relaxed. Now, all she had left to worry about was the inevitable teasing from the rest of her party that was sure to follow.

Berwyn leaned down and whispered in her ear, "How about we give everybody something to talk about?"

Kira tilted her head from side to side. "I guess."

Almost as soon as the words left her mouth, he dipped her almost to the floor in sync with the music. Her body seemed to weigh nothing as she let out a surprised laugh that drew the attention of the couples around them. Many altered their paths to give their host more room.

From her angle, Kira caught a slack-jawed Farnsworth practically hanging over the railing above. If the *Shield* had been drinking any punch, she would have spit it right over the balcony. Oh, and Max did indeed look quite smug.

Berwyn lifted her back up slowly, making the move appear rather seductive. The act would have made Kira uncomfortable if it wasn't for a certain experience that she'd had back in college. One that had actually prepared her for this moment.

After a few more steps, he removed his hand from her back and spun her out with one arm outstretched. Her gown swirled around her legs, the tiny morning stars embedded in its folds sparkling as he pulled her back in a fluid motion.

She let out another laugh that blended with the music of the orchestra. If she was going to get made fun of later, she was going to give them a good reason to.

The rest of the couples drifted further to stay out of their way, a decision that proved wise when they both pranced down the entire side of the floor in an exaggerated grapevine that ended in another twirl. This time, he wrapped his arm around her on the return so that she spun into an embrace, her back resting against his chest.

She let out a squeak as the intimacy of the move caught her by surprise. Fortunately, he didn't wait too long before releasing her into another twirl, which he followed with another sprawling grapevine. "How 'bout a big finish? There's something I've been wanting to try."

He was clearly having a good time.

That was when Kira noticed that none of the other couples were dancing anymore. Instead, they were all watching from the sides. Ginger beamed at her, pride evident on her face.

"Lead on." Kira gave Berwyn a nod.

"Okay," he lowered his head to whisper in her ear, as if conspiring, "just try to bend one leg up and point the other one."

"Umm, what?" Kira pulled her head back.

"Don't worry, just go with it," he advised before spinning her backward again. Instead of holding her there, he crouched to her level and raised one of her arms over his shoulder. When he rose back up, he took her with him, both of her feet leaving the ground as he stepped in a circle.

She hadn't been expecting it, but as he'd suggested, she went with it. In a way, it reminded her of flying. He spun twice, then a third time, increasing his speed before slipping her off and placing her back to the floor. She landed with momentum that she directed into a twirl that spun her around her partner like a top.

What the hell, why not give them something to talk about? she thought, getting carried away as she flicked a few points of mana into the spellwork of her wings. Shimmering pixie dust filled the air around her, receiving a few audible gasps from the crowd.

Finally, Berwyn pulled her back into his arms and dipped her just as the music stopped.

The room fell silent.

"Wait for it." Berwyn held her there with one hand supporting what little weight she had.

The crowd erupted in cheers and whistles.

"And there it is." He shot her a wink and lifted her back to her feet. Taking one step back, he bowed to her, this time placing a kiss on her hand without hesitation.

He raised his head and turned to the crowd, holding his hands out toward Kira. She gave a polite curtsy that she thought seemed appropriate for the situation. She would almost certainly regret it later when listening to Max's comments.

Berwyn clapped his hands. "I think that's probably a good note to end on," he called out as the crowd settled down. "Once again, thank you all so much for coming, and I'll be counting on your support in the months to come. So, safe travels and all that. And have a lovely night." He gave a wave that carried a sense of finality that declared the night over.

He turned back to Kira and clasped her hand. "Thank you for making my night. I should have asked you to the floor earlier. Unfortunately, I probably need to return you to your house."

"That's okay," Ginger's voice answered from behind, clearly acting like Kira's skills on the floor had not been a surprise. "I'm sure you'll get another chance."

Berwyn slipped back into his formal persona. "I certainly hope I do." He sighed, glancing back at the palace doors. "However, right now, I should probably go meet with Mr. Holiday before he gets worried that I've forgotten about him. Sometimes, running an empire is not all it's cracked up to be." He clapped his hands together, pointing a finger at Kira. "Anyway, next time? Definitely."

"Sure." She smiled and inclined her head.

"Great, have a wonderful rest of your night." He backed away, keeping his eyes on her as he vanished into the crowd.

Kira immediately slouched and let out an exaggerated sigh that droned on for longer than necessary.

Ginger opened her mouth to speak, but Kira shot her a look that said, 'I don't want to hear it.'

That's when Max's voice spilled onto the house line in mid-guffaw, as if he had started laughing before raising his ring.

Ginger raised her ring to her mouth. "Okay, I think someone has some explaining to do. Since when can Kira dance?"

"Wait, so it went well?" Kegan asked from somewhere hidden in the palace.

"Oh nothing," Ginger answered, "just Kira putting everyone to shame on the floor. I mean, screw using me as bait for this thing. I think you just stepped onto center stage."

"Yeah, 'cause that's something I wanted." Kira snatched a cocktail sausage off a stray plate and began walking toward the exit.

"Okay, spill it. Where did you learn that?" the *Coin* prodded.

Max answered for her, "She took a semester of ballroom dancing in college."

"It wasn't by choice," Kira added, crossing her arms.

"So, you were forced into becoming a dancer?" Ginger snorted.

Kira blew out a sigh. "Okay, what happened was the school's computer screwed up and dumped my whole course load senior year, and I had to re-register for all my classes."

"So?" Ginger continued to probe.

"So, I needed one gym credit to graduate, and almost all of the classes were full by that point. It was either ballroom dancing or pay for another semester, and I didn't exactly want to increase my student debt."

"That sounds like the plot of an eighties movie," Kegan chimed in. "Were you also a nerd that discovered you were beautiful all along?"

Kira ignored the question as they headed through the doors back through the entryway. The others were surprisingly silent, as if her explanation actually made sense. Then Ginger caught onto one small hole in her story.

"Wait a sec. You're a guy out in the real world. If that was what happened, shouldn't you only know how to lead?"

"Yes, Kira, why don't you tell us all that?" Max urged, looking smug as he appeared at the stairs with Farn to meet them.

"Because," she fidgeted with her dress for a second, "I wasn't the only student it happened to, and it just worked out that most of the class were dudes. Since I am relatively slender, the instructor made me learn the other side." She spoke as fast as she could, hoping that they might let it pass.

They did not.

The house line filled with laughter. Even Piper and Corvin could be heard in the mix with a few chuckles each. About the only one that seemed to leave it be was Farn, who looked sympathetic as she greeted her friend with a comforting smile at the door on the way out. From there, it wasn't long before they were back aboard the Cloudbreaker.

Kira threw herself into the back and folded her arms.

Farn settled in beside her. "I thought you were amazing out there. I don't care what the others say."

Kira chuckled. "Meh, it was kinda funny, and I kind of deserve it considering how much I antagonize Max and everyone else." She rested her head on the fur trim of the *Shield's* cape. "Thanks for not making fun of me."

Farn nudged her arm. "Why would I? That took more courage than I have. You really were amazing out there."

Kira smiled, appreciating that someone could see past the opportunity to embarrass an easy target. "I was, wasn't I?" She let a hint of pride into her voice.

Farn sunk into her seat. "Sorry Berwyn was all over you."

Kira shrugged. "It's okay. He didn't seem that bad."

Farn's face shifted to a frown that bordered on a scowl. "Maybe, but I don't trust that guy."

CHAPTER TWENTY-TWO

Mack_the_Ripper climbed the stairs to Berwyn's study. The fingertips of his clawed gauntlet dragged along the railing as he moved. He wasn't sure what his Lord needed a *Shield* for in the palace library, but he was the First Knight of the House of Serpents. He wasn't about to question Berwyn's requests. At least, not after everything the man had done for him.

It had only been a year since his Lord had found him and elevated him from Noctem's PVP scene and given him a purpose. Up until then he had spent his nights taking the lives of every player that crossed his path. It had been fulfilling for a time, but after a while, it wasn't enough. Killing in the name of something, on the other hand, gave him more. He could actually feel something again, knowing that his opponents could lose more than just experience points. It still wasn't real, but there was something satisfying about taking away a player's throne.

Life should be about consequences.

At least, that was what he'd told his friends last weekend when he refused to go out to the woods for beers. His parents would never let him get online if he got caught, and the Serpents needed him. He couldn't take that chance. It wasn't like he liked any of his friends anyway. They were a bunch of sheep, just doing whatever the rest of his school thought was cool.

"Ah, Ripper, there you are." Dartmouth, the Archmage, met him at the landing.

Ripper walked past the elf without slowing. It wasn't that he hated the guy, just that he didn't respect him. The elf was useless in a fight. He just happened to be a good assistant and therefore held his position simply by being a convenient choice.

Dartmouth let out a huff. "Oh, we all get it. You're mysterious and anti-social. So brooding." The elf stepped forward to block his path.

"What do you want, Mouth?" Ripper grumbled.

"I don't want anything," the elf pouted, "but Berwyn wanted me to tell you there is a man waiting in the study. His name is Holiday, and Berwyn wanted you to keep an eye on him. He requested for you to be vaguely intimidating."

Ripper glowered at the elf. "Sure."

Dartmouth patted his arm. "Yes, just like that. Now, go play nice with our guest."

Ripper shook his head and kept walking toward the door.

The study was full of books, so full in fact, that it took up two floors with a spiral staircase connecting them. Rich, mahogany shelves and brass railings lined both. Only one wall was left bare to house a wide floor-to-ceiling window made up of hundreds of diamond-shaped panes of glass. Through it, Ripper could see the entire city of Reliqua. Below, the guests from Berwyn's party strolled back to their ships out on the dock.

Ripper didn't care for the event, but he had never been forced to participate, so there was nothing to complain about. He turned away from the window.

A blond man sat, tapping his fingers on the arm of a leather padded chair across from a desk.

That must be Holiday.

Ripper said nothing to the man, opting for imposing silence as he paced the shelves near the desk. A few books marked with the crest of the House of Serpents sat in a neat pile on top. Probably Reliqua's ledgers, the ones that Berwyn used to assign the city's hard to bounties or to replenish farming areas. They didn't look like they had been touched recently. It made sense since Berwyn had been ignoring all that in favor of his conquest.

Ripper passed behind Holiday, making the man flinch when he got close. A bead of sweat trickled down his brow. Ripper smiled, then dragged the clawed tips of his gauntlet along one of the shelves, creating an unnerving, scraping noise.

Suddenly, the door swung open.

Holiday stood immediately to greet the Lord of the palace but was struck dumb when his eyes fell on Nix.

The unkempt reynard girl carried a tray piled high with an assortment of food from the party. It looked like she had scavenged the leftovers of multiple trays into one. Her ears flipped back and forth.

"Oh, Ripper, you're not who I was looking for."

He crossed his arms and spoke without looking at her. "Berwyn is on his way up."

She swayed a little, counteracting the weight of the tray. "That's nice, but I was really just looking for Aawil. We were going to patrol the palace to make sure everyone gets the hell out before logging."

"Well, she's not here." Ripper tilted his head to gesture to the room around them.

"Yes, I can see that," Nix said sharply, making it clear that she didn't appreciate his tone but that she wasn't looking to start anything about it. She held the tray out as a peace offering. "You want some?"

"No thanks," he responded, making nice for the sake of his Lord who had hired the idiot and her partner. Honestly, he understood why Berwyn kept Dartmouth around. The elf was at least useful, but why the Lord of Serpents wasted good hard on the pair of useless mercenaries was beyond him. He had only seen Nix fight once during the siege of Torn, and that had been nothing more than a sneak attack. It hadn't even been one on one. No, mostly, he just saw the irritating fox girl lounging around the palace like a freeloader.

Ripper didn't mind her partner Aawil; she, at least, kept quiet and didn't bother him. Nix, on the other hand, was a pain in the ass, always seeming to be where she shouldn't be and never where she should. If he had a plate of hard for every time he'd seen her drop her gun, he would have enough to start his own empire.

Nix finally pulled the tray away and held it out toward Holiday, making a humming sound that suggested an offer.

He declined.

That was when Berwyn appeared in the doorway behind her. "I'll take one."

She immediately stepped into the room further to let him through before holding the tray in his direction.

He leaned over, placed a finger on his chin, and hummed in an exaggerated manner.

Holiday stood awkwardly like he was unsure what to do as he waited for his host to finish.

Eventually, Berwyn grabbed a spring roll and popped it in his mouth. Still chewing, he wandered over to a globe near his desk and flipped it open, revealing a set of tumblers and a bottle of brown liquid. He grabbed the tumblers and set them on the desk, pouring a couple drinks and handing one to Holiday without asking if he wanted one.

The man didn't argue, taking the glass in both hands.

Berwyn leaned on the front of his desk and swallowed a mouthful of spring roll. He took a sip from his tumbler. "Ahh, I realize the system is just pulling a memory of bourbon from my mind to recreate it, but I have to say, it really nails the flavor."

Holiday tipped his glass back. "I guess so."

Berwyn shifted his view back to Nix. "Thank you for the snack, Nix. You know, I think I saw a tray of chocolate covered strawberries downstairs that you and Aawil might like."

Nix sighed. "Why is it that men think that all women want is chocolate? Like I'm gonna run my ass down there and load up."

Berwyn didn't respond. Instead, he just stared at her until she finally got the hint.

"Oh, you meant that I should leave so that you can talk business. Gotcha, nice to know where I stand on the totem pole." She started to leave but spun back around, the tray wobbling in her hand. "You know what, I am going to go down there and load up on those strawberries. In fact, I'm gonna eat all the chocolate I can find in this place. And do you know why?"

Berwyn rubbed his eyes with his fingers. "Why?"

She placed one hand on her hip while holding her tray like a waitress in the other. "Because I'm lactose intolerant, and in the real world, eating that much chocolate would send me on a one-way trip to diarrhea island."

Holiday snorted his bourbon, coughing as he inhaled wrong. The idiot fox girl looked pretty damn proud of herself as she marched out of the room. Ripper slammed the door behind her.

Good riddance.

He couldn't help but feel superior about the fact that he was allowed to stay. He took up a position directly behind Holiday to reaffirm his intimidating presence.

Berwyn gave his attention back to Holiday as he struggled to recover from a brief coughing fit. "Sorry about her. She's a bit unorthodox, but she is a good mercenary. Wouldn't have been able to take down the shield surrounding Torn's palace without sending her and Aawil in first."

Ripper had his doubts about that, but he wasn't going to question the claim.

"But that's enough about Noctem." The Lord of Serpents paused to take a sip. "Our business concerns the real world." He set his glass down and placed his hands together, pointing at the man with his fingers. "You, sir, owe me a lot of money."

Ripper's jaw fell open. He couldn't believe what he had just heard. Berwyn had always been secretive about any details of his real life, but now, he was actually letting Ripper in.

"Yes, I know." Holiday looked relieved, like he had been dreading the conversation all night and was glad to get it over with. "Ever since we lost that shipment, we have been trying our best to recover. I just need a couple more—"

"I'm well aware of your little mishap in Boston. You've been using it as an excuse for a while now." Berwyn picked up his glass and swirled the bourbon around in it. "It's been two years, you know?"

Holiday winced. "Ah, yes, I know, but we're back on track now. I should have the funds together in a couple days."

"Well that's good." Berwyn sounded pleased. "However, there is a problem. You missed the deadline."

"I did. Obviously, I'm very sorry about that, and I understand if you need to adjust the payment to compensate." Holiday lowered his gaze to the floor. "It's a lot of money already, but your organization is the best, so I'm happy to accommodate any request in favor of keeping a good relationship."

Berwyn nodded. "That would help. I've had to keep your shipment in storage longer than anticipated. And obviously, due to the nature of your purchase, that does increase the risk of my end of the exchange."

"I certainly understand that." Holiday's shoulders relaxed a little.

"Oh, you know what?" Berwyn suddenly slapped a hand against his thigh. "That would still leave me with a problem."

"Whatever it is, I'm sure—" Holiday started to say but was quickly cut off.

"You have to understand; I've been doing this a long time, and I have other clients. Clients that pay on time and don't leave me stuck holding a shipping container full of... contraband. If I let you get away with this now, what stops—"

"Cline, I have the money," Holiday interrupted. He immediately cringed the second the words left his mouth.

Ripper's ear pricked up at the name, Cline, wondering if it was Berwyn's real one. From the sudden irritation on his Lord's face, he guessed that he was right.

"Sorry, Lord Berwyn." Holiday corrected, bracing like he expected to be slapped at any second.

With that, the Lord of Serpents sighed. "Do you know why I choose to do my negotiations here in Noctem?"

"Ahh–" Holiday started.

"Obviously, it makes it easy to meet with clients all over the world, that's true for any business. But really, it's about safety. You know what I mean? In the real world, you and I are both considered… dangerous, but online, we can simply stop by and have a chat without worrying that one of us might end up face down in the harbor. That gives people peace of mind. Which, in turn, helps business move forward." He grinned. "I mean, do you have any idea how much my client list has grown since Carpe Noctem came out?"

Holiday shook his head.

"Well, let me just say, business is booming," he pulled out his player journal and flipped to the back where his inspector lay, "but do you know what the best part is?"

Holiday shook his head again, sweat pouring down in buckets.

"The best part is that same feeling of safety is just as fake as this bourbon. It's a false sense of security." That's when he dug his inspector from his journal and dropped it on the desk.

An image of a rather portly man sleeping peacefully in bed, a Somno unit clearly visible on his head was displayed. The shadow of an unknown man fell across him.

Ripper's heart skipped a beat, unable to believe what he was witnessing. The implications of the image were clear. Berwyn actually had a man in Holiday's house in the real world.

The Lord of Serpents leaned down to his prey. "I would not have pegged you as the type to wear pink pajamas."

"Oh god," Holiday gasped as he pushed back into his chair as if trying to get away from the image. His hand shot to his other wrist to activate his system menu that was blended into his stat-sleeve. His finger hovered around the sign off option.

"I wouldn't do that if I were you." Berwyn placed his hand on top of Holiday's wrist to cover his menu. "It takes around ten to fifteen minutes to fully wake up after logging out, and I can guarantee you that I can send out a kill order in that amount of time. So how about you just stay here and listen to what I have to say?"

A wave of heat rushed through Ripper's skin. It was real. This was actually happening. Berwyn held a man's life in his hand. There were consequences.

"Please, I can get you the money." Holiday's hand slipped away from his menu. "I can get you anything you want."

"Oh, I don't doubt that. But can you save my reputation? Because there is a reason that clients pay up, and sadly, it's not because of my winning personality." Berwyn sighed. "No, in the end, even through the veneer of safety that this amazing technology allows, it all comes down to good, old-fashioned fear. I built my reputation on it decades ago, but a side effect of running my business through Noctem has been that people start to forget that. So I'm sure you can understand, examples must be made."

Holiday gripped the arms of his chair hard enough to make the wood creak. "But you'll be left without a buyer for the shipment."

Berwyn simply waved a hand as if it didn't matter. "There's always someone who wants to blow something up."

"Oh, god, please," Holiday begged, his eyes filling with tears. "I can fix this."

Berwyn leaned back on his desk casually. "Well, that's the thing. Even if you could, it would be too late. You were dead before I even entered the room."

Holiday's mouth fell open.

"It was just a tiny injection. Right between the toes."

"But..." Holiday trailed off.

Berwyn turned back to Ripper. "Have you ever seen someone die while logged in?"

Ripper couldn't hide his curiosity. He'd seen the light fade from a player's eyes dozens of times, but that was just pretend. This was real. He shook his head and stepped closer. His heart raced.

"It happens every now and then. But I've seen it a few times, from well, less natural causes, and it's," Berwyn paused, looking back at the man as he clutched at his face, "interesting."

Holiday looked broken, momentarily reaching for his menu, only to drop his hand to his lap. Then without warning, he lunged at Berwyn, tears streamed down his face.

"I'll kill y—"

Ripper moved fast, catching the man by the collar and drawing back his claws to strike.

Berwyn held up a hand to stop him. "He's not a threat."

Ripper forced Holiday back into the chair, feeling the man tremble as he resisted.

"This is it." Berwyn leaned in closer, staring into Holiday's eyes. "Watch, there's a moment when the spark fades from their eyes."

The man fell back, no longer fighting Ripper's grip. His head lolled, his eyes staring at the ceiling. It was fascinating. Nothing like when a player disconnected. It was more subtle than that, just a shift in the tone of his iris.

Ripper held his breath. He hadn't felt anything like it before.

Berwyn waved him away from Holiday's empty shell. "This is where things get interesting."

Strangely, the body didn't disappear. Instead, Holiday was still talking. No words came out, but that didn't stop the thing from trying. It just mouthed the word 'please' over and over in a silent plea for mercy.

"Why doesn't he die here too?" Ripper placed a hand on its shoulder.

"There's a delay, I think." Berwyn folded his arms and

tapped his chin with one finger. "He's gone, but the system didn't receive a logoff command, so it's still trying to represent him. He's like an echo." He leaned back on his desk.

"So why does he keep begging? Where does that input come from if he's gone?"

"I think it comes from us. At least, that's my theory. From what I've seen, I think that when the system stops receiving from him, it looks for information elsewhere." He picked up his glass again. "In a way, he's the same as this bourbon. The system just pulls the necessary data from our memories. But we don't really know him well, so all we get is this pathetic mess."

Finally, the man fell limp as the system caught up to what had happened, leaving Ripper captivated as the particles began to dissipate, taking the body with them.

Berwyn walked away as if losing interest, stopping at the window to finish his drink.

"Ripper?"

"Yes?" He paused as the last of the glowing fragments drifted past his fingers.

"I trust you won't mention this to anyone."

"Of course." Ripper nearly tripped over himself as he crossed the room to his Lord's side.

"Good. I won't have to send anyone to your house then." Berwyn gave him a sideways smile.

Ripper let a laugh slip, not sure if Berwyn was joking or not.

"Stick with me, kid. I think you have a bright future ahead of you." The Lord of Serpents patted him on the back before finishing his bourbon. "Now, let's see if we can spot that breathtaking little fairy I had so much fun with tonight."

CHAPTER TWENTY-THREE

Wyatt woke to sunlight shining through the narrow slits between the blinds of his new house. The memory of landing the Cloudbreaker a few miles outside of Reliqua before logging out was still fresh in his mind. He rubbed at his eyes and motioned to run his hand through his hair. His fingers, however, only met with the bare skin of his scalp, unapologetically reminding him that he was in the real world.

He groaned.

His hair was really the only difference between him and the avatar that he'd created online as MaxDamage24.

He sat up and sighed, then immediately laughed to himself as he remembered Kira's performance on the dance floor. That was when a squeaking noise coming from the balcony of his bedroom drew his attention.

As mentioned, the house he lived in was new. It had been his one big purchase after receiving the payout from the mission the previous year. It wasn't anything fancy, just a simple two-story duplex in Sarasota, Florida. It had left him with plenty of money left over. Not enough to retire, but enough so that he didn't have too much to worry about in the immediate future.

He still worked for the time being but not very hard. As such, he had taken a few days off so he could focus on the heist since that seemed to be the responsible thing to do. Hell, it might even be able to bring in enough so that he wouldn't even need a day job afterward.

Again, he heard a high-pitched squeak from outside the sliding door that lead to his balcony. He shoved his body out of bed and walked over to open the blinds. With the pull of a string, they slid to the side. He yawned, then gazed out at the sky and stretched as if the source of the irritating squeaking wasn't there. Then he turned and walked out of the room.

A moment later, he came back and unlocked the glass door so that Seth, who had been pressing his face up against the window for the last minute and a half, could get in.

"You could at least react," Seth complained as he slid open the door, letting the sound of their neighbor's sprinklers in behind him. "I don't do this for my health, you know. I'm just trying to brighten your day."

"Shut up and get inside, twinkle toes."

Seth wrinkled his nose. Even on his scruffy face, it was easy to tell that he and Kira were the same person.

Outside, Wyatt's balcony sat on the back of the house with only four feet between it and the balcony belonging to the other side of the duplex. Of course, that side had been purchased by Seth.

Despite the fact that they always logged out at the same time, Seth usually woke up first. Ever since they'd moved, he had hopped the gap between balconies every morning to entertain Wyatt. Sometimes, he would show up simply waving like a goon, while other times, he had performed puppet shows using a variety of socks. It was, well, really stupid.

Wyatt went down to the kitchen, his friend following behind him.

Seth took the blender from the cabinet and began grabbing things to make a well-balanced protein shake. It was all he could really digest with his defective stomach.

Wyatt, on the other hand, had no problem with solid foods. He poured a bowl of the finest breakfast cereal to ever grace a table, Cinnamon Toast Crunch. He opened his mouth to speak but wasn't able to get out any more than a, "So–" before Seth turned on the blender.

Wyatt sighed and waited patiently before starting again. "So–"

Seth flipped it back on. "Sorry, I can't hear you."

Wyatt shoved a spoonful of cereal in his mouth.

Seth shut off the blender. "What were you trying to say?"

Wyatt chewed fast and swallowed so that he could speak. "So–"

Seth hit blender again, grinning like an idiot before turning it off.

This time, Wyatt didn't speak. Instead, he just sat and stared at his friend with his arms crossed while letting his cereal get soggy. Finally, after almost a minute, he started again, "So–"

Seth flipped the blender on again, this time, forgetting to hold the lid on so that the contents spurted out the side.

"You deserve that." Wyatt laughed as Seth struggled to turn it off again without knocking it over.

"Yeah, I know, instant karma." Seth groaned as he wiped his shake off his cheek with the sleeve of his shirt.

"So, last night went well. Hopefully, the guys can get us in tonight when we get back on." Wyatt stirred his cereal a little.

"Yeah, I can't believe how smooth everything went. We might actually be criminal masterminds. Well, minus the dance-off."

"Ha! That was the best part. I mean, forget sneaking back in, I bet you get a personal invite to the palace before the day is out."

"How'd Farn sneak off to get the guys in, by the way?" Seth changed the subject.

"Oh, she performed an amazing stealth maneuver using ventriloquism to throw her voice and distract a guard."

"Really?"

"No, not really." Max shook his head. "She fell into one of the servers and spilled champagne all over herself. The guards had to take her to a washroom to refresh her gear."

"Ah. That makes more sense." Seth poured his shake into a tall glass, then paused as if debating on saying something or not. "So, speaking of Farn. You ever gonna ask her out?"

Wyatt nearly choked on his cereal. "What makes you ask?" He did his best to avoid the question.

"Nothing much, just that Ginger was pushing Farn to ask you out the other night, so I thought I'd ask."

"And what did you say while Ginger was playing matchmaker?"

Seth tilted his head from side to side. "Farn hasn't dated in a while, so I tried not to pressure her."

Wyatt assumed he was being intentionally vague so that he wouldn't betray the *Shield's* trust.

"Besides, I figure I can just pressure you instead." Seth smirked.

"That's kinda crappy logic," Wyatt commented through a mouthful of cinnamon perfection.

Seth shrugged. "So, why haven't you?"

"I don't know, man." Wyatt slumped back. "It's not like I'm head over heels in love with her or anything."

"But you do like her, right?"

"Well, sure. We have fun when we play together."

"That sounds like a good place to start." Seth took a sip of his shake. "You could just go for it and see where it leads."

"Yeah, but," he paused, pushing the last few bites around in his bowl, "if I ask her out, it will change things. And I feel like I should have stronger feelings than just liking her to take that risk."

Seth looked at him incredulously. "You're my friend, so I don't want to call you a stupid baby. But you're a stupid baby."

"Yeah yeah, ha ha. I'm bad at dating, I get it. But if I ran around asking out every woman I liked, I'd just make a mess of things. Hell, I probably would have asked out Ginger back when we first met. How do you think that would have turned out?"

This time Seth almost choked. "You had a thing for Ginger?"

"No, not like a thing." Wyatt made air quotes around the word 'thing.' "But you know, back when we first met, maybe I would have been interested. But that was before I got to know her."

"Ouch." Seth scrunched up his nose and winced. "That's a burn on Ginger."

"That's not what I meant," Wyatt defended.

"Is it 'cause you found out she has kids?" Seth guessed.

"No."

"Cause she's older?"

"No."

"'Cause she sleeps with men for money?"

"No. I just find her…" Wyatt hesitated before adding, "intimidating." He let out a sigh. "She knows a lot more than me about the world. Plus, she teases me a lot."

"I guess that makes sense. She teases me a lot too, but anyway, back to Farn. What can I say to make you ask her out before this mission is done?"

"You sound like a car salesman."

"Sorry." Seth leaned back. "To be honest, I care about Farn," he sounded uncharacteristically serious, "and she deserves to be happy. That's why I think you should go for it. You're the best guy I know. So if someone is going to date her, I'd rather it be you than some jackass she meets at work or something."

"Aww, you mean I can take your BFF to prom?" Wyatt joked dismissively.

"You know what I mean." Seth took a sip of his shake.

"Okay, let's say I ask her out." Wyatt leaned forward. "What happens to you?"

"What about me?" Seth frowned.

"I mean, are you just going to third wheel it all over Noctem with us?"

Seth laughed, "Oh, I'm fine with that. I'd be like the front wheel of a tricycle. That's the most important one. It has the pedals. Besides, without me, you'd just be a bicycle, and then you'd never get anywhere."

"Why not?" Wyatt asked, not realizing the trap he had walked into.

Seth's smile grew, almost touching his eyes. "Because then you'd be two-tired."

Wyatt simply laid his forehead down on the table and attempted to ignore the grinning idiot across from him. He rocked his head back and forth as if repeatedly saying no. After about a minute, he shot back up, feeling a little dizzy from the sudden movement.

"Wait a sec, you've been on me all morning about my love life. What about yours? You haven't even gone out with anyone since before last year, and you've never been single that long."

Seth laughed. "I got problems. You know, that damn apocalypse thing screwed me up. I got my brain messed with, fought a bunch of zombies practically naked, and almost died. I have issues to work out." He picked up his leg by the cuff of the athletic pants that he wore as pajamas and dropped it onto the table. "I shaved my legs the other day. I didn't plan on it. It just kinda happened, and I don't know, I might keep doin' it. It's comfortable." He let his leg fall back to the floor. "My point is that I'm kind of a mess. So dragging someone else into this situation seems like a bad idea."

Wyatt laughed despite the seriousness of the problem. It seemed like the best way to help his friend relax. "So did you stop at your legs, or did you just go all out with the manscaping?"

Seth answered with silence and a very telling expression.

"Oh god, I didn't want to know any of that." Wyatt recoiled in mock horror.

They both fell silent for a moment before Wyatt started again.

"So, no judgment here, but you're okay, right? I mean, do you think you should stop playing or create a new character or something?"

"Can't," Seth answered immediately.

"Why not?"

"That damn pendant can't be deleted, which means Kira can't either. So it's not possible to link me to a different character." Seth hesitated. "But honestly, I don't think I could delete her even if it was possible."

"Why not?"

Seth tipped his glass, coating the side with liquid. "I know Kira started out as just a goofy character that I played while online, but it's been four years now. She's kind of a part of me, and she's a lot of fun. So even if I'm happy with myself here in the real world, I'm also happy being her. So the idea of deleting her feels wrong. Like I'd be hurting someone or something important to me. I don't think I could do that. I know it's weird, but this is me now, I guess."

Wyatt breathed a sigh of relief. "Obviously, you're my friend, and I would support whatever you choose. But to tell you the truth, I don't think Noctem would be the same without Kira. Besides, maybe this is just because I've known you for a long time, but I don't really notice much difference between you and her anymore." He grinned. "Well, except that ass."

"How sweet." Seth rolled his eyes.

"What? It's a nice butt. At least I'm honest. If you ever decide to switch teams, let me know."

Seth groaned. "Well, unfortunately for you, I have standards."

"Sure you do." Wyatt fell silent again, afraid to ask the next question on his mind. "You are okay, though, right? I mean, with everything Carver did to you? I know you don't, but technically, you can still control the system and everything."

For an instant, Seth winced. "That's a whole other issue."

"What does that mean?" Wyatt prodded, understanding that it was a subject that his friend avoided. He had ignored it for the last few months and let him get away with vague answers, but he was starting to get worried.

Seth let out a heavy sigh. "It means that whatever I let enter my mind last year is still there in my head, and I'm not sure what that means."

"What do you mean, you let something in?" Wyatt furrowed his brow.

Seth shook his head. "Carver had you all trapped in your own personal hell, and I wasn't strong enough to get to you alone. So I asked for help."

"From what?"

"From whatever Carver wanted me to. I don't know. But whatever it was, it became a part of me there." Seth looked apologetic. "I know it's not evil or anything, I'm sure of that. But I think it was what attacked you guys at the end. I sealed the deal and finished the quest when I touched it."

A memory streaked through Wyatt's mind of himself and the others screaming in agony as a clone of Kira stood over them. It had seemed frightened as if it didn't understand what it had done. The strange part was that he remembered the moment but not how it felt. He could recall being in pain, but not how it felt.

"Do you know what it wanted?"

Seth nodded. "It wanted me, and I gave it exactly what it wanted. If you and Farn hadn't refused to leave me behind…" He stopped to stare out the window without finishing his sentence. "The problem is that whatever it was didn't leave." He touched his temple. "It's still right here, waiting for me to need it again. Every time I ask it for help, to change anything in Noctem, I feel the line between us get thinner. And that just feels…"

"Wrong?" Wyatt finished his sentence for him.

"No, that's the thing. It feels right. Like it's what's supposed to happen. And that scares the hell out of me. So yeah, I avoid using that ability so it won't get worse. Not to mention that it's kinda overpowered. I mean, what if I asked it for help and it went overboard? I'm not sure where that thing's limits are."

"True, that could be a problem for everyone." Wyatt nodded just as his phone buzzed on the counter where he had left it the night before.

They both jumped at the sound.

Seth motioned for him to see who it was, probably grateful to have an excuse to end the conversation there.

Wyatt grabbed the phone and tapped in his eight-digit pass-code to unlock it. He would have just used the standard four-digit code, but Seth had been guessing it too easily and changing his keyboard shortcuts ever since he got it.

He opened Noctem's messaging app and selected the Lock-heart text chat that came with their house rings.

"Looks like our Kegan and Corvin stayed online a bit after we logged out."

"Nice," Seth snapped out of the somber mood that had been forming around him. "I'm gonna go find my phone."

"Okay, but don't forget to wash the blender," Wyatt shouted as his friend ran up the stairs.

Seth shouted back, "Yes, dear, I will."

CHAPTER TWENTY-FOUR

House Lockheart Chat – Timestamp 9:36 AM

Kegan: So we have this whole place to ourselves.

Corvin: Provided you don't count the NPC guards.

Kegan: Well yeah, but they're not really much of a problem.

MaxDamage24: Any luck finding the vault?

Corvin: Not yet, but we're heading down. It's probably below ground level.

Piper: That makes sense.

GingerSnaps: Piper, you're at school. Put your phone away.

Piper: Don't worry, I have it hidden behind a book.

GingerSnaps: I'm pretty sure that wasn't the response I was looking for. At least your brother turns off his phone in class.

Drakenstein: Yeah, I'm the good one.

GingerSnaps: Ha, that was a trap! I knew you were on here too. I can see your name in the notifications at the bottom!

MaxDamage24: Busted.

Drakenstein: Doh…

Kirabell: Max, can you call my phone. I can't find it.

MaxDamage24: How are you typing then?

Kirabell: I'm using the computer. Now make with the calling.

MaxDamage24: Okay.

Kirabell: Found it!

Farnsworth: Where was it?

Kirabell: ...I don't want to say.

Farnsworth: Now I have to know.

Kirabell: It was in the fridge.

MaxDamage24: Yeah, that sounds about right.

Farnsworth: That's probably not good for it.

Kirabell: I know. It was all laggy for a bit. I'm glad I found it now and not tonight. It might not have worked.

MaxDamage24: Well, now that that crisis has been averted. We can worry about more important things. How you guys doing in there?

MaxDamage24: Guys?

MaxDamage24: Kegan?

Kegan: Sorry, we were hiding from a patrol.

Corvin: We're on the second floor. There's more activity in the palace the closer we get to the bottom.

MaxDamage24: Okay, keep at it.

MaxDamage24: Kira, I still have a blender in my sink waiting to be cleaned.

Farnsworth: That was random.

MaxDamage24: Sorry, she left it there.

MaxDamage24: When I was a kid, I used to watch the movie *Howard the Duck* and pause it during that scene with the topless lady duck.

MaxDamage24: I still think about it sometimes in the shower.

Farnsworth: Well, that was far more information than I ever wanted.

MaxDamage24: It was hot.

Corvin: I remember that scene. It's on the list of things I wish I could unsee.

GingerSnaps: Max, my kids are reading this.

Piper: Yeah, that's messed up.

GingerSnaps: Turn your phone off in class!

MaxDamage24: It was hot.

MaxDamage24: It was hot.

MaxDamage24: Kira! Darn it. I can hear you laughing through the wall. When the hell did you put all that in my shortcuts?

MaxDamage24: And how the hell did you know I would use those words in that order.

Kirabell: Bwa ha ha ha. You have no idea how long I have been trying to get you to put a question mark at the end of my name. I figured if I didn't respond right away, you might finally do it. Also, you always type either 'damn it' or 'what the hell' when I do that. So I just used both interchangeably.

Farnsworth: I have to ask; did you also leave the blender in the sink to give him a reason to use your name in the chat?

Kirabell: I plead the fifth.

Farnsworth: That's… just devious.

MaxDamage24: You see what I live next to. I deal with this every day.

Farnsworth: How is it that you can plan a prank like that, but you leave your phone in the fridge?

Kirabell: I dun know.

Kegan: Well, now that everyone knows about Max's duck fetish. If anyone's interested, I think we've gone as far as we can here. The first floor is too busy.

Corvin: We could try to keep going, but we might get caught.

Kirabell: Probably don't do that then.

MaxDamage24: Yeah, wait until the rest of us are on. I don't want to press our luck. We can try to come up with a distraction.

Corvin: Okay, we'll head back up and log out.

MaxDamage24: Cool.

GingerSnaps: Hey, Max, do you think I should send Berwyn a message or anything? Just to say we had a good time. Or I should just offer him a night with Kira in exchange for everything in the vault?

Kirabell: You will do no such thing, thank you very much.

Farnsworth: Yeah that might be crossing a line there.

Piper: Yeah, Mom, your kids are reading this.

GingerSnaps: Oh relax, I was kidding.

GingerSnaps: About giving him Kira. Not about sending a message. And I'm hiding your phone charger, Piper, so have fun watching it slowly die. Bahahaha… ha ha ha… ha

MaxDamage24: No, that might seem suspicious if we send him a message so soon. I feel like we should wait a day before contacting him. Don't want to seem too eager.

GingerSnaps: Sigh… spoken like a true man.

Kirabell: Ha!

MaxDamage24: Last time I checked, you were on my side, bro. So quit laughing.

Farnsworth: What do you mean by, the last time you checked?

GingerSnaps: Yeah, just what kind of relationship do two you have?

MaxDamage24: I didn't mean it like that.

Kirabell: It's okay, Max, there's no use hiding it. Our love needs to be shared with the world.

MaxDamage24: You are not helping.

Kirabell: Did you expect me to?

MaxDamage24: …No.

MaxDamage24: Anyway, how about we all meet up in the Cloudbreaker when we get on tonight and figure out our next move?

GingerSnaps: I don't think that will be necessary.

MaxDamage24: Why is that?

GingerSnaps: Because I just got a message from Berwyn. It looks like some men don't worry about seeming too eager.

Farnsworth: What's it say?

GingerSnaps: House Lockheart has been invited back to the palace. Everything is going according to plan.

CHAPTER TWENTY-FIVE

NIGHT THREE: THE VAULT

Kirabell hummed to herself as she adjusted the item bag on her belt. "That should do it."

She spun around in front of the dusty mirror hanging on the wall of Sully's Bait & Tackle. Obviously, she wasn't there to purchase supplies. Fishing had never been her thing. If she was honest, she felt bad for the fish, even the virtual ones.

No, the place just happened to be the nearest item shop with a quick-change panel. She couldn't wait to get out of that damn ball gown from the previous night.

It wasn't that she didn't like the dress. The thing had actually been more comfortable than she'd expected. The attention it got her was another thing altogether. After last night, she'd had just about all the attention she wanted.

It probably would have made more sense to kick Max and the others out of the Cloudbreaker and use the ship's cabin as a changing room. That was what Ginger had done. Though, after fighting a horde of zombies last year in her underwear, Kira avoided disrobing if she could help it.

Fortunately, they had some time to kill before heading back to the pyramid in Reliqua. Arriving too soon might make it obvious that they had landed so close the night before. Considering that, Port Han seemed like a convenient detour with it being just across the sea on the coast of a neighboring continent.

Kira stepped away from the mirror and up to the shop's register, tossing her journal on the counter.

Sully, the shopkeep, ignored her, picking at the curled horns that bracketed his head. He'd been quite interactive when she entered a few minutes ago, but after she'd turned down the same fishing quest three times, he seemed to have given up.

She flipped her journal open to her message page and wrote the word 'new' along with a check mark.

- New Message -
To: Larkin
From: Kirabell

Thanks so much for the beautiful dress. It really was a hit at the party. Please don't repeat this to anyone, but I really liked it. It made me feel pretty in a way that I don't often admit, but after the effort you clearly put into the dress, I felt I owed you some honesty. You are an amazing crafter.

I don't have much need for a gown now that it has served its purpose, so I'm sending it back attached to this message. I hope you'll find a good use for it.

-Thanks again, Kira

She scrawled the words 'attach item' at the bottom. Then she selected the gown that Larkin had named A Promise Kept. She wrote the word 'send,' followed by another quick check mark. The text vanished from the page, and she snapped the book shut.

"Thanks for letting me use the quick-change panel." Kira waved to Sully as she turned to leave.

"Yeah yeah," the NPC responded in a gruff tone before slapping a hand down on the counter. "Oi, have you heard about Ol' Sawtooth?"

"No thanks, but good luck with that." She waved back at him. *At least he's persistent,* she thought as the door closed behind her. The Cloudbreaker waited in the distance.

Kira took a deep breath and blew it back out, deflating as she walked toward her coach. *Well, let's get this honeypot underway.*

Of course, Berwyn's invitation hadn't explicitly requested a romantic evening with Kira or anything of the sort. No, it had been sent to Ginger in the interest of forming an alliance between their two houses. A mutually beneficial relationship, as Berwyn described it. As far as what kind of benefits he was hoping for, Kira wasn't sure how much she should read between the lines. Fortunately, she felt confident that Farn wouldn't leave her alone with him if she could help it.

She settled into the ship's cabin without saying much to anyone. Instead, Kira just stared out a narrow window for the remainder of the trip. There was too much to think about, and she only had so much space in her head.

The Cloudbreaker touched down, shaking Kira out of her thoughts. It had felt like they had just taken off, like she had only left Sully's a minute ago.

The palace dock was busier than expected, with a number of visitors coming and going. Apparently, running an empire took more networking than she thought.

Max hopped out and pulled the ramp from below the door, this time with considerably less effort than last.

Ginger exited the ship, back in her usual gear—canvas pants, a shirt, and an armored, leather corset. A hooded cloak topped it all off. The woman had seemed comfortable in the gown the night before, but Kira suspected the *Coin* was more at home wearing something more substantial. After all, most players weren't accustomed to wandering around with so little defense like she was. Considering the number of mercenaries coming in and out of the palace, Kira didn't blame her. It was a tough crowd.

A couple members of the House of Serpents greeted them as Kira and Farn set foot on the airship dock. Berwyn's men seemed a little more relaxed than the hired guards from the night before. The palace must have returned to business as usual, no longer the high-security fortress that it had been. A number of players even came and went without an escort. Hopefully, Lockheart would be able to shake theirs as well. At least, Kira hoped so. She gave a glance to Max to see if he'd noticed.

He nodded back without a word.

The lack of security was a good sign, but that didn't mean that things were going to be easy. With the number of people up and about, it was going to be difficult for Corvin and Kegan to move around without being spotted.

As soon as they stepped into the palace entryway, Berwyn was already in sight. He had been in the middle of speaking to a couple elven men. The pair took one look at Kira and made their exit but not before whispering something to Berwyn. From there, he rushed over to take Ginger's hand.

"Thank you so much for coming."

"Of course, I wouldn't skip out on the chance to see the inner workings of Noctem's first empire." She gestured to the room and all of the players passing through.

"Spoken like a strategist. I like it." He shook her hand, then bowed to Kira. "And it's obviously nice to see you again, Kirabell."

She hesitated, not expecting to be called by her full name. "Oh, just Kira is fine. Who has time for three syllables anyway?"

"Okay then, Kira." He nodded before shifting to Max and Farn who were standing around as if they weren't really sure what to do. "You must be the dual-wielding *Fury* that Nix mentioned."

"Ah, yeah," Max stepped forward, clearly unsure if he should shake the man's hand.

Ginger jumped in to save him, "Yes, MaxDamage and I have been through quite a lot. There's no one that I'd rather have as my personal guard, as long as you don't mind letting one of the fastest guns in Noctem into your palace."

"Of course not." Berwyn threw out his hand. "You should stop by our training hall at some point. I'd love to see what you can do."

Max grinned and gave him a firm shake. "Sure, if we get the time. And if you don't mind having to repair the place afterward."

The brag got him an approving smile from Ginger. "Yes, there is actually quite a bit of truth to his name."

Berwyn raised his eyebrows at the claim before flicking his eyes to Farn. "And will your *Shield* be destroying my training hall as well?"

"No," Farnsworth answered, politely as usual. She paused a moment later. "But you may have trouble finding me a decent sparring partner."

Kira smiled. It was nice to hear the *Shield* giving herself the credit she deserved. Even if it was just for show.

"Awesome," Berwyn rubbed his hands together, "and I assume you will be protecting Kira then?"

"I won't be letting her out of my sight," the *Shield* fired back with a knowing grin, almost like she was issuing a warning.

"That's certainly reasonable. Although, I do want to express that the safety of my guests is very important to me. So feel free to relax while you're here. You're in good hands. Bodyguards are always welcome, but not necessary."

"Thanks, we'll try our best to remember that." Ginger gestured to Max to stand at ease. "I guess that leads to my next question. When would you like to sit down and talk shop? Alliances can be complicated, after all."

Kira almost laughed at the *Coin's* bluff, considering that

there wasn't really anything to talk about. House Lockheart was nothing more than a front.

"Oh, you just got here," Berwyn brushed off the question. "I don't want to rush you into a meeting. And besides, I'm in the middle of a lot of things tonight. I'll have someone show you upstairs to the guest suites? You can set one as your home point and just enjoy what the palace has to offer for a few days before we get down to business. I figure if we're going to be working together, you should get to experience the benefits first hand."

"I'd like that." Ginger touched his arm. "It would give us the chance to get to know you and the rest of your Serpents here as well. That would certainly make me feel more comfortable about working together."

"My thoughts exactly." Berwyn smiled as he began to walk backward. "I'll catch up with you later." He waved to a sullen-looking faunus near the wall. "Aawil, do you mind showing our guests to one of the suites?"

The quiet woman had been standing around like she had nothing to do. From the exaggerated eye roll she gave, she would have preferred to continue doing so. Despite that, she obeyed like a good minion, greeting the party with a slight bow before walking off down the hall without saying a word.

The trek up to their suite took longer than one would expect with the sprawling nature of the floor plan. Aawil made little effort to fill the silence. Though, she did at least take the time to point out a few locations.

Compared to some of the other palaces in Noctem, it truly was a paradise. Everything a player could want in a luxury vacation spot was right at their fingertips. It was beginning to look like an alliance might actually be a good idea.

Berwyn had certainly chosen his capital well. It may have been inconvenient to get around, but it gave him plenty of ways to keep his snakes happy. After all, a happy snake was a loyal snake.

Dartmouth met them on the top floor, freeing Aawil of her duty. The silent *Coin* abandoned them almost immediately.

"Thank you for coming." Dartmouth began walking down the hall. "I hope you like the palace. Lord Berwyn spared no expense to make it the paradise that you see now." He gestured to a row of large, potted plants that lined the hallway, evenly spaced between each door. "The hibiscus flowers here, for example, were brought in from the Isle of Wane. We actually had to have the pots specially coded by Checkpoint to override the system clocks, since the rest of the palace resets itself every night to repair any kind of damage. Otherwise, the flowers would never change, but with the override, they grow naturally." He cupped one of the flowers in his hand. "Beautiful, aren't they?"

"Sure." Max touched one of the flowers, clearly humoring Dartmouth's boasting as the prideful elf continued down the hall.

"The palace is full of details like these. I suggest you all stop by the beach downstairs. It's one of our crowning achievements. You should have seen the pyramid before when we got here. It's come a long way." He stopped at a door near the middle of the hall and pushed it open. "This one is yours. I hope everything is to your liking."

Ginger didn't skip a beat, strutting into the room as if she owned the place.

"Holy crap." Kira stopped short next to Farn, who staggered for an instant.

A large sitting area rested in the center of the room. A stone coffee table, holding a bowl of crystal blue water, sat between a sofa and chairs. Roses floated on the liquid's surface. Against one wall ran a small bar and desk. The other held two gold-encrusted doors made of dark wood.

Dartmouth bowed with a satisfied smile on his face. "I'll leave you to get settled in then. Please feel free to explore once you're ready."

"I could get used to this." Kira hopped into the space as soon as he was gone.

"It's a palace. Did you expect less?" Ginger plopped herself onto a chaise lined with green velvet.

The room was gorgeous, but what really hammered things home was the view. One entire wall was simply missing. In its place were three wide archways that led out to a balcony. The city sparkled across the scene as the sea reached out to the horizon. Kira ran to the railing and leaned out.

"Don't get too comfortable. We're not on vacation." Max smirked, leaning against the side of one of the archways.

She ignored him and spun back to the room, exploring the other doors. One lead to a bright and sparkling washroom complete with floor to ceiling mirrors and the largest marble tubs she had ever seen. The other lead to a bedroom that boasted a king-sized canopy bed.

Kira scrunched up her nose at the piece of extravagant furniture as the others followed her into the room. Max took one look at the bed, then blushed. Farn cleared her throat, probably to break the silence.

"That's a lot of pillows."

Ginger made a point to bump into Max with her hip, shoving him towards the *Shield*. "Looks like the palace is equipped for all kinds of activities."

Kira shrugged off the implications and did what any reasonable mage would do. She dove onto the mattress belly first, only to bounce back up onto her knees with laugh.

Max snorted, then jumped onto the opposite end of the bed with all of his weight. Kira fell, toppling into the pillows as Max rolled over on his back. Farn let out a laugh.

"I gotta say…" Ginger leaned against the bedpost. "Considering how close you two are, I'm not surprised to see you end up in bed together."

"Meh, I could do worse." Max brushed off the comment, obviously trying to deny Ginger the satisfaction of making him uncomfortable. Kira took the opening to call his bluff and rolled back over to flop on his chest with mock adoration.

"You mean we can finally be true to our feelings?"

"Get off of me, you ass." He shoved her away without much effort.

Her silver hair fell in her face, and she let out an annoyed huff to remove it. She proceeded to kick at him with her bare feet.

He shielded himself with a pillow. "Dude, keep your gross feet away from me."

"Shut up. They're dainty and cute," Kira argued.

Ginger shook her head at the display, then leaped into the fray as if it was unavoidable. She landed on her knees next to Kira, continuously bouncing to keep her from being able to get her balance enough to fight back.

Farn smirked. "Now you guys are making it weird." She added a surprised, "Yurk!" as Ginger snagged her cape with one hand like she was stealing an item from a dungeon boss. The *Shield* fell directly on top of Max as he squirmed to get out of the way.

Ginger slapped a hand to her face and let out a disappointed sigh as he squandered the opportunity to be smooth. Eventually, when the stupidity faded, Kira and Ginger settled into the pillows at the head of the bed while Max and Farn sat at the foot. Ginger elbowed Kira.

"I'm pretty sure my honeypot idea is working. So you should probably get used to the bed here."

Kira let out an elongated sigh and pulled a pillow over her face. "Could someone just hold this down for me?"

"Happy to." Max reached out to assist with the request. Farn grabbed his collar and yanked him back before he could apply any pressure.

"Hey, no choking me," Max coughed.

"What? I'm supposed to be guarding her. So no, you can't smother her right now." Farn tugged again at his collar.

Kira tossed the pillow at him, then turned back to Ginger.

"If you haven't noticed, I don't exactly have the same seduction capabilities as you do. So, I'm not sure how long it will take before he gets bored and kicks us out of here."

Ginger smiled. "Don't worry. Just be the same lovable goon that you always are. You'll have him begging to keep us around to spend more time with you." She tousled Kira's hair, leaving her staring through a curtain of silver locks, her lips pouting with annoyance. Ginger snorted. "Yeah, you'll do just fine."

Kira grumbled and got up, padding her way back to the coffee table to set the room as her home point. That way, she could teleport the four of them back now that they had been registered as guests. As for Corvin and Kegan, they would have to fend for themselves.

That was when a system chime sounded in Kira's ear.

CHAPTER TWENTY-SIX

Max slapped a hand to his face and sighed.

"Let go of the damn chair," Ginger grunted, attempting to pry an uncooperative fairy off the furniture.

"I've changed my mind. You can go without me." Kira gripped the arm of the sofa, its legs inching across the floor at a steady pace.

Is this really my life now? Max asked himself just as a sound drew his attention to the balcony.

Behind him, Corvin rested in a cat-like crouch on the railing. Kegan dropped down beside him a moment later. The elf landed silently, then hopped into the room.

"Sorry we're late. This guy was taking his sweet time getting online." He gestured at the reynard behind him.

Corvin bowed his head. "Sorry, I got a call from my parents right before I got on."

Kegan slapped him in the shoulder. "Shoulda just told them you have a heist to perpetrate."

"Like that would have gone over well," Corvin muttered.

"Anyway, I was hoping all of you welcomed guests here could run interference for us as we sneak down to the vault…" Kegan trailed off, his vision settling on the tug-of-war going on in the sitting area. "Ah, what's going on in here?"

Max rested his hands on his hips as if there was nothing out of the ordinary. "Berwyn sent Kira a direct message inviting her to a movie in the theater downstairs. She's freaking out a little."

"I see. Well, we don't have all night," the *Leaf* said.

"True enough." Max started walking as he stuck a finger in his mouth, slipping it in Kira's ear a second later. The fairy slapped her hands to her head for protection.

"Ha!" Ginger claimed victory as her prey came loose.

"Ack." Kira rubbed at her ear. "Not fair."

"I know, but we have things to do. And you have a date to get to." Max wiped his finger on his pants.

She folded her arms in a huff. "Fine, but Ginger's coming with me. I'm gonna need a buffer to keep things PG."

"I can do that." Ginger nodded.

"And you'll need your bodyguard too." Farn stepped forward. "Can't let you out of my sight."

"Okay, great. Now get moving." Max began shooing them to the door. "We've got a lot of ground to cover." The others fell in line behind him.

The upper floors proved easy to navigate with most of the palace guests spending their time down on the ground level. The automated guard patrols were still there, but Max had little trouble keeping his uninvited companions hidden.

It wasn't until they reached the first floor that the situation got hairy. Somehow, it had gotten even busier, like the entire House of Serpents, plus several parties worth of guests, were wandering around at once.

Makes sense, Max thought as he scanned the hall. Several open doors lead to the inside of the pyramid and its private beach. Not to mention there was a theater, a tavern, and even a tiki-bar over near the beach.

Sneaking the guys through was going to be difficult. Too bad the stairs didn't lead all the way down to the vault floor below ground. Max chewed his lip. At least the stairs provided a place for them to hide.

"Any ideas?" Kegan asked, peeking out from behind the crystal obelisk that stood at the center of the stairwell. Corvin's ears poked out below him.

"Maybe." Max tried to look inconspicuous. "It looks like there's a smaller stairway a few hundred feet down the hall. There are no guards on it. That's probably your way in."

"Great. And how do we get there without being spotted?" the *Leaf* questioned.

Max leaned against the obelisk. "There's a little shop close to us, but most of the players around seem more interested in the beach. Ginger, can you scout it out to see if it's empty?"

"On it." The *Coin* got moving, ducking into the shop a moment later. "Good call, just an NPC behind the counter," she reported over the house line.

Max smiled. "Okay, Kira, Farn, stay close. We'll walk down there together. Kegan and Corvin, you guys just stay between us and the wall. Hop into the shop as soon as we get there. Got it?"

"Yup."

"Yes."

"Gotcha."

"Aye aye, my captain."

Max rubbed the bridge of his nose for a second. "Okay, let's go." He pushed off the obelisk, the others taking their positions alongside him. He held his breath.

To his surprise, no one so much as looked at them. Other than Berwyn and a handful of his higher-ranked housemates, the rest of the Serpents just did their own thing. Max exhaled as Corvin and Kegan passed through the shop's door. He backed through it as well, bumping into Kira as soon as he was inside.

"Hey, don't stop in front of the..." Max spun around. "Oh." That was when it occurred to him to that he should have read the sign outside the small shop.

Ginger stood in the middle of the space with her arms held

out wide like a model on the Price is Right, showing Max what he'd won. He let out a sigh as a display of women swimsuits confronted him.

An NPC wearing a one piece with a sarong wrapped around her waist stood patiently behind the counter. "Please let me know if anything interests you."

"I'm thinking this one." Kegan held the skimpiest one he could find out to Kira.

"Har har." She proceeded to slap it out of his hands, then continued to swat at him.

"Alright, alright," he pleaded, not that there was much she could do to him anyway. As soon as she stopped, he pointed beside her. "Hey, check it out, chainmail bikini." This time Farn slapped him.

That one probably hurt.

Ginger browsed the selection. "In all seriousness though, we are going to need bathing suits if we're going to be hanging around here. It would be suspicious if we didn't."

Kira groaned. "Fine, who cares. All of you saw me naked last year anyways. Do your worst, Ginger."

The *Coin* grinned. "I will. But not now. These are nice and all, but I wonder if Larkin can hook us up again. After the stellar job he did with our gowns, we'd be stupid not to ask him."

"I'm okay with that." The fairy nodded. "He has good taste."

"But what I do want is this." Ginger pointed to a bracelet hanging by the checkout counter. She touched her forehead. She whispered the words, "Five Finger Discount." The NPC suddenly turned around to organize a shelf as if she had been compelled to. Ginger swiped the accessory off the rack and grinned, just as the NPC shook her head and returned to the counter.

"Did you just shoplift?" Max gave the *Coin* a sideways look.

"Kind of. I do it all the time. Why do you think I have a near endless supply of bombs? They're basically free if the skill works. It makes the clerk turn around." She twirled the bracelet around her finger. "Common items are fair game as long as you don't go overboard."

"And what if you do go overboard?" Max asked.

Ginger gave him a wink. "It would explain why I'm banned from a number of shops in Lucem."

"Glad to know I've brought the right player for this mission." Max grabbed the bracelet from her hand. "What did you want with this if it's just a common?"

She snatched it back and held it up to show a charm dangling from the chain. "It's a pyramid, like the palace. And it's not for me. It's for Kira."

"Ah, thanks, I guess." The fairy held out her wrist.

Ginger ignored her outstretched arm and crouched down to fasten the item around Kira's ankle. "Don't thank me too much. I'm trying to give Berwyn a feeling of ownership."

"Kind of like subliminally marking her as his belonging." Corvin scratched his chin.

"That's messed up." Farn frowned and crossed her arms.

"Yeah, well, men are pretty messed up creatures." Ginger stood back to admire her handiwork. "They like to own things."

"I resent that." Max snorted.

"So do I," Kira furrowed her brow, "and I resent being referred to as a 'thing' too."

"I calls 'em like I sees 'em." Ginger turned her palms up and shrugged.

Max brushed off the comment. "Well, personal feelings aside. Let's go scout ahead, see if there's anywhere else for these guys to hide on the way to the stairs."

Ginger followed as he turned back to the door.

Panic gripped him the instant he set foot into the hall. Berwyn was standing right there. Dartmouth stood at his side.

"Ahh, hello." Max's mouth went slack as Ginger bumped into his back.

"Hey, don't just stop in front of the door…" She took a

sharp breath. "Oh, Berwyn! We were just coming to see you. As long as you don't mind us tagging along to the movie."

Berwyn hesitated but smiled a second later. "Of course not. I'd be glad to have you join us. I was just heading over there now." He gestured to Dartmouth. "You can handle things from here without me, right?"

"Of course, sir." The Archmage of Serpents bowed and continued down the hall.

Berwyn watched him go for a moment, then gestured to the sign next to the door. "Were you doing some shopping?"

Ginger nodded. "Oh yes, Kira had wanted to stop in for a souvenir. It's her first time in a palace."

"Let me tell the shopkeep not to charge her. One of the perks to being king."

Max's heart leaped against the inside of his chest as Berwyn took a step forward toward the door. Fortunately, Ginger stepped in his way. It was probably the most suspicious thing she could have done, but it was better than letting him walk in on a couple uninvited guests.

"Sorry." Her eyes darted around. "I'd give her some time. Kira gets self-conscious, and she'll never pick something if someone's watching her."

"Oh, never mind then." Berwyn stepped back immediately.

Max released the tension he'd been holding as Ginger made small talk. He waited a minute or so, then raised his house ring. If he didn't report back soon, someone was going to come looking for him. He had to say something.

"Sorry to interrupt, but if you're ready in there, we ran into Lord Berwyn outside if you want to say hello."

There was a sound from inside, like people bumping into each other.

Kira emerged a few seconds later. Berwyn's eyes lit up as soon as he saw her.

"Find anything interesting?"

The fairy said nothing until Ginger nudged her in the shoulder. "Oh, yeah." She held out her foot to show off the miniature pyramid. "Ta-da."

Ginger probably would have liked for Kira to have lifted her skirt a little too show off some more leg. Max smirked at the thought. *Can't have everything you want.*

"Oh, that suits you well." Berwyn gave her a smile.

"So what sort of movie are we seeing?" She slid her leg back and clasped her hands behind her back.

"How about you pick? I don't really know what's available anyway. It's been a while since I've had the time to see anything with all this." He gestured around the hall as he spoke. He started walking, only looking back briefly to make sure his date was coming.

Kira let out a nervous squeak and jumped up to his side. Farn followed close behind. Ginger joined them as well, beckoning back to Max with urgency in her eyes.

He glanced to the shop's entrance where Kegan and Corvin were no doubt pressing their ears against the door. "You're on your own guys. Good luck."

With that, he jogged to catch up.

CHAPTER TWENTY-SEVEN

Keegan held the shop's door open a crack to watch as Max and the others walked away down the hall. "Damn, they just ditched us." He was starting to feel like they were getting the short end of the stick.

A fuzzy ear flicked against his chin.

"That's going to make moving around out there harder," Corvin said from below.

Kegan stepped back into the small shop. "Well, we can't stay here with Susan McNPC." He gestured at the woman behind the counter.

"Let me know if you find something that interests you." The NPC gave a polite bow.

"No thanks, we're fine." Corvin stepped away from the door without looking at her. "You're right. Eventually, someone is going to come in here, and they'll probably wonder what two guys are doing in a women's swimsuit boutique."

Kegan picked up a hanger containing a yellow one-piece and held it up against Corvin's chest. "I don't know, the color's working for you."

"You're not helping." Corvin glowered back before

changing the subject. "The guards aren't even the problem here. There're just too many players out there. It's like the expo-hall at an anime con out there.

"But without schoolgirl costumes." Kegan sighed.

Corvin chuckled. "Actually, I think I saw an elf girl a little down the hall whose gear is close enough."

"Really?" Kegan hopped back to the door and peeked out at a *Breath* mage wearing a pleated skirt with a light tunic and scarf. "Oh yeah, that counts." He had never been much into anime. Not like Corvin was, at least, but he couldn't complain about the costume designs.

Corvin leaned against the wall by the door. "A lot of armor and clothing in Noctem has been inspired by comics and anime. Which makes sense, I mean, my character is basically a gender-swapped fox girl." The *Blade* twitched his tall ears.

Kegan picked up another hanger containing a bikini bottom with an attached skirt and held it against Corvin's waist. "So we should put you in a schoolgirl costume then?"

"You're still not helping."

"I know." Kegan tossed the item back on a shelf as Corvin went back to the door to peek out.

"Okay, this might sound crazy, but what if we just walked out there?"

Kegan couldn't believe his ears. "Weren't you the one giving me dirty looks for throwing a rock at those guards last night?"

"Yeah, but hear me out on this. We haven't been invited, so the guards will recognize us as intruders on sight since they're just bots. But the patrols are predictable, so we can avoid them. The problem here is all the players wandering around."

"Your point?"

"My point is that there's a ton of them, so how will they know that we're not supposed to be here?"

Kegan thought about it. It was actually a good point. "We could just walk out there like we own the place, and they might not even notice." He couldn't help but grin. "It's stupid. I like it."

"Okay, then we wait until the next patrol passes, then jump out there and try to act natural."

Kegan took his place at the door, watching for the next patrol to pass. Then on the count of three, he held his breath and stepped out into the hall. He winced, half expecting to be outed immediately. The image of everyone pointing at him and shouting streaked through his head. To his surprise, no one batted an eye.

This might actually work.

Then he caught a glimpse of his partner who kept fidgeting with his item bag and sword, like a nervous mess.

"You call that acting naturally?"

"I don't know what to do with my hands," Corvin answered back, a touch of panic entering his voice.

"Just put them in your pockets, man."

The *Blade* proceeded to shove his hands into his pockets so hard that it looked like he was trying to fight his own pants. From the looks of it, he was losing.

About halfway to the stairs, the girl in the schoolgirl looking gear arched an eyebrow at them. Trying to distract from his awkward companion, Kegan raised one hand as if touching the rim of an imaginary hat. He inclined his head as the word, "Howdy," escaped his lips.

"Howdy? How is that natural?" Corvin fired back in a frantic whisper. "And you're not even wearing a hat."

"I don't know. I panicked. It just came out," Kegan's skin started to prickle as his forehead began to sweat. The rogue 'howdy' had been just as surprising to him as it must have been to his partner. Even more surprising was that he felt himself make the same gesture to another player. This time adding an old west sounding accent. "Partner."

Corvin jabbed him with his elbow. "Seriously? You're an archer, not a gunslinger."

"I know, I can't stop," he responded as they finally reached the stairs and ducked down out of sight. Kegan immediately swatted Corvin to pay him back for jabbing him. Corvin slapped him back. A few seconds of flailing at each other later, Kegan let out a sigh of relief. He was kind of glad the others hadn't been there to witness his performance.

The stairway continued down for several flights before they reached a narrow hall. Kegan did the math. "I think we're underneath the pyramid."

"So that would mean that all that water is right over our heads." Corvin looked up.

Kegan decided not to think about it. "Does it seem odd that there are no guards down here?"

"Maybe, or it might just mean that whatever is waiting in the vault's entry corridor is serious enough to not require anything more."

Kegan swallowed. "That doesn't make me feel good about this." Just as the words left his mouth, they reached an ornate door.

It was made of gray stone, carved with a stylized design of waves flowing around its edge. A large skull was carved at the center with four triangular buttons resting in its mouth. Two of them faced up, while the others faced down. Horizontal lines bisected half of them. The words 'Choose that which life requires' curved below the skull.

"Well, that's obviously a puzzle lock." Kegan slapped his partner on the back. "Good luck, man."

"Thanks." Corvin sighed as he stepped up to examine the lock. "Glad to know Checkpoint Systems is getting its security ideas from Umbrella." The *Blade* scratched one of his ears. "At least this is an easy one. The buttons represent the elements in alchemy. Since Reliqua is filled with water, and life needs water to live, that should be the right choice."

"How do you even know what those symbols are?" Kegan arched an eyebrow at him.

The *Blade* shrugged. "Books, I guess."

Kegan placed his hands to the sides of his mouth as if he was about to shout but whispered instead, "Nerrrrrrrddddddd."

He elongated the syllable for effect before adding, "How did you not get beaten up in school?"

Corvin's face went white at the question.

Guilt stabbed at Kegan's chest as he remembered how quiet the kid had been back when they had met last year. *Of course he got beaten up in school.*

"Oh sorry, I didn't mean to—"

"No, it's okay," Corvin let out a sigh, "and yes, I did get beaten up. But not for being a nerd. That just got me made fun of."

Kegan debated on asking a follow-up question, unsure if he should push the subject. "What did you get beaten up for?"

Corvin gave him a sad smile. "I brought a gun to school."

"What do you mean?" Kegan's heart dropped into his stomach like a rock.

The young *Blade* shook his head. "Nothing sinister. It was a stage prop for the theater department."

"Oh my god. You scared me." Kegan placed a hand on the kid's shoulder.

"Yeah, that was pretty much the response when it fell out of my locker in front of everyone. I was beaten half to death out of panic. Lost a bunch of teeth and broke several bones, including a skull fracture. I was unconscious for days. Plus, I got expelled when I woke up."

Tears welled up in Kegan's eyes, catching him off guard. It was easy to forget how young Corvin was. At nineteen, he wasn't even half Kegan's age. No, Kegan hadn't even thought about it in the last year. Corvin was just Corvin, the fuzzy-eared *Blade* that he'd been helping level most nights for the last year. He hadn't even noticed that the kid had become his best friend.

Oh, what the hell?

Kegan surprised himself as he threw his arms around the *Blade* and hugged him tightly.

"Umm okay, not the response I expected." Corvin patted him on the back. "That's probably enough."

"Shhh, shhh. Just let it happen," Kegan whispered.

"Are you crying?"

"Shut up." Kegan sniffed.

"Umm, we still have a vault to open," Corvin reminded as the hug began to go on too long.

Kegan released him, shoving aside his instinct to make light of the situation. "I'm sorry you had a rough time in school. You're stronger than I was at your age."

"Ah, thanks." Corvin scratched at the back of his neck.

"Okay, now let's get this door open." Kegan reached for one of the buttons. "This one means water, right?"

Suddenly, Corvin grabbed his hand. "Wait."

"What?" Kegan furrowed his brow.

"Sorry, but I'm just thinking about the writing on the door. We need to pick the one that life requires."

"And that was water, right? 'Cause we're in Reliqua and water is so abundant."

Corvin pointed up to the ceiling where millions of gallons of water rested just above their heads. "What do you think happens if we're wrong?"

Kegan's blood ran cold as he yanked his finger away from the button. "The hallway floods. Oh man, that's why they don't need guards down here. That's just sadistic."

Corvin nodded. "If that's true, and the question of what life requires refers to this hallway specifically..."

"Then what we need is air," Kegan finished his thought.

They both slowly turned toward the buttons. Kegan's shoulders suddenly felt heavy with the imagined weight of the water.

"I hope you're right."

"So do I." Corvin reached for whichever button represented air.

"Wait!" Kegan stopped him.

"What?"

Kegan took a deep breath, then gestured to continue.

"Good call." Corvin inhaled as well. Then he pressed the button.

CHAPTER TWENTY-EIGHT

Corvin winced with his entire body as several strange clicks came from inside the door. The pressure of the situation was immense, and he didn't want to let the others down. He expected a torrent of water to crash into him and wash him away any second.

It didn't.

"Oh, thank every god in the pantheon." Kegan released a lungful of air as the door rolled into a pocket in the wall. Corvin exhaled as well, almost dropping to his knees.

"That was terrifying."

Beyond the first door was another stairway. They made it down the first few steps before a sound like the door moving came from behind.

"And the door just closed behind us, didn't it?" Kegan slapped a hand to his head.

Corvin looked over his shoulder. "Yup." Then he noticed a single button on the inside. "Whew, there's a switch to open it again." He tested it just in case, feeling better as the door rolled back into the pocket. With that, they continued down toward the rest of the corridor.

Kegan stopped short before reaching the bottom. "Let's take a peek before walking in there." He activated his Light Foot skill and slipped his inspector from his journal. "Ready?"

Corvin nodded and held out his hand. They had explored enough dungeons together to have figured out some interesting ways to check a room without entering it.

The *Leaf* took his hand and crouched, letting Corvin lower him back until he was hanging upside down over the next few stairs. He held his inspector over his eye. "Damn, so much for not having any guards down here."

"How many?" Corvin pulled him back up.

"Twelve, six on each side. Stealth is only going to get us so far. I think the gloves have to come off here. At least with the door closed up above, no one will hear us murder these guys."

"Okay, let me see." Corvin borrowed the inspector and repeated the maneuver to get an idea of their enemies' positions.

The first two had *Shield* gauntlets, the last held daggers. Probably *Coins*. All the ones in between had swords. Looking through the inspector, he could see each of their health bars. According to the color, which was yellow to indicate caution, they were close to his level in the mid-range. At least they weren't red.

Beyond the guards was another large door with a single button. A chain with a pull ring hung to the side of it. An alarm, from the look of it.

Can't let any of them reach that. Not after everything Max and the others did to get us here. He pulled himself back up with the help of his partner, and they crept back up a few stairs.

Kegan leaned into Corvin's ear. "What do you think?"

"What color were their health bars for you?"

"Green. I should be able to one-shot them if I can land some criticals, but those *Shields* are going to be a problem if they get their gauntlets up."

Corvin nodded. "I'll go for them first. You aim for the *Coins* in the back. I'm willing to bet they go for the alarm instead of fighting."

"And the rest?"

Corvin answered with a shrug.

"This is gonna be a shit-show." Kegan sighed.

"Probably. I think I'm going to need this." Corvin pulled off his patch to expose his yellow basilisk eye, making sure not to look in Kegan's direction. "It can only hold one of them at a time, but at least that's something."

He drew his katana, swiping two fingers down the back of the steel. The weapon hummed with power as he whispered the words, "Phantom Strike."

"Ready?"

"As I'll ever be." Kegan drew a handful of arrows.

Without another word, Corvin simply stepped forward, using gravity to take the remaining stairs in only two large strides. He burst into the hall before either *Shield* knew he was there.

They almost looked surprised as Corvin slashed up, releasing the phantom blade into the first guard at point blank range. He sprang up with the momentum of the follow through and turned to come down hard on the second *Shield's* shoulder. His sword dug in as he put all his weight into the strike, letting out a wild cry and streaking crimson light down the guard's body. Both *Shields* staggered back, but neither fell.

It wasn't enough.

In his peripheral, he caught a glimpse of the two *Coins* at the back making a break for the alarm chain.

An arrow whistled through the hall, so close he felt the displacement of air against the fur of his ears. It hit one of the *Coins* in the back with a sickening thunk.

"Down!" Kegan roared as he appeared from the stairs, letting off another arrow. It impaled the other *Coin's* neck just before his hand touched the alarm chain.

Corvin dropped to a crouch as another arrow finished off

the *Shield* behind him. He sprang back up and pushed his sword into the other, feeling the guard go limp.

Four down, eight to go.

In the past, when confronted by a group of more than two enemies, most games would use a mechanic called slotting. This meant that despite the size of the conflict, there would only be a limited number of active spaces, or slots, for enemies to take. Any opponent not slotted would simply strafe around and wait their turn to attack. It was a system meant to keep the player from being overwhelmed as well as convey a feeling of badassery.

Noctem, however, expected more from its players.

The eight NPC *Blades* rushed forward, using their numbers to their advantage and forcing Corvin to step back. He tried to lock one of them down with his eye, but everything happened so fast that all he could do was raise his weapon.

Steel scraped steel as he blocked a hit and used it to push himself to the side. With a little distance, he swiped at the group, then pushed into them.

They fell back as he rushed low, hooking the blunt edge of his sword behind one of their legs to yank them off balance. The guard fell with an armored crash as Corvin dropped down to pierce his heart. He ducked an attack at the same time, his mind firing on all cylinders to keep him from taking a hit.

The moment was short lived.

Pain streaked across his back, dulled by the system as it faded to a numb tingle. A boot connected with his shoulder, sending him to the floor hard. A glance at his wrist showed his health drop twenty percent. The slash had been shallow. There was still a chance.

Stomping boots filled his ears; a memory of the day when three of his teeth had been kicked from his skull shot through his mind. He growled to chase away the thought as silver glinted across his vision.

He kicked off one of the guard's legs, throwing himself a

foot to the side as a sword came down. It hit the floor with an ear-splitting screech, like a car door being keyed.

Two arrows hit his attacker from out of nowhere.

"I got you, man," Kegan shouted through the chaos.

Another couple arrows forced the group back.

Corvin pushed himself up from the floor with a grunt just as one of the remaining guards made a break for the alarm. Kegan loosed an arrow, only for a sword to swat it out of the air.

"I don't have a shot. Cover me." The *Leaf* dove into the fray, landing on his knees in a slide.

Corvin didn't even have time to think before two swords streaked toward his partner's head. He lunged, blocking both as he braced his foot against the wall. Kegan slid underneath like a spider escaping a rolled-up newspaper.

The *Leaf* pushed back up onto one knee and let loose three arrows, stopping the runner hard only a foot from the pull chain. He stood and turned just as one of the guards rushed him, his weapon aimed for a critical thrust. Without a sword of his own, Kegan parried with the last arrow in his hand. It snapped but deflected the blow just enough to miss his heart as the sword slid into his chest.

Kegan gasped, but he had the health to take it. He didn't struggle. Instead, he simply dropped his bow and grabbed the strap on the guard's chest plate as he fell back. The momentum threw him to the floor but not before placing a foot against the man's abdomen. Kegan pushed off as he hit the ground, throwing the guard head over heels into the wall.

Before the guard could recover, Kegan pulled two arrows from his quiver and stabbed him in the neck. The act was horrible, even if there was no blood.

Corvin's stomach flipped as he impaled another nameless guard and pushed him back until the tip of his sword hit the stonework behind. An instant later, another enemy did the same to him from behind, burying their weapon in his back up to its hilt. He almost cried out. It hurt, but not anywhere near as much as it would if it had been real. His stat-sleeve showed his health drop below half.

The NPC had missed his heart. It pinned him to the body in front of him, or at least, it would have if he hadn't gotten a foot up in time to push back. He let out a stifled growl as he shoved back, sending the three remaining *Blades* sprawling.

They recovered quickly.

He didn't.

The problem with fighting against Noctem's enemies was that they never got tired. Corvin, however, was exhausted. Not to mention that he couldn't reach the handle of the sword sticking out of his back. He rolled to one side to put a small amount of distance between himself and his opponents. Then deflected a slash with a weak parry, almost losing his grip on his own weapon in the process.

With few options, he reached forward, grabbing the sword sticking out of his chest and shoving it back hard enough to dislodge it. It fell with a clatter that seemed to go on forever as his chest heaved and his heart raced.

His stat-sleeve ticked down another ten percent. Without a healer or time to get a health vial out of his bag, he had reached his limit. There was a reason he avoided taking on large groups, after all.

The guards closed in for the kill.

Kegan suddenly rushed the group from behind, jumping onto the back of the middle guard and pulling him to the ground. Without his bow, the leaf simply punched the enemy in the face to keep him down.

Corvin took the opening with an uncoordinated lunge. He didn't even bother to maintain his footing. Instead, he slashed into one guard's chest with as much momentum as possible, letting it carry his katana and him in a circle until it struck the back of the other.

Neither guard fell.

Corvin hit the ground with a thud that took the wind out of him. He wheezed and scrambled across the floor, finding

Kegan's bow laying to the side. "Catch," he coughed to his partner before lobbing the weapon in his direction.

The *Leaf* rolled off the guard and snatched up his bow, scooting back on his rear to gain some distance. He reached for his last handful of arrows.

The three guards turned to rush him.

Kegan drew back his bow and shouted, "Hold them still!"

Corvin raised his head, locking his yellow eye with the first target. The guard froze in place, leaving his throat wide open. The sound of a bowstring struck the air. Corvin didn't wait to see where the arrow hit before flicking his eye to the next target. He didn't want to watch.

The three guards fell like dominos. After that, the hall fell almost silent. Only the heavy panting of the victors filling the space.

"That sucked." Kegan gasped as he crawled. "You alive?"

"Yeah." Corvin pushed himself up against the wall and fished a health vial from his bag. Kegan did the same, scooting up next to him. They clinked the vials together before downing the contents. Even after their health was full, they still waited a full minute before finding the strength to stand.

Bodies littered the room.

Kegan nudged one of the lifeless forms. "I'm just gonna say it because it's kind of the elephant in the room, but this is pretty messed up."

"I know," Corvin answered, trying his best not to look down at the bloodless carnage. "There aren't any human type enemies in the rest of Noctem. They're just here in the cities. We're not really supposed to kill them. I read online that Check-point had decided that fighting people would be too disturbing to include them as a common enemy."

"Well, they're right." Kegan shuddered. "I've killed plenty of players in my PVP days, but this is probably the worst I've ever felt about winning. I mean, I just drove an arrow through a man's throat." Kegan shivered. "It's all just too—"

"Intimate?" Corvin finished the thought for him.

The *Leaf* took a breath. "That makes it sound weird, but yeah."

Corvin tapped a few options on the menu woven into his stat-sleeve, hoping to have access to the collect loot option now that the room had been cleared. At least that way, the bodies would disappear. He let out a sigh of relief when he saw it highlighted. The bodies began to dematerialize as he pressed it, depositing any item drops gained from the fight into their virtual inventories. "That's better."

"Outta sight, outta mind. I feel less morally bankrupt already." Kegan gave himself a nod.

"They'll probably respawn when we leave, if it works like other dungeons. We should learn everything about the vault we can now so we don't have to go through that again."

"I hear that. Let's get on with the breaking and entering."

With that, Corvin punched the button on the next door. At least it wasn't locked with another ridiculous puzzle. The door rolled off to the side, just like the first one. Kegan let out a low whistle at what lay beyond.

"That is one hell of a laser grid."

"Mana fence," Corvin corrected.

As expected, in classic heist fashion, a crisscrossing web of blue beams filled the space. Many were positioned so close together that it seemed impossible to get through without crossing one.

Corvin just stood there for a moment in awe of the monstrosity; it was actually really cool to see in person. "At least it's visible without having to blow fog into the hall or something."

"But how the hell are we going to fit through there?" Kegan scratched his head.

Corvin crouched down to get a different angle. "Simple. We're not going to fit in there. It's way too small for either of us to crawl through. But we do have a pint-sized fairy on our side that might be able to help us out. Maybe if we ask nicely."

"Kira's going to hate this." A grin crept across Kegan's face.

Corvin chuckled and pulled out his inspector. "This as far as we go for now. I'm going to snap a few photos of the setup. If I can get enough angles, I can use the perspective to map it out. Maybe we can recreate it somewhere to practice."

"Good thinking."

Corvin motioned to step through the door, but before his foot could touchdown, Kegan grabbed the back of his vest. Startled by the sudden contact, his inspector slipped from his hand.

What did I miss? The question shot through his mind like a bullet as the world slowed.

A look of horror was plastered to Kegan's face. His eyes locked on the small pane of glass as it tumbled end over end. Corvin followed the path of the falling inspector to the floor.

His heart nearly stopped. It wasn't marble like the rest of the palace. It was metal with an out-of-place carving of flames at its edge. Even worse, he recognized it from a dungeon he'd done with Kegan back when first he'd changed classes. It was from the Fire Tomb, and it was a trap.

The entire floor was a pressure plate.

Corvin's hands shot out for his inspector as he leaned forward past the door. His partner held tight to his vest so he didn't fall in. He willed the item to his hand with every fiber of his being until his fingertips touched the glass. It teetered back and forth, balancing for an instant before falling to the floor.

Corvin held his breath as a deafening silence filled the hall.

CHAPTER TWENTY-NINE

Max shifted in his seat, feeling out of place sitting in a movie theater while wearing a pair of pistols in a shoulder holster. He usually stored them in his inventory whenever he visited one of Noctem's more modern facilities.

Actually, modern wasn't the right word. Sure, there was a screen behind the red velvet curtains at the back of the stage, but that was about it. The rest of the extravagant room was covered in gold leaf and filigree from floor to ceiling. Max felt more like he was spending a night at the opera.

"This is not what I expected to be doing tonight."

Farn sat back into her plush leather seat. "I can't complain. There are a few things that I wanted to see playing. I kind of feel bad that we don't get to sit with our friends though. Being a bodyguard sucks."

Max turned his attention a few rows ahead where Kira and Ginger sat with Berwyn. "Yeah, sitting in the back doesn't really sit well with me either, but it's probably for the best. We'd probably just get in the way down there." He leaned on the armrest that he shared with the empty seat between himself and Farn.

After the conversation that morning about asking the *Shield* out, he was uncomfortably aware of the fact that they were now seeing a movie together. Hence, why he had left the empty seat as a sort of social buffer between them. Obviously, he didn't want to make things weird or send mixed signals.

Max gestured at their housemates in front to lessen the tension he was imagining. "Is it me, or do you feel like we're parents taking our daughter to her first movie with a boy?"

Farn slouched in her chair and folded her arms. "If Berwyn pretends to stretch and put his arm around her, I'll break..." she trailed off as someone began shuffling down their isle.

"'Scuse me, sorry." Nix scooted past Farn, carrying an armload of snacks and a beverage. She dropped into the empty seat between Max and Farn, spilling loose popcorn on him in the process.

Clearly, the reynard didn't require a social buffer, as she seemed oblivious to her status as a third wheel. She definitely wasn't a helpful one either like on a tricycle. More like that one on a Reliant Robin, the three-wheeled car from Mr. Bean that was notorious for flipping over.

Max eyed her suspiciously.

"What? Free movie," she said, leaning back into the leather cushion as if that explained everything.

"Fair enough." Max found the mercenary hard to read, similarly to when he had met her. She was either kind of dumb and just wanted to see a free movie and make new friends, or she was keeping an eye on them. He leaned back and tried to ignore her.

One of Berwyn's Serpents brought down a tray of popcorn and drinks for Ginger and Kira. It made Max smile. He could almost see the inner conflict that must have been raging in the fairy's head.

An imaginary Kira dressed in the frilly, white dress she had worn a year ago, perched innocently on her shoulder. "Remember the mission. It's just popcorn. Act like a lady and eat slowly."

On the other side, a second tiny Kira dressed in the black

dress of the Rasputin form she once had barked commands. "Shovel fistfuls into your face!"

For a moment, Max was a little worried that the dark side might win. He relaxed when the fairy politely tossed a couple of the buttery puffs into her mouth. He sighed a minute later when Berwyn turned to talk to Ginger and Kira took the opportunity to shove in as much popcorn as she could fit into her face. It was actually pretty impressive.

"Your Archmage really likes popcorn, huh?" Nix commented while tossing a kernel up in the air so she could catch it in her mouth. It hit her in the eye and bounced onto Max's lap.

Farn gave an awkward laugh. "Yeah, Kira likes pretty much anything that she can fit in her mouth."

"You may want to rephrase that one there." Max flicked Nix's dropped popcorn off his leg.

Farn paused for a second before her eyes went wide in understanding. "Food! She likes any food that she can fit in her mouth."

Max shook his head as the lights dimmed, and the curtain raised. He leaned back and settled in. At least his seat was comfortable.

That was when alarm bells filled the air.

CHAPTER THIRTY

Max almost jumped out of his seat when the theater lights snapped back on. The sound of dozens of bells bombarded his senses.

Nix launched her popcorn into the air, clearly just as startled. It rained down in buttery clumps as the reynard wiped her spilled drink from her skirt.

Ginger stood, signaling for her bodyguards to come to her defense as if she feared for her safety. Max drew his pistols and jogged down to meet her. Farn took up a position in the aisle facing the door, ready to confront the threat.

It was a good act.

Max had a pretty good idea of why the bells were ringing. *What the hell did you guys do?* A ridiculous image of Kegan and Corvin running for their lives while being chased by the entire House of Serpents passed through his head. He shook off the thought and joined the others.

Berwyn placed a hand on Kira's shoulder as she shrank back near Ginger. The act was probably meant to calm her, but from the look on her face, it didn't. Actually, it probably stressed her out more. What was odd, though, was that his first act had been out of concern for her. Max would have expected that he'd be more interested in the security breach. Apparently, he considered her a priority.

Nix strolled down to join them, her gun held limply at her side. Max tried to get a look at it but couldn't see the weapon well without it being obvious that he was looking. She leaned close to Berwyn so that he didn't have to yell over the alarm. He said something that Max couldn't make out before turning to Kira.

"We're going to head to the center of the pyramid. It's the safest place in the palace. The rest of my men will form a perimeter around the throne room. That's the protocol for something like this." He made eye contact with Nix for an instant. "Take the lead."

The reynard shifted her stance to grip her gun with both hands as she moved up to the door. Farn joined her, activating her new gauntlet's barrier to give the reynard some cover. Nix gave her a nod and moved forward into the hall.

Max tore his attention away from the other *Fury* and fell back to join Ginger. She gave him a concerned look that said volumes. Max glanced to his house ring.

Why haven't Corvin or Kegan checked in?

It wasn't like them to leave everyone in the dark. He resisted asking over the house line, since raising his ring would have been suspicious. As far as Berwyn knew, there weren't any other members of Lockheart in the palace.

With nothing left to do in the current situation, Max just held his guns at the ready and followed the group out of the theater. Besides, with all things considered, there was only one explanation. His friends had been caught. There was nothing he could do to change that.

If it came to it, he could just stand back and pretend he didn't know them. As unpleasant as that sounded, it was an option. Hell, it was the only option. Max ground his teeth. Watching his friends get executed wasn't high on his list, but at least his cover wouldn't be blown.

Suddenly, his forehead broke out in a cold sweat as a realization hit him. Kegan and Corvin were wearing their house rings. Rings which had Lockheart's crest emblazoned on them. If they had been caught, then all of their covers would be blown the moment Berwyn's Serpents marched them into the pyramid. All the Lord of Serpents needed to do was glance at their hands, and the whole heist would go south.

He should have told them to remove their rings as a precaution. It was a rookie mistake, and now it was only a matter of time. Max choked down his terror; he wasn't going to help anyone if he let himself freak out.

His party followed Nix to the enormous throne room within the pyramid. Moonlight shined down, casting a foreboding pallor across the sand. The sound of waves drifted through the air. Berwyn took a moment to assure them that everything was going according to protocol once more. Then he broke away from them and joined some of his house members near the patio where he and Kira had danced. It was far less magical than the night before.

Most of the palace's other visitors had been directed to the same area, all of them standing in the sand with Max. Having them all in one place must've made them easier to protect. Then again, it also made it harder for anyone to escape.

Ginger stepped closer to him. From her expression, she was thinking the same thing. Kira and Farn moved closer to each other as well. They had to get out of there.

Max scanned the perimeter, making note of how many of Berwyn's men were guarding each exit. The doors to the upper levels were closed, probably locked from what he could tell. Using flight magic was out. That just left the ground floor. It would be tough, but they could make a break for it. Fight their way out if they had to.

Most of the Serpents weren't much to worry about. The only ones that might be a problem were Nix, Aawil, and Ripper. Though, he didn't see Aawil or Ripper. They were probably the ones taking down his friends as he stood doing nothing. That just left Nix, whom he still wasn't sure was an idiot or not.

Watching her with his peripheral vision, Max finally got a better look at her gun. What he saw filled him with a sense of dread, not because he didn't recognize the gun but because he did. Like his, it had a modern design, without all the silly details that most fantasy guns had. Instead, it seemed to be based off a Beretta M9 with an extended magazine and folding fore-grip. She held it at a low angle with both hands, her finger resting to the side of the trigger guard.

Like his, the gun had a third position on its select fire switch. If it was true to the model of gun it was based off, then it was probably a three-round burst. He only recognized the gun because he had used it in over a dozen games over the years. As far as he knew, the pistol wasn't available in Noctem. The only explanation was that it was a contract item. Even worse, having a contract could only mean one thing—she was dangerous.

Just as Max was debating on whether to rush the other *Fury* or not, he heard a commotion at one of the doors to the pyramid.

Ripper and Aawil emerged, followed by a group of Serpents. They seemed to be walking in formation, as if leading their captives while keeping them surrounded to make sure they couldn't escape. That was when the alarm bells stopped.

Max tightened his grip on his guns.

"We've got the intruder," Ripper declared, almost sounding eager.

His words sent a chill down Max's spine as if the guy couldn't wait to execute his friends. He had to act fast, holding his breath as he started to raise his guns. Then his mind crashed into a detail that he had almost missed. *Intruder? Had Ripper just said intruder? As in, singular? Did one of them get away?* If so, then they might not be as screwed as he thought. The only question was if it was Kegan or Corvin.

Ripper stepped aside as the Serpents lead their captive into the middle of the beach. Suddenly, everything changed.

It wasn't either of them.

An elven woman stood proud as if she had no regrets. She had pink hair and wore a ridiculous set of gear that suggested a Japanese school uniform. The emblem of a *Breath* mage adorned her hand. She glared daggers at the Lord of Serpents before her, defiance burning in her eyes. Ripper gave her a shove hard enough to throw her into the sand.

"Hold on there." Berwyn stepped between them. "No need to be rough."

The *Shield* backed off. "We caught her in your study going through the books. She ran but didn't make it far."

Berwyn knelt down to the elf. "Oh, Luka." He sounded sad. "You've been a part of our house for over a month. Why would you betray us now?"

That was when Max noticed she wore the same house ring as the rest of the Serpents.

The woman laughed. "You think you have it all figured out, don't you?" Her voice was dripping with venom.

Berwyn deflated. "Have I not been good to you?"

She pushed herself up to her knees slowly, as if stalling to choose her words. "Sure sure, but there's more to life than a bit of hard and private beaches. The rest of the world won't stand by while you destroy it."

He sighed and lowered his head, only to raise it up again a second later. "Okay, who's paying you, and what city are you reporting back to? Thrift? Lucem? Maybe even Tartarus? I always figured those rogues would be a problem at some point."

"Paying me?" She smirked as if he had missed the point completely. "Are you really that simple? I have a conscience, unlike the rest of your snakes." She gestured towards Ripper. "I actually care about the world. I don't need to be paid."

"So you're a rebel then? That how you see yourself?" He opened his journal and scratched in a couple lines. With a final, decisive slash of his pen, her house ring melted off of her finger, leaving a puddle of gold in the sand. "Fine, you want to be treated like an enemy, so be it. You're out of the house. I'll advise you not set foot in my territory again. I'll be giving orders to kill you on sight." He put away his journal and turned away.

"Do whatever you want to me—throw me out of the house, kill me, or put bounties on my head. It doesn't matter." Her nostrils flared. "Someone else will take you down." She started to stand, and for a moment, she made eye contact with Max.

He could have sworn he saw her smile at him.

"Ripper, make sure she leaves the palace however you see fit." Berwyn didn't even look back at her, his voice holding a layer of disdain.

From the look of Ripper's excited grin, it was obvious to Max how he would choose to remove her from the palace. Execution was about as efficient as one could get, but strangely, he didn't draw his sword. Instead, he just held out a hand, his clawed gauntlet outstretched in her direction.

Suddenly, the woman bent backward and fell into the sand. Her entire body twitched as if she was in pain. She spat a slurred insult at Ripper as her spine locked in a heaving arch. Glowing particles of crimson light began to drift from her body to his claws. Patterns of spiraling lines burned across the surface of his gauntlet. The class emblem on her hand dimmed and faded as her health drained.

Max couldn't believe his eyes. Ripper hadn't even touched her.

The dark *Shield* slammed his fist closed as if crushing an insect, tearing what remained of her life from her body. A cloud of embers burst from her form in one bright mass, like a root pulling free from the ground. Then the elf fell limp in a crumpled mess.

A wave of nausea rolled through Max's stomach as her body began to dissipate, drifting out across the sand. His gaze snapped back to Ripper's closed fist.

The gauntlet was definitely a contract item, but even with that, it was overpowered. Whatever the ability was, it had hit her from over ten feet away. From what Max could tell, it couldn't be dodged. Otherwise, the poor elf would have done something. It wasn't that insta-kill abilities were uncommon when it came to contracts, but most had a drawback, like only working once or carrying a heavy cost to use. Hell, even Amelia's blade required her to at least cut skin for its venom to work. Whatever Max had just witnessed was just broken.

Berwyn stepped up the stairs to the patio area to address the rest of his house along with his guests. He spoke in a voice loud enough to be heard without yelling. "This might be a House of Serpents, but that doesn't mean that we can have snakes within our ranks. I don't mean this as a warning but as a plea. We may be building an empire, but I am not Vader. I ask you all to stay with me through the months ahead. Continue together, so that the rest of Noctem can follow our example. As one house, one empire, and one world."

His words must have washed away the memory of the moment before because the rest of the Serpents gave applause without hesitation. In turn, their excitement relieved the other guests, many of them joining in as well. Even Ginger clapped; granted, she also looked like she might throw up. Max followed her example, shoving his conscience to the back of his mind. His stomach rolled again.

The only holdout was Kira, and Berwyn's gaze fell to her as she stared at the spot where Luka's body had been. As the Serpents and their guests began to disperse back into the palace, their Lord returned to Kira's side.

"I'm really sorry you had to see that. Sometimes running an empire," he let out a long sigh, "well, let's just say it gets messy. I know that's not really an excuse and Ripper's Death Grip doesn't really make us look like the good guys. I hope you won't let it ruin your time here."

"Yeah, that was a bit much." Kira gave a weak smile.

"But spies have to be dealt with," Ginger added before Kira got herself into trouble, "and might I add, that is one hell of a contract item. What did you call it?"

"The Death Grip?" Berwyn glanced back at his Knight.

"It's easily one of the most powerful items in all of Noctem. It's Ripper's claim to fame."

"I'll say." Max nodded, trying to seem envious about the overpowered ability. "It makes our contracts look a lot less impressive. Right, Farn?" He nudged the *Shield*, indicating that they both had at least a couple contracts between them without saying more.

Farn let out a surprised laugh as his elbow rubbed against her ribs, but she recovered quickly. "Speak for yourself. Mine are pretty epic."

"That's pretty big talk." Berwyn smiled once again, just as charming as before. "Maybe you could knock Ripper down a peg or two. Honestly, he could use it."

"Maybe." Farn laughed.

"Anyway, I'll have to go through my study and make sure she didn't see anything that could be a problem. I'm sorry that this kind of spoiled the evening, but why don't you head back to the theater and finish the movie? There should be time enough for that before you have to log out. Oh, and if you want, visit the beach tomorrow night. It's one of the best places to swim in all of Noctem."

"That sounds like a good idea to me." Ginger gave an eager smile. "And Kira loves the water."

Kira's eyes widened.

"Perfect. I hope you like it." Berwyn grinned.

"Thanks, I will." Kira's face flushed as she looked at her feet.

Berwyn bid them farewell and headed off to his study.

Max watched him go, then exhaled, releasing the last thirty minutes of tension from his body all at once.

"What the hell did we get ourselves into?"

CHAPTER THIRTY-ONE

Kira stood on the beach, staring at the sand where the elf, Luka, had died. Her fists were clenched so tight her knuckles went white. "I did this. That contract is horrible. And it's my fault it exists."

Her words cut right to Ginger's heart. "No, it's not."

"I broke the contract system. That thing exists because of me."

"Don't be an idiot." Max holstered his pistols. "Contracts are pulled from the user's subconscious; it has nothing to do with you. If anything, it just tells us about what kind of sociopath Ripper is."

After everything that happened on the beach, Ginger didn't really feel like going back to the theater and sitting through a movie. Fortunately, neither did anyone else. Somehow, even Kira had lost interest in shoving handfuls of popcorn into her mouth. Considering all that, Ginger thought returning to their suite upstairs was for the best. Plus, they still had a couple house members missing in action.

They didn't stay missing for long.

Ginger narrowed her eyes as soon as she walked into the suite.

"Well, well, well. Glad you could make it." Kegan sat on the couch, wearing a smug grin. He sipped a club soda that he must've taken the liberty of pouring himself from the bar.

Corvin sat beside him in one of the chairs, a little less smug with his hands folded in his lap. Kira raced across the room, jumping on the couch next to the *Leaf* so that he almost spilled his glass.

"We thought you'd been caught."

"Yeah, what the hell happened?" Max walked over with a little more dignity.

Kegan set his glass down as Kira bounced on the cushion next to him. "No idea. We had just made it into the second part of the vault corridor when the alarm bells sounded. Thought for sure we were toast, so we made a run for it. You can imagine our surprise when the alarm shut off with us still running free."

Ginger glanced at their hands, noticing that they didn't have their house rings on. "And you took off your rings so you wouldn't blow our cover if you were caught. That's why you weren't on the house line?"

Kegan leaned back with his hands behind his head. "We're really thinking like criminals now. Pretty smart, huh?"

"It really was, actually." Max sat down across from him. "It dawned on me way too late that the rings would blow our cover. I was starting to freak out."

"We all were," Farn added, leaning on the back of the couch behind Kira.

"I wish I could take credit, but it was all this guy's idea." Kegan hooked a thumb in Corvin's direction.

The reynard froze, avoiding eye contact for a second, then accepted the compliment with a nod. Then he leaned back and threw his feet up on the table in victory. The sight warmed Ginger's heart. It was nice to see the *Blade* resisting his meek tendencies and showing some pride.

"How did you both get away with Berwyn's people all running around?"

"Umm, we hid." Corvin deflated.

"I don't like the sound of that, umm." Max frowned.

"It wasn't a big deal." Kegan poked at his drink, pushing it along the table's surface nonchalantly. "We just ducked back into that shop on the first floor that you guys ditched us in."

"And?" Ginger raised an eyebrow.

Corvin took over, "We kind of hid behind the counter on the floor. The NPC just ignored us since we were on her side of the counter."

Kegan cleared his throat and swiped his hand back and forth near his throat, giving him the international signal to stop talking. Corvin's ears twitched as he glanced between the *Leaf* and the Lady of his house before he continued. "We dove behind the counter when someone came in to search the place. We were just lucky they didn't look down and that the NPC ignored us."

"No points for style, but at least you didn't get caught." Ginger laughed, picturing the two curled up together around the NPC's feet.

"Yeah, but more importantly," Kegan leaned forward, getting to the meat of the discussion, "if it wasn't us that set off the alarm, who the hell was it?"

Ginger shuddered, remembering the unfortunate *Breath* mage. "It was just some random *Breath* mage named Luka. Seemed to have infiltrated the Serpents and broken into the royal study. She got caught pretty fast though, so I doubt she found what she was looking for."

Max let out a defeated sigh. "And then Berwyn's *Shield* killed her with some overpowered contract that literally tore the health from her body without even touching—"

"Wait a sec," Kegan interrupted. "Was this Shield named Mack_the_Ripper by any chance?"

Max furrowed his brow. "I didn't check his full name, but Berwyn calls him Ripper, so probably."

"Crap, the Death Grip's here." Kegan slapped a hand against his head.

"What? You know him or something?" Farn asked.

"Not personally, but damn, this just got a lot worse." Kegan grabbed his drink and downed the last of it in one gulp. "He used to run in the same PVP circles I did. He wasn't much to worry about before he got that damn gauntlet, but man, after, he was pretty much unbeatable. The only reason I never got paired with him was because I wasn't considered a challenge. Eventually, no one was. That's when he stopped doing matches altogether, or more accurately, people stopped betting against him so the guys that ran the cages in Tartarus wouldn't let him fight. He sort of disappeared after that. I guess he found a new calling."

The room fell silent as that sunk in.

"I think I should fight him." Farn blurted out almost casually, getting puzzled looks from the entire room.

"I'm sorry, what?" Ginger questioned, having trouble comprehending what would prompt such an insane suggestion.

The *Shield* shrugged. "If we're worried he'll be a problem, then we should learn everything we can about him and whatever that Death Grip thing does. Maybe I can find a weakness if I challenge him."

"And what if he kills you?" Max threw out his hand in her direction.

"Then my death will probably kill the romantic mood that Berwyn is trying to build and buy Kira another night without him putting the moves on her." Farn patted the fairy on the head. Kira leaned into the gesture and nuzzled the woman's hand like a loving pet.

"Aww, thank you for the sentiment, but I still prefer that you not die for me."

"I don't like it," Ginger thought about the idea, "but we do need to learn about that Death Grip ability. So picking a fight with him might make sense."

"Maybe I should challenge Nix while we're at it." Max

leaned forward. "I'd like to know what she can do as well. Something about her has me worried."

"She seems harmless enough, but then again, she is a mercenary, so you never know." Ginger shrugged, then turned back to Kegan. "What did you guys find out about the vault's entry corridor?"

Both members of Lockheart's black-ops team shuddered in unison. Kegan spoke first.

"There's a puzzle lock at the entrance, and we're pretty sure the hallway fills with water if you get it wrong. Beyond that, we ran into twelve mid-level guard NPCs."

"Twelve?" Max's eyes widened.

"Yeah, we had to murder them. It wasn't fun."

"That's kind of impressive." Max gave a whistle.

"Yes, it was. We're pretty badass."

"Sure, sure, and after that?" Ginger skipped past the *Leaf's* boasting.

Kegan chuckled. "Oh, the second hall's a laser grid."

"Mana fence," Corvin corrected.

"Whatever."

Corvin pulled out his inspector and held it out to display a series of photos he'd taken. Ginger leaned over to see, the others crowding in behind her.

"Damn." Max rubbed at the scruff on his chin. "Think you two can get through it?"

"No way in hell." Kegan let out a mirthless laugh. "The beams are too close together for a full-sized player."

The room immediately turned to look at Kira.

"Blarg." The fairy slid lower in her seat. "It's not enough that I have be the honeypot, but now I gotta crawl around on a floor under a bunch of laser beams too."

"Mana beams," Corvin corrected.

Max laughed. "At least you'll be earning your cut."

"Yay." Kira rolled her head back and forth on the couch cushion. "One more thing to worry about."

"Actually, it's two things." Corvin swiped to a different image of a metal floor. "Recognize this?"

Ginger squinted at the picture. "No. Should we?"

"It's the same floor that's in the Fire Tomb. Kegan and I did it again when I first switched classes."

"Oh, now I remember." Max's eyes rolled up and to the side. "That's the floor that sets off a fire trap if you step on it."

"Wait, so I can't even touch the floor?" Kira sat up straight. "How is that gonna work?"

"Maybe, maybe not." Corvin fidgeted with his inspector. "The floor seems to have a tolerance, so a fairy might not weigh enough to set it off. I'm going to need to stop by the Fire Tomb to test that theory, though."

"I'll come help," Kegan stood abruptly. "I don't really want to be stuck on the roof by myself until logout. Can we get a teleport to Thrift? It's closest to the Tomb."

"Wait a sec." Ginger glowered at the pair. "What makes you think the pressure plate has a weight tolerance?"

"Umm," Corvin froze for a second, "because I kind of dropped my inspector on it, and it didn't go off."

Max snorted. "Yeah, that makes sense."

Ginger shook her head. "Well, on that note, I'm going to make a trip back to Fashion Souls and see what Larkin can do to hook us up with some beachwear. Think I could get a ride in the Cloudbreaker?"

Max got up. "Sure, I actually had something I wanted to ask Larkin about."

"Thanks. And hey, you can help me pick out something cute for these two." She winked at Kira and Farn. They both grimaced as Max made a show of rolling his eyes. Ginger grinned, noticing a pinkish hue that invaded his cheeks to betray him. Her chest warmed at the sight. He was still fun to tease.

Kira snapped open a caster to set up a teleport for the others while Farn remained where she was standing behind the sofa. For a moment, the *Shield* opened her mouth but then closed it again without saying anything.

"You want to go back and watch the movie, don't you?" Kira guessed.

Fan nodded sheepishly.

Kira laughed. "Okay, I'll join you after I teleport the guys. But let's go find a different theater. I've had enough of the palace for one night."

CHAPTER THIRTY-TWO

Max struggled to think of something to fill the silence as he walked next to Ginger through the alley that lead to Larkin's shop. They had seen each other pretty regularly in the last year but almost never alone. At least, he knew she wasn't interested in him. She might've teased him every now and then, but he could roll with it, knowing that she didn't actually mean anything by it.

He shoved his hands into his pockets, resigning to walk in silence all the way to Fashion Souls.

Ginger had other plans.

"So what says Lady of House Lockheart more—a tasteful one piece or something that shows everything?"

"Whatever you think is best." Max rubbed at the back of his neck as he escaped the question.

Ginger narrowed her eyes. "You know, it kinda defeats the purpose of asking your opinion if you don't answer."

Max forced himself to look straight into her eyes. "Go with less. You'll be more distracting to Berwyn's Serpents."

"I agree, just be sure you don't get distracted too. You might miss a shot or something if you're too busy with the view." She punctuated her warning by humming a couple notes.

"I'll be a perfect gentleman."

"Oh, really?"

"Absolutely."

"Not even a glance?"

"Of course not, I have too much respect for you."

She eyed him for a moment. "You're no fun."

"Sorry, we're friends. Checking you out might give me a really weird boner."

Ginger burst out laughing. "I take it back, you're still fun."

"I know."

"Well then, how about Kira?" She gave him a playful nudge. "What would you like to see her in?"

Max snorted. "A freaking parka if I have a say."

"Yeah, 'cause that will keep Berwyn interested. I was thinking something tempting that shows off her finest feature." Ginger thrust out her rear. "By which I mean her backside."

"Yeah, I got that. You're not subtle, and good luck getting her to wear it." Max thought about the prospect. "Watching her fight you tooth and nail would be entertaining for me, though."

"You might be right. I should ask Larkin to make her something cute rather than sexy. That would fit her better, and she might not put up too much of a fight if we're reasonable." Ginger tapped one finger to her mouth. "But there's no way I'm gettin' her a one piece. That would be blasphemy."

Max thought about it from a practical standpoint. "Just make sure not to get her anything with frills or loose strings."

"That is weirdly specific." She raised an eyebrow.

"I mean for the heist." He shook his head. "She's going to need something form-fitting in order to get through the laser grid without crossing a beam."

"Mana fence," Ginger corrected.

Max ignored her. "Kira can't wear her gear for that. So I figured she would feel more comfortable in a swimsuit than crawling through in her underwear."

Ginger chewed her bottom lip. "That's… really considerate of you."

Max shrugged. "She's been going through some stuff after everything that happened last year. I don't blame her. She did almost die. Plus, I'm a little worried about the direction this mission has headed in, so I don't want to make it harder on her if I can help it."

Ginger stopped walking for a moment before jogging a few steps to catch up. "Okay, but now that we've covered the fact that you have no interest in seeing me and Kira in something sexy, I have an important question." She grinned and rubbed her hands together. "How much of Farn would you like to see?"

"What's that supposed to mean?" Max asked, despite knowing exactly what she meant.

"I know she's acting as Kira's guard, but she should still get to enjoy the beach. I mean, when are we going to be back there? And you know, you might want to take the opportunity to find out what she looks like under that armor."

"I don't think she would appreciate me ogling her." Max crossed his arms. "Hell, she'd probably kick my ass."

"True, true." Ginger waggled her eyebrows. "But you are going to ask her out at some point, right?"

Max just let out a long sigh and stared up at the night sky visible between the buildings. "Kira was just bugging me about this. Do I really need to get it from you too?"

"I'm sorry that we bug you, but we care about you both. Is it wrong to want to give you two a little push in the right direction?" Ginger gave him an affectionate punch him in the shoulder.

Max stayed quiet for a moment, deciding whether or not to let her in on the real reason he still hadn't asked out Farn. He glanced to the woman beside him, her eyes pleading with him. It was obvious she meant well, and he did trust her, even if she was a bit of a busybody. Case in point, the current conversation.

He furrowed his brow. Ginger was actually the smartest person he knew. Last year, when he'd been nursing his bruised ego and terrified of losing his best friend, she had been the one that said the words he needed to hear. He respected her for that, so maybe she could help him with the dilemma that he had been worrying about alone for months. It would actually be good to have an accomplice.

He took a deep breath.

"Okay, for starters, I will not be asking Farn out, ever."

Ginger flinched at the words, like each one hurt. "But I thought you liked her?" Her gaze fell to the ground, crestfallen.

He exhaled slowly. "I do like her. She's one of the best women I know. She's smart, cool, and really fun to be around."

"But?"

"But I can't ask her out. Not when I'm not the right person for her."

"What?" She stopped dead in place, then tilted to the side.

Max placed a hand on her shoulder. "Okay, what I'm going to tell you is something that you can't tell anyone."

Her eyes grew wide, suddenly flooded with a curious sparkle. She dragged two of her fingers across her lips and twisted them as if turning a key. Max braced himself.

"As much as I hate to admit this, I have spent enough time in social situations to know when I'm a third wheel."

"And?" she asked, sounding confused at the sudden change in direction.

"And in the last year, that's exactly how I feel when I hang out with Kira and Farn."

Ginger leaned closer. "Wait, what?"

Max thought back over the year, feeling a warm ache in his chest. "For example, remember the other night when you three started Lockheart together. Wouldn't you say that the two of them are a little too in sync?"

Ginger stared off into space for a moment. "Okay, yeah, they do finish each other's sentences and play off each other well. But that doesn't mean—"

"Did you see how Kira snuggled into Farn's hand back in the suite when she touched her hair? Have you seen that little goon that happy without food in front of her? Or how protective Farn is of her?"

Ginger's mouth dropped open. "Do you think they have feelings for each other?"

"Maybe," Max sighed, "but I don't think they've realized it. Kira seems dead set on avoiding her personal issues to a point where she's sworn off dating, and Farn is just an awkward mystery."

Ginger's cheeks swelled like she might explode as a growl erupted from her throat. "Oh, that stupid little fairy, why can't she just be honest with herself? And why the hell has she been trying to help me get you together with Farn?"

"Mostly because she is an idiot and just wants to make her friends happy." Max lowered his head. "I've been single for so long; I think she's prioritizing being a wingman to help me out. Either way, Kira and Farn have a minefield of problems standing between them, what with one of them having a different body in the real world. I'm not even sure Kira knows what to identify as."

Without warning, Ginger slapped him in the arm, continuing to do so repeatedly.

"Hey! What did I do?"

"You could have brought this up with Kira at any point to help her work through things. But instead, you let months go by because god forbid you talk about each other's feelings. Not to mention that you never asked Farn out because of the bro code. You're all a bunch of idiots."

"Sorry. I didn't know what to do, and I want them to be happy too." Max rubbed his arm, noting the loss of a small amount of health.

"Fine, I guess that is pretty sweet of you." Ginger let her arms fall to her sides. "But you're still a bunch of idiots."

"Why are you so hell-bent on getting people together anyway?"

Ginger's shoulders fell. "I guess because it lets me live vicariously. I missed my chance at love already, so I try to push my friends ahead before they do too."

Max scoffed. "Now who's the idiot? You're only," he paused to do the math in his head, "nine years older than me. I doubt you've missed your shot at romance."

She smiled, though her eyes still seemed sad. "I supposed I'm not that old, but I've had two kids. I love them, don't get me wrong, but it didn't do much for my figure. I don't exactly look like this in the real world." She held her hands out to draw attention to her body.

"And I'm bald in the real world. Who cares?"

She snorted a laugh. "True, but most guys aren't looking for an instant family."

"I guess, but your kids are cool, so you did something right there."

"As long as they don't start a life of crime now that I've led them down a dark path."

"Probably keep an eye on Piper. She's a little too eager to help with this heist."

"She's always been too devious for her own good." Ginger gave a weak laugh before continuing, "When it comes down to it, I may be taking a break, but I did work at a brothel for years. I personally don't feel like there's anything wrong with that, but it doesn't exactly make for good first date conversation. Some people are still a little repressed, if you know what I mean."

"Meh," Max shrugged, not really sure what he thought about it. "That doesn't really change who you are."

"And who am I?"

"Someone I respect," Max answered without hesitation.

"Thanks." A smile found its way back to her face. "I'm sorry I called you an idiot. You can say the right thing sometimes."

"Tell that to my love life."

"Well, if you're not going after Farn, I'm sure someone will be happy to be with you." Ginger rested her head on his shoulder with her eyes closed. "I might even snatch you up." She smirked and jabbed him in the ribs. "Even if you are bald."

"Ouch, low blow." Max feigned an injury.

They shared a laugh that Max found strangely comforting. He hadn't really realized it before, but Ginger was actually the one person he was most honest with. She never held anything back with him, and there was something to be said for that. He appreciated it.

Suddenly, Ginger's face fell as she raised a finger to point behind him.

"Nice try," Max resisted whatever prank she had in mind. "I'm not falling for that."

She stepped away, her bottom lip trembling in fear as a shadow grew across the cobblestone from behind him.

"Oh damn, I'm not going to like what's behind me, am I?"

Ginger shook her head "No."

"Great," Max muttered as he reached for his pistols.

The shadow behind him stretched further until they both were shrouded in darkness. A chorus of voices, like nails on a chalkboard, cried from behind him.

"Fashion!"

CHAPTER THIRTY-THREE

"What the shit is that?" Max leaped backward as a mass of writhing bodies slammed into the ground where he had been standing. Hundreds of tiny hands reached for him, many holding tiny knives or scissors.

"Fashion!"

"It's the dolls," Ginger screamed as she fired a grappling line at one of the buildings that bracketed the alleyway that lead to Larkin's shop. She shot upward just as the mass of creaking ball-joints swirled toward her, snagging her ankle before she could escape.

"I knew those things were creepy." Max took aim and fired at the glob of porcelain bodies that was climbing up Ginger's leg.

The beast collapsed, sending dolls falling to the ground. They picked themselves up from the stone and started running toward him.

"What did we do to piss off Larkin?" he shouted as he kicked away a pair of tiny assassins dressed in Victorian dresses. More piled on, tripping him as he tried to run. He hit the stone just as a doll in a sparkling, white gown climbed atop his chest.

Max did a double take at the thing, it's violet eyes gleaming with murderous intent through silver locks of hair. It looked like a miniature Kira. He swatted it away.

"What the hell is wrong with Larkin?" Max kicked himself free and stood up.

"I don't know. The guy likes dolls." Ginger clung to a wall. "It's some kind of weird hobby."

"That's the truth— oh my god."

Pocket-sized Kira leaped into his face, poking him with what looked like a hat pin. Max grabbed her with one hand, ignoring the spikes of damage he took as she stabbed him in the wrist.

"Damn it, stop doing that." Max aimed his pistol directly in the creature's face but felt weird about pulling the trigger. Instead, he just holstered his gun and snatched the doll's hairpin away. Ginger dropped down next to him just as the rest of the dolls were reforming into a mass of shabby hands.

"Shit, does that one look like Kira?" Ginger looked sideways at the tiny but considerably more violent version of the fairy.

"Yeah. It's way more annoying too." Max tossed it to the *Coin*.

"What the hell?" Ginger cried as it climbed into her hair and started trying to rip it out. She ran in a circle before attempting to smash it into a wall, doing more damage to herself than the little monster.

Max took aim at the blob of dolls and fired repeatedly, stopping them from reforming into the giant monstrosity that they were before. He couldn't tell if he was doing any real damage, but at least he was slowing the things down. Then the slides of his pistols locked back empty.

"Shit!"

Max began the process of reloading both guns as the heap of bodies surged together into a towering behemoth.

Suddenly, a familiar voice shouted from the door of Larkin's shop, "What are you two doing loitering out here? Get inside before the marionettes stab you to death." Larkin held open the door. "And stop shooting my handiwork."

Max made a break for the door, followed by Ginger close at his heels. The mass of dolls slithered after them, the chorus of voices screeching.

"Fashion!"

Max looked back, immediately wishing he hadn't. Tiny limbs worked together to propel the writhing mass of nightmare fuel forward at breakneck speed.

"Must run faster."

Ginger sped up, ignoring the miniature Kira clinging to her head and shouting, "Fashion," in a squeaky voice as it waved around a fist-full of her hair.

Together they dove through the door, Larkin slamming it behind them just as a tidal wave of bodies slammed into the shop window. Hundreds of faces pressed against the glass as Max and Ginger clung to one another on the floor of the entryway.

Miniature Kira climbed back up onto Max's chest, squealing a furious battle cry. He swatted her into the empty shelves, then glared up at Larkin.

"What the hell, man? I thought you were on our side."

The man just stood there looking down at them.

"Hurry up and get upstairs. You have no idea what you've done."

Larkin dropped his inspector on the table of his crafting studio. Checkpoint's message boards lit up its surface. Ginger took one look at the screen and immediately clasped a hand over her mouth.

"Oh no…"

"Oh no is right." Larkin picked up the pane of glass and handed it to Max. "When I said your house should stand out, I didn't think you all would take that advice so literally."

The bottom dropped out of Max's stomach as soon as he saw the title of the first post.

[Where did House Lockheart come from?]

Max scrolled further.

There were dozens more like it.

Many speculated how a house as unique as theirs had stayed hidden. Others questioned why they had chosen to reveal themselves now. The fact that they had been invited to the Jewel of the Sea had even sparked a debate as to whose side they were on.

He kept scrolling, finding scores of players arguing about what it all meant that they were loyal to the fallen city of Rend. It seemed that they had accidentally reignited the debate that had surrounded the enormous dungeon for years.

A post with over a thousand comments caught Max's eye. All it contained was a photo of Kira twirling around Berwyn on the dance floor surrounded by sparkling pixie dust. Apparently, that dress had made quite the impact. There were entire threads on it, wondering where she had purchased it. Larkin snatched back his inspector while Max was still reading and set it down on the table.

"I made the mistake of commenting on one of the posts that I had made Kira's gown." He gestured to the dress form in the corner that now wore the sparkling, white garment. "It was a moment of weakness for me. It is one of the finest pieces I've ever made. So I was proud to see so many people admiring it." He dropped his hand back to his side. "But now my inbox has been flooded with hundreds of requests, and customers have been showing up nonstop. I'd have a line down the alley and out into the street if my shop was easier to find. As it is, I've had to increase the aggro of my dolls downstairs just in case one of my clients has a case of loose lips."

"Yeah, thanks for that, by the way," Max grumbled.

"Sorry, but it really was necessary."

"And was this thing necessary?" Ginger held up a birdcage that now held the miniature version of Kira clawing at the bars.

"Yes, well, I had some leftover fabric from Kira's gown, and I felt inspired. Sue me." Larkin tossed a scrap of fabric over the little prisoner. "She should go dormant if she doesn't see anyone for a bit." The cage rattled back and forth for a minute before going silent.

"Anyway," Larkin picked up the birdcage and placed it on a shelf, "thanks to your antics over in Reliqua, my inbox has been flooded with requests."

"Isn't getting more requests for work a good thing?" Max leaned on the table. "You should make more money, right?"

"I make enough money already, and besides, I don't craft items for just anyone. I'm an artist, and I prefer to work with the best quality materials as possible." He ran his hand through the folds of a piece of stray cloth. Then he gestured to Ginger. "The canvas is just as important as what you put on it."

"I'm not sure if I should take that as a compliment or not." Ginger shifted uncomfortably.

"You should. I don't give out many." Larkin shot her a wink.

Max tugged at the bottom of his vest, understanding a little more about the man that gave it to him. "Thanks for the compliment, I guess."

"Not you, Max." Larkin waved away his words. "You're just a guy I can unload my hand-me-downs on to."

"Oh." Max fidgeted the strap of his shoulder holster. "I kind of thought that might be the case."

The eccentric crafter grinned. "Oh, don't look so morose. You look great." He then spun on Ginger. "But you! You are the Lady of House Lockheart. How do you expect to impress anyone in this?" He tugged on the end of the short cloak she wore.

She looked down at the garment. "What's wrong with this? I'm a *Coin*, it makes me look stealthy, and I can hide items under it." She rummaged around for a second, producing a handful of small explosives that she no doubt had stolen from a shop.

Larkin scoffed and started pulling the cloak up over her head. "Nope, you can do better than this. Thanks to your high-profile escapades, you represent me now. I can't have you parading around in something so basic."

"Hey, ask before you pull someone's gear off." She squirmed.

"Sorry, but I've spent all day working on something special for you." Larkin tossed the cloak to the floor like a discarded piece of trash.

Ginger stood, looking shocked and disheveled, her hair sticking up on one side from having her hood removed. The fashion-obsessed *Rage* took a moment to brush it back down with his hand. He took a step back and leaned his head to the side.

"Good enough."

Suddenly, he turned and raced into a closet, leaving Max and Ginger alone to stare awkwardly at each other. A moment later, Larkin burst back into the room with something draped over his arm.

"I think you're going to like this." He beamed with pride as he dropped a dark gray frock coat over her shoulders and pushed her toward the mirror. "Now, this is how the Lady of House Lockheart should dress."

"That is pretty badass." Max nodded in agreement as Ginger stood there with her mouth open.

She shoved her arms through the sleeves and ran her fingers down the row of silver buttons that lined the front. One sleeve was cut short to display her party readout with a small cape, bearing their house crest, hanging off her side to cover her arm. "I look like a pirate." She spun around to check the fit, adjusting its hood and flipping the collar up as she winked at her reflection. "A sexy lady pirate."

"Yes, certainly, but that's not the best part." Larkin held the side of the coat open and gestured to the lining. Stripes of two different shades of green ran through the interior of the garment. "This is what is left of your dress from the night before. Which means—"

"That it has the same passive Venom Bite ability!" Ginger clapped her hands excitedly.

"See, told you you'd like it. Also, the defense is much better than whatever that cloak you had on before had. Each of those buttons was made from a mimic tooth that I infused with five different types of ore. So right now, that coat is giving you the same protection as a set of plate mail." He strolled back to his work table, looking pretty damn pleased with himself.

Ginger admired the coat a bit more, then grabbed Max by his tie. "Avast, I claim this wench as my bride." A smile spread across her face that looked more carefree than usual.

Max accepted his fate, letting her shake him about until she got bored.

"You done?"

The *Coin* straightened his tie before letting go. "I am, thank you."

Larkin shook his head. "Now that you look a little more appropriate for your title, let's talk swimsuits?"

Ginger threw herself into a chair with one arm slung over the back like a buccaneer lounging in a tavern. "Yes, I was hoping for something similar to our dresses from before but, you know, covering less."

"I can do that; I have some leftover material that will work for yours. Kira's will be a little more difficult to find a way to incorporate the morning stars into something so much smaller than a dress."

"It has to be completely form-fitting too, for, umm… reasons," Max added.

Larkin eyed him suspiciously.

"Sorry. We need Kira to fit through somewhere, so there can't be anything hanging off of her. And she'll have to wear her bathing suit most of the time under her regular gear so she can strip down when the time comes."

Larkin tapped his fingers on the table for a second, then grabbed pad of paper and started sketching. "That gives me an idea. I've never tried it, but maybe I can set it so that her swimsuit takes up her undergarment slot instead of an armor slot. That way, she can keep the extra thousand mana and its regeneration rate no matter what she wears on top of it."

Max leaned on the table, trying his best to hold in a laugh. "So what you're saying is that you're going to make Kira some magic underpants?"

Larkin smirked. "That gives me another idea of how to get all those morning stars in there." He stopped sketching and glanced across the table at Ginger. "You would describe Kira as a unique character, yes?"

"To put it mildly."

"And now that she's all over the message boards as part of House Lockheart, would it be appropriate to think of her as somewhat of a house mascot?"

Ginger laughed. "I guess that would be accurate."

Larkin nodded with a smile and continued sketching. "Okay, while I finish this, do you have any requests for Farnsworth?"

"Just something comfortable would be good," Ginger said, giving Max a wink. He rolled his eyes.

Larkin continued to sketch. "That's easy enough. I can have these ready and sent to you by the time you log on tomorrow night. So you may as well leave me to it."

"Actually, I have one more request." Max tapped the skull tattoo on his wrist to open his stat-sleeve. He navigated to his inventory list and selected an item. An oversized, dusty robe materialized in his hand, its ends in tatters.

A parting gift from the Nightmare of Death the year before.

It felt heavy, reminding him of the fight that he'd received it from, the fight where he had missed a shot and wasted a powerful contract in the process. The one that had taught him a hard lesson about himself. It seemed right that he kept it close to stop him from making the same mistakes.

"Oh my god, you kept that?" Ginger placed a hand over her mouth.

"Yeah, it didn't seem right to throw it out. Even if I can't use it for anything." He placed the robe on the table. "Have you ever seen anything like this, and can you make anything out of it? Its description is just a bunch of question marks."

"Where did you get this?" Larkin immediately dropped his sketchbook and grabbed the fabric. "Was it from a rare monster? Something one of a kind?"

"You could say that." Max took a step back, not expecting the crafter to be so interested. "It's the Robe of Death; it was a Nightmare fight hidden in Rend. We were the only players to ever face the boss as part of a unique quest that put us through hell last year."

Larkin arched an eyebrow. "Rend again? There seems to be a thread of destiny between your house and that city. Interesting."

"I'm not sure about destiny, but am I to take from your interest to say that you know what this is?"

Larkin poured over the material, checking its description with his inspector. "It's an enemy-class item. I have only encountered one of these before, dropped by a rare monster. Though, I get the feeling that this item is more powerful, having come from a Nightmare."

"So it's like a contract item?"

Larkin shook his head. "It's far more than that. Whatever item I craft with this will bond to your character and grow as you level like a second character class. With enough time and experience, it could give you a whole new set of skills." He tore his gaze away from the robe and looked straight into Max's eyes. "I take it back. You're a more interesting canvas than I thought."

CHAPTER THIRTY-FOUR

NIGHT FOUR: THE TURN

Farn stood in the corner of the palace suite, struggling not to grin as Ginger offered Kira what could only be described as a work of art. Larkin had outdone himself.

"You can't be serious." The fairy tilted her head to the side like she was observing something otherworldly.

"Oh, I assure you I'm quite serious." Ginger held up the white pair of bikini bottoms, stretching them playfully.

"What the hell? Why does Farn get a one-piece and I get that?"

"I'm happy with mine." Farn admired the sensible bathing suit that Larkin had sent over. It matched the color scheme of her new armor.

Ginger smirked. "Oh, I'm sorry, would you prefer to see Farn in something more revealing?"

Farn's ears perked up at the question.

"No," Kira snapped back, driving a spike through Farn's hopes.

Ompf, right in the feelings. Farn clutched her swimsuit to her chest to absorb the emotional impact. Though, despite her answer, Kira did turn a rather cute shade of pink that soothed away the ache in Farn's heart. *Maybe there was interest after all?* She shook off the thought as Kira continued to argue.

"But that covers less than my underwear."

Ginger shrugged. "It's not my fault you wear granny panties."

Kira winced.

"You don't like the word panties, do you? That's adorable." The *Coin* stretched the offending swimsuit and fired it at Kira like a slingshot. It hit the little mage in her cute, pink face.

Kira snatched the garment off the ground. "Oh shut up, a lot of people don't like… that word."

Farn let out a laugh before covering her mouth with one hand and adding a quick, "Sorry."

Kira turned even redder, then plopped down into a sofa and crossed her arms.

"Okay, fine." Ginger's tone shifted, sounding a little more nurturing. "I get it. You're not wild about wearing something like this in public. But you'll get to play in the water, which I know you'll like if you give it a chance. Then you'll forget all about what you're wearing. Plus, it will give Berwyn a more enticing view while still having Farn close by to cock block him if need be."

"That's true. I am excellent at ruining the mood." Farn wished she had something more impressive to boast about, but there it was, her claim to fame.

Kira smiled but continued to sit with her arms crossed in protest.

Ginger handed her the top that came with her bathing suit. "Okay, here's the deal. We can argue about this for the next half hour and eventually give you a guilt trip about how this is important for the heist. Or, you can just go in the washroom now and change so you can get down there and start having fun in the water sooner."

Kira sat silently for a moment before letting out a defeated sigh. "Fine, but I'm going down the hall to find a quick-change panel. Getting undressed for real still weirds me out."

Ginger rolled her eyes at the fairy. "Oh, be a grown up and get changed. We can't have you roaming the halls looking for a quick-change panel when we have our own suite. That would be suspicious, and besides, Farn and I are going to get changed in here. So unless you want the awkwardness of us getting naked in front of you, then you should probably get moving now."

"Oh yeah?" Kira stayed sitting. "I dare you."

Farn's eyes widened at the thought. Ginger shrugged and started unbuckling the clasps on her corset.

"Okay then, this is happening. Farn, start stripping."

Farn was tempted to go for it, her heart racing at the thought. Guilt immediately pushed the desire from her mind, as if taking advantage of the situation would have been wrong. She sighed.

I would have chickened out anyway. I am so not ready for that. Farn gestured for Ginger to proceed without her. "Nah, I think you have that covered."

The *Coin* dropped her corset to the floor, then paused, giving the stubborn fairy a chance to escape the room before things got uncomfortable.

Kira stayed put and let out a harrumph.

"Suit yourself." Ginger pulled off her shirt without hesitation.

"Oh god, fine, fine." Kira blurted as she raced into the attached washroom, slamming the door behind her.

"Well, I should have done that sooner." Ginger stood proud with her hands on her hips. "Never underestimate the power of boobs."

"Ah... yeah," Farn turned toward the balcony and unbuckled her armor.

A few minutes later, they were both ready for the beach. Ginger draped herself over the chaise, looking comfortable in the little green two-piece that Larkin had sent her. She sat back up a second later and eyed the washroom door.

"What the hell is Kira doing in there? It doesn't take this long to get changed." She marched over to the door and knocked as loud as she could. "Hey, quit looking at your lady parts in the mirror and get out here!"

A fairy-like squeak came from the room, followed by the sound of someone bumping into things. The mage emerged a moment later, avoiding making eye contact.

"Everything how you expected? No surprises?" Ginger swept her gaze up and down the fairy's body.

Kira simply crossed her arms and turned up her nose. "Like you wouldn't look."

"True." Ginger nodded. "I'd do a whole lot more than look if it was me."

"It's good to know which one of us has more self-control."

"That's fair. I suppose there is a reason I have two kids," Ginger commented on her own lack of will power, "but more importantly." She twirled her finger in a circular motion.

The fairy groaned and turned around.

Farn immediately lost her composure, laughing so hard that she had to lean on the furniture. Larkin really had outdone himself. A design of morning star crystals sparkled across the fairy's rear end to form Lockheart's house crest, a keyhole at its center.

"What the hell is that?" Farn blurted out mid-snort.

"Kira's our mascot. We have to make sure everyone knows it." Ginger smirked.

"Ha ha, very funny. I have a heart on my butt. Let's all have a nice laugh about it." Kira spun back around.

"Sorry." Farn calmed down, letting out a few more chuckles, partly to hide how interested she was to see a little more of Kira.

The mage planted herself back onto the couch. "You know what, I'm fine with it. It may not cover much, but this has the same stats as my gown from the party. So I have an extra thousand mana stored on my ass. Wearing this might be embarrassing, but it's worth it." She dropped her voice to a low grumble. "Although I don't love the implication of the keyhole back there."

"Oh, that's the best part." Ginger threw herself back down on the chaise. "It's like an invitation."

"Don't remind me." Kira slouched into a pose that could only be described as unladylike.

The room quieted down as the pressure of the mission settled in. They had already come so far, mostly thanks to Berwyn's interest in Kira, who had proved to be more than a little distracting. Now, the question was how long could they keep the charade going and what Kira might have to do to keep their cover.

Farn shuddered, not wanting to think about it.

The question had been weighing on her mind all day. If it was Ginger, she wouldn't have worried. Seduction was a way of life for the *Coin*, but putting Kira in that position was something else entirely. The thought turned Farn's stomach. She had pined for her for months, so of course she wasn't comfortable with the situation. Even if there was no hope of being with Kira, Farn couldn't stand the idea of letting Berwyn lay a finger on her.

She shoved the thought down before it took her over. Then, as if sensing the tension in the room, Ginger brought it all to the surface.

"Sorry to bring this up," the *Coin* gave Kira a weak smile, "but are you okay with everything?"

"Like what?"

"Like being thrown into this honeypot. Things have gone well so far, but it's mostly been flirting and dancing so far. I know none of us want to think about it, but what if things go further?"

"We don't need to talk about this." Farn squeezed the couch cushion. "It won't come to that."

"But what if it does?"

"It won't."

"I'm sorry for starting all this," Ginger's voice grew quiet, "but there's only so much we can do to stall without blowing our cover. It is possible that we'll run out of options, and we all know where this road ends. So the question is, do we quit the mission if that happens or do we stand aside?" She let her eyes fall to Kira. "Would you actually want to go through with it?"

The question hung in the air. The meaning of the word 'it' was clear, even if Ginger didn't spell it out. Farn wanted to cover her ears so that she didn't have to listen to the conversation.

Kira sat up straight and rested her hands in her lap, staring at the floor. "Would I go through with it?" She sat silently for a moment. "Well, I am a guy, sort of. So thinking about it from that perspective, the choice is obvious."

"Well, yeah," Farn took solace in the other fact that she had tried her best to ignore, "obviously you wouldn't sleep with him."

"I would," Kira stated without hesitation, with a tone of finality in her voice.

"What?" Farn flinched as if she'd been struck by the words. It certainly wasn't the response that she expected.

Ginger's mouth fell open. "Really?"

"I'd be an idiot not to. If I'm gonna be a man about this, then this is just an avatar. Placing that much importance on my body would be crazy. It doesn't matter what happens to it. It's not me."

Farn's heart nearly broke from the way the fairy spoke so cavalierly about herself, like the woman she had fallen for was worthless. She dropped into a chair, her legs giving out from the shock.

"Look, it's a lot of money." Kira shrugged, clearly forcing a laugh. "I'm not so delusional to think that I don't have a price. And nine million in hard is one hell of a payout. That's plenty for each of us. It's the kind of money that can change our lives. It would be selfish of me not to do whatever it takes to make sure we all win."

Farn covered her mouth. She would have thrown up if the system had allowed it. The thought that Kira would leap into the fire for the sake of her friends was too much. What's worse, she was right. Farn hadn't valued herself any more. She'd done plenty of things she regretted, back when she was still trying to pretend to be something she wasn't.

"I guess I've done more for less." Ginger sat up a little. "I'm comfortable with my choices, but I understand where you're coming from."

Farn's clenched her teeth until her jaw hurt. Then she closed her eyes and took a breath, struggling to remain reasonable. "But what if you…" she hesitated, "what if the you here is more than just an avatar? What if you think of things as Kira?"

The fairy fell silent, and for a moment, her eyes welled up. "I don't know." Her gaze fell the floor as she fidgeted in her seat, her legs pressed together. "Thinking as myself, it's just so personal. Letting someone…" She trailed off and shook her head. "I don't want to, but I'm not sure which me is right."

Farn couldn't help but feel that there was something more honest about that answer. Maybe it was just wishful thinking. Ginger stood from her seat, signaling that the uncomfortable conversation had gone on long enough.

"Whatever you decide, don't push yourself. It's your decision. Everyone will support you no matter what you do. Okay?"

Kira nodded but said nothing.

"And if you want to get out of this, all you have to do is ask." Farn leaned on the sofa behind her to make sure she didn't feel alone. "I'll stab the first person I see. That should really put a damper on the mood."

"It's nice to know that you have such violent tendencies." The fairy snorted. "Thanks."

Ginger tied a thin piece of fabric around her waist like a skirt and made her way to the door. "I guess we should let Max back in. He has been surprisingly quiet, waiting in the hall." She adjusted her swimsuit top. "I almost want to reward him for being so patient."

CHAPTER THIRTY-FIVE

- New Message -
From: Larkin
To: MaxDamage24
Subject: An interesting canvas indeed

I honestly can't believe what you brought me last night. That ratty old cloth was more of a challenge to work with than you might think. There were so many tears and holes, not to mention it had been worn thin all over. Not much of it was even salvageable.

But you're in luck.

You've got me.

I treated it with several different recipes to reinforce it to the point that I could work with it and ended up with just enough to craft a scarf. However, it was too basic for the system and wouldn't accept it as an equipable item as it was, so I had to get creative.

I dyed it black with the ink from a mind flayer, and yes, that was hard to get. I tracked the monster down in the ice caverns near Rend. I could have gone somewhere else, but I wanted this item to mean something for you. It had to be Rend. Long story short, I got sprayed by the damn things multiple times and ended up with an insanity ailment that messed with my vision and hearing for almost an hour. During that time, I either killed a number of ice poplos on my way back through Rend or a couple dozen low-level players.

I fear it was the latter judging by the fact that a few of the poplos I killed dropped human bones. But that is the price we pay for art, and I was able to grind the bones into a powder that made a pretty nice ink. I used it to add a subtle design that I think fits the item. I topped it all off with a pin to keep it from falling off.

All in all, I am quite proud of this item. It is one of the most interesting pieces that I've crafted. I will let you see it for yourself, though. I wouldn't want to ruin the surprise, but after reading the description, there may be more to this item than just a unique drop. I'm not sure how, but it may have been meant for you.

-Larkin

Message Attachment,
    Accessory - slot, neck.
    Accept?

Max stood in the hall of the palace while Ginger and the rest got ready for the beach. His pen hovered over the word 'accept'.

Larkin had done it. He'd actually made something of Death's robe. Max had carried the thing around for the last year, unable to figure out what to do with it. Crafting had never been his strength, so meeting Larkin had been a godsend. That man was a treasure, worth his weight in hard to be sure.

Max drew a check mark on the page, feeling a sense of anticipation swell as his pen scratched across the paper.

Out of nowhere, a system chime sounded in his ear, somehow different from any other. It was deeper, as if filled with power. The message text faded away only to be replaced by a flood of system messages.

Max's hand shook, almost dropping his journal.

NEW ITEM RECEIVED: THE MANTLE OF DEATH
Description: Death is coming for us all. Thus, the world must have a Reaper. By defeating the Nightmare of Death, you have agreed to take on its mantle.

This item grants the wearer a unique sub-class that may be activated by wearing this item in its active state. While active, all main class skills will deactivate and be replaced by any unlocked sub-class skills. Main-class weapons will remain effective, however, new weapons may become available as they are unlocked.

REAPER SUB-CLASS DISCOVERED!
Class Description: Wield the power of Death. This sub-class will consume HP while in use.

NEW SKILL UNLOCKED: UNBREAKABLE DEFENSE
Call forth the blades of Death to deflect any incoming projectile attack. Does not guard against area of effect abilities, non-physical, or magic attacks. Activated by holding one's breath.

NEW TITLE ACQUIRED: PALE RIDER

Max gasped as the black fabric materialized in his hands. A subtle, gray pattern of bones and teeth flowed across the scarf, one end holding a silver pin bearing a skeletal hand.

He stared at it for a solid minute, admiring the craftsmanship. Then he ripped off his necktie and threw it in one of the potted plants that lined the hall. *Good riddance,* he thought as he wrapped the scarf around his neck. The pin on the end shifted to grip the rest of the scarf in its boney fingers.

Larkin may not have been able to salvage much of the original material, but there was still more than enough to cover his neck and shoulders. He waited for the item to activate, excited to try out his new sub-class.

Then nothing happened.

"Any time now." Max tugged on the garment. Still nothing. "Well, crap, leave it to me to get the most badass item in Noctem and not know how to use it." He leaned back against the door of the suite and folded his arms.

"At least I look cool– oh no!" he shouted as the door he leaned on opened.

CHAPTER THIRTY-SIX

Max spilled into the suite, hitting the floor with a cartoonish thud. Ginger stood over him, dressed in a green bikini with a piece of fabric tied around her waist. The view felt like he was looking up her skirt.

He shut his eyes tight out of respect.

"You know I'm wearing a bathing suit right? You can look at me."

He peeked out from under one eyelid. "Yeah, but it's, um, a revealing angle."

"I don't mind." She made no motion to move, staring down at him with a playful smile. "Nice scarf. Is it everything you hoped it would be?"

"Yes and no." He opened his eyes and tried to ignore the view altogether.

"Why so vague?"

"Because…"

"Because why?"

"I don't know how to use it."

"That sounds about right."

"Yeah, well, I take it y'all are ready to go?" Max pushed himself up off the floor.

Kira and Farn got up from the couch, answering his question by walking toward the door. The *Shield* picked up her sword and held it at her side, apparently still acting as the fairy's guard. It looked entirely out of place alongside the tall woman's simple one piece.

"You might as well store your sword in your inventory. There's no need for both of us to stand guard. I doubt anyone is going to start anything with us, and I'll be ready just in case." Max made an attempt at sounding cool. In truth, he was trying to be a good wingman by giving the pair an opening to spend time at the beach. Maybe something might click.

"Thanks." Farn tapped a few options on her stat-sleeve, and the sword vanished.

"We should be on our way then." Ginger threw her new coat over her shoulders.

"Wish I had a nice, big coat to hide under," Kira grumbled, holding her arms in an awkward self-embrace. Before she had a chance to complain further, Farn draped her cape across the fairy's shoulders like a gentleman on a date.

"Ompf!" Kira immediately fell to the floor with a crash.

"Oh, sorry!" Farn dropped to her knees to help. "I forgot how much the scale armor weighs."

"I'm fine. I'm fine." Kira shifted around under the cape, hoisted herself back up, and pulled the cape around her shoulders. "I appreciate the gesture. Just wasn't expecting it is all. Thanks."

"Sorry." Farn cringed and covered her face.

Max shook his head, then glanced to Ginger as if to say, 'see what I mean?'. The *Coin* gave him a somewhat frustrated nod, then stepped out the door without any further comment.

◆———————◆ ◆———————◆

The sound of waves met Max's ears as soon as they entered the pyramid below. He took up a position at the rear so that he could keep an eye on the party as they made their way across the patio area.

Fire pots and torches lined the beach, blanketing the sand in a warm, inviting glow. Flickering light glistened across the water's surface as a relaxed atmosphere settled in, unlike the night before. Max couldn't help but notice the others glancing at the spot where Luka had been executed.

Kira leaned close to Ginger. "So, how do I go about luring Berwyn?"

The *Coin* hesitated. "You know, you're a little different than most women."

"Obviously," Max commented.

Ginger glowered back at him before continuing, "I think your appeal is just as much about who you are as it is about how you look. So just have fun. That's really when you shine. If Berwyn stops to watch, then we'll know he's hooked. And probably show off that sparkling butt of yours."

Max arched an eyebrow, wondering what the *Coin* meant by sparkling.

Suddenly, a voice called from a distance behind. He looked back to find Nix running toward them, swinging a small bag and wearing a frilly two-piece under a short, hooded robe that looked like part of a *Venom* mage's starter set. It obviously didn't match her class, but it functioned well enough as a coverup.

Once she arrived on the patio, Nix took a full thirty seconds to catch her breath. The ridiculous reynard bent over panting and held up one hand as if to say, 'hang on a sec'. "You going swimming?" she got out between breaths. "Mind if I come?" Her ears stuck straight up in a way that seemed hopeful.

Max deferred to the Lady of House Lockheart for her decision.

Ginger's eye twitched for an instant before answering, "Sure, we'd be glad to have you. Will Aawil be coming too?"

"Nah, she's doesn't really like water. Which is probably why

I don't get many chances to swim. It's weird to play on the beach alone. That's why, when I saw you guys from the window, I threw on a suit to catch up." Without saying anything further, she tapped her stat-sleeve a couple times, materializing a multi-colored leather ball. She tucked it under her arm and stepped into the group next to Kira.

Max kept the reynard in his peripheral, still wary of the woman. It could be just that she wanted to make friends and have fun at the beach, like she said, but he wasn't so sure. It would also make sense if she was, in fact, keeping an eye on them to make sure they weren't up to anything. Her presence would make sure they couldn't act on anything or do any planning. Combined with the realization from the night before that her pistol was a contract item, Max was almost sure she was dangerous.

That was when she dropped the ball she carried and proceeded to chase after it like a child, dropping her bag in the process. The simple pouch hit the stone of the patio with a heavy clank as her pistol fell out of it. Her eyes went wide as she looked back and forth between the ball and her weapon, like she couldn't decide which was more important. A low whimper emanated from her chest combined with an annoyed growl.

"That's awkward," she commented, sounding less embarrassed than she should have been.

"I can carry this for you if you want." Farn picked up the ball from where it had come to rest a few feet away.

"Thanks." Nix stuffed her M9 back into her bag and continued walking as if she hadn't just made a fool of herself. Her tail wagged as she went.

Max kept his eye on her, just in case.

CHAPTER THIRTY-SEVEN

Kira smiled as soon as her toes touched the sand. It was soft and warm under the light of the fire pots that surrounded the beach. She breathed in the salty air, almost forgetting she was still inside.

An NPC manned a small bar at the edge of the patio while a few of the palace guests and Berwyn's Serpents roamed about. Other than that, the place felt somewhat private. It made Kira feel a little better about what she was wearing underneath Farn's heavy cape.

Honestly, how is a cape this heavy?

She smiled, feeling the weight of the armor on her body. There was something strangely comforting about it. She shrugged off the cape, catching it before it fell. She didn't want to return it covered in sand, so she gently folded it over the patio railing.

Suddenly, a black robe and canvas bag flew past Kira's head. Both landed in the sand as Nix took off down the beach, running out onto the stone bridge that lead to the throne. She jumped off the side and tucked her legs up close to her body so her tail trailed behind her like a comet.

"Cannonball!"

She hit the water face first with a splash that seemed dispro-portionate for a character her size. Ginger let out an exhausted sigh as she picked up the discarded robe and bag and placed them on a lounge chair.

"She's worse than my kids."

Kira watched the reynard splash about. "At least she knows how to have fun."

"That's one way to put it." The *Coin* untied the sheer fabric from her waist and tossed it at Max as if he was her servant. The skirt hit him in the face as he looked out across the water.

"Thanks." He squinted back at her as she lay down on the sand, positioning herself like she was ready for a photo shoot.

"You know it's nighttime, right Ginger?" Max pointed to the pyramid's ceiling.

"I do."

"You're not going to tan."

"Yes, but Corvin and Kegan are off working on something for later so there's really nothing else to do right now. I'm going to take this time to relax the best I can while this fire pot next to me is nice and warm."

Max sighed and stood beside her like a good bodyguard.

Kira snickered and leaned over closer to Farn. "They're kinda cute, in an old, bickering, married couple sort of way." Farn snorted a laugh at the comment.

Ginger glared back at them, clearly overhearing the comment. "Shouldn't you both go play with Nix?"

"I think she drowned." Farn pointed out at the water.

Kira followed her finger to where Nix should have surfaced. Eventually, a pair of pointy ears poked up like a periscope. Then a moment later, the rest of her head followed as she doggy-paddled her way back to the shore.

As far as characters went, Nix could be described as pretty. Well, could being the operative word. At the moment, she looked more like a drowned rat crawling onto the beach on all fours. She wobbled as she got to her feet, like the weight of her waterlogged tail was throwing her off balance.

"I have to check something." Max grabbed the leather ball from Farn and launched it in Nix's direction. "It's dodgeball time."

"Wha—" was all Nix got out before being hit in the head and falling back into the waves.

"Sorry! Thought you were looking." Max sounded less sincere than he should have.

Kira cast an accusing glare in Max's direction.

"What? I thought she'd have better reflexes."

"I'm okay. I'm okay." The spunky reynard sat up out of the water, coughing and shaking her ears like a dog. "Just swallowed some water."

"You might want to stop being suspicious of her." Farn gestured to the mercenary. "She might not be a genius."

"I really thought she'd catch it."

Farn shook her head and walked off toward the water.

Kira let out a sigh in his direction.

"Fine, I feel bad about it, okay?"

"You probably should," Kira said as she motioned to join Farn.

Max laughed as soon as she passed him. "Nice butt, by the way."

Kira thrust her hands over the sparkling heart on her rear. She'd actually forgotten about it.

"You know what, I'm owning it." She puffed out her chest and marched the rest of the way to the water. "I'm a mascot, and it's cute."

Slipping into the water, the artificial ocean surrounded her like a blanket of happiness, washing away whatever she had been concerned about a moment before. Kira really did love the water. Even if the last time she'd gone swimming had been a year ago, back when she'd been shackled with the pendant that still clung to her throat. She ducked under and let the water strip away that worry as well.

Everything will be fine, she thought as she surfaced.

Of course, that was when Farn chose to belly flop off the throne.

The *Shield* crashed into the water beside her, sending a wave over her head. Kira brushed her dripping hair out of her face as her friend rose to the surface.

"How'd that feel?"

"Not great but still fun." Farn let out a wheezing laugh.

"Well, I guess it's war then." Kira turned away without another word and swam to the throne. Moments later, a fairy-sized cannonball plopped into the water next to the *Shield*, barely sending more than a few droplets in her direction.

Kira frowned.

Farn seemed equally unimpressed.

That was when Kira remembered she could fly.

She suppressed a grin as she flicked a few points of mana into the spellwork of her wings, shooting into the air. Thirty feet up, she swiped open her spellcraft menu and glanced at the fifty hit points displayed in the readout on her wrist. She was going to need some protection. Glyphs spun into place, activating a defense spell with water resistance.

That should do it.

She dove.

Below, Farn scrambled to get out of the way.

Too late. Kira flattened out to give her body the maximum surface area possible as a thunderous clap hit the air, followed by muffled laughter. Kira floated back to the surface, holding her chest as her entire front burned from the full body slap.

"I regret nothing. Tell my family I died how I lived. Being totally awesome." She let herself sink back down for the sake of comedy.

She almost swallowed a mouthful of water when she noticed her stat-sleeve.

5 out of 50 HP remained.

Damn, that was a little closer than I expected.

She surfaced and sent some mana into her wings, fluttering

in place, to heal herself with the dust they produced. That was when a quiet voice came from the side.

"Oh wow." Nix stared up at her, floating with her beach ball held against her chest. "You can actually fly."

It wasn't surprising that she was impressed. After all, it was rare to see a fairy with a level high enough to have wings, let alone one that could actually use them. Most just crashed into things since the control system was difficult to master.

Kira nodded, trying not to make a big thing of it.

Nix's ears pricked up and she squeezed her beachball tighter. "How high can you go? How fast are you? Can you touch the top of the pyramid? Can I see?"

"Whoa, slow down." Kira looked up at the crystal above, not really sure where the top was. "I guess I can show you something."

She floated gracefully into the air. Then took off like a bat out of hell. It was good to fly, as good as swimming even. Especially considering that she hadn't had much opportunity to stretch her wings in the last few days.

Kira made a lap of the beach before setting her sights on the pyramid above. She reached out, letting her fingertips glide against its crystal surface, slowing as she reached the apex. Her reflection surrounded her on four sides in endless lines of fairies. It was dizzying.

She let gravity take her, dropping straight down and forcing a torrent of mana through her body. Reflections of a falling star shone in the crystal until she stopped dead above the water. Her toes dipped in the gentle waves.

It was then that Kira noticed the other players on the beach were looking at her with the same expression as Nix. Some even watched from the balconies. Heat rushed through her body, reminding her of how much skin she was showing. Her first instinct was to duck into the water in embarrassment. She shoved it back and locked it away. She was, after all, a mascot. It was time to own it.

Suddenly, a voice shook her out of her thoughts.

"I heard that a fairy was flying around in here so I thought I'd come to see."

Berwyn stood on the beach, holding his hands behind his back and smiling. He wasn't wearing his regular gear, just his crown and a linen shirt. He looked comfortable yet stylish. A less casual Ripper still accompanied him, standing a few dozen feet away at the edge of the beach. Fortunately, the night had left Kira in a good mood. She drifted through the air toward him.

"I might know something about that."

His eyes widened as she floated in a slow circle around him. Delicate sparks flaked away from her wings like embers in the night air. Kira stopped short.

Holy crap, I'm flirting, and successfully, I might add.

She took a breath and committed to her role, stopping in front of him so that she hovered at eye-level. Her feet dangled a foot from the sand. She made a point of getting close enough so that her dust could dance across his skin.

"You're quite good at that."

"Thanks, I practice." She winked.

"I guess you do. I've heard flying isn't easy." He glanced down at the rest of her, then quickly brought his eyes back up.

Kira ignored the stolen glance and smiled her most enchanting smile before floating back down and sinking her toes into the sand. She tucked her arms behind her in a way that seemed innocent enough but also displayed her barely clothed form. Glancing away across the water, she gave him the chance to take in the view without being caught.

"You should have come out to swim earlier."

He sighed. "I definitely would have rather been here than inside working all night."

"Is it worth it?" She turned back to him. "The empire, I mean?"

He shoved his hands in his pockets, slouching in a way that made him seem more familiar. "Sometimes, or at least, it can be rewarding. I do have a palace, I suppose, but I do wish I had more time to relax." He looked back to her eyes. "I think that's part of what draws me to you."

Kira flushed instantly but suppressed the urge to look away.

He smiled. "Sorry, what I mean is that your house has a freedom that I don't. It kind of makes me remember why I started playing this game in the first place. Before I got caught up with all this." He gestured weakly back at the palace as if it was less important than spending a few minutes with her.

"Well, it's never too late," she chirped.

Berwyn laughed. "You're right about that. Might as well start now. Would you want to get a drink with me over at the bar? Since we're here."

Kira thought about it for a second, wondering if that would be letting things move too fast or if turning him down would be moving too slow. She didn't really want to go on a date alone with him, even if her friends were close by. Not that she was worried he'd try something but more that he might try something tomorrow night if she gave him too much encouragement. There was also a part of her that felt surprisingly guilty about leading him on.

She shook off the thought. It was best to worry about the heist first. Besides, what could one drink hurt, right? She settled in at his side, landing with a quiet, "Sure."

Ripper followed them like a distant shadow, drifting far enough behind to give his Lord some space. His presence made Kira's skin crawl as she walked past the rest of her party. She wanted to stay close to them. There was safety in numbers.

Ginger sipped a drink from the bar while Max avoided eye contact, both preserving their cover as the honeypot went according to plan. Farn, on the other hand, was less covert, squeezing the beach ball hard enough to depress the leather.

The *Shield* nodded as if to say, 'I'm ready when you need me.' Kira breathed a little easier knowing Farn was there for her.

That was when Berwyn placed a hand on her lower back, sending a chill surging up her spine to the base of her skull.

Kira resisted the urge to flinch for fear of sending the wrong signals. It wasn't that she was bothered by being touched. Well, she was, but there was more. He was charming and gentle, but as his fingertips traced her vertebrae, something felt off, something that she didn't notice until he touched her with more intent than just dancing.

Whatever it was, it scared the hell out of her.

Apparently, Farn didn't like it either because Kira didn't even have to signal for help. The *Shield* had already sprung into action, creating a distraction in the most awkward way possible.

By starting a fight.

"So what's so special about this thing here?" Farn grabbed at Ripper's gauntlet as he tried to stay out of the way.

"Cut it out." Ripper yanked his clawed hand away, drawing the attention of his Berwyn and the others.

"Relax, I was just looking," Farn answered as if channeling Nix while coming across as vaguely antagonistic.

"Oh, I can give you a look at it. You just might not live through it." He gave her a grin that didn't seem appropriate when directed at a woman in a swimsuit.

Berwyn dropped his hand from Kira's back to call to his Knight. "Ripper, play nice."

"I'll take that challenge." Farn gave a decisive nod.

"Huh?" Ripper questioned, clearly unaware that he had issued one.

"I'd kind of like to see what I can do against you." Farn sounded like she was sure she'd lose but still wanted to try. She turned her attention to Berwyn and Ginger without giving Ripper time to back out. "Would that be okay?"

"As long as it's fine with our host." Ginger stirred her drink with a little umbrella.

"It's fine with me. I'd love to see what your house can do as well."

"Great, I'll run back to the palace and get my gear on." Farn turned back toward the patio. "Then we can meet back in the training hall."

"Actually," Ripper smiled, "there's a washroom by the patio with a quick-change panel. So we can do this right here." He pointed down at the sand.

Kira gave Ginger a dirty look for making her change upstairs when she could have just changed easily at the beach's washroom. The *Coin* ignored her, pretending to be more interested in her drink.

"That's perfect." Farn clapped her hands together. "I'll be right back." She ran off toward the patio, only to come back moments later back in the stylish armor that Larkin had given her. She practically radiated power as she casually grabbed her cape off the patio railing and swept it around her. "You ready?"

Berwyn stepped between them. "Okay, I do feel I have to say a few things. First, this is a friendly duel, so there's no need to go and kill each other." He gave a stern look to Ripper. "That being said, Ripper doesn't really do nonlethal. It's a big reason why I made him my First Knight. So try not to get killed."

"Thanks for the vote of confidence," Farn responded.

Kira ran to her savior, grateful for the rescue. She tugged on the *Shield's* collar which was stuck under her cape, mouthing the words, 'thank you' as she popped it back up in a way that looked cool. "Don't worry, I believe in you." Kira made sure to squint at Ripper to let him know who she wanted to lose. *A little psychological warfare couldn't hurt.*

With that, the two *Shields* took positions further down the beach where there was more room to move.

Kira sat down next to Berwyn, who was using one of the lounge chairs as a bench. She tried to stay calm, but in truth, she was doing her best not to think about the elf, Luka, who died so horribly the previous night. The beach suddenly felt a lot darker than it had before. She stood back up and swiped open her spellcraft menu, spinning glyphs into position to activate her strongest light spell.

A sphere of pure energy gathered in her hand just before she tossed into the air. It took off like a flare, climbing high above the sand where it stopped and hovered like a miniature flickering star. She couldn't help Farn fight, but she could at least help her to see her enemy.

Farnsworth stared up at the light pulsing above, then lowered her eyes to her opponent. "So is there some kind of signal to start, or do we just start swinging at each other?"

Ripper smiled.

Then he stabbed her in the stomach.

CHAPTER THIRTY-EIGHT

Pain ignited Farn's senses as Ripper twisted his sword through her virtual kidney. How he had known exactly where would hurt the most was uncanny. It was as if he was challenging the system to keep it under control as it soothed the sensation back down to a dull numbness.

Farn didn't bother checking her health. Her defense could take it. It wasn't going to kill her. She doubted that was Ripper's goal anyway. Judging from the uneven grin on his face, he wouldn't have ended things so soon. No, right now, he was having fun. Stabbing her was just a greeting. He hadn't even waited until she was ready. *Damn, I was practically in mid-sentence.*

Farn's brain caught up quick. Synapses fired, sending one of her legs out to kick him away before he could do any more damage. She fell in the sand and scrambled to get her fingers through the brass knuckle grip of her Feral Edge. No luck, there wasn't time.

All she could do was get a hold of the sword's extended handle, leaving her with little leverage as Ripper prepared to strike. There wasn't time to get her gauntlet's barrier up either. She cursed herself for leaving herself open. Then she cursed

Ripper for starting the duel with a cheap shot. That gave her an idea.

If you want to fight dirty, let's see how you react to this.

She grabbed a handful of sand as obviously as she could. Ripper's eyes widened as he pulled back and activated the Death Grip's shield generator. A construct of crimson energy appeared, projected by a glowing, red stone embedded in the back of his clawed hand. He ducked behind it to shield his face, clearly expecting a handful of sand to be flung at his eyes.

Gotcha! She was never one to fight dirty. It didn't sit well with her. Instead, she dropped the sand and used the opening to roll back and get to her feet.

The glowing wound on her abdomen faded before her opponent realized he'd been tricked. He lowered his shield just as Farn activated her own. Larkin's White Rose bloomed from her wrist to form an oval shell of light.

Farn gestured with her head at the Ripper's shield, its size only that of a standard buckler. It was clearly meant for offense rather than protecting others. The corner of her mouth tugged up into a smirk.

"Mine's bigger."

She drew her Feral Edge, flipping the sword so she could thread her fingers into the grip. Then she took her stance. He looked pissed.

Sparks flew as hits came at her in a furious push of raw aggression. Farn struggled to block, almost losing her footing in the sand. She slammed a closed fist against her chest and spat out the word, "Sure-Foot," to activate her new house skill. The loose ground beneath her feet suddenly firmed up, giving her the traction she needed to push back.

She rammed forward with her shield and attacked, hitting a wall as soon as he too activated Sure-Foot. *Damn, probably should have expected that*, she thought as he parried a thrust that she'd aimed at his head. He caught her arm with his claws as her attack flew off course. Then he pulled her close, drawing back his sword to impale her other kidney.

Before he could follow through, she head-butted him in the eye. Okay, maybe she wasn't that against fighting dirty. Without her weapon bonus, the blow didn't carry much damage, but at least it surprised him. Plus, it sent a clear message that she wasn't food that he could play with.

Ripper hopped back, holding his head for a moment before refocusing on her. He extended his claws as his energy shield blinked out, leaving the Death Grip burning with an angry, red glow. He held it as shimmering particles began to spill from the gauntlet. They trickled from his palm like blood from a wound.

In retrospect, Farn probably shouldn't have given him time to prepare the weapon. She froze as she recognized the sparkling, red light dripping from his palm. It was the health that he'd drained from Luka the night before. Farn gasped. The Death Grip could actually use a player's life force as fuel.

Shit, like that thing wasn't overpowered already.

Ripper rushed forward, planting his foot on the base of one the fire pots. He kicked off, knocking the support structure down in a crash of embers as he leaped into the air with his claws drawn back to strike.

For an instant, Farn debated taking the hit to her shield. If she survived, she could strike back while he was unguarded. *No, too risky.* All the unknowns that surrounded the Death Grip echoed through her head. *What if it kills me outright?*

Acting fast, she rolled to safety as Ripper's glowing fist came down. She was glad she did. He hit the beach with an ear-splitting crack, shaking the ground. Even stranger was the wave of scalding steam that exploded from the wet sand. It actually wilted the leaves of the potted plants nearby. Farn gasped as the steam cleared.

Ripped stood at the center of a crater of jagged glass. Shards of crystallized sand jutted out on all directions around him.

"Still comparing sizes?" His voice was raspy with a touch of madness. "The Death Grip stores the lives of everyone it kills. That attack was Luka's. You remember her, right?" His words turned her stomach as he stepped forward, crushing shards of glass under his boot. "I've been busy, and I have plenty more lives stored up. Just think of what I could do with yours."

Again, she couldn't believe the raw power that a single contract item had granted him. Even with her shield up, she wasn't sure she could have survived a direct hit from the gauntlet. How an item like that even existed was insane. Of course, she knew exactly where it had come from. It was born from the user's mind, a representation of his mental state. The thought sent chills slithering down her body.

She glanced down at her sword and wondered what part of her the Feral Edge represented. It was power with a price, damage in exchange for her defense. She had always considered herself a protector, so why did her mind produce a weapon made for all-out attacks? It was a risk, and she hadn't taken a risk in years.

She shook her head before she fell down that rabbit hole. Now wasn't the time to be thinking about her past. Ripper was still coming.

Without his shield active, he was free to attack with both hands. Claws bit into her arm, tearing streaks of red light across her stat-sleeve. Her health dropped fifteen percent as she realized his weapon bonus was applied to the Death Grip as well. *Of course it does.* She wasn't even surprised anymore.

He was fast.

Too fast.

Too aggressive.

She had to even the odds.

Farn dove behind the nearest fire pot and deactivated the White Rose's barrier. A little time, that was all she needed. A little time to breathe.

Claws carved through the base of the pot. The wooden supports splintered and buckled under the weight of the steel bowl of flames. It rang like a bell as Ripper slammed his armored fist in the side, sending fire raining down in Farn's direction. She was out of options.

Finally, she grinned.

Light erupted from her sword as the blade's edge split apart. A plane of razor-sharp energy poured out, almost twice as long. Farn cleaved the fire pot in half with a streak of crimson ferocity as she dashed through the explosion of embers, thrusting forward with both hands.

"Mine's still bigger!"

Ripper's face twisted in anger. He tried to block by raising his arm. If he'd had his shield active, he might have been successful. Instead, the Feral Edge impaled his wrist, coming to a stop with its tip resting in his shoulder. He gritted his teeth with a growl and prepared to strike back with his claws.

"I don't think so." Farn planted her boot in his stomach and shoved. Her Sure-Foot skill gave her all the footing she needed to send him flying into the small bar by the patio. The NPC ran for his life as Ripper crashed into the counter.

Farn didn't stop there.

Ripper shook his head, recovering enough to duck a swing that severed one of the supports that held up the bar's grass roof. It collapsed, taking the shelves of bottles with it. A cacophony of shattering glass echoed across the beach.

Farn caught Max in her peripheral, clapping his hands while giving her an approving grin. *Didn't he say something about destroying a bar in Tartarus earlier in the week?*

Suddenly, a bottle flew at her head as Ripper made a break for the water's edge at the center of the beach. His claws began to glow.

"Not that again." Farn sprinted to close the gap, hoping to stop him from burning another life to fuel the Death Grip's special attack.

He retreated onto the stone bridge that lead to the throne.

Farn followed, the water surrounding her on both sides. *I'm not letting you off that easy.* She let out a wild growl from the back of her throat.

Swords clashed, steel against crackling energy. Ripper fell back again, apparently unable to strike without canceling his gauntlet's charge. Finally, he ran out of space. Farn landed a hit to his leg that dug into Berwyn's throne behind him. Somehow, she didn't feel bad about it. In fact, from what she could tell, she was actually winning.

That was when Ripper made his move.

He grabbed the hilt of her sword, allowing her to cut deeper into his thigh. Then he backhanded her in the jaw with his gauntlet.

Stars detonated across Farn's vision as thunder cracked against her skull. For a moment, she wasn't sure if her head was still attached to her body. She couldn't feel the ground beneath her feet as gravity shifted around her, the beach flipping end over end. *I guess this is as far as I go.*

That was when a whisper pushed through the confusion, sounding close, like she was right there next to her, "Don't give up."

Kira?

The fairy's voice reached over the house line, snapping her impact-rattled mind out of her stupor. Water splashed around her as she landed in a crouch with nothing but the sea beneath her. Then things got weird.

She didn't sink.

Confusion returned as Farn slid backward, skimming the surface of the waves like it was covered by a layer of wet ice. Light from Kira's spell danced all around her in a cascade of droplets of water thrown up in her wake. She threw her arm out, holding her sword to the side for balance as she came to a stop in the middle of the artificial surf.

One question consumed her. *How the hell am I doing this? Either I've suddenly become Jesus, which I doubt, or...* The answer hit her like a palm to the forehead.

Sure-Foot: Temporarily fight while standing on any surface.

Her heart leaped for joy as she stood back up. She couldn't find much in the way of traction, but she wasn't about to complain. It wasn't every day that she found out she could walk on water.

Farn suppressed her excitement and glanced at her stat-sleeve. She immediately wished she hadn't.

HP: 50 out of 5888

The irony was not lost on her as an imaginary weight settled across her shoulders. *This is what it's like for Kira all the time.* One wrong move. That was all it would take.

She shook off the thought. Fifty hit points were better than none. In fact, she might have gotten lucky. From what she saw of the Death Grip's power, a charged attack should have one-shotted her. Maybe she survived because he hadn't hit her with a full punch, just a backhand to the mouth.

Farn clenched her jaw and flicked her sights back to Ripper. His horrible smile cracked across his face as he stepped onto the water's surface like it was merely a continuation the land. Obviously, his Sure-Foot skill was still active, too. His claws began to glow.

Farn gripped her sword. She wasn't going to win, that much was clear. She just hoped she could force him to use his killer move. That was the whole point of challenging him. If she couldn't learn anything, then it would all be for nothing. Well, not nothing. She'd at least ruined Kira's date.

Farn rushed him, not wanting to give him enough time to charge. Each step sent a ring of sparkling droplets up around her feet. She swung with a growl as her blade tore through the air.

Ripper dodged, jumping back before countering with a swipe. His claws streaked past her face, leaving ribbons of crimson light lingering across her vision. Flashes of red lit up the night as the Feral Edge and Death Grip clashed.

Her reach was greater, but he was faster. They were both low on health. It was a fair fight. After trading blows across the water, they had circled back to stand on the stone bridge that lead to the throne at a stalemate. An icon of a boot faded from Farn's wrist as she stared down the length of her blade at her enemy.

"Looks like Sure-Foot just wore off. Want to call it a night? We seem to be evenly matched."

"No fight is even, best you learn that," he growled as he raised his gauntlet the same way he had with Luka the night before. He was done with her.

The attack hit unlike anything Farn had ever felt.

There was no warning.

No animation.

No moment to dodge.

Just a sudden feeling of discomfort and… loneliness.

The sensation gripped her spine and sent her virtual body into spasms. Farn's knees buckled, her face hitting the wet stone of the bridge. She swung her arm wildly, hoping to catch his leg with her sword. The blade of energy shattered along with her heart.

Ripper grinned as he stood just out of reach, his claws held up as if picking fruit from a tree. "I've heard that it doesn't really hurt. It's uncomfortable, but that's not what does the job." He crouched down as if to see her eyes better. "No, it's the loneliness that kills you. It makes you give up."

The world went cold as the life in her body began to seep out in a trickle of red light. She cried out a defiant howl as raw anger burned her throat. Her chest throbbed. It was as if he had reached inside her, his claws caressing her fragile heart.

She struggled to cling to something, to someone, but images flashed through her mind, one after another. The family that cast her out. The friends that turned their backs. The birthday cake she never ate.

It wasn't fair.

She was happy with who she was, so why wasn't anyone else? Then it just stopped, like the hand crushing her heart had been slapped away.

"Enough!"

A sound like a clap of thunder exploded, followed by a roar of wind. Ripper vanished from the bridge, launched by some kind of impact. A string of confused expletives erupted from the man as his body skipped like a stone across the water before sinking.

Farn's discomfort faded as a healing spell swirled around her, washing away the loneliness. In its place, she felt warm. She rolled over to find Kira hovering over her. The fairy tucked her hands behind her as her bare feet touched down on the stone.

"Sorry to interrupt. I couldn't watch that again."

"What did you do to him?" Farn pushed herself up on her elbows.

"Overcast pulse, like what I did to Ginger the other night," she lowered her head sheepishly, "but with one hundred percent of my mana."

Farn observed the splashing man struggling to stay above water while in full *Shield* gear. "You didn't kill him."

"Nope, it still doesn't do much damage. But it looked cool, and it knocked him away from you, so I'll take the win."

"You broke the Death Grip's hold."

"Must be a range thing." Kira shrugged.

"Good." Farn let out a sigh of relief. "For a second, I thought you might have asked your pendant for help."

"I'm not that dumb." Kira reached down to help her up.

"Thanks for coming to save me." Farn took her hand but made sure not to put much weight on her.

"No problem." Kira glanced back at the others standing on the beach, looking worried. The rest of the pyramid's guests had gathered around to watch as well. "I should probably get back to being a good honeypot. I hope I didn't mess things up."

Without another word, the fairy shot into the air, only to drop back down in front of Berwyn a second later. She rubbed at the back of her neck and bowed as if apologizing. He seemed to laugh in response.

Farn walked back to the beach, passing Ripper's panting form as he swam to shore. Max and the others ran to join her as soon as she reached dry land. Even Berwyn came to congratulate her.

"That was one hell of a duel." His attention quickly shifted to Kira. "I'm not sure you need a guard after that, though."

She brushed his praise away with a musical laugh. "Not quite, I used all my mana."

He eyed her incredulously. "Then how did you fly back here?"

"Oh!" Kira's blushed a little before spinning around and hooking a thumb over her shoulder at the crystal heart on her rear. "Magic butt." Berwyn cocked his head to the side as Ginger stepped in to explain.

"The emblem is a backup mana supply. Our crafter has an odd sense of humor."

Berwyn glanced down before suddenly snapping his eyes back up as if he hadn't realized what he was staring at. "Umm, yes, quite funny."

"Sorry that Kira disrupted the duel though." Ginger inclined her head.

"Yeah, sorry," Kira added.

"Nonsense, it was entirely understandable."

Nix joined in, "Plus, it never hurts to remind Ripper not to rely on his contract, no matter how powerful it might be."

"True, in that case, you did me a favor." Berwyn nodded.

"Probably going to take a rain check on that drink, though." Kira gestured over to the rubble off to the side where an awkward looking NPC stood next to a pile of broken glass. "You know, 'cause the bar is kinda closed."

Berwyn laughed. "Yes, tomorrow might be better after the palace resets."

That was when Ripper crawled out of the water, breathing heavy while resting on all fours. Nix took the opportunity to humiliate him further.

"You just got your ass handed to you by a *Breath* mage." She offered him a hand, but he slapped it away and stood up on his own.

"Shut up, the fairy got me by surprise."

"Said no one ever," she continued as she splashed around

him. He responded by placing a hand directly on her chest and shoving her with all his strength. She fell backward in the shallow water. He then stormed up the beach, recovering his poise as he reached his Lord's side.

Farn took the moment to show that she was a good sport. "I think the win technically goes to you, considering I was saved by the player I was supposed to be guarding."

Ripper glared back at her but eventually nodded.

With the fight over and the formalities done, the two groups parted ways for the night.

Farn fell in line behind Max and Ginger as Kira bounced along beside her on the way back to the suite. As soon as they made it inside, Ginger went into the washroom to change, throwing Kira's gear out before closing the door. The fairy shrugged and wriggled back into to it, keeping her bathing suit on underneath. Once that was done, she threw herself onto the sofa.

Farn stretched before sinking in beside her. It felt good to sit down. She kicked her feet up and settled into the cushions, shutting her eyes for a moment to help herself relax.

"I wouldn't get too comfortable."

She cracked one eyelid again, finding Max standing over her. She groaned. "I think I've done enough for tonight."

"That's okay." Ginger reappeared to join him. "It's this one that we need anyway." She tousled Kira's hair which was already pretty messy from the beach.

"I think I've done enough too," the fairy pouted.

Max leaned down with a smug smile plastered across his face. "Too bad, you're not the only one who has been busy."

Ginger joined him. "Yes, and we have a surprise for you."

CHAPTER THIRTY-NINE

"Ta-da!" Kegan posed like a magician at the end of a trick.

A latticework of string filled the hallway behind him where he and Corvin had slaved away on for most of the night.

Kira blew out an unenthusiastic sigh. "I guess I should have expected this when this guy dragged me into bowels of the Fire Tomb?"

"Oh, I didn't drag you here." Max stepped past her.

"I don't know. I saw some shoving." Farn folded her arms.

"Gentle shoving," Ginger added.

Kegan gestured to the hall. "Well, what do you think?"

"It's good enough." The *Coin* shoved her hands into the pockets of her new coat.

"Good enough?" Kegan marched over to her. "I'm sorry, is it not impressive enough for you? I mean, we only built an exact replica of the laser grid in the middle of an active dungeon.

"Mana fence," Corvin called from the other end of the hall where he inspected their work.

"And how did we get it so accurate, Corvin?"

"We mapped it out during the day based on a few photos."

"And how did we map it so accurately?"

"Math."

Ginger ignored him and began to walk forward into the hall. Kegan threw out an arm to block her path. "And why did we build this in an active dungeon?"

"The Fire Tomb has the same pressure plate as the vault corridor," Corvin answered.

"Oh yeah." Ginger's eyes fell to the floor.

"How did you do all of this on a booby-trapped floor?" Farn asked.

Kegan hopped backward to the pressure plate, watching everyone cringe, clearly expecting him to be immolated on contact. He pointed behind them. "There's a deactivation switch under a statue over there."

"I kind of wish I'd known that back when I ran this dungeon a couple years ago." Farn furrowed her brow. "What did you do about the monsters?"

Kegan answered her question by whipping an arrow out of his quiver and firing it past her head. "That."

"Ah, that makes sense." She didn't even turn around as a quiet yowl followed by a dying gurgle came from the flame goblin sneaking up on her. "And what about the other players that wanted to get through?"

"Bribery," Corvin called from the other end.

Keagan slung his bow over his shoulder. "There've only been a few parties since it's a low-level dungeon. But they've been pretty happy to turn back in exchange for some credits."

Kira hopped onto the pressure plate beside him. "How much weight can it hold without setting off the trap?"

"Fifty pounds."

Her eyes bulged. "I weigh forty-five pounds."

"Don't worry. If you set off the flame throwers in the walls, the strings are all enchanted to be fireproof. So they won't go anywhere."

"Oh great, never mind about me getting burned."

"Probably step lightly then." Kegan smirked.

"We can keep the floor deactivated until you feel comfortable getting through the strings," Corvin added.

Max clapped his hands together. "Great! So take off your clothes and get in there."

Kira glowered at him before shrugging and pulling her gear up over her head. She dropped to the floor and took a breath. "Here goes nothin'."

Kegan snorted as soon as she slid under the first string. "Is there a heart on your ass?"

"I'm aware, and I'm owning it."

"Fair enough." Kegan laughed.

Kira pushed her head and shoulders up and arched her back to pass between a few more strands.

Max cleared his throat. "I'm going to, umm, go watch the entrance for monsters." He glanced at the fairy's form slipping through the hall then immediately turned away.

Ginger laughed. "I'll join you. I've seen enough of that girl's ass for one day."

"Yeah, I supposed I should go too," Kegan added. "It's fun and all to make Kira uncomfortable, but she probably needs to focus."

"That's very mature of you," Kira commented as she thrust her butt into the air while extending one leg to pass between two strings. It looked like a solo game of Twister.

Kegan cleared his throat at the provocative display, then called to Corvin, "Enjoy the show, buddy."

The *Blade* immediately averted his eyes.

Farn broke away, sliding down to sit against one wall. "I'll stay and keep an eye on her. I mean, who would want to miss that?" She hooked her thumb back at Kira.

"This has gone wrong." The fairy had run out of places to put her hand that were not already occupied by imitation lasers. Her body was contorted into a position that strained her arms.

Max laughed.

"It's not funny, jackass."

"It's kinda funny," he corrected.

"Try moving your leg to the side," Farn coached.

She did, freeing up a little space. "Damn," she let out a long breath, "this is going to be a lot harder than I thought."

CHAPTER FORTY

The morning sun shined in through Seth's window as he pulled off his Somno unit and sat up in bed. He rubbed at his shoulder for a few seconds before he realized that it didn't hurt. He had spent much longer practicing as Kira in the Fire Tomb than he had intended. It was already ten in the morning. A glance at the nightstand clock told him he had been logged in as the fairy for over thirteen hours.

He winced.

It wasn't smart for him to stay in that long, considering everything Carver had done to his brain. He shrugged and tapped the power button on the side of his headset to shut it down. Seth let out a sigh when the familiar chime of its startup sequence sounded instead. Apparently, the system had lost its connection during the night and just powered itself off when it wasn't needed.

He winced again.

His screwed-up brain had started doing the work on its own again. He was due for a break.

Seth growled.

The timing was bad with the heist coming up. Taking time off now was out of the question.

I'm sure a few more days won't kill me.

"Famous last words," he said out loud as he set his headset on its charger.

Seth threw himself back into the mattress for a full body stretch before hopping up, wandering over his dresser to grab something to else to wear. It was late after all; the day couldn't wait forever.

Making his way to the kitchen, he grabbed a popsicle from the freezer. It was too late to make breakfast so he figured something quick would be best before he went over to bother Wyatt next door. Sure, a popsicle wasn't much of a breakfast, but he was an adult, and he could do what he wanted.

That was when he heard a knock at the door.

Seth jumped and glanced around the room as if looking for someplace to hide. He wasn't expecting anyone, and Wyatt had a key, which only left one option.

A stranger!

Seth did what any reasonable person would do. He waited by the door for them to go away. 'Cause really, what kind of monster would actually come to your door at ten in the morning?

They knocked again, making it clear that they weren't going anywhere.

Seth crept his way to the window and pulled back the curtain just enough to peek out at the uniformed police officer on his porch. He immediately jumped like a cat encountering a cucumber.

"Oh, crap!" He almost dropped his popsicle.

Seth fidgeted in place for a second, debating on what to do. Then again, he did what any reasonable person would. He licked his popsicle before it dripped on his hand. Then he opened the door.

"Hello, what may I do for you, officer?"

"Seth Hase?" the officer asked in that tone that most cops

seemed to prefer, the one that seemed kind of rude but expected to get what they wanted regardless. It was meant to intimidate.

And intimidate it did.

Not so much because of the tone but because the man had used his full name. There was no doubting it. The officer was definitely there for him.

That was when Seth heard the door next to his open. He leaned forward and looked to the side, unintentionally ignoring the officer's question. What he saw worried him even more.

A second cop was standing in front of Wyatt, asking him to identify himself as well.

Seth remained reasonable, waving awkwardly to his terrified friend. Wyatt didn't wave back.

"Mr. Hase!" The officer shifted his posture in a way that felt vaguely threatening. "That is you, isn't it?"

Seth leaned back, redirecting his attention to the man on his porch. "Umm, yeah, is there somethi–"

"You're going to have to come with us," he interrupted, "your friend too."

"Are we in trouble?" Seth asked almost in unison with Wyatt next door.

"Not at this time, but we need you to answer some questions down at the station."

"Umm, okay. Just let me get my shoes," Seth added as he slipped into a pair. Moments later, he was sitting in the back of a squad car next to his best friend. Wyatt looked at him sideways as if questioning the fact that he was still holding a half-eaten popsicle.

Seth shrugged and attempted to bite off the side to finish it faster. The whole thing fell off the stick.

Wyatt's eyes bulged as the orange piece of ice hit the floor.

They both looked at each other, then at the officers in front.

The cops didn't seem to notice.

Seth stuffed the stick in his pocket. Then he looked back to his terrified friend, as if to say, 'I didn't just drop a popsicle in a police car and have no idea what you're on about'.

Wyatt tried to ask what they were needed for, but the officers just blew him off, like they didn't want to be there either. From there, they just stayed quiet until they reached the station. Seth tried his best to be cooperative, especially since they hadn't done anything wrong. Well, except planning a heist of millions worth of virtual currency, but that wasn't really illegal.

Right?

They were shown into a plain-looking interrogation room. The walls were a bland, off-white with a table and chairs in the middle. The table was cheap, the kind that was covered in paper printed with wood grain to make it appear nicer than simple pressboard. A couple fixtures of fluorescent lights buzzed above. The room lacked a bright light hanging from the ceiling like in the movies.

They waited quietly at the table for a few minutes before Seth started humming the theme to *Law and Order*. Wyatt clearly didn't appreciate it. He didn't have to endure it for long because the door opened shortly after.

A man and a woman entered, both wearing suits. Seth's humming trailed off into a stunned silence as they sat down.

Wyatt swallowed audibly.

The letters F.B.I. read clearly on the face of the laminated identification cards clipped on each of their lapels.

"Hi there," the man said with a smile that failed to put Seth at ease. His suit didn't look expensive, but he wore it well, and his short black hair was styled professionally. His face, however, was covered in a day's worth of stubble, as if he had been too busy to shave. He looked old enough to be either of their fathers, which didn't make things easier.

Seth waved weakly in a way that seemed to add a question mark to the gesture, as if he was unsure if it was the right thing to do. A glare from Wyatt told him it was not.

"Can we get you anything?" the woman asked. Her hair was streaked with gray and tied back, giving her a serious appearance. Her voice, however, sounded almost excited. "Coffee or a donut?" She paused. "Oh, sorry, Mr. Hase. We could get you something else if you want."

Seth started to sweat when he realized how much the agents already knew. They must have pulled his medical records before coming in, knowing that he couldn't digest solid foods.

"No thanks." His voice wavered as he answered.

"Okay, let us know if you change your minds." The man placed his hand down on the table. "Anyway, I'm Agent Dawson, and this is my partner Agent Delgado. We're part of a special cybercrime division within the F.B.I."

Delgado took over. "Yes, and for the last few years, we've been handling criminal activity within the popular game Carpe Noctem."

Not good! thought Seth as soon as he heard the word Noctem.

"Are we in some kind of trouble here?" Wyatt's voice almost cracked.

"Let me start with telling you what we know." Dawson leaned forward so that his elbows rested on the table. "We know that you play the characters MaxDamage24 and Kirabell." He glanced at Seth as if questioning if he really was the fairy in question. "We know that you both received a large payment from Checkpoint Systems a year ago, as well as four other players.

"At first, we thought it might have been some kind of legal settlement. But then we noticed that the timing seemed too coincidental with the firing of Neal Carver and that whole dragon incident that he set off afterward.

"After comparing your party to the descriptions provided by players concerning the event, it wasn't hard to figure out that your team was at the center of it. We don't know the specifics, but we assume that the payment was for services rendered in stopping the situation." He leaned back. "Now, none of that's illegal, but it did put your team on our radar.

"So you can imagine our surprise when your people were spotted within the pyramid in Reliqua, mere breaths away from the Lord of Serpents." Dawson folded his arms. "Naturally, we thought that you had been hired by Checkpoint to stop Berwyn's conquest since it has been hurting the gameplay lately. But after looking into the legality of that, we've found it to be unlikely that whatever you're doing there would be on the books. Apparently, getting directly involved would be against the game's rules, so if you're not being paid to be there, then that begs the question—what are you doing there?"

Wyatt started to answer but was cut off by Agent Delgado. "You see, we have a theory. One about a vault and what would happen if someone were to break into said vault."

"Wait a second," Wyatt interrupted, his face suddenly widening into a grin as his shoulders relaxed. "You said that we were spotted in the palace, which implies that you have people in there as well. So that begs the question, what were they doing there?"

Seth answered before they had the chance. "Holy crap, Luka was one of yours."

Delgado sighed and lowered her head

Dawson chuckled and nudged his partner. "See, told you they'd figure it out."

"Yeah, yeah, you told me so." She raised her hand. "That was me, actually. I use the character, Luka, to run ops online. It took me months to build my cover and get into the Serpents."

"And now you've been kicked out," Wyatt added.

"Yes." She sighed again.

"That's why we need your help," Dawson continued.

Seth leaned back as he realized what was going on.

"We're listening." Wyatt did the same, looking a bit more smug than he should.

Dawson chuckled and pulled out a file folder from a bag below his chair. "Okay, for starters, you've stepped into a bigger mess than you realize. Not to mention the fact that we're pretty sure that you're planning a theft. So wipe that look off your face."

"Sorry." Wyatt stopped smiling.

Dawson flipped open the folder. "Let's start by letting you in on some details. Do you recognize this man here?" He held up a photo of a man that looked around sixty. He wore a fancy suit with his hair slicked back despite the fact that most of it was gone. At one point, he might have been attractive, but his looks had long since faded.

Seth shook his head in the negative along with Wyatt.

Dawson set the photo down on the table. "His name is Roger Cline, but you know him as Lord Berwyn."

Wyatt picked up the image. "Damn, you danced with this dude."

Seth crossed his arms and looked away. "Yeah, I know. It was embarrassing the first time. I don't think the Feds care."

Delgado smiled. "Actually, I was there. You have some moves."

Seth rolled his eyes.

Dawson ignored the exchange. "Anyway, Cline is suspected on over a dozen counts of murder. So, you know, he's probably not the best choice for a dance partner."

A familiar chill slithered through Seth's body, the same as when Berwyn had touched him as Kira the night before. He suppressed a shiver. "What were the motives?"

"Mostly business disagreements. However, we can't prove anything or even find him. He served a few years in prison decades ago and disappeared when he got out. We only found him again online when Noctem came out, and like the majority of legitimate businesses, he's been using it to run his ever since. We tried tracing his account, but unfortunately, it's too easy to hide where connections come from."

"What kind of business does he run?" Wyatt asked.

"Smuggling and selling illegal goods." Dawson pulled out a few more pages of text that didn't mean much to Seth but clearly did to him. "We believe he has a global network set up to traffic everything from military grade ordinance to biological threats. We've caught some of his people here and there, but he compartmentalizes his operation in a way that no one really knows much more than their own role. The result is that we can't get anywhere near him, and now that he has a damn empire online, we can't get to him in Noctem either."

"And that's where you come in," added Delgado, closing the file.

"Okay, but I don't think he's going to start talking about that stuff around us," Wyatt argued.

She pulled out another folder. "You're right. He won't even send messages through anything that he doesn't consider secure. But there may be something that can change that."

"And that is?" Seth slid to the edge of his seat.

Delgado leaned forward as well as if she was about to tell a secret. "We found a book in the possession of one of his people in Noctem after he had been caught storing shipments in the real world. They had hidden the book in a shop online that they had a deal with."

"Why didn't he just store it in his inventory?" Wyatt asked.

"It seemed to be just part of a larger contract item, so it can't be stored in a virtual inventory unless it's brought together with the rest of it."

"Ah, so it's like the rings that I share with Farn." Seth rubbed at his finger where the item would be if he was logged in as Kira. "I can't store it by itself, so I wear it on a chain whenever I take it off."

Wyatt nodded. "I've had the same problem with Farn's Shift Beads before. They only dematerialize as a set."

"Exactly." Delgado pulled out a number of photos from in game. "And what we found inside this contract item changed our approach to the case." She spread out the photos across the table. "What does this look like to you?"

Each image showed a page from the book in question. There were dates and times as well as names and locations all written in the same handwriting. At the top of each entry was a number four, while a page number sat at the bottom. Another photo showed the book's cover, which contained an ornate four in gold leaf.

Seth thought about it but waited to hear more before making a guess.

Delgado handed them another few photos. "These are from a second book that was found under similar circumstances." This time, each entry showed a six at the top, and as expected, the photo of the cover had a gold number six on it.

"So you think the books you found are mirroring the contents of another?" Seth surmised.

"Yes. We think they're part of a set of ledgers and that he must have a master copy that has the contents of all the others. He probably just writes which volume he wants the page to appear in at the top of each entry, and it shows up in it no matter where the book is in Noctem. The thing that's really interesting is that only a few minutes after we found each volume, they suddenly turned blank from cover to cover. So he must also have a way to erase them when one becomes compromised."

"He probably just tears out the pages," suggested Wyatt.

"That's what we think too. Obviously, you can see why this master ledger might be important."

Dawson leaned in. "It's basically an untraceable means of communication that gives him the ability to coordinate his business from anywhere in the world. As far as why a game would create an item like that and give it to a guy who would use it to run a criminal organization, that's beyond me. And Checkpoint has not been very forthcoming about it either. They've refused to give us information on the contract system."

Wyatt looked to Seth knowingly but didn't say anything. It was obvious to them why Checkpoint wasn't helping. The contract system was broken. Checkpoint couldn't help even if they wanted to. Berwyn's contracts would have been created by his subconscious. The content of them was probably stored in his brain as well, according to what they had learned last year. That would mean the books could only be read while he was online.

"And that is why I went in as Luka to try to find it. We know that it's too big for him to carry on his person based on the other books we found, so he must be storing it somewhere."

"But you got caught looking through his study." Wyatt leaned back in his chair.

"Yes and blew a four-month op in the process. Fortunately, he just assumed I was working for another city in the game and not the Bureau. I had time to search the study thoroughly, so I know it's not there. So that just leaves one place."

"The vault." Wyatt slapped his hand on the table as he realized it.

Dawson nodded. "Yes, and hypothetically, if there was a team with the intent to break into said vault, then they might be so kind as to grab the book in question while they're in there."

Wyatt sat quietly for a moment before speaking, "I guess, hypothetically, that might be a possibility."

"Great, because we've already gone through the trouble of beefing up your team's cover IDs as well as concealed your finances so that Berwyn won't find anything if he decides to look into you," Dawson explained as if it was that simple.

"Wait, what?" Wyatt froze in his chair.

"It was a necessary precaution. This way, you're protected by another layer of anonymity. It wasn't hard for us to figure out your real-world identities, so it would have been just as easy for Cline to do the same if he got suspicious. And if he finds out that Kirabell is played by you, Seth, then that might ruin your chances, considering he's almost certainly trying to sleep with you."

"Don't remind me." Seth dropped his face to his hand. "How much danger could we be in if we get caught by him?"

Dawson looked hesitant. "If things go badly, we may have to relocate you."

"Like, witness protection relocate?" Wyatt lurched forward.
"Yes."

"Well, crap." Seth sunk into his seat.

Wyatt's face fell, suddenly looking more serious than Seth was used to. "We'll have to discuss things with the rest of our party. Can you meet up with us online? I think it would be best if you explained the situation. We can take a vote after that."

"That's fair." Delgado took back some of the photos.

"Okay, we'll be at the Hanging Frederick in Valain at nine tonight," Wyatt said, taking charge of the situation.

Dawson frowned but agreed anyway, "We'll be there." He stood, signaling that the meeting was over. "It will be good to meet the rest of your team."

Seth and Wyatt got up as well, the two agents offering their hands to shake, as if sealing their unlikely alliance.

"Oh, one more thing." Dawson continued to shake Wyatt's hand longer than necessary. "It should go without saying that nothing that has been said here should be shared with anyone that we have not approved. Currently, the only people that know about this operation are in this room. I expect that it stays that way. Understand?"

Wyatt nodded slowly before Dawson finally released him.

"Good, I'm glad we see eye to eye."

With everything settled, Seth followed Wyatt as he got the hell out of there. The interrogation room had started to feel a little too small for comfort.

Delgado waited until the pair of gamers were safely out of the room before speaking again, "We should have told them everything."

Dawson picked up the folders and shoved them back in his bag. "Yeah, but they're civilians. I'd prefer not to involve them at all."

Delgado nodded. "True. I don't like using them either. But they're good at what they do, and we don't have the time to find anyone else. There's too much at stake."

CHAPTER FORTY-ONE

The orange shell of a teleport spell dissipated, dropping the team back in their room at the palace as if they had never left.

"I swear, I better not get relocated to Florida because of all this." Ginger didn't skip a beat. "That's the last place I want to raise kids."

"What's wrong with Florida? Kira and I grew up there, and we turned out fine," Max defended the state of his birth.

She leveled a blank stare at him as if his statement had just proved her point.

Farn dropped onto the couch and put her feet up on the coffee table while the two continued to bicker.

Kira sunk into the cushions beside her with a lengthy sigh. It had been a stressful evening so far, and she felt like having a good slouch was the right thing to do.

It had only been moments before that they had sat in the back of the Hanging Frederick with Luka and a bland-looking avatar named Rando404. Rando had turned out to be Agent Dawson's online persona. Luka had explained that she had made his avatar for him and had assigned him the name when he had told her that he didn't care what she chose.

Rando's unremarkable appearance was also by design since his only request was that she make him something that wouldn't stand out. Apparently, he wasn't much of a gamer.

After a very long conversation filled with plenty of questions, everyone was still on board with the heist. They had also voted to help the two agents take down Berwyn.

Ginger wavered a bit when they brought up the possible consequences, but as everyone raised their hands in agreement, she'd given in. Her response had been a simple, "Fine, but I hate all of you."

Kira could sympathize. She didn't want to back out, not with everything that was on the line. Still, the thought of playing the honeypot now made her skin crawl. Before she knew who Berwyn was, she could fool herself into thinking his intentions weren't so sinister.

"Well, look at it this way. Even if we ended up being relocated to somewhere crappy, at least we'll be rich." Max grinned at Ginger as he appealed to her more practical temptations.

"Yeah, well, I still hate you," the *Coin* pouted. Though, Kira suspected that it was just for show.

He shrugged as if he was fine with it.

After waiting enough time for Corvin, Kegan, and Piper to get into position outside, Farn stood. "I suppose I should probably help the guys sneak back in." She tugged on the strand of Shift Beads on her wrist as she raised her house ring to her mouth. "You guys ready?"

"Sneaking through the bushes as we speak," Piper's voice reported back in response.

"Okay, hold onto each other." Farn touched her bracelet with two fingers, vanishing in an instant. In her place stood Piper holding hands awkwardly with Corvin and Kegan.

"Wow." Piper's eyes went wide at the sight of the lavish interior of the room as she let go of their hands. "This place is amazin–"

Suddenly, Farn reappeared in her place as if she never left.

"Oh, come on, guys. You could at least let me stay for, like, a minute," Piper complained over the house line.

Ginger raised her ring. "Sorry, dear, I said you could help, not that you'd get to have fun."

Piper scoffed over the line without saying anything else.

"Now I kind of feel bad." Farn stared at the Shift Beads on her wrist as if debating on swapping out again.

"Don't." Ginger shook her head. "Keeping her out of this is best. I already regret letting her get involved this much. I don't know what I'd do if something happened to her." She wrapped her arms around herself. "It would be my fault."

Kira's stomach rolled as the reality of the situation sunk in. She had thought she had come to terms with it. Nothing had really changed. The plan was still the same. Helping take down Berwyn wasn't much more than a convenient detour. Still, they weren't playing a game anymore. She touched the pendant that clung to her throat, feeling a little like she had the year before. Things had gotten a little too real.

Back together with everyone, Max went over the plan so far. "Okay, there are still another two nights before Checkpoint refills the vault's hard. So we're in a holding pattern 'til then."

Corvin leaned on the sofa. "We could make a run on the vault anyway. Get the book early and forget about the money."

"No," Ginger said without hesitation, getting a number of accusing looks in response. "Oh, I get it. I'm greedy."

"You are a *Coin*." Farn smirked.

"Ha ha. And no, it's not because I want the money. That's just a bonus." She leaned on the table. "If we do this now, he will almost certainly link the theft to us. And if the Feds don't get him, we're all going straight in witness protection. Plus, if we wait until the vault is full, Berwyn will be distracted with continuing his conquest. That makes everything safer for us."

Max tapped his fingers on the back of her chair. "So we have to steal the hard to cover the theft of the book. It will slow his reaction time."

"So what do we do tonight then?" Kira hoped that she might not have to entertain their host.

"Beach?" Ginger shrugged. "I wouldn't mind swimming. You'll probably have to have that drink with Berwyn, though."

"But we can keep an eye on you," Farn added.

Kira sighed and began awkwardly pulling her gear up over her head. Her belt got stuck halfway, wrapped around her chest. She felt like a child having trouble putting on her winter jacket.

"Little help?"

Max begrudgingly assisted, but as soon as she got the dress off, there was a knock on the door.

Everyone fell silent.

"Were we expecting anyone?" Farn pointed at the door.

Kira gasped and immediately started trying to put her gear back on again. Ginger hopped up and snatched it away before pushing her to the door.

"It's probably Berwyn, and we want him distracted." The *Coin* then turned to Kegan and Corvin who were still standing in the room as if they weren't trespassing on the palace grounds.

It was a fact that they quickly remembered as they dove behind a chair. Kira snickered as Kegan's butt stuck out from the side and Corvin's ears poked up from the top.

"What's wrong with you two? Get in the bedroom and close the door," Max whispered in a tone that gave the impression of yelling.

They poked their heads up and glanced at the bedroom door as realization washed over their faces, leaving them both with expressions that said, 'duh'.

Once the two intruders were hidden away, Kira turned to the door. Before she could open it, Farn ran over to straighten her hair, which was still a mess from when she had taken off her gear. Then she ran back to the sofa with the others to act natural.

Kira turned the knob and pulled.

An excited smile shined on Berwyn's face as soon as he saw

her. For a moment, she couldn't help but picture the aging man in the photo she'd seen earlier that day, the man that had killed at least a dozen people to settle business disputes. Every muscle in her body tightened. She had been worried about talking to him since the moment she'd found out. At least now, she didn't feel bad about deceiving.

Kira swallowed her fear and shoved it down, returning his smile with one of her own. It was almost painful.

An equally-excited Nix stood behind him. She waved silently as if they were already good friends, her tail wagging as she did. Apparently, Berwyn had decided not to bring Ripper to her door after the events of the previous night.

"Hi," Kira chirped in a tone that she hoped would come across as being happy to see them.

He glanced at her swimsuit. "Oh, were you going to the beach?"

"We were thinking about it." She pretended that he had not just blatantly checked her out. "Why, did you have something in mind?" She assumed he did. Otherwise, he wouldn't have come by.

"I was thinking of going down to the Catacombs later tonight, and I wanted to ask if you and Lady Ginger would like join me."

Kira wasn't sure what he was asking. She didn't know what the Catacombs were. It sounded like a dungeon. She answered regardless, "Sure." Then she turned back to Ginger as if to ask if it was okay.

Ginger rested one arm on the back of the couch. "We'd love to."

He placed his hands together as if signaling that he had gotten what he'd come for. "Great, how's two o'clock sound?"

"That works," Kira chirped.

"Fantastic, we'll meet you at the gates out front then."

"Oh, did you want to come to the beach with us before we go?" Kira asked before he had the chance to leave. She'd only asked to seem interested since she was pretty sure he couldn't.

He had spent much of his early nights meeting with people that she now realized must real-world business contacts. Probably just as guilty as he was.

"Definitely," he answered without hesitation. Then he glanced at Nix and sighed. "But unfortunately, we still have things to do before I get to have fun."

Kira forced her warmest smile. "That's okay. There'll be time eventually, and the beach isn't going anywhere."

He laughed. "True. I'll see you later, though."

"Okay." She tried to sound disappointed.

He smiled and headed off down the hall with Nix in tow.

Kira closed the door and immediately turned to Ginger. "What the hell are the Catacombs?"

Down the hall, Nix followed Berwyn like a loyal mercenary or, at least, a well paid one. Granted, she didn't exactly look like she was ready to defend him at a moment's notice, mostly because she had her hands shoved in her pockets and was staring at the carved stonework of the ceiling as she walked.

"So what's so special about Kira anyway?" she asked, sounding a little more familiar with her boss than she should.

"What do you mean?"

"I mean, I get it. I wouldn't kick her out of bed, and I pretty much just sleep with guys. But seriously, you have an empire. You could have a different woman every night and put in way less effort." She didn't mince words, leaving no room for vague answers.

He paused before answering, "Let me ask you, Nix, have you ever been intimate with a fairy before?"

She snorted. "Gonna go with no on that."

He laughed. "Obviously, you know that they're more graceful than other races in Noctem."

"Yeah. Something to do with them weighing so little."

"Well, let's just say that the same effortless grace translates into other activities."

Nix nodded. "Right, right, so you're just looking to bang her then?"

"That's putting it a bit too simply."

"Really? I can't imagine that you're in love with her or anything."

He laughed again. "Oh, god no, but even you must be able to tell she's not very experienced. It's written all over her body language."

"Ahh, so you're all about the deflowering then." Nix mouthed the word, 'gross,' without saying it out loud.

"I'm not that immature," he said as if accusing her for suggesting it, "but someone like Kira isn't going to just jump into bed with anyone. No, it's about the negotiation. Someone like her needs to be convinced. She needs to be treated well and guided until she thinks it's her idea. Then she'll just give herself away. Not to anyone, but to you. That's when you know you've won her."

Nix grimaced. "And what happens after that?"

"Does it matter?" he answered her question with a question.

"Kind of. If you dump her immediately, you're not gonna keep her house on your side. They might even vow to take revenge, and I'll be honest, Ginger doesn't seem like someone I want to piss off. Not to mention Farn and Max are pretty protective of her. It actually warms my cold, mercenary heart to see how much they care 'bout each other."

The Lord of Serpents simply shrugged. "Eh, what are they going to do to me?" He tapped his crown to remind her that he was essentially immortal. "Besides, I have plenty of people. I don't need Lockheart's loyalty. They would be helpful on our side but not necessary."

Nix hesitated for a moment, looking back up at the ceiling. "Well, you're certainly one hell of a douche, aren't you?"

Berwyn stopped short, forcing her to stop so that she didn't run into him. "Nix, you are one of the best mercenaries I've found, and I consider you a valuable piece on the board."

"Aww, thanks, boss." She smiled with feigned modesty, throwing her hands behind her back.

"But," he turned to look down on her, "don't think for a second that you are in a position to speak to me with disrespect. I know how much Ripper would love to get his Death Grip around your throat."

Nix rubbed one hand around her neck and swallowed. "Okay, point taken."

Berwyn started walking again. "Great, I'm glad we had this talk then."

CHAPTER FORTY-TWO

Max checked over his shoulder for the fourth time. The alleyway was just as dark and empty as it was the last time he checked.

Kira waved at him, clearly noticing how uneasy he was.

He attempted to ignore her, but a small smile worked its way through his facade of tactical awareness. She was surprisingly calm despite the weight that had been dropped on her shoulders. Especially with Berwyn walking beside her.

Max checked over his shoulder again.

Of course, he wasn't worried for his own safety. Berwyn, on the other hand, well, more than a few players would've been glad to see the man's rule ended with extreme prejudice. With that on his mind, Max found himself on edge.

He didn't like it.

Berwyn had brought Nix and Ripper along for added protection, and he was still technically unkillable, thanks to his crown. Although, that didn't mean it would be out of the realm of possibilities for someone to try something. That was all Max needed, some random house making a move and ruining things when they were so close.

He clenched his fist. Why Berwyn had chosen now to leave the palace was beyond him. Honestly, he wasn't sure what made the Catacombs so special. Certainly not worth taking such a risk. Berwyn's priorities seemed out of order.

Max brushed off the thought. Worrying wasn't going to help now. They were already in way over their head. Besides, maybe he could figure out a way to make the situation work in Lockheart's favor.

He pulled out his journal and sent a quick message, then flipped to his map before anyone noticed.

At least the Lord of Serpents had the sense to map out the city's back alleys so that they would have an undisturbed path to their destination. Apparently, it was a necessity for all royalty. It was best to keep off the main streets as much as possible.

Nix lead the way, playing some kind of word game with herself as she walked. It seemed like it was as much for entertainment as it was to annoy Ripper who walked beside her. Behind them, Kira made small talk with Berwyn while Farn stayed nearby. Ginger kept close to Max.

There was a palpable tension in the air as they turned down a side street and into a small nondescript door. Inside was just a storeroom of barrels and bins filled with coconuts. It smelled sweet, like one of those tropical drinks served in a hollowed-out pineapple.

According to Berwyn, there were numerous entrances to the Catacombs, some of which were quite secret. It was to the point that players had to spend hours searching message boards just for their locations, only to have them change a few days later. Being the ruler of Reliqua, Berwyn had them all marked automatically on his map as a perk of his position. It was a point that he happily mentioned as they walked down a row of barrels, only to stop at a solid brick wall.

He touched one of the bricks three times. It responded by glowing a gentle blue, like the water of a swimming pool as if lit from below. He tapped four more so that five glowed in a pattern like a star. Then the whole wall slid backward,

D. PETRIE

revealing a narrow, spiral staircase twisting down into the dark.

Kira glanced back to Ginger before being urged forward into the lead. Snapping her casters open, she called up a low-level light spell to help the others see. She also materialized her wings for added light to help her navigate the narrow stairs. Under the moon, it wasn't that noticeable how brightly the fairy glowed, but here in near darkness she shined like a glittering beacon.

She swallowed once, then descended to a landing where a hallway stretched into the distance. The sound of rushing water reached back to meet Max's ears. It grew louder as they walked until he realized that it was mixed with something else from beyond. Something even louder.

He fought the urge to hold his breath.

Ahead, a curtain of water fell across their path from an opening in the ceiling. It flowed seamlessly into a second matching hole in the floor so that the water passed straight through the subterranean corridor without so much as splashing back at their feet.

Berwyn didn't stop. Instead, he walked straight toward the curtain of falling liquid as if it wasn't there.

Max flinched, expecting the man to be thrashed into the floor as soon as he came into contact with the torrent. Suddenly, a stone moved above, as if locking onto his movement like the automatic doors of a convenience store. It cut through the water, splitting it so that it fell to either side to make an opening wide enough for him to step through, remaining completely dry.

Berwyn looked back. "You coming?"

Kira took a step back before forcing herself to hop through the opening like she was exiting an elevator that she feared might fall.

From there, the group passed through several more walls of rushing water that parted in the same manner. The noise beyond grew, almost rhythmically as it became less distorted

344

with each barrier they breached. Dim light shined ahead, a welcomed sight after making do with only a fairy's glow to guide them. Finally, the hall widened as one last waterfall barred their entrance. Far larger than the rest, it parted wide enough for the whole party and, in turn, revealed their destination.

The beat surged into Max's ears as vibrations reverberated in his chest.

He didn't like what he saw.

A massive underground space lay exposed, its walls decorated with figures carved into the rough stone. Water flowed from openings everywhere, even from the carvings themselves. It poured from the carved mouths of snakes and wolves. A trickle fell from the eyes of a beautiful woman clothed in only palm leaves of chilled rock. All of it flowed into a reservoir below that rivaled the pyramid's private beach.

Dozens of stone slabs balanced impossibly, held up by only a few narrow pillars to form a networking of levels connected by bridges and stairways. Some were filled with high-top tables and chairs. Others were more private spaces, cordoned off by golden chains.

The rest were packed with players.

Their bodies writhed and swayed with the sound of a heavy, electronic beat that came from a stage near the back. Most were dressed in either gear that could also double as club-wear or non-game clothing designed to be provocative.

One platform, far larger than the rest, sat at the center, featuring the most spectacular bar that Max had ever seen. It stretched across the edge at least the length of a basketball court. A dance floor covered the rest.

There were no railings or barriers of any kind on the platforms or stairways, making the place the most dangerous nightclub ever conceived. Some patrons even dove off the edge into the water below where they swam and splashed about. Most of them were wearing swimsuits, though some could be described as being less prepared. Near the edges of the water, couples joined hands and led each other into the mouths of dozens of half-submerged caves, whose shadows provided an element of privacy.

Max shuddered at the idea of diving into the human soup below. It might have all been virtual, but that didn't make him feel better about it. *I should give Kira a heads up before she dives in without noticing.* It seemed like something she would do.

Max followed Berwyn and Nix up to a platform near the one wall with a view of the bar and dance floor. It was one of the quieter spaces reserved for VIP's, which made sense considering they were traveling with an emperor.

Kira settled into a velvet sofa next to Berwyn as Farn took up a position close by. Ginger pulled up close to Max and spoke a drink order into his ear so that he could hear her over the music. He pulled back, confused, unsure if he had heard her right.

"You want how many shots?"

She responded with a simple nod.

"Alright, it's your funeral."

"Put everything on my tab." Berwyn reached his arm across the back of Kira's seat.

Nix fell in at Max's side with a bounce in her step. She had an order from her boss as well, so together, they made their way down to the bar. Ripper sneered at them as they passed him on the stairs.

There were several bartenders below, and as Nix approached, one of them ignored the other patrons as to give her their undivided attention. *Berwyn must bring the mercenary here a lot,* Max assumed from the preferential treatment. Nix seemed to be important, and by extension, so was Max. It wasn't something he was used to. In the real world, he was always the guy hovering at the end of the bar struggling desperately to get the bartender's attention. It was a refreshing change of pace for him. He could get used to being important.

Max leaned one elbow on the counter like the VIP he was. "Twelve shots of vodka." He started to hold up his fingers to indicate the number but stopped as he realized he didn't have that many. The bartender, an elven man in a silver waistcoat, eyed him as if he saw right through him but presented him with a tray of small glasses nonetheless.

Moments later, Max returned to his party just in time to catch Kira's idea of date conversation.

"…and so the termite asked, is the bar tender here?" She sat with her mouth open as if proud of herself.

Berwyn smiled politely.

Farn covered her mouth to hold in a laugh, reminding Max why her and the fairy worked so well together. It took a special kind of bond to laugh at Kira's puns.

"Thank god, the drinks are here." Ginger hopped up.

Nix set down a tray with a couple girly looking drinks and a glass of brown liquid. She also got three waters for herself, Max, and Farn. She got nothing for Ripper. He didn't seem to care, resigned to watch from the stairs alone.

Max set down the tray he carried, containing twelve one-ounce glasses, each filled to the brim. He wondered who the hell they were for, considering only Ginger, Kira, and Berwyn would be drinking. Four shots each seemed like a lot.

Ginger immediately picked up one for herself and handed another to Kira. Then when Berwyn wasn't looking, the *Coin* set a second one in front of the fairy.

Kira sipped her first with an incredulous look.

Ginger simply nodded and pushed the fairy's glass up with the tip of her finger.

Eventually, Berwyn apologized and stepped away to handle something he'd heard over the Serpent's house line. He insisted that he wouldn't be long before running down the stairs and taking Nix and Ripper with him.

That was when Ginger began shoving shots into Kira like they were going out of style. The fairy shrugged and obeyed.

Farn spoke up after four. "Umm, why are we pouring shots into a girl that weighs less than fifty pounds?"

Ginger passed Kira a fifth glass. "Alcohol works off memory here, not body weight. Her tolerance is going to match her real body. I'm just trying to get her a little tipsy, so Berwyn will think he has a shot at getting her to his room tonight. Plus, she'll be a little more fun, and hopefully, she'll stop with the puns."

"Like that's gonna happen." Kira laughed. Then she laughed again.

That was when Max chimed in. "She's kind of a lightweight in the real world so that might be plenty. And if anything, she's going to make more puns."

"Oh." Ginger took a shot out of the fairy's hand as she was trying to drink it.

"And what happens when he tries to get her to his room later?" Farn leaned over Kira's seat like a loyal guard.

"Not a problem." Ginger grinned. "He won't get the chance."

"Why not?"

"Because then we're just going to pour the rest of these shots in her and get her completely wasted."

"Won't that just make it easier for him?"

"Nope, thanks to Checkpoint's forethought in building this world," she gestured around them, "you can't give consent if you're tanked. So the system will just activate her cage while her judgment is impaired. Berwyn won't even able to touch her with the system protecting her. So that option will be off the table."

"Oh." Farn's voice wavered a little.

Kira grabbed the girly drink in front of her that Ginger hadn't taken away. "Don't worry. Alcohol is a solution," she took a sip, "chemically speaking."

Max immediately slapped his hand against his head. "And it starts."

Suddenly, Kira froze, her eyes darting around as if searching. "I think there might be a ghost in here."

"Why?" Farn leaned closer.

Max glowered at her for falling into the trap.

Kira smiled wide in a way that made her violet eyes sparkle. Then she hopped up onto her knees and turned so that she could face the *Shield*. "Because of all the booooooooze." She made a point of wiggling her fingers like a spooky ghost.

Farn laughed.

Ginger groaned. "Don't encourage her."

"It's best if you don't respond. She'll get bored eventually." Max rubbed at his eyes.

The string of bad jokes ended when Berwyn returned. At that point, it became clear that four drink Kira was actually a decent flirt. She sat close, leaning into the Lord of Serpents, even touching his leg in a way that clearly gave him ideas. Not that he didn't already have ideas in the first place. Even more surprising was the fact that she'd actually stopped chattering, letting him talk about himself for most of the night. She only asked questions to keep him engaged.

Eventually, Berwyn brought her to the dance floor. Four drink Kira wasn't as graceful as she had been a few nights before, but Berwyn seemed to be having a good time regardless.

Max couldn't help but feel bad for his partner. Clearly, she was trying her best to play her role, not that she had a choice with everything on the line. He'd known her a long time, and if there was one thing he understood, she would put herself through anything if it would help her friends.

He sipped his water to wash away the taste in his mouth. It didn't help.

I just hope she doesn't have to do much more.

Finally, Max leaned to Ginger and suggested that it was time to move onto phase two of her plan to put the fairy out of commission. She agreed and took her first opportunity to pour another five shots into the little mage, who was pretty coopera-tive now that she was already half gone.

With Kira trashed and safe from the Lord of Serpents' advances for the night. Max checked the time on his stat-sleeve. It was getting late. He decided to take a patrol around the plat-form, walking its perimeter and exploring the stairs that led to the connecting areas. He spent a few moments looking around at the carvings on the walls, smiling when he saw one of a skeleton throwing back a mug of ale. Water poured out of its mug and into its bony jaws, only to flow out from its ribcage and down the wall. He chuckled at the use of the environment.

That was when a familiar face waved to him from a platform not far from his. A predatory mouth grinned wide enough to show teeth. Excitement danced in her eyes.

Max's heart sped up as he popped off the leather strap that secured his guns into his shoulder holsters. Then he watched as Lady Amelia turned and disappeared into the crowd.

House Winter Moon had arrived.

CHAPTER FORTY-THREE

"Damn, that girl's messed up." Nix leaned over to Max, her hand held in front of her mouth as if she didn't want anyone else to hear while also speaking at full volume.

Max tore his attention away from the platform where he'd seen Amelia just a moment before and glanced back to find twelve-drink Kira. The fairy was dancing on a table and singing along with the club's music despite there being no lyrics. She was going to be pretty embarrassed about it when she sobered up. He chuckled.

"At least she's having fun."

"Huh?" Nix stared off to the side, clearly not paying attention to the conversation that she had started only seconds before.

"I said. At least she's having fun."

The mercenary looked back to the hot mess on the table. "There are worse things to do while you're drunk." Her attention drifted away again, almost immediately.

Max followed her line of sight as she settled her gaze on a group of players sitting down at a nearby table.

Like most of the club's patrons, they were dressed in lighter gear that passed for something appropriate for the club. *Hmm,* Max raised an eyebrow. They were armed. Not with anything heavy, but still, it was strange if all they were looking for was a night out.

It probably wasn't a coincidence that they were seated a few tables over from Berwyn, who was enthralled by Kira's antics. His charming smile shined up at her. Albeit, a slightly disappointed smile since it was clear she was in no condition for any other activities.

Nix nudged Max with her elbow and gestured back to the armed group at the table. "You notice anything about those guys over there?"

"They just sat down a few minutes ago," Max responded, being intentionally vague in the hope she might provide some more insight into how she thought.

"And?" She seemed to be playing the same game.

"And they sat at a table between Berwyn and the stairs that lead toward the nearest exit." He shoved his hands into his pockets like he didn't consider them a threat. "It's what I would do if I wanted to stop someone from escaping."

She grinned at his answer, adding another, "And?"

"And they all have their house rings turned inward so we can't see their crests." He frowned, knowing it couldn't be a coincidence. Not with Amelia lurking somewhere in the club. He folded his arms across his chest and added, "Pretty sure they're members of Winter Moon."

"What makes you think that?"

Max smiled back, finally getting glimpse of her tactical side. She was smarter than she looked, but not so smart to have known everything. "Well, it would be a safe bet, considering that you guys just overthrew their city, that they would be looking for some revenge. But honestly, I just saw Amelia in the crowd over there." He hooked a thumb over his shoulder.

Nix's eyes widened. "Oh…"

Max's shoulders relaxed. He had been playing at espionage all week, and frankly, he wasn't good at it. A fight, on the other hand, especially one in a location as unique as the Catacombs, that was something he could handle.

Nix's face shifted to one more fitting of a mercenary. "Looks like we'll be working together." Her tone grew cold, almost predatory, as she released the strap that secured her pistol in her holster. "Watch my back. I'm checking them out."

Max nodded and raised his house ring. "Ginger, we have company. It's Amelia's Moons. Tell Berwyn, and get Farn and Ripper ready to shield him. Kira... just try not to fall down."

He lowered his ring and locked his attention on Nix as she approached the table of six potential enemies. One question hung in his mind. Would she prove to be the clumsy oaf that she seemed to be, or would she reveal herself as the danger that he had been sensing since they had met?

Then she tripped over her own feet, her arms and legs flailing with an undignified oomph as she crashed onto the table in front of the players in question.

Drinks shattered to the floor.

Max cringed.

It was obvious that she wasn't a threat, and if the players had only been there for a night out, they would have treated her as such.

They didn't.

Whether she was a threat or not didn't seem to matter. She had startled them, and now, they had to act. Two went for their weapons on reflex, *Coins* by the look of their daggers.

Max reached for his pistols only to hesitate the moment Nix rolled onto her back. Her expression stopped him cold.

The fall hadn't stunned her. No, there wasn't even a hint of confusion. Her eyes darted across each of the players. The simple fact that their first reaction to her falling in their laps was to attack spoke volumes.

Two words left her mouth, "Thought so."

She fired.

Her M9 let out a pair of three round bursts at point-blank

range into the two players to her left. Both fell as multiple hits ensured a critical.

Max didn't even see her draw the gun. She must have reached for it as she rolled over to keep it hidden.

Strangely, she had chosen to take out the two players that had yet to draw their weapons rather than the two at her feet who were already brandishing daggers. They seemed surprised by it as well, and she took the moment to kick one of their weapons out of their hand. It flittered off the platform, catching the light as she fired another burst to her right, eliminating another member of the group.

Max couldn't believe what he was seeing. It was as if she was assessing each of their threat levels by her position and her capability to acquire them as targets. The two at her feet might have seemed like a problem since they'd already drawn on her. Though the fact was, she could see them and, therefore, could take them out fastest. Instead, she focused on the ones that remained in her peripheral.

That's when a *Blade* class directly behind her plunged his sword down at her head. She had been ignoring him. Maybe because his weapon was largest and it had taken the most time to draw.

She reacted, only moving her head a few inches as he struck the table at full force, embedding his sword into the wood. It was as if she had kept her head there on purpose to bait him, prepared to move from the start.

Her fingers moved in an efficient blur, switching the M9 out of burst mode. With half of the group handled, she didn't need the additional firepower. She grabbed the *Blade's* shirt as he struggled with his sword and yanked him forward. He fell beside her. She fired two shots, one to his neck and another to his chest as she used his weight to pull herself away from the two *Coins* at her feet.

Nix slid backward off the table, landing on the floor between it and a chair. With a kick, she shoved the table into the shins of the remaining two players.

It knocked them forward, forcing them to use their hands to catch themselves. Their mistake was obvious as they raised their vulnerable heads in surprise. One of them opened his mouth.

"Oh, fu—"

She popped each of them once.

The club's music pulsed, and for the most part, no one noticed the fight or the shots fired. Hell, it had ended so fast that the first body hadn't even started to dissipate. Max stood, stunned, his hands still reaching for his guns. He hadn't even had time to draw them.

Nix was a monster.

There was no grace or style to her movements. Just raw, unfiltered damage. It was unlike anything he'd ever seen.

He finished drawing his pistols. Now wasn't the time to stand there with his mouth hanging open. There was no way those players were alone. His mind raced forward, connecting the details.

Nix seemed to be doing the same as she got to her feet.

Most likely, the six Moons at the table were a distraction to draw their attention, which meant that the real threat was elsewhere. A dozen Star Wars memes flashed through his head as he looked up.

The high ground.

It made sense for Amelia's people to take the platforms above. It's what he would have done. They were probably already surrounded.

He was right.

Ten players emerged from the edges of the platforms above. The fight had only just begun. Max glanced back to the rest of his party to make sure they were ready for what was coming.

Farn and Ripper formed a protective wall in front of Berwyn and Kira, while Ginger pulled up her hood, leaving her face hidden in shadow.

Good idea, Max thought, as he remembered the photo of Kira that had made the rounds online, the one of her dancing with Berwyn. The fight ahead was about to get very public, and the last thing he needed was his face plastered all over the message boards.

He tugged his scarf, the Mantle of Death, up over his mouth and nose, realizing just how convenient the garment was.

The fabric shifted in his hand, clinging to his face to remain in place as if it had always been meant to be used as a mask. At the same time, a system chime sounded in his ear, the same as before when he had received the item. It was heavy, like it carried a weight along with it.

Max suppressed a maniacal laugh as he realized that he had just activated his new sub-class. The *Fury* emblem on his hand transformed into a simple, black coffin. A banner with the word *Reaper* appeared across his skin beneath it. His health began to tick down every two seconds.

- 20 HP

- 20 HP

He did the math. 3,603 hit points in total meant he could keep his *Reaper* class active for around six minutes before it killed him.

Good enough.

Arrows flew down from all sides as Max took in a breath and held it. A blur of spectral steel cut through the air as the sound of snapping arrows met his ears. The players above stood dumbstruck with their heads cocked to the side as five gleaming swords drifted around him.

Max let out an awkward laugh. They were the same weapons wielded by the Nightmare, Death, the year before. "Huh, that was interesting," Max commented to himself as player aimed a pistol down at him.

"Block this!" the enemy *Fury* shouted before unloading the gun. He continued to yell until his pistol locked back empty.

"Um, okay." Max exhaled, prompting the spectral swords of Death's Unbreakable Defense to blink out of existence like a dream.

The *Fury* above pulled the trigger of his empty pistol twice more, the gun clicking. "What the—"

Max cut off his words with a bullet as the other members of Winter Moon's ambush team fell back, using the platforms above for cover. They took turns popping up to take a shot at him. He fired back and held his breath to block.

\- 20 HP

\- 20 HP

His health continued to tick down. The *Reaper* sub-class was keeping him safe, but it was also killing him slowly. Six minutes wasn't a lot of time, and it was difficult to land a critical on the players above over the distance. Then suddenly, Nix slid to his side on one knee firing up.

"Looks like you could use a hand?"

"I'll take what I can get."

She stood and took up a position against his back, her body pressed up against his. "Good because I don't know what kind of ability you're using here, but I'm guessing the safest place to stand right now is close to you."

"Glad to be of use." Max smirked.

A green coil of smoke swirled around them while a *Venom* mage laughed from above.

Damn. Wrong time to get cocky.

"So those things don't block poison, huh?" Nix pointed to her wrist as her health ticked down.

Max glanced at his stat-sleeve.

\- 20 HP

\- 30 HP

\- 20 HP

\- 30 HP

Not good.

He turned back to the others. "Hey, Kira? You sober enough to get us a heal over here?"

The fairy answered by opening her spellcraft menu and spinning the rows of glyphs into something that passed for an incantation. The spell danced around them, shifting colors from white to blue to red. Somehow her magic seemed as tipsy as she was.

Max checked his wrist to find the poison cured. He noted the addition of fire resistance and a buff to his melee damage as well. Kira wobbled and gave a triumphant salute.

"Close enough." Max shook his head at the little drunkard.

"You got Custom Rounds?" Nix pulled a new mag from her pouch and reloaded.

"Yeah," Max answered on reflex before remembering that his *Fury* skills were locked by his sub-class. "Wait, no. Not while this is active." He gestured to the scarf the wrapped around his mouth.

"It's up to me then." Nix held her M9 vertical in front of her face and whispered the command, "Fracture Rounds."

Max arched an eyebrow as she activated the lowest level of the custom rounds skill, meant only for weakening armor ... or structures.

His eyes went wide.

Nix took aim at the narrow pillar holding up one of the platforms and fired two bursts. Chunks of stone shattered on impact. She immediately slipped past Max like a dance partner and released another two bursts into the other platform's support, filling the air with shards of gray shrapnel.

For a moment, nothing happened.

Then everything did.

The weakened pillar on the right practically exploded under the weight of the platform, dropping the entire level, bystanders and enemies alike. A chorus of screams passed by as it fell, followed by a deafening crash from below.

The sound turned Max's stomach.

It was just a game, but killing dozens of innocent players just to take out a few targets was never an option that had crossed his mind. He tried not to think of the swimmers that had been caught underneath.

Then from the other side came an ear-splitting crack.

Max ducked on reflex.

Unlike the first pillar, the second snapped in the middle. The platform tipped back, slamming into the wall of the cavern just above where he stood. The impact destroyed a carving of a fish spitting water from its mouth. A torrent burst from the wall, gushing down the leaning platform like a waterfall. It poured down onto the floor near where Farn and Ripper stood.

The *Shields* both rapped their gauntlets against their chest plates, no doubt activating their Sure-Foot skill to keep from being washed away. Ripper gripped Berwyn's coat with a firm hand before he slipped. Farnsworth, however, had a little more trouble wrangling Kira. The fairy lost her footing almost immediately, landing on her rear before finally latching onto the *Shield's* leg. Ginger let out a groan at the sight of her Archmage before firing her grappling hook into the floor.

Max and Nix dropped to one knee in unison as the wave of water hit their feet. The mercenary leaned against his side for support.

Clubgoers screamed from the platform, struggling to hold on for dear life. Most were washed away along with the Winter Moon's attack team. All but one enemy fell.

A lone *Caldron* mage slid down, jumping from his platform to Max's. He hit the floor with a splash, his arm thrust out as a circle of power contracted into a single point of yellow light. He slammed his hand into the water, sparks flying from his fingertips as a current of electricity surged across the surface.

Every nerve in Max's body lit up at once, vibrating in a chaotic buzz that sapped all his strength. He fell forward to catch himself with his elbows. Through blurred vision, he caught the readout on his stat-sleeve.

- 300 HP

- 20 HP

- 300 HP

He checked the rest of his party. They were fine. Out of range of the spell.

Nix wasn't so lucky. The brunt of the spell hit her along with him. She fell, draping herself across his back.

Max clenched every muscle he had to fight the continuous spasms. The spell didn't actually hurt, but still, his jaw ached. It felt like his teeth were trying to vibrate right out of his skull.

Nix gripped his shoulder tight and pulled herself close. "Sorry, but I have to borrow you." Her voice wavered as she pressed her shaking body against his and lowered her gun to rest on his back for stability. She pumped three rounds into the mage.

The vibrations ceased the moment the man's body washed past Max's side. Shimmering particles began to float from the corpse just as it slid over the edge.

Nix slipped off of Max's back and slapped him in the shoulder. "No time to rest. More incoming."

He raised his head.

A party of six appeared halfway up the stairs to the platform, each wading through the water that poured down the steps.

Max exhaled, his health ticking into the red as he pushed himself out of the water. *No time to rest.*

Suddenly, a spiral of white light streaked around Nix and himself. Max smiled. He still had the most powerful healer in Noctem on his side. Though, he did wonder how Kira had been able to cast while clinging to Farn's leg.

The answer slid by a second later along with a slurred, "I'm going with the flow."

She must have let go.

Kira looked back as the water carried her to the edge. "At least I'm staying current."

Max shook his head as she vanished over the side. "That makes sense."

CHAPTER FORTY-FOUR

Kira tumbled end over end, not really sure which way was up. The world had been spinning long before she had fallen off the platform. If she didn't do something, she would hit the water below.

It was fine. She had wings. Everything was fine.

She hit the water's surface with a slap.

"Ow!" Kira blurted, swallowing a mouthful as soon as she did.

Was I not flying?

Apparently not.

Kira rubbed at her side, glowing red from the impact. Pins and needles prickled over her skin. Checking her wrist, her health remained full. She immediately reached to her item bag to check for her bone charm.

It was gone. Sacrificed to take the damage.

At least it saved me from the fall.

For a moment, she let herself drift. The water was comfortable and warm.

She shook off the feeling and flicked a few points of mana

into the spellwork rooted in her back. Her wings ignited in a blaze of shining particles as she shot out of the water.

Woah, no! Stop stop stop.

She scrambled to choke off the flow of energy surging from her body as she shot up toward the platforms above. It was hard to do anything gently, like trying to close a door while drunk without slamming it. Instead of a few points of mana, she'd dumped half of it into her wings.

Oops.

The cavern lit up as if in daylight as Kira came to a stop and cut off the torrent of pixie dust.

Whew.

Max was staring up at her, wearing his scarf like a bandit's mask. A pattern of white teeth had formed a wicked expression across his face. Kira checked his health. At least the shower of energy she'd released had topped off his health.

Nix ejected a spent magazine and slapped in a new one before turning her sights to the stairs leading up to their platform. Another party of Amelia's Moons crept toward her.

Two *Shields* in front brought up their gauntlets, activating a set of glowing barriers. A pair of *Furies* aimed their pistols from a position behind them along with a pair of *Blades* waiting with their swords drawn. They pushed forward.

Nix rushed them without hesitation.

Kira couldn't help but watch, enthralled by the mercenary as she threw her magazine at one of the *Shields*.

He raised his gauntlet to block his face on reflex. Nix took the opening, firing two shots low, hitting the man in both feet. He swore and lowered his barrier. She put one more in his head at close range.

Without a railing on the stairs, his body slumped off the side, leaving the other *Shield* open. Slipping past, Nix fired two in his back from inches away.

One of the *Furies* behind thrust his gun in her face. She caught his arm with her free hand, yanking him towards her. His gun was left aiming uselessly over her shoulder while his body blocked the line of fire for the rest of his team.

With her attention occupied by the struggling player, one of the *Blades* pushed past for the kill. She was faster, catching the edge of his sword with the trigger guard of her M9 and twisting to redirect it safely to the floor where she stomped it out of his grip. He looked confused when she shot him in the chin.

The other *Blade* attempted the same. She dodged by turning into the *Fury* she still held, wrapping his arm around her neck in the process. For a moment, the player looked like he had just been given a present as he pushed his wrist into her throat. The remaining *Blade* moved to take advantage of the opportunity. From there, he could run her through easily.

Nix raised her legs as if to protect her chest and stomach while reaching back and putting three rounds in the side of the *Fury* that held her. They weren't lethal, but he loosened his grip. She kicked the *Blade* square in the chest.

Well, kick wasn't really the right word. It was more of a push. One hard enough to shove both players in opposite directions, sending them flying off the sides and into the water below as she dropped safely to the stairs. She finished by unloading the rest of her pistol into the last of them to make sure he was down without needing a critical.

Kira hovered with her arms dangling limp, staring at the brutal display of tactical violence that the small reynard mercenary had demonstrated.

The crowd on the central platform did the same, finally realizing there was a fight going on. Several players moved toward Nix, though it was hard to see them mixed into the crowd. More of Amelia's Moons, no doubt.

Nix spat out a breath, her ears flicking back as over a hundred casual players gawked at her laying on the stairs. She tapped the magazine release on her pistol and flipped it to the side to eject the spent mag before slapping in a fresh one.

Max approached the top of the stairs and fired two rounds into the air, shouting, "Clear the floor!"

The crowd just stood there staring up at him, leaving him looking a bit awkward, clearly at a loss of what to do next.

Nix pushed herself upright. "It's a game. Warning shots are useless." She switched her M9 back into burst mode and fired directly into the crowd.

Kira froze at the sight of the mercenary shooting into a packed dance floor. The situation suddenly felt too real as the horrific act turned her stomach.

Screams erupted as panic took over the crowd. They ran, many opting to dive off the platform, taking their chances with the fall into the water. It was like there was something about being shot in a nightclub that overwrote the knowledge that it was all just a game.

"That got them moving." Nix smirked.

Guilt stabbed at Kira's breast. She was an accomplice.

Then she felt worse.

Not because of the shady morality of what her temporary teammate had done but because there were far more players holding their ground than she expected.

At least twenty.

They must have been Amelia's main force.

Nix reloaded again, but before she was able to fire off another round, Max leaped clear over her from the top of the stairs. With the bystanders gone, he was free to unleash hell.

Fire and smoke erupted as he came down, landing on the floor in a roll that ended with him back up on one knee for a moment before hopping back to his feet. He never stopped firing.

Kira let out a cheer, just happy to see Max back in the fight. Things were black and white again. Her best friend against Amelia's Moons.

Max stopped in the middle of the dance floor surrounded by well over a dozen enemies. The slides of his guns were locked back, empty, after letting loose on the way down the stairs. The players circled him, adjusting their positioning. As soon as he ejected his magazines, they would rush him. Even Kira knew that much.

Max did it anyway. There wasn't a choice. Hopefully, his *Reaper* class could keep him alive, though he could only hold his breath so long, and without range on his side, he was a sitting duck.

Just as his spent mags hit the floor, Nix ran into the fray, firing at anyone who made a move. The timing was perfect. A moment later, Max's guns were full and ready to go, just as Nix's M9 ran dry.

The Moons rushed from all sides, using their numbers to overwhelm them. Spectral swords flittered in and out, slapping away any projectile as Max and Nix thinned out the melee classes who might have landed a hit.

Max's hands moved independently of each other as he fired, only letting his enemies get close enough to ensure his hits. He spun, firing forward, backward, and sideways. Players fell with every movement.

The Moons didn't stand a chance.

From what Kira could tell, their level had been closer to Corvin's, down in the mid-range. If they had been closer to Max's, things might have been different.

Kira wondered where Amelia's best fighters were. It was a large house. Surely she must have had a few high-levels. Even more surprising, there wasn't a single *Fury, Leaf,* or mage on the floor.

That was when she realized the trap. She scanned the platform as Max finished with the group of mid-levels, looking for where the Moons might have set up their ranged classes.

Then it was obvious.

The bar.

Two *Furies,* five *Cauldrons,* and two *Leafs* popped up and took aim from behind the counter. Max could block the bullets, but the magic could still take him out. Kira willed herself to shout a warning, but all she got out was a confusing, "Trap is here!"

There was nowhere for Max to run.

Then with an epic roar, Farn slid in, putting herself in the line of fire, dropping low so that the energy projected from the White Rose protected her whole body. Apparently, she had figured out the trap first, and being completely sober, had acted fast.

Max and Nix huddled close together at her back to reload as the players behind the bar gave them everything they had.

The *Reaper's* translucent swords swirled while a hail of crystal shards pinged against Farn's barrier. She braced, losing twenty percent of her health in spillover damage.

That was when a brewed spell from each of the *Cauldrons* rose around her in a gust of wind and fire, combining in an explosion of colored smoke. Kira lost sight of her friends and checked their health as their totals plummeted, only stabilizing in the red. Nix probably hadn't fared any better.

As soon as the smoke cleared, Max stood with both guns drawn, his scarf pulled down from his face. A full-auto barrage of explosive rounds poured into the bar. The sound of shattering glass filled the air as bullets riddled the players and bottles alike.

Kira counted on her hands.

That's three bars we've destroyed so far this week.

Finally, Max's pistols locked back, leaving just a couple of the Moons for Nix to handle. They both smirked at their handiwork. Then another trap sprang.

From all sides, players began stepping onto the floor, surrounding them again.

That's where the high-levels were. Kira slapped her forehead.

The only members of Winter Moon missing were Amelia and her two commanders, Klaxon and Kashka. Obviously, the first wave of mid-levels had been just to soften them up. Amelia had saved her best for last.

With Max's health and ammunition running low, things were looking grim.

Kira smiled and cracked her knuckles. *Good thing they have one of the best Breath Mages in Noctem on their side.* She dove straight toward them, her casters snapping open to cast two of her strongest heals from her quick-cast queue.

The air began to glow as shimmering particles of white and green rose from the floor and swirled around... a set of chairs.

"Oh dang." Kira fluttered to a stop.

She was, of course, entirely trashed, thus making casting an area effect spell a bit difficult to target while flying.

Max looked up at her with one eyebrow raised.

"Oh man, sorry," she blurted as she opted to fly in a circle around them, dumping pixie dust like a crop-duster.

Well, sort of. It wasn't quite a circle.

She veered off course, floating to the left when she meant to go right, only making it worse the more she tried to correct it.

Good enough.

She slowed, throwing her hands on her hips in satisfaction just as a *Leaf* from below fired an arrow at her.

"Ack!" Kira dodged to the side and took off to keep moving. Looking back, she shouted a loud, "Nice try!"

Then she looked forward again.

"Ack!"

One of the platforms somehow flew straight at her. Then she realized it was her that was flying toward it. She corrected her path just in time to avoid hitting it directly. Instead, she just skimmed its surface in a ridiculous display of flailing arms and wings.

A few patrons of the club who had been hiding there watched with confusion as she jogged past, unable to stop her momentum. She kept running right off the edge.

Kira closed her eyes and screamed, forgetting that she could fly for a moment and remembering just in time to swoop up above the main floor again.

"Ha ha!" she laughed in an attempt to sound victorious as she passed over Max and the others. Their health climbed back to where it belonged.

Then a bowstring thumbed from behind.

She didn't even see it coming.

An arrow burst from her chest almost in slow motion as it streaked through her heart.

That's… not… good…

CHAPTER FORTY-FIVE

"No!" Farn cried as an arrow tore through Kira's chest with a burst of crimson light.

The fairy's health crashed to zero as her body did the same, smashing into the bar at full speed and falling out of sight behind it. It happened so fast; she couldn't believe it. Even Nix looked shocked.

"Shit!" Max put a round into an attacking *Blade* before turning back to Farn.

"No," she repeated, unable to shake the image of Kira's limp body hitting the shelves of broken bottles.

"Umm, Farn?" Max pointed at her hand.

She looked down at the black onyx ring on her finger. The one that tied her life to Kira's in a one-way bond.

It was glowing.

Suddenly, the display of Kira's health woven into the Celtic knot-work on her wrist ticked back up by one. At the same time, a countdown appeared next to Farn's name. Kira's death had been passed to her.

5:00 minutes ticked down.

A few minutes of power and the life of her friend in exchange for her own. It was a price worth paying.

Farn stared down at the ring, not knowing what to expect. Her gauntlet deactivated involuntarily, its barrier of white light blinking out as her arm began to burn. The sensation was familiar. Her Feral Edge was taking over, drawing power across her body from her gauntlet.

The instant it reached her heart, her world ignited.

A new energy welled up from within her. It tingled the way the dust from Kira's wings did on her skin, except this time, it was from inside and far stronger. It surged into her, filling her to the brim with warmth and strength.

Her sword split, now glowing purple as light gushed out to form the weapon's energy blade. Farn glance back over her shoulder at Max and Nix.

"Make sure Kira's alright." Then she flicked her eyes to the *Leaf* responsible for the arrow that had struck her friend. "You're so dead." She dashed forward as purple sparks flew from her footsteps.

An enemy *Shield* stepped in front of the *Leaf*, only to be struck with a strength unheard of. The player blocked, but it made no difference as her Feral Edge radiated with power. He flew over a dozen feet with a slash of crimson light nearly a foot wide staining his body. A trail of shimmering particles poured from his corpse as it slid across the floor, tripping another enemy before his form dissipated.

The rest of Amelia's Moons took a step back.

Farn gave them a smug grin as she twirled her sword around her, from which her message was clear.

Bring it.

Without her Gauntlet's barrier, she took hits. It didn't matter. The contract item on her finger regenerated her health faster than her enemies could hurt her. She had no clue as to what her stats were, but even with the drop in defense that came along with using her sword's contract ability, they must have been off the charts.

The Feral Edge felt impossibly light in her hand as she cut through Amelia's Moons like they were paper. Her body felt the same, like she weighed half as much, making each move feel effortless.

Enemies either fell by her sword or were launched off the platform as she darted across the floor in streaks of purple light. The timer on her wrist ticked down as the sands of her life slipped through the hourglass.

Farn let out an enthusiastic growl.

She was going to go down swinging.

Max dove over the bar's counter, mostly to get to Kira but also to stay out of the way of Farn's rampage. Just as he landed, an enemy *Coin* slammed into the shelving nearby, his corpse dissipating as he landed. *Damn, remind me never to piss Farn off,* he thought.

That was when Nix jumped headfirst over the counter, tumbling into the narrow space and landing on her face.

"I meant to do that."

Max ignored her and crawled to the other end where he found Kira rubbing her head.

"You okay?" Max shouted over the noise and screams of the fight on the other side of the counter. The fairy just stared at him with a puzzled look that said she was unsure and still completely wasted. He repeated his question, this time adding that she had taken a fatal hit.

Kira glanced at her health through her drunken haze, taking a moment to figure out which wrist it was displayed on first. It took her another few seconds to process what the single hit point next to her name meant. She scooted back against the counter like she was trying to get away from the readout on her wrist.

"I'm so stupid. I got careless."

"It's okay." Max reached out to steady her. "This is what you have that contract for. It had to get used at some point."

"No, it didn't." She shook her head.

Max sighed. His partner had always had trouble sorting out her emotions in regards to what was real and what was virtual. In her inebriated condition, it was a lost cause. To her, Farn was going to die, and it was her fault. It didn't matter that her friend would respawn. She would still blame herself.

Kira shut her eyes tight with tears trickling down her cheek. Max touched her shoulder. Her body trembled as she furrowed her brow and scrunched her nose in concentration.

Then she really did do something stupid.

"Oh, no you don't." Max squeezed her tighter, knowing that it was already too late.

It was easy to forget that Kira still held the power of a god in Noctem thanks to the entity that she had been bound to the year before.

Carver's parting gift.

Alastair had warned her not to use the power in the vault or around the hard they were trying to steal, as it could nullify the legal loophole they needed. On top of that, Kira had even said that she was afraid of losing herself to the other whatever it was that lurked inside her mind. Using that power was out of the question, but now, they were nowhere near the vault, and Kira wasn't exactly in her right mind.

Max couldn't stop her.

He froze, having no idea what the inebriated fairy might do with the power of a god. Ultimately, she could tell the game's system to do anything—spawn bunny rabbits, open the gates of hell, or summon something entirely unimaginable.

It was all on the table.

Not even the medical team at Checkpoint that treated her knew what her limits were. The result could be a nightmare.

Kira opened her eyes, revealing two bright pools of crimson power in place of the dreamlike purple irises that Max had gotten used to over the last year. It was only a moment before her eyes faded back to violet, but he was sure it hadn't been his imagination. He didn't understand what it meant, but it scared the hell out of him.

Max glanced at Nix out of the corner of his eye, hoping she hadn't noticed the brief color shift. The mercenary didn't seem to react, which could've meant anything at this point. She could've been pretending to be oblivious. Max couldn't be sure.

Without a word, Kira braced her weight against the bar and stood, her legs wobbling under the influence of several shots. Her lip quivered as soon as she saw Farn. The *Shield* simply tore through the last of Amelia's house as Kira clasped her hands against her chest.

That was when Max noticed something new.

The ring on Kira's finger that had traded Farn's life for hers had changed. Gone was the black gemstone that represented death. In its place, a brilliant ruby sat at the center of the silver band.

Such a small change.

Max wondered what it could mean.

Farnsworth let out a ridiculous howl as she cut down the last three players in a rapid attack that flowed from her like poetry.

She couldn't help it.

It was awesome.

Never in her entire life had she felt as powerful as she did at that moment, but nothing could last forever.

As the few seconds of the contract timer slipped away, she twirled the Feral Edge in a flashy display of pride before slamming the tip down into the floor to strike a final pose. If she was going to die, she was at least going to look cool.

Her sword returned to normal, the blade of violet energy shattering like glass. Farn fell to one knee as the power drained away from her body.

She missed it already.

Weakness consumed her as if weeks of exhaustion had caught up with her all at once.

This is it.

Farn let her body fall to the side and roll onto her back. She closed her eyes and waited for the world to fall away. The moment seemed to last forever.

Umm, I don't remember respawns taking this long.

That was when she felt a gentle tap on her cheek.

"Poke."

Farn cracked one eye open find Kira squatting on her toes and hugging her knees with one arm. The fairy's hair was damp, leaving it messy and fluffed as it fell across her eyes. She poked her again.

"I'm not dead?" Farn furrowed her brow.

Kira winked and raised a finger to her lips. "Shhh."

Farn's blood immediately began to boil as she realized how she had been saved. She had half a mind to chastise the fairy right then and there in front of the Lord of Serpents and everyone else. Kira knew better than to use that power; to put herself at risk just to cancel out a meaningless death was insane and stupid. Farn would have just respawned in ten minutes.

She pushed herself up onto her elbows and looked up at the fairy, the little idiot's drunken expression faltering into that of a worried friend.

The anger faded.

Max jogged up behind her, glancing around before adding a suspiciously awkward, "I never thought you'd use that contract. I guess it was worth saving."

Farn eyed him suspiciously before figuring out what he was doing. It probably wasn't a good idea to let on that their *Breath* mage had an artificial god hiding in her brain.

"Oh yeah, sorry, had to use that one. It took a lot more out of me than I expected," she added, explaining away the ability she'd used as a contract. It was half true. Berwyn didn't need to know that the contract was supposed to kill her.

Kira stood and offered a hand to help her up. Considering the fairy's lack of balance, Farn wasn't sure she was the best person the reach for. She reached up regardless, making sure not to put too much weight on the little mage. Kira made it worse by overcompensating, nearly falling backward once Farn was on her feet. Fortunately, Max was there to catch her in an embrace that left her clinging to his chest in a way that looked a little too romantic.

"That's awkward," Ginger commented as she stepped down the stairs onto the floor.

"I picked the right house to invite out tonight." Berwyn appeared on the platform behind Ginger, taking in the destruction that had been delivered upon the Catacombs. His vision drifted back to Kira. "I was worried, though. Are you okay?"

She started to step away from Max, only to stumble back into his arms a second later.

"We should probably get her out of here and sober her up." Farn jumped to her other side to help.

The fairy responded by letting out a seemingly random laugh at nothing in particular followed by a drunken, "You're pretty," and a boop to Farn's nose.

Berwyn gave a somber smile. "You may be right. Tonight might be beyond salvage. I'll take care of things here. Hopefully, I can keep us all from getting banned from the Catacombs."

Farn cringed at the wreckage around them, noticing for the first time the number of players peering down from the higher platforms. She was just glad that she didn't have to deal with the aftermath. "Thanks."

"It's the least I can do. I should be able to blame everything on the Winter Moon anyway, although I'm not sure why Amelia never showed herself."

"It was probably just a poke." Max passed Kira off to Farn. "I bet she was just checking your defenses."

Berwyn seemed to consider it. "That would mean she's planning something else for another time."

"Probably, but we can worry about that after we get this

one's drunk ass out of here." He held his finger in front of the fairy's face and swept it from side to side. "You think you can manage a teleport out of here?"

She followed his fingertip with her eyes, then nodded and opened her spellcraft menu without bothering to ask where they were going. Ginger and Max stepped in close.

Farn watched as Kira spun the glyphs in seemingly random order and swiped down to activate the spell.

Then just as the orange shell of the teleport solidified around them, Kegan's voice erupted over the house-line. He sounded frantic as if racing to get the words out.

"Get out of there now! Our cover's blown!"

CHAPTER FORTY-SIX

Corvin lay on his back, minding his own business and working his way through the last level of *Altered Beast* on his third-party emulator.

Kegan slumped against the window of their hiding place, the same narrow rooftop gable where they'd waited all week. The crystal pyramid filled the view behind him.

"So now we're just waiting here while everyone else has the time of their lives down in the Catacombs." The *Leaf* drove his chin into his palm. "I mean, I like clubbing, or at least, I did at one point in my life."

"Ugh, no thanks." Clubbing was the last thing on Corvin's mind.

"Don't be so quick to exclude yourself. It's never too late for a social life."

"Not really the dance club type."

"I guess not. There's no need to go out when you have a cute little teen fawning all over you." Kegan waggled his eyebrows, referring to the blatant crush that Piper had developed on Corvin during his tutoring.

"What the hell, man?" Corvin paused his game in horror. "She's sixteen, which is to say very illegal."

Kegan laughed a little too loud. "Relax, I'm kidding."

"I would hope so." Corvin added, "I have enough to worry about with that whole situation. I don't need you making it worse."

"Plus, Ginger would probably kill you."

"Yeah, I don't intend to find out. Piper's a nice girl, but obviously, she needs to find a guy her own age." He laid back down and un-paused his game. "Any advice for me on that front? I'm not really experienced with rejecting the advances of young ladies."

"You should probably just tell her the truth and let her down easy."

Corvin froze immediately.

It was good advice, but the problem was that Kegan hadn't said it. Instead, it had come from Aawil who was leaning against the other end of the narrow hall.

The faunus sat, casually picking at one of her fingernails.

Corvin stared at her, equally surprised to see the *Coin* as well as to have heard her speak. Aawil hadn't said a word from what Max had told him. Actually, the only reason he recognized her was due to her horns. They were thick and curled forward to frame her head in a way that made her look more like a dragon than a ram.

"What?" She gestured with a finger. "I'm not mute, you know."

The three of them sat in silence for a long moment, none of them moving until finally, Kegan's eye widened. He slapped one hand over his house ring to cover its emblem.

Aawil responded with a grin that said it all. It was too late. She'd seen everything.

Corvin fumbled with his emulator, trying to get up. They couldn't let her escape or send a message. The moment she did, it would be all over.

Kegan reached for an arrow, but she was faster. Her arm

shot out, firing a grappling line from her wrist. He ducked the barbed spike as it buried itself into the side of the window behind him with a sharp crack. She retracted the line as soon as it dug in, using it to close the gap before they had time to react.

Corvin was still fumbling with his emulator when she landed on his chest. The line continued to retract as she hooked her knees under his arms and dragged him across the narrow space into the wall. His head rammed into Kegan, knocking the *Leaf* through the window and onto the roof outside.

Corvin hit the bottom of the low sill hard. His head whipped backward so that he hung outside with an upside-down view of the shining, crystal pyramid. He pulled himself back inside to find the faunus still on top of him. The horned *Coin* straddled him in a way that would have seemed erotic if she hadn't been trying to kill him.

Aawil flicked her dagger out of the sheath at her lower back using only one finger. It twirled through the air for an instant before she snatched it with one hand. It was a plain-looking weapon with a ring at the base of its handle. She slipped her thumb through the brass circle and gripped the weapon back-ward as she drove it down toward Corvin's chest.

He grabbed her wrists in defense. There wasn't time to draw his sword, especially since he had removed it from his belt and left it on the floor a few feet away.

Corvin let out a rasping breath. She was only using one hand but still had the strength to make him struggle even when he used both of his. If she chose to use her other hand, she could kill him easily.

"Get off my friend!" Kegan fired two arrows at her head from outside.

Aawil tilted her head, dodging the first without taking her eyes off Corvin. Her free hand blurred to catch the second. She flipped the shaft in her hand and immediately stabbed it down through Corvin's shoulder.

He saw his health drop ten percent on his wrist as he struggled to hold her back. Pain and numbness radiated through his shoulder.

Kegan loosed two more arrows.

She followed the same pattern as before, dodging the first and catching the second, only to stab Corvin with it in the same shoulder. He let out a growl.

"Damn it, Kegan, stop giving her weapons!"

The *Leaf* took the hint and stopped shooting, opting to rushed her instead. "Catch this!" He plowed into her shoulder first, knocking her off his partner.

They tumbled to the floor, Kegan scrambling to disarm her. He failed.

Aawil rolled to get behind him, only to curl her arm around his neck. With her other hand, she plunged her dagger toward his heart. Keagan thrust his hand up fast enough to block, only succeeding in becoming her new captive.

"This isn't. How. I envisioned this," he choked out.

Corvin snatched the two arrows from his shoulder and tossed them to the side. Now that the *Coin* was off of him, he lunged for his katana, passing the pair struggling on the floor. His fingertips only brushed the grip of his weapon before she hooked her foot around his ankle. Aawil yanked his leg out from under him, sending him toppling back down.

He scurried back, too close to her legs, not realizing how dangerous they were. Her ankles snapped around his neck before he knew what was going on. Then through an impressive display of contortion, she juggled him up to her thighs where she held him like a vice.

Corvin let out a muffled yell, his face smooshed into her, well, parts that he wasn't exactly used to being close to. Which, again, might have been erotic if she hadn't been trying to crush the life out of him. It didn't help that she kept thrusting his head into Kegan's rear in an awkward humping motion.

"Oh come... on... move... your ass!" Corvin shouted in rhythm with her movement.

"No, you get your head out of my ass!" Kegan complained

back as he struggled to stop the faunus from stabbing. He pushed with all his might against her. "How are you this strong?"

She didn't answer.

It was a valid question since physical strength didn't actually change based on a player's level. Their weapon damage did, but that was it. Thinking about it, there was no way that she should have been able to grapple with two players at once without breaking a sweat, unless she was somehow that strong in the real world and the system was using that as a basis for her avatar. For that to be true, she would've needed to be something entirely inhuman.

There had to be some kind of exploit in play.

Either way, there wasn't time think about it now, not as long as Corvin wanted to keep his head from being shoved halfway up his partner's rear.

He caught a glimpse of something on the floor within reach. He didn't care what it was, just that it was something they could hit her with. Corvin reached out and flicked it with his fingers so that it slid up to Kegan.

The *Leaf* braced one arm against his captor and grabbed for the object, catching hold with his fingertips just enough to drag it toward him. With a push against the wall to gain some leverage, he cracked her in the head with it.

Aawil didn't seem to care, especially since it had only connected with one of her horns. Kegan growled in frustration as he followed the attack with several rapid whacks.

Aawil let out an annoyed squeak as he struck her in the eye with the corner of what turned out to be the leather-bound book that housed Corvin's third-party emulator. In the process, he also bumped the un-pause button, filling Corvin's ears with the background music of the sixteen-bit classic, *Altered Beast*.

Aawil let go of them both but not before slapping the third-party device out of Kegan's hand and sending it flying into the wall. The emulator bounced, landing directly in front of Corvin as he finally got free from the grip of the *Coin's* thighs. He let out a disappointed grumble finding his game had been un-paused in the middle of his character's beast transformation, just in time to die instantly.

"I was on the last level!" He pinned his ears back.

Aawil hopped back to the window before either of them could get back to their feet. Kegan didn't waste time, grabbing Corvin's sword from where it lay and sliding it back to his partner.

He caught it.

For a moment, the *Coin* looked like she might flee, which was something they couldn't let happen. She had seen their house rings. If she escaped, it wouldn't be long before she messaged Nix.

They had to buy time.

Fortunately, the *Coin* didn't flee. Instead, she rushed forward, jumping to the side and kicking off the wall to weave around Kegan so that she could take a swing at Corvin.

He tried to draw his sword in the narrow space but ran out of room. The weapon's sheath hit the wall before exposing more than a few inches of blade. It was enough to block. He immediately rotated his blade, still in its scabbard, and cracked her in the ribs with the blunt end. It wasn't a true hit, but she seemed surprised nonetheless.

He smiled.

So did she.

Her body slipped to the side just as Kegan fired three arrows at her back.

Corvin let out surprised, "Yar!" as they flew at him instead. He deflected one and pressed himself against the wall to dodge the others. *Damn! We have to get out of this hall.* The space was too small to fight in.

Kegan must have realized the same thing because he turned and ran toward the window, hopping through it as the *Coin* pursued him. She must have decided to kill him first so she could focus on Corvin without worrying about being shot in the back.

The *Leaf* turned and fired three more arrows, bellowing a frustrated growl when she blocked them all without flinching.

She darted to the side and fired her wrist line a second time. It hit a gabled section of roof behind him, splitting the ceramic tile. In an instant, she was on him, using the line to launch herself. She tucked her body with her knees in front like a cannonball.

Without time to dodge, the *Leaf* took the hit square in the chest, throwing him in a diagonal path down the roof. The incline wasn't steep, but with the added momentum, he slid straight toward the edge.

Corvin watched in horror as his partner vanished over the side. There was nothing he could do. Aawil turned her attention back to him, looking pretty damn pleased with herself.

He would have rushed her, but a glance at Kegan's health demanded he be cautious. Instead, he crept back as if he didn't want to risk falling off the edge himself.

The *Coin* twirled her dagger around her thumb for a moment before catching it backward and readying it in front of her. Clearly, it was meant to be intimidating.

She darted toward him, swiping low at his leg as soon as she was in range. He blocked it, but she streaked around his back and swiped again, this time at his spine in an upward arc. He stepped forward to dodge, seeing through the move. A feint followed by a critical. It was what he would have done.

"Nice try." He flipped his blade back and thrust it blindly at where he thought she would be.

The attack caught her off guard, forcing her to deflect with her hand since her dagger was out of position. She back-stepped away, her palm glowing with a bright red stripe.

This time, she looked a little less pleased with herself.

Corvin didn't let up, keeping his attacks quick and using only the tip of his sword to poke or swipe at her while staying out of range of her knife. Unfortunately, she blocked everything with little effort. In fact, she was fast enough to deflect his strikes all day, which would have been fine since he was only trying to buy time. But that would have been boring and, as Corvin was beginning to learn, Aawil didn't do boring.

Without warning, she slapped his blade away hard with her dagger, sacrificing her positioning to create an opening. She moved in regardless. Corvin's mind raced to see what she had planned—another dagger, an item, a bomb?

Then she bit him.

He yelped in surprise as she clamped down on the meat of his shoulder, letting out a savage snarl. The pain was dull, and the damage was negligible, but it felt worse due to the shock of what had happened. Corvin stumbled but shifted his weight just in time to kick off one of the roof's gabled peaks and shove her away.

Aawil tumbled back, sliding to a stop by using her dagger for traction and splitting the tiles in her wake. She looked up, her eyes wild, a smile growing across her face. No, not a smile, she was baring her teeth. A low growl rumbled from inside her.

From there, the fight changed completely.

Corvin ran, turning to block a hit only to have her use the momentum to slip past him. He spun just in time to deflect another lunge for his throat. He swung back with a Phantom Strike that she dodged. The *Coin* landed to the side on all fours like an animal before kicking off, running at him at full speed. Again, she slipped past him, this time taking three strides right up the side of a window and leaping off. The dull shine of her dagger streaked around her as she cut the air with a high-pitched whistle.

Sparks flew as he blocked.

They both alternated between running and clashing until they had traveled all the way to one of the corners of the palace, its obelisk glowing brightly as they darted around it. She pushed him back, leaving him nowhere to go but up.

Fine, this is happening, he thought as he sprinted up the side of the crystal pyramid at a forty-five-degree angle. Turning near the top, he dropped to his knees and slid back down, his sword ready to strike the snarling woman chasing him on all fours.

Aawil blocked and shoved, sending them both in opposite directions, sliding halfway down the pyramid before stopping.

Corvin gasped for air and leaned on his sword as he got back to his feet, standing wide to account for the steepness of the structure. For a moment, he became aware of the ridiculousness of what was happening, battling an enemy atop one of Noctem's palaces. His heart raced. He kind of wished that Max had been there to see.

Corvin pushed aside the thought. It was time to use his trump card. He ducked low to hide his face and ran, his boots squeaking against the crystal surface beneath him. Aawil was sure to block. He was counting on it.

The clang of steel against steel reverberated through the night air as Corvin locked eyes with her between the razor-sharp edges. His eye patch dangled around his neck, revealing the bright yellow basilisk eye staring her in the face.

He grinned.

Then she grinned.

Corvin let out a confused, "What the hel–," just before she head-butted him in the nose, which had been where she had been looking to avoid making eye contact.

Somehow she had known.

He fell back, slipping down the smooth surface until he hit the roof below with hard thud that took another ten percent from his health. The *Coin* followed, dashing down the pyramid at full speed.

Corvin braced and raised his sword, just as she leaped clear over him. She landed in a crouch on the roof behind him, her dagger thrusting forward before he even had the chance to turn.

Then an arrow punched through her chest.

Her face contorted as the emblem on her hand faded to indicate a near lethal drop in health.

"It's about time." Corvin breathed a sigh of relief. He had been waiting for Kegan to get back into the fight ever since he noticed his health bar hadn't depleted after he had slipped off the roof earlier.

"Sorry, used my last Shift Arrow to save myself, and I ended up on the second floor. Had to climb all the way back up." Kegan nocked another arrow.

Aawil spun on her heel just in time to deflect before taking another hit that would have killed her.

She looked pissed.

Kegan, however, looked pretty damn pleased with himself.

Aawil reached to her item bag for a health vial, but another arrow aimed at her head demanded her focus. The fight was over. There was nothing she could do.

She let out a furious growl and ran toward the *Leaf,* deflecting arrows one after another. Desperation took over as she threw her dagger, her only means of defense gone.

The weapon hit Kegan the shoulder, doing little more than to delay his next arrow. He ignored it and fired.

Then shock flooded Kegan's eyes as the wild *Coin* snatched the arrow out of the air and leaped straight at him. She tucked her legs into a crouch, hitting him feet first before plunging his own arrow into his neck. Together, the momentum carried them off the edge of the roof. She grabbed her dagger and kicked him with everything she had left, ensuring his fall while launching herself back to safety. She hit the tile roof in a heap as the *Leaf* disappeared over the side.

Corvin froze, unable to process what had happened.

Kegan's last words rang out over the house line. A warning for the others. "Get out of there now! Our cover's blown—" It was the only thing he could do before his words were cut off by the ground.

This time, his health crashed to zero.

Aawil pushed herself up, using her dagger for support. The tip of the blade scraped against the tile with an awful screech. She crouched and turned her attention back to Corvin.

Without hesitating, she rushed forward.

He did the same. There was only one option left.

Corvin thrust his sword at her head with both hands in an all-out attack that left him open. She ducked and plunged her dagger into his stomach. Shoving upward, her head rested against his shoulder, his arms around her in an embrace of simulated pain.

"This one's for Kegan," he rasped in her ear as he closed the trap he had set using himself as bait. All he needed was an opening. It was simple.

Throwing one arm around her back, he held her tight and ran her through, impaling them both.

She gasped against his neck, and for a moment, her body relaxed. Corvin fell to his knees with her in his arms as he waited for the world to fade.

Then together, they drifted into the night air in a single cloud of shimmering light.

CHAPTER FORTY-SEVEN

"Damn it!" Max punched the wall of snow-covered stone that surrounded the teleport point of Mount Feech.

They hadn't arrived there for any particular reason other than that it had been the first place that their drunk-ass teleporter had picked. It was as good a place as any to regroup since it was quiet and secluded.

Only ten minutes had passed before Kegan and Corvin respawned. It had taken even less time for Luka and Rando to pick them up before teleporting to the rest of the group for debriefing.

"We were so close." Ginger eyes watered with a crestfallen expression. She rested her chin on Kira's head as she held the wobbling fairy against her chest to keep her from wandering off.

"Quit clingin' on me," Kira complained.

"No, you might fall down if I don't." The *Coin* held her tighter. "Plus, you're fun to squeeze, and I need something to make me feel better.

"I'm really sorry," Corvin said, clearly blaming himself for blowing everything. "Aawil just snuck up on us. There was no time to hide our house rings."

"It's not your fault. Things happen." Max waved away the apology.

Rando stepped up, looking just as bland as he did before when they first met. "What's important is that we try to salvage the op."

"How do you suggest we do that?" Max threw up his arms. "Our cover's blown."

"Well, there's really only one way," answered Rando, sounding a little condescending. "Just teleport yourselves back to the palace before they revoke your access."

Max scoffed at the idea. "Yeah and walk right into a trap."

"Actually, he's kinda right." Farn stepped forward. "Nix and Aawil are mercenaries, so they aren't really loyal to Berwyn. Just his money. And if I was them, I'd wait to find out more before doing anything. They might not have told on us yet. So teleporting in might be the fastest way to find out if our cover really is blown."

Max flipped through his journal to see if his base point was still set to their room in the palace, which it was. "They haven't kicked us out, and they've had enough time to do it already. But that could also mean that they're waiting there with a team to kill us all as soon as we appear."

"That does seem like something Berwyn would do," commented Luka, provoking an annoyed glower from Rando.

"Either way, we should probably get this one sobered up a bit first." Farn gestured back at Kira who was trying to get free of Ginger's arms by going no-bones and dropping to the ground like a child.

"I'm fine," argued the fairy while leaning against the *Coin's* legs for balance.

"I know you are, but just in case, why don't you have a snack and rest a bit anyway." Farn crouched down and materialized the last lagopin bun from her inventory.

Kira immediately snatched the item and scarfed it down.

There were no further arguments.

About a half-hour later and few more food items from

everyone's supply, Kira was relatively stable, or at least, stable enough to build a small family of snowmen. Well, snow-people. She gave two of them breasts.

"Oh great, I feel better about this already," Max said sarcastically as he stepped toward her for a teleport along with Farn and Ginger.

"Report back as soon as you know where things stand." Rando stood back with the others.

"Yeah, yeah, we know the drill." Max tried to act as if covert operations weren't anything new. "Make sure you take us to the right place this time," he added in Kira's direction.

She gave a harrumph but took her time selecting the correct glyphs from her menu just in case.

Tendrils of orange light weaved a sphere around them, replacing the cold of the mountains with the collective, uncomfortable warmth of four bodies breathing.

"It's probably a good thing that none of this is real," Kira rubbed at her stomach, "'cause I would totally throw up on all of you right now."

Max tried his best to keep his distance.

As expected, the shell of mana dispersed in a burst of light and color.

They moved fast.

Weapons were drawn, and casters snapped open. They were ready for anything.

Well, almost anything.

"Hi, guys." Nix sat in one of the chairs, ignoring the guns, sword, and dagger pointing in her direction. Her tail peeked out from under her, swishing happily. On the arm of the chair, just within reach, was her M9. "I was afraid you all might not come back."

"Hi, Nix," Max breathed through his teeth without lowering his pistols. "What the hell are you doing here?"

"Now, is that any way to talk to your new partner?"

Max gave a low snort meant to sound sarcastic. "And when exactly did we become partners?"

The reynard's ears twitched back and forth for a moment before letting out a long sigh. "Okay, so I'm just gonna lay everything out on the table here. Aawil and I might have an ulterior motive for working for Berwyn. And I assume, judging from the two jackasses that you guys have had hiding up on the roof all week, that you might not be here just to join up with Berwyn either. After watching you for a while, I can only assume that you are after the same thing as us."

Max started to say something but stopped just short, not wanting to give her any information. "And what's that?"

"The vault." She rolled her eyes as if it had been obvious.

"Okay, so why didn't you tell on us? Shouldn't you want us out of the way?"

Nix shifted in her seat, almost seeming embarrassed. "Well, we sort of need your help here anyway."

Max said nothing, forcing her to continue.

"Both Aawil and I are too big and heavy to get through the laser grid."

"Mana fence," Kira and Farn corrected in unison.

Nix ignored them.

"So you need our help then?" Max assumed, letting a smug grin crack onto his face.

She ignored that as well and gestured to Kira. "Well, you have such a perfect solution right here."

"That's true. We do," Max agreed before repeating the words, "We. Do," with more emphasis. "So the question here is why do you think we need to take you two on as partners?"

"True true." Nix nodded. "For starters, we're not greedy. So we're happy with just a cut of the hard, even though we were here first. And as for what we have to offer, well, we just won't tell on you."

Max decided to play hardball. "But what's to stop us from just telling on you first?"

"That's simple, I have Aawil in position to tell Berwyn right now that she just killed two Lockheart spies on the roof, and of

course, I'm already right here to take prisoners." Her eyes
flicked to her gun, still resting on the arm of her chair.

Max adjusted his aim to draw her attention back to his
pistols. "You really think you can take the four of us?"

"You think I can't?"

Max didn't answer. Instead, he just let out a pensive,
"Hmm." He wasn't sure. He could call her bluff, but that
would blow the whole plan. Then again, if they took her on as
a partner, she might jeopardize everything anyway. Not to
mention that they would be adding two players into the split of
the take when things were over. He was stuck between a rock
and a hard place, and it showed when he let the silence go on
too long.

The others to looked at him awkwardly as if they were
wondering if they should still be aiming their weapons at the
mercenary.

Nix clasped her hands together. "I'm sensing that you might
need a little more convincing. So I could sweeten the deal a bit."

"Oh yeah, how?" Max said, partially hoping it would be
enough to justify the risks of working with her as he let his aim
fall to a more relaxed position.

She hesitated a moment, her ears twitching. "I wasn't going
to get involved in your problems, but hey, I'm curious." Her
gaze drifted to Kira. "I could get that pendant off you."

Max raised his guns back up so fast that she may as well
have issued a threat. Instead of firing, he looked to Kira who
was just as stunned, clasping the amethyst gem that clung to her
throat with one hand.

Farn stepped closer until she pressed against the fairy,
shielding her with her body just in case.

"How do you know about her pendant?" demanded Max,
practically shouting before realizing that he should keep his
voice down.

A Cheshire grin crept across Nix's face. "You'd be surprised
what I know about what goes on in this world. I am rather well
informed."

"Then do it. Get it off her now!" Farn jumped into the conversation, sounding a little desperate.

Kira nodded along with her.

"Not so fast." Nix shifted in her seat, turning her eyes to Kira so that she could address the fairy rather than letting everyone else discuss her fate in front of her. "We haven't even gotten into the vault yet. Besides, getting that thing off isn't as easy as it sounds. But if you stick with me on this, I can promise you that it won't be a problem much longer." She looked back to Max. "And don't worry, I'll answer whatever you want when this thing is over."

He wanted to say more but wasn't sure how to respond. Kira's situation had sat at the back of his mind ever since she had almost died the year before. Having it brought up now by someone as shifty as Nix in the middle of the heist threw him for a loop.

She raised an eyebrow. "Should I take it from your lack of shooting me that you're on board here?"

"I guess, but—" he started to say before being cut off.

"Perfect." She got up, making sure to pick up her M9 as non-threateningly as possible before slipping it back into her holster.

"I'm glad we could work this out." She held out her hand to shake as if they had all just become the best of friends. However, when it became obvious that none of them were putting down their weapons, she just gripped the muzzle of one of Max's pistols and shook it instead.

"Well, I'll be logging off, but I'll be on tomorrow night bright and early. So we can all hang out then and go over the plan. There's still one night left to kill before Checkpoint deposits the city's hard anyway. Might as well get prepared while we wait."

With that, she slipped out of the room, leaving Max with his eye twitching. He let his guns drop to his sides and stared at the door where she'd been.

"What the hell just happened?"

CHAPTER FORTY-EIGHT

NIGHT FIVE: THE HONEYPOT

Max wrapped his knuckles against the rickety door of a small shack near the edge of Port Han.

There was no answer.

"Is this the right place?" Corvin swiveled his head around the street of the quiet fishing village. The lantern hanging by the door bathed the scene in an eerie light.

"Yeah, it kinda gives me the willies." Kegan furrowed his brow. "Or is it the heebie-jeebies?"

"Keep thinking about that. I'm sure you'll figure it out." Ginger checked the time on her stat-sleeve despite having only just logged in for the night.

"Is it possible to have the willie-jeebies?" Kegan continued. With Kira and Farn absent, he seemed to be taking it upon himself to lighten the mood.

Max hadn't wanted to leave them behind, but it seemed prudent to keep a presence back at the palace to keep an eye on their new partner, Nix. He didn't want to take his eyes off of her for a second, but he had questions, and right now, answers came first. He banged on the door of the shack hard enough to make the lantern beside it rattle.

"Hey, Luka, open up. We don't have all night!"

Finally, an annoyed elf answered the door, "Are you trying to call as much attention to our secret field office as possible?"

Max gave her a humorless stare, then gestured back to the empty fishing village.

"Point taken. Come on then." Luka nodded before showing them inside and down a stairwell that lead beneath the structure. Max followed her down the creaking planks until they reached a plain-looking door. She pushed it open.

Max let out an involuntary, "Whoa," as he took in the brightly lit, modern hallway that lay beyond. It was as if he had just stepped out of Noctem and into an office building in the real world.

"We get that a lot." Luka chuckled at his dumbfounded expression.

"I had no idea something like this was sitting here under Port Han." Ginger blinked and glanced around.

"Actually, I'm not sure if it is." She directed their attention down the hall where a dozen more doors lined the wall. "These all lead to different places all over Noctem, so technically, this hallway could be anywhere. Though, the Bureau rents the space from Checkpoint Systems, so I always assumed it existed in Valain."

"Yeah, I get it, it's all very impressive, but we do have to get back to the palace," Max tried to speed things up, coming off a little rude. He wasn't comfortable leaving Kira and Farn alone with Nix.

If Luka was offended, she didn't say anything. Instead, she led them to a door at the end of the hall which housed an office. A number of terminals of floating glass, similar to a player's inspector, lined one wall.

Rando stood in the center. "Sorry to call you out here, but we didn't think it would be good to keep meeting in the open."

"What were you able to find out, Rando?" Max asked,

cutting to the reason they had come. After being forced into a partnership with Nix, he had thought it wise to have Rando and Luka find out what they could about her during the day. The mercenary had to be more than she appeared. He was sure of it.

"You can call me Dawson down here; this location is secure. And sorry to disappoint, but Nix is clean."

"That's it?" Max asked, unsatisfied with such a basic answer.

"That's it." Dawson held his hand out empty. "I can't tell you much about her since you're not cleared to go digging into the private information of a civilian, but she's just your average college student. Average grades. No record. Nothing out of the ordinary. If you can work with her, you should still be able to pull this off without—"

"You're wrong." Max interrupted.

"What?"

"You must have missed something."

Dawson glowered at him. "We were thorough, I assure you. So unless she's somehow better than us at putting together a cover, then I think she's just a normal girl."

"What if she is better than you?"

Dawson arched an eyebrow. "What makes you think—"

Max immediately drew his guns and pointed them at the bland-looking man.

Dawson stepped back. "What the hell do you think you're doing?"

"What am I doing wrong?" Max answered his question with a question.

"I'm sorry, what?"

Max adjusted his aim. "You're an F.B.I. guy, right? So you've had firearms training?"

"I have."

"Then what am I doing wrong?"

Dawson relaxed and ran his eyes over Max's pistols. "The safety is off, you're pointing them at a person that you don't intend to shoot, and your fingers are on the triggers."

"Exactly." Max holstered one gun while twirling the other dangerously around his finger. "It's called trigger discipline. I looked it up before logging on."

"And what's your point?" Dawson leaned against a desk.

Max ceased his twirling and pointed his gun at the man as if gesturing with his hands. "My point is that I learned everything I know about guns and fighting here, online. So for me, things like trigger discipline don't matter. If I was to shoot someone by accident." He swung his pistol to the side, aiming at Kegan's leg.

"Hey, watch it." The *Leaf* jumped out of the way.

Max ignored him. "If I shot Kegan here, what's the worst that could happen?"

"I would be extremely annoyed."

"Exactly," Max said again as he holstered the pistol. "Worst case scenario, I accidentally land a critical that kills him, and he respawns in a bit. Which is why, for me, being responsible with my weapons doesn't matter. I'm a gamer, not a soldier. Who cares?"

"And how does this relate to Nix?" Dawson crossed his arms.

"She's the opposite. I've watched her, and she never puts her finger on the trigger until she's ready to fire. Plus, she keeps her gun aimed low and away from people."

"So you think, what? That she trained in the real world?"

Max tapped the tip of his nose. "Also, she knows something about what happened last year. About all the stuff with Carver and whatnot. I'm not sure how much she knows, but for starters, it's more than you guys."

Dawson's eyes widened.

"So let me ask you," Max continued, "if we really are dealing with someone that can build more convincing cover IDs than the F.B.I. and has real-world training, then what would someone like that want with a few million in hard? I would think they would be able to get money in other ways. So that just leaves one possibility."

Luka gasped. "You think she's after Berwyn's book."

Max tapped his nose again. "I bet the information in there is far more valuable to the right people."

"Shit." Dawson slapped the desk he leaned on. "That's actually a good point."

Max nodded.

"Shit." Dawson slapped the desk again. "If she's after the same thing as us, she'll almost certainly double-cross you when the time comes."

Ginger stepped in. "And if she double-crosses us and things go bad, we could get stuck holding the bag with Berwyn after us." She shifted on one leg and crossed her arms. "I hate to say it, but I'm not sure we can take that kind of chance."

Dawson shifted his focus to her as his face lost some of its color. "You can't back out now."

"That's not up to you," Max retorted, feeling guilty at the prospect of letting so many people down. "This has all gotten out of hand."

"Like Max said, we're gamers, not soldiers." Ginger lowered her eyes to the floor. "We're just regular people. We're not cut out for something this important."

"I wouldn't say that." Luka slammed her hand down on a desk, making the rest of the room jump. "You have gotten further in a week than we did in months."

Ginger laughed half-heartedly. "That's just because Berwyn is a perv and we have a cute fairy on our team."

Max threw up his hands. "Yeah, that doesn't really qualify us for much. And Kira will certainly be happy to be done with this. So, I'm sorry to let you down, but—"

"Tell them," Luka interrupted, staring daggers at Dawson. "We should have told them from the start."

Max froze. "Tell us what?"

Dawson fell silent for a moment, staring at the floor before finally speaking. "There is a shipment."

"What kind of shipment?" Max asked, assuming he wasn't going to like the answer.

"A dangerous one," Dawson said, clearly trying to keep it vague.

"What kind of shipment?" Max asked again, this time growling his words through his teeth.

"Something biological and deadly." Luka locked eyes with him. "That's all we could put together from the other books we got a hold of, and that's why we need Berwyn's copy, so we can see all the information and stop the sale."

"And we don't have time to find another way. No one has come this close to Berwyn's operation. Right now, you're all we have." Dawson let out a long, defeated sigh. "I understand we're asking a lot, but if we don't do this, a lot of innocent lives could be lost."

The words slammed into Max like a truck, the weight of the responsibility almost crushing him. "And when does this sale take place?"

"Three days." Dawson held up three fingers.

"But that's so soon. Doesn't he have to get his product here?" Ginger cupped her hands over her mouth. "Oh god, it's already in the country," she guessed through her fingers.

Dawson broke eye contact and nodded.

Max wanted to punch the guy. To shove everything he'd told them right back at him and walk out. He didn't. Instead, he just leaned against the wall, tilting his head back in defeat. "Well, I guess there's no sense wasting time here then, is there?" He looked around the room at his team for any arguments.

There were none.

"Can I borrow Lockheart's ring box for a sec?" He held his hand out to Ginger.

She pulled the item out of her bag and passed it over. Max opened and closed it twice, producing two house rings. He set them down on the nearest desk.

"Welcome to House Lockheart. I guess we should let you in on the plan."

CHAPTER FORTY-NINE

"Thank god you're here," Farn said as she swung open the door of the palace suite. An enthusiastic voice came from the room behind her.

Max leaned to the side to peek past the *Shield*. Ginger did the same. Together, they tilted their heads to the side as Nix awkwardly positioned herself on the couch with her rear in the air. She gestured one hand behind her in a senseless, yet vaguely obscene manner.

Kira sat as far away from the mercenary as possible, cramming herself into the end of the sofa, tucking her knees in front like she was trying to hide. Max arched an eyebrow at the scene.

"So, what's going on in there?"

"Nix is explaining, umm," Farn fidgeted in place, "how to pleasure a man."

"Yikes," Max said, not really sure exactly what act the mercenary was trying to explain. "And why is she doing this?"

Farn closed the door behind them. "Berwyn stopped by and asked Kira out for a walk on the beach later. He specified that it would be just the two of them without their guards since their last few attempts have been interrupted."

Nix took a break from her demonstration to lean over the arm of the couch in a position that still seemed inappropriate with her tail curling up over her back. "If you think about it, this will be like, their fourth date. So you know, things might happen." She lowered her voice to a whisper before adding, "Sexy things."

"How 'bout no?" Kira shifted to a more comfortable position and straightened her dress.

Max laughed, which actually surprised him after the news that he had been given back at Port Han earlier. "So you have to make out with him for a bit. You'll be fine."

Nix ears stood up straight. "Oh, you're probably gonna have to do more than that."

"Okay, maybe second base." Max stepped into the sitting area.

Kira groaned and slouched in her seat.

Nix leaned closer to her, clearly having a little fun. "Probably third."

The fairy let out a squeak and sat up straight. "Nope, I'm out. I'm gonna go hide in the bedroom, and you can tell him I died suddenly. Yeah, that'll work. Problem solved." She brushed her hands together as if finishing an imaginary task.

Max sat down across from her. "I'm not sure that will—"

"I said, problem solved," she repeated before he could finish and glared back at him as if daring him to argue.

"I could try to get in the way again." Farn dropped into the chair next to Max. "That worked before."

Nix rolled over and lounged against the armrest. "True, but Berwyn's getting impatient. I can tell."

"Oh great, more pressure. Awesome." Kira grimaced.

"Look, no one expects you to sleep with him or anything." Max tried to ease her fears.

"Berwyn does," Nix added.

Max glowered at her. "You are not helping."

"What? I'm just saying."

"Yeah, well, do you mind giving us some time to talk about this?"

"Sure, go right ahead." Nix tilted her head back into the cushion as if exiting the conversation without really leaving.

Max continued to stare at her in silence.

"Oh, you mean you want time to talk without me in the room."

Max continued to glower.

"Fine, I guess Kira could use the support of her friends, which I apparently don't rank yet." She placed a hand across her heart as if wounded. "I can go find something else to do, but I'll be back later to go over the plan for tomorrow."

"Thank you." Max relaxed, a little surprised with how cooperative she was being after forcing her way onto the team the night before. Even more surprising was how disappointed she looked as she left. He actually felt a little bad about kicking her out. Then he reminded himself that she was probably planning to double-cross them and turned his attention back to his real friends.

Farn moved to sit down in the space Nix had left and leaned towards Kira. "Don't worry, you don't have to do anything you don't want to."

"Actually, you might." Max sighed.

"What?" responded both of them in unison.

"Things have changed." Max took a deep breath, then told them what he had learned about the arms deal that they had been tasked with stopping by Dawson. He also mentioned his theory about Nix's intentions.

After that, everyone sat in silence to process what it all meant. Max expected Kira to argue or possibly lock herself in the bedroom. Instead, she just flopped over, resting her cheek on the arm of the couch, deflated.

"So that's it then. We can't afford to take risks. How can I say no?" Her voice came out thick like it was stuck in her throat.

Her response hit Max harder than any argument could. She had always been a person that put others before herself. It was one of the traits that he'd always admired about her. Hell, she had almost sacrificed her life the year before, and back then, there wasn't nearly as much on the line. Now, from her reaction, it seemed like she might do whatever it took to make sure no one else had to suffer.

"Maybe he won't try anything," Max suggested, trying to remain hopeful.

Kira scoffed. "He almost certainly will."

Max leaned forward. "If he does, I'm sure you can stop him before it goes too far without upsetting him."

"That's a lot harder than you think." She closed her eyes.

"She's right," added Ginger as she sat down on the coffee table between her and Max. "Guys don't always take it well when you try to slow things down, especially when they are used to getting their way. Saying no can be a bit of a minefield."

Kira tightened her arms around her chest, hugging herself. Ginger brushed away a lock of silver hair from her face.

"I'm sorry. This was my dumb idea. You just got caught up in it. If I could take your place, I would."

"I know. It's not your fault. Everything else aside, there wouldn't even be a chance to stop anything if it wasn't for your plan." Kira touched her pendant absentmindedly.

"True," agreed Max, before adding, "at least you'll be getting more action than I do," in an attempt to lighten the mood.

"Now you're the one not helping." Farn scowled at him.

"No, you're not," Kira added before continuing, "I just wish it wasn't him."

Max snickered. "Oh, don't worry, no one is going to think you're gay."

Kira immediately sat up and glared at him. "You jackass, do you actually think that's the part that is bothering me?"

"Umm, I don't know," he said, not really prepared to defend himself.

The fairy stood up and laughed, but not in a 'fun, that's funny' sort of way. No, it was more of an angry, 'I can't believe you said that' kind of way. She looked down at him, and for a moment, it looked like she was going to let him have it. Then she just sighed and placed a hand on her forehead.

"You really are terrible with women."

Max wasn't sure how to respond. "I didn't mean—"

"I'm going to go get this over with." Kira turned away. "If you don't hear from me, I'll talk to you in the morning." Without another word, she stomped out the door.

"Wait here." Ginger leaped up and ran after the fairy.

Max sat there, still confused and unsure if he should follow as well. "What did I do?"

"You really have no idea, do you?" Farn stood up abruptly and stormed into the bedroom, slamming the door behind her.

Max sunk into his seat, alone in the empty room.

"What just happened?"

CHAPTER FIFTY

"Wait!" Ginger ran from the suite to catch up to the fairy, only to run into her a few feet from the door. Apparently, Kira hadn't gone far. "Ompfm, sorry."

The fairy shook off the impact. "I'm okay. You don't have to—"

"Oh, shut up. You are not." Ginger jabbed a finger in her direction, getting sick of beating around the bush. The girl's insistence on sacrificing herself was infuriating.

"Okay, sure, but there isn't much left to say." Kira rolled her eyes.

Ginger threw her arms around her friend without hesitating. "I'm so sorry."

"I know." Kira's body relaxed her arms.

Ginger pulled away, looking her over. She really was a breathtaking creature. It killed her to see the girl being forced into making so many choices—choices that Ginger had made years prior. She'd never regretted any of it, but still, everyone was different. What was right for her wasn't right for everybody.

"Look, I just wanted to tell you not to do anything you're uncomfortable with."

Kira smiled. "I appreciate that."

"I mean it. If you decide that this isn't how you want your first time to be, that's okay. It's your choice, no matter what anyone else says. And I can't believe I'm saying this, but forget about the hard and everything else."

The fairy's face turned bright red. "Oh god, Ginger. Are you giving me 'the talk'?"

"Someone has to."

"I know all that stuff already."

"But you need to hear it again anyway."

The fairy groaned up at the ceiling like a frustrated teenager. It reminded Ginger of her daughter.

"I know, I know. You'd rather not talk about this, but I have to add, if you do decide to go through with things, that's okay too. Everyone is different, and there's no wrong way to lose your virginity."

Kira hid her face in her hands. "I can't believe you just said that. You do know I'm twenty-eight years old, right?"

"I mean it, some people wait for the right person to come along, but others just get it out of the way. And there's nothing wrong with either choice. Just do what's right for you. You'll still be the same person tomorrow, and all of your friends will still love you."

"Are you done?" The little mage dropped her hands to her sides.

"I am." Ginger nodded before throwing her arms around the girl again and squeezing her tight.

"I should probably get going." Kira struggled to escape the embrace until Ginger finally released her.

"Okay, just remember what I said."

"I will." Kira stepped back, then paused to give her a smile before turning away down the hall.

Ginger watched her go, surprised by her own words. She hadn't known what she was going to say when she chased after the fairy. In the end, she just wanted Kira to make up her own mind without fear or regret.

She blinked away a tear and turned back to the suite.

CHAPTER FIFTY-ONE

Farn paced across the bedroom of the suite, stomping back and forth hard enough for her armored boots to rattle. Nonsensical grumbles narrated her tantrum.

I can't believe Max just sent her off to do whatever with whoever. Does anyone even care?

She stopped dead in her tracks and stared at the bed that occupied the room, feeling sick to her stomach.

"Nope, I can't do this."

Farn immediately made for the door, bursting back into the suite's main room.

"Okay, I can't stay quiet. I thought I could, but I can't."

Max ducked as Farn rattled her way toward him.

Ginger entered the room at the same moment from the hall, stopping short as she took in the room. For an instant, she looked like she might turn right back out again. Farn couldn't help but notice that the *Coin* hadn't brought Kira back with her. She scowled at Max as she flew off the rails.

"I just can't believe you."

"I have no idea what I did." He let out a groan and buried his face in his hands, pushing his fingers into his eyes.

Farn stomped one foot like a bull, ready to charge. "Really? You have no idea? Your best friend is going out for a romantic evening with a murderer, and all you can do is make a joke about her being gay!"

Max threw up his hands. "I'm sorry. I was trying to lighten the mood. I didn't know what else to say."

"That's easy, you tell her not to go," Farn growled.

"I couldn't do that, not with everything on the line."

He was right. Farn knew that much, but that didn't make her feel any better. She couldn't stand the idea of Kira and Berwyn together. Rational thinking wasn't on the menu.

"Calm down." Ginger stepped in.

"Thank you," Max said.

"Max's choice of words earlier was idiotic," Ginger started.

"Hey, wait a sec?"

Ginger held up one hand to stop him from speaking. "But he's not wrong. I don't like the situation, but Berwyn is dangerous."

Farn closed her eyes and tried to keep her mouth shut. Saying more wasn't going to help, and it would only make her outrage more suspicious. Ginger was right; she had to let it go.

That was easier said than done.

She let out a frustrated growl and gave in to her jealousy. "But this is Kira we're talking about. She's never even kissed anyone before."

Max tilted his head. "Umm, I used to share a wall with her back in our apartment, and trust me, she's been kissed plenty."

"That was different. That was Seth, not Kira," Farn argued, fully understanding that she wasn't making any sense. "It just isn't right. Kira shouldn't have to do this. She shouldn't be with him. She should—"

"Be with someone else?" Ginger finished the sentence.

Farn froze, realizing she had said too much as Max swirled his head between her and Ginger like a confused dog. Suddenly, Ginger blew out a long sigh and fell back into a chair.

"I am an idiot. A great, big, dumb idiot."

"What, why?" asked Max.

Farn took a step back toward the door. She knew why.

Oh no!

She could practically hear the pieces falling into place as Ginger figured her out.

"I'm so sorry, Farn." The *Coin* shook her head and stared at the floor. "I was trying so hard to push you and Max together the other night. I never stopped to think. I was being nosy and a busybody, and I'm sorry."

Farn cringed as if bracing for a car accident that she saw coming but couldn't do anything to stop. She even held her breath. The *Coin* raised her head and locked eyes with her.

"So tell me, how long have you been in love with Kira?"

There it was.

The one thing Farn had been trying to hide, out in the open. Half of her felt relieved. The other half freaked the hell out. Either way, there was no point denying it now. Farn collapsed to the sofa with a groan. Her armor clanked as she fell to the side, planting her cheek into the seat cushion. She continued to groan until she ran out of air. Finally, she spoke.

"I don't know. Since last year, maybe."

With that, Ginger let loose, hopping over to sit by her feet. "How did I not see it sooner? I mean, is my worldview really that narrow?"

"Most people's are," Farn commented.

"When did you realize it?"

"Oh my god." Max's mouth fell open. "I knew it. I am the third wheel."

Farn ignored him. "It was back when Kira was in quarantine after the mission last year. I didn't see her for two weeks, and it destroyed me how much I missed her. When she got back online, that was it. It was too late."

"So, is this a new attraction just for Kira," Ginger raised an eyebrow. "or is it—"

"It's not a phase." Farn shot back. "I knew what I liked before I even knew what that meant."

"Why didn't you say something?" Max asked.

"Oh, I don't know, Mister No-one-is-going-to-think-you're-gay."

"Oh shit. I'm an asshole." Max slapped himself with both hands.

"Kinda."

"I need to start keeping my dumb mouth shut." He threw his head back and stared at the ceiling.

"Eh, you didn't know." Farn waved his comment away.

"That's no excuse. You're my friend, and I'm sorry."

"We're both sorry," Ginger added.

"I know." Farn tucked her head down until her chin touched her chest plate.

Ginger leaned closer. "We may be idiots, but we would have accepted you. You could have just come out."

Farn pulled away from the *Coin*. "I like who I am, and I don't need to be accepted. Plus, everything happened so fast back when we met, what with Carver and his mission. There wasn't really a good moment to bring it up."

"That's fair." Max nodded.

"Not to mention, I got outed back in high school. It didn't go well, so sorry if I didn't want to go through that again."

Ginger eased back, giving Farn some space. "I'm sorry. That must have been hard. You grew up in the south, right?"

Max crossed his arms. "The south isn't that bad..." He trailed off, ending with a simple, "Oh."

"Yeah, my family obviously had trouble fitting in." She didn't need to say more. Instead, she just gestured to her face. The color of her skin said the rest. "Church was the only thing that tied my parents to the community. It was important to them, and they followed it to the letter. So you can image how thirteen-year-old me felt when she realized why she liked the Little Mermaid poster on her wall."

Ginger laughed, clearly caught off guard.

"I get that, actually." Max placed a hand on his chin and nodded. "The seashells kind of worked for me too."

"I know, right?" Farn let a smile show, finding some common ground. "Anyway, my parents weren't quiet about their opinions, so I grew up thinking there was something wrong with me. I tried to pretend it wasn't true. And that worked for a while."

"But?" Ginger asked in a sympathetic tone.

"Then I met a girl."

"That's always trouble," Ginger joked.

Farn didn't laugh. She couldn't. Her chest still ached from old wounds. "We didn't have much in common, but we went to the same school, and there was an attraction there. It didn't take long before we started sneaking around."

"But?"

"But then another student caught us making out. The rest of the school found out in record time. Our parents found out a day later."

"What'd you do?" Max asked.

"We decided to face things together. Tell our parents that this was who we were and if they didn't like it, then that was too bad."

"Didn't work, did it?" he asked as if knowing the answer.

"Nope, she backed down. Who could blame her? She was able to return to school without much of a problem, while I was left to face my parents and become an outcast. I haven't dated anyone for real since."

Ginger winced. "I probably would have stopped dating too. Did you fare any better with your family?"

"They went through all my movies, video games, and manga, throwing out anything that they considered question-able. Then they monitored everything I bought to make sure I didn't get anything they didn't approve of."

"What'd you do?" Max asked again.

"I tried to change."

"Seriously?" Ginger looked at her incredulously.

Farn laughed. "What else could I do? I had been taught that was how it worked my whole life, and I didn't know any better. I thought I could change. Eventually, things settled down, and people forgot about it. I got a boy to take me to prom and fell in line along with everyone else. My parents were thrilled."

"That's horrible." Ginger looked like she might cry.

"I know. I was faking it, and it was killing me. Eventually, I couldn't take it anymore, so on my eighteenth birthday, I blew out the candles on my cake and came clean. I said that this was who I am and I wasn't changing. I told my parents I loved them and that I would always be their daughter."

Ginger looked a little proud. "And?"

"We didn't even cut the cake." Farn felt all the strength leave her as if experiencing the moment all over again. "I left home that night without even a change of clothes. I walked six miles to a motel."

Both Max and Ginger's mouths fell open.

Farn shrugged. "In their defense, I don't think they expected me to really go, and even after I did, I don't think they realized I'd stay gone. But I had enough money saved up from working part-time to get me started, and from there, I scraped by."

Ginger's response was instant, "Now you're the idiot."

"What?" Farn pushed up on her elbow.

"You go through all that, and now that you have a chance at happiness, you hide and wait a year without even saying anything." The *Coin* slapped her in the boot. "And why the hell did you snuggle up so close to Max back at karaoke when you had plenty of room next to the girl you like?"

"Because Kira's my best friend, and I feel guilty." Farn dropped back down. "I don't want her to figure things out, and it's hard to keep up a front when I'm close to her. I just know I'm going to do something to give her the wrong idea."

"Like what?" Max asked.

Farn rolled over to face the back of the couch. Somehow, not looking at them made things easier to talk about. "Like a friendly hug that goes on too long or a stare that borders on leering. Hell, she might catch me smelling her hair when she leans close."

Ginger snorted a laugh. "Oh man, Farn, you're kind of a creep, aren't ya?"

"Ginger, I haven't had sex for almost a decade. So yeah, I've gotten a little weird."

"Ouch." The *Coin* patted her leg.

"Plus, she smells nice. I'm not made of stone." Farn rolled onto her back and placed her wrist across her forehead. "It's even harder to be alone with her."

Ginger gave a mischievous grin. "Because you just want to rip off her clothes and have your way with her?"

Max snorted an uncomfortable laugh that trailed off awkwardly, prompting a firm eye roll from Farn.

"It's not like that. I just," she hesitated, letting her fantasies rise to the surface of her mind, "I just want to take her home, curl up somewhere warm, and binge watch the entire series of Farscape together. I want to watch her stuff her face with food and laugh with her mouth full. I want to tell her everything I feel." She cringed at her own words. The longing in her voice was almost palpable.

"And then you want to rip off her clothes and have your way with her?" Ginger added again, this time getting a sly smile in response.

"Oh, god yes. I would do everything to her." Farn pulled her cape over her face to hide. "Which is why I don't trust myself. I can't stop rehearsing conversations in my head. So much that I'm almost sure it will be the next thing out of my mouth the next time I'm alone with her."

"So why don't you just say it then?" suggested Max, as if it really was that easy.

"Oh yeah, and how would that work?" Farn asked, not expecting an answer. "I know it's easy to forget, but Kira is a character played by your bro Seth. I love her, but I'm terrified that she's not even real."

"I get that," Max tapped his foot on the table, "but you're wrong. I've thought about this a lot, and I don't think it really matters what world you're in. They are the same person. Kira and Seth aren't different people, just two sides of the same coin. The longer she lives this way, the more those sides blur together. She doesn't really seem to be one or the other."

"That's what I mean. What kind of relationship would that even be?"

"Well, there would have to be compromises on both sides," Ginger folded her arms, "but if the feelings are there, then that shouldn't be a problem."

"Maybe in a perfect world, but it doesn't take a genius to see that Kira is going through some stuff of her own. How could I just drop all of this on her while she's trying to sort out her own identity? How would that be fair?"

"True. Even I've noticed that Kira is dealing with her own personal discoveries." Ginger leaned to one side. "But if there is one thing that I've learned from watching her, it's that—"

"She's lazy," Max finished her sentence, sounding more serious than usual.

"What?" Farn glared in his direction.

"He's right." Ginger nodded. "Kira is lazy."

"Why do you think she never takes anything seriously?" Max leaned against the arm of his chair. "You don't have to deal with your problems if you just make jokes and pretend they don't exist."

Ginger continued where he left off, "And I'm willing to bet she'll never work through her issues if she doesn't have to. She'll just keep running away from herself," then a smile cracked across the *Coin's* face, "but I'd also bet that if the right carrot was dangled in front of her, then she might actually put some effort into moving forward."

Farn scoffed. "And you think I'm the right carrot?"

Ginger's smile shifted into a smug grin, answering her question without a word.

"Hold on. What do you know?" Farn shot up straight, her heart racing.

The *Coin* crossed her legs and bounced one foot while

tapping a finger on her chin. "Remember your fight with Ripper on the beach?"

"Yeah."

"Well, while you were fighting, I was watching our little fairy."

Max leaned forward. "What did she do?"

"Nothing really." Ginger shrugged before holding up a finger. "But I have been in enough adult situations, and if there is one thing I can recognize, it's arousal."

"What?" Farn nearly went cross-eyed with shock.

Ginger held her hands out empty as if she had nothing more to offer. "I'm just saying. All that running around like a badass, growling at Ripper on the beach, seemed to work for Kira. You were cool and strong. You know, it gets her—"

"Okay, that's probably enough." Max held up his hands, wincing a little.

"Holy shit." Farn let herself fall back against the back of the sofa. She didn't really know what to do with the information.

"I think you know what you have to do now." Ginger gave her a warm smile.

Farn leaped up from her seat and made a fist with her gauntlet. "I have to kill Berwyn!"

"What? No." Ginger grabbed her by the cape and pulled her back to the sofa. "You have to tell Kira how you feel."

"But that's so hard." Farn buried her face in her hands.

The *Coin* placed a hand on her back. "I know, but sometimes you have to take a risk to get what you want."

Damn it. She was right.

"I can't believe I let her go. I said nothing, and now, she's gone." Farn cursed herself for letting everything get away from her. "I feel sick."

"I get that." Max lowered his head. "I don't like the situation either."

"But it doesn't matter," Ginger added. "Kira will always be Kira. Whatever happens tonight won't change that."

Farn raised her head. "I know, but I can't just sit here and wait." She checked the time—still several hours left before morning. "I'm going to log out. Maybe I'll feel better if I just sleep the night away."

"That sounds good." Max nodded. "We don't have anything left to do tonight, and Ginger and I can keep an eye on things."

"Just worry about yourself," Ginger added. "I'm sure every-thing will look better tomorrow."

Farn stood up and navigated to the logout option on her stat-sleeve, starting its count down. Her stomach turned as a mix of jealous snakes and hopeful butterflies fought for domi-nance. She tried to ignore them.

"Thanks for the talk."

Max and Ginger smiled back as her sign-off counter hit zero, and the suite fell away.

Butterflies fluttered through her dreams.

CHAPTER FIFTY-TWO

Max sunk into his chair just as Farn vanished from the room. "Told you she wasn't interested in me."

"I guess so." Ginger got up and walked over to the bar. "You weren't even in the running."

"Ouch, right in my pride." Max placed a hand over his heart.

"You didn't even have a shot."

"Well, you don't have to keep saying it."

"Sorry." Ginger poured two glasses.

"Don't be." Max threw his feet up on the coffee table, feeling like things had worked out for the best. "I've been single for years. A while longer won't kill me. I'll just be glad if the two of them are happy."

Ginger set one glass in front of him. "That's actually sweet. You might be an ass sometimes. But at least you're a lovable ass."

"Aww thanks," he accepted, not really thinking about it.

"I mean it." She sat down beside him, a little too close. "Not many people would support their friends like that. You stepped aside, and while it may not have mattered in the end, you're still a good friend."

She fell silent for a while before mumbling to herself. "Sometimes you just have to take a risk."

"What?"

"Nothing, just thinking." She set her glass down. "You want to hear something funny?"

"Sure."

"Last year, when you turned up in my room at the brothel to recruit me for Carver's quest..." She fidgeted with the buttons of her coat for a moment. "I would have."

"Would have what?"

"You know..."

Max tilted his head to the side, not understanding what she was getting at.

Ginger started to roll her eyes but stopped halfway, opting to look at the floor. "I would have taken you as a client."

"Oh! I, ah," Max stammered, not sure how to respond to a statement like that. Eventually, he settled on a joke in order to cover for his lack of charisma. "I would hope so. I did pay and everything."

Ginger frowned, finishing the eye roll she started a moment before.

Maybe a joke wasn't the right response? he wondered.

"True, you did pay." She sighed, then smiled again. "So technically, I still owe you."

With that, Max's mind kicked into gear as if he had just entered the most dangerous dungeon of his life. Thoughts fired off at speeds that pushed the boundaries of the human mind. The first of which was, *Holy crap!* Which was immediately followed by, *Is she coming onto me?*

She was smiling. It was nice. She leaned against him, her green eyes sparkling, inviting him to make a move.

Do I even think of her that way?

The question hit him like a bullet.

Sure, in the beginning.

It was true, he had definitely fantasized about her. *But why would she be interested now?* Then it dawned on him, so obvious he felt stupid.

She's messing with me.

It was last year all over again. She had made him squirm back when he had gone to her room to recruit her. She was probably just blowing off some steam.

He swallowed a lump in his throat.

Not this time. Two can play this game. Time to take charge.

"I guess you do owe me, huh?" He called her bluff, making a point to sound as smooth as possible so that she would have to back down first.

Her face went blank, clearly caught off guard. She shook it off and regained her focus, adding a wry smile to her attack. "So should I just climb on and ride you 'til morning."

There's no way that grin is serious.

"Hop aboard." He doubled down, patting his lap.

Ginger almost looked away but brought her gaze back to him. Her eye twitched for a second, but she didn't give in. Instead, she shifted her weight and stretched one leg over him until she was straddling his waist.

It felt a little too real.

His heart raced, but he held his ground, praying that she couldn't feel it as she placed one hand on his chest. Then for a moment, she closed her eyes and hesitated.

That's it. That's her limit. He expected her to laugh and admit defeat.

Then she kissed him.

His mind went blank as he responded with a startled, "Blarg," that forced air into her mouth, making a brief but ridiculous noise that startled her right back. "What the! Why didn't you stop?"

"Why the hell would I stop?" she spouted right back.

"You were messing with me."

"No, I wasn't."

"You weren't?"

"No!"

"Then why?"

"Because I like sex, you ass!"

"Oh, god," he said in horror as she pulled away. She frowned, looking hurt more than anything else. It hammered in how bad he had misunderstood. She hadn't been playing with him at all. No, she was taking a risk, just like she had told Farn to. "I'm sorry, I didn't realize…"

Ginger leaned forward, lowering her head to rest against his. "Thank god."

"What?"

She looked back up at him with a relieved smile on her face. "You were being so aggressive; I wasn't sure what was going on. I mean, sure, confidence is sexy, but it didn't feel like you."

"Oh, so my lack of confidence is what works for you? I'm not sure how I should take that." Max expected her to get off of him now that the mood had been thoroughly murdered.

"Sorry, it's just, you've always made me feel comfortable. I haven't gotten to be myself for a long time, so I wanted a break. Especially with everything going on. I thought it would be good for the both of us to relax."

"And that means, ah, doing… the sex."

She groaned. "You could just say sex like a normal adult."

"I thought you liked my lack of charisma."

"Shit, I did say that."

"You did."

"Fine, yes. I meant do the sex."

Max couldn't help but laugh. "Sorry I ruined the mood."

She shook her head with laugh of her own. "I still want to."

"Oh." He cringed at how awkward he sounded.

"Why do you think I'm still sitting in your lap?" She threw her arms around him and attempted another kiss.

"Woah, wait a sec," he blurted. "Shouldn't we at least, like, get to know each other first?"

The *Coin* let her head fall in defeat before raising back up and eyeing him incredulously. "We've been friends for years. I think we know each other well enough."

"Well, sure." Max squirmed a little. "But what would this make us? A couple?"

Ginger stopped and stared past him for a moment. "Umm, I was thinking something like casual lovers. You know, nothing serious." She leaned in again and whispered, "Just fun."

Max opened his mouth to say something else but found no words as her lips touched his.

Then to his surprise, he kissed her back.

Her response was instant, pushing closer as she shrugged off her coat and threw it to the floor. She shifted in his lap and reach forward to unbutton his vest.

Max fumbled with the clasps of her corset, not really sure how to get it off her. It was well broken in, enough for easy movement, but still, it was snug, and there were buckles everywhere.

"Damn fantasy armor." Ginger pulled away and tugged at one of the clasps. "Honestly, a chainmail bikini would be more practical right about now." A full minute later, she was finally free. "Ooh, I forgot what it felt like to breathe," the *Coin* moaned as she untucked her shirt and rubbed at her sides.

Max let his hands rest on her hips, feeling her relax as she got out of her gear. After a good stretch, her attention fell back to him as she loosened the straps of his shoulder holsters enough to slip off his pistols. She tossed them over the back of the sofa, then pulled off his shirt.

Collapsing against him, her mouth found his, her hands against his chest.

Max held her close, slipping one hand under her shirt. She let out an enthusiastic growl as she pushed him down and shimmied out of her pants. Her hair swept across her face as she positioned herself on top, wearing nothing but a loose shirt.

Max's heart stuttered.

She had always been beautiful, but now, it was like seeing her for the first time, like he was catching a glimpse of the woman behind the avatar. Max slid the back of his hand down her stomach, her back arching in anticipation. There was no turning back.

Suddenly, the main door of the suite flew open as Nix burst into the room. The mercenary skidded to a stop, immediately shielding her eyes.

"Gah! I looked right into it."

Everything crashed to a halt.

Ginger let out a whimper and sat up so that her shirt hung down enough to cover her for the most part.

Max jumped with an undignified, "Eek," immediately snatching his vest off the back of the couch and holding in front of his shirtless chest. "What do–" His voice cracked. Clearing his throat, he started again, "What do you want, Nix?"

She didn't answer, opting to stare at the floor, examining the discarded articles of clothing. She nodded to herself, then thrust forward an enthusiastic thumbs up. "Nice job, Ginger."

"Huh?" Max uttered, feeling confused. He shook it off and got back to what was important. "Why are you here, Nix?

"I just wanted to check in to see what's up." She suppressed a laugh. "You know, besides that." She pointed at his lap.

Max threw his vest over his… situation, then folded his arms across his chest.

Ginger slumped against the back of the sofa and glowered at the mercenary. "At least close the door."

"Oh, sure." Nix pushed the door shut, then continued to stand there looking vacant.

"I was kind of hoping she would have done that with her on the other side," Ginger whispered back to Max as she let out a sigh. "Okay, Nix, what's up?"

"Um, I did say that I was going to come back to go over the plan, didn't I?"

Max groaned, realizing that he had forgotten about that with everything else going on. "The plan's not real complex. We can go over it first thing tomorrow. There will be plenty of time before we have to move."

"Oh, okay, I guess." Nix deflated a little. "I'll let you two get back to, ah, you know…" She trailed off, finishing her statement with an exaggerated pelvic thrust, followed by a pause for laughter that went unfulfilled. Finally, the mercenary took the hint and made her exit.

Max sighed and rested his hands on Ginger's waist, feeling her body relax.

"Now, where were we?" She back leaned in.

"One more thing," Nix announced as she burst back through the door.

"What!" yelled Ginger and Max in unison.

"I ran into Kira a few minutes ago, and she said to tell you," Nix paused and glanced up to the side, "umm, her date is over, and she's fine, and that she's going to go swimming if you don't need her for anything."

"Oh." Max softened his voice, grateful for the update. "Did Kira seem okay?"

"She said she was fine." Nix shrugged.

He checked the time. "That was a short date. I guess nothing happened with Berwyn."

"I hope that's true," Ginger squeezed Max's hand. "but these things don't always take that long."

"I should go check on her." Max gave her a sad smile. "She might need a friend right now."

"Yeah, it wouldn't be right to indulge ourselves while she's out there all alone." Ginger climbed off of him and searched for her underwear. "The mood's been thoroughly killed anyway."

"Sorry." Nix's furry ears drooped like a scolded puppy.

"It's okay." Max pulled on his shirt. "Thanks for reporting back to us."

"And there will be other chances," Ginger added, tugging on her pants.

"There will?" Max couldn't help but sound hopeful.

"Of course, I'm not going anywhere." She leaned down and gave him a peck on the lips.

"Aww." Nix clutched her hands over her heart and fluttered her eyelashes.

"You're not helping." Max buttoned his vest.

"I know." Nix nodded in agreement.

"Do you want me to come with you to find Kira, or is this more of a bro thing?" Ginger changed the subject.

Max considered what would be best for his friend. "You've done enough for everyone tonight, and I need to make up for being a jerk earlier." He shrugged his guns back on. "This is something I should do alone."

CHAPTER FIFTY-THREE

A sick feeling crawled through Max's stomach as he reached the beach beneath the crystal pyramid. The only thing he found was Kira's dress and item bag laying in the sand like a discarded candy wrapper.

He knelt down and picked up the pouch. It felt heavier than he expected. Setting it back down, he drove his fist into the sand.

Damn, Farn was right. I never should have let her go. I should have stopped her. Screw the heist. Screw the money. Screw the mission.

He sat down and raised a handful of sand, watching it sift through his fingers.

"Well, you look awfully pensive."

He dropped the sand as Kira snuck up behind him, holding a coconut with a bamboo straw poking out through a hole. The white fabric of her bathing suit seemed to absorb the moonlight through the ceiling of the pyramid. Her hair was wet, as if she'd just gone for a swim. She raised the coconut to her mouth, staring down at him while blindly searching for the straw with her lips.

Max relaxed, only now realizing how tense he had been.

Kira took a long pull from the coconut then winced and rubbed at her forehead. "The bar has frozen pina coladas."

"Oh, great. How drunk are you?" Max eyed her with suspicion.

"It's a virgin, thank you very much. I didn't want a repeat of last night."

"That makes sense," Max let his vision drift away from her, "and can the same still be said for you?"

Kira answered his question with a frown and leveled a stare on him that could have bored a hole through steel. She finished by letting herself drop to the sand, slowing her fall by materializing her wings for a fraction of a second.

"It's been a strange night."

Max moved to sit next to her. "Do you want to talk about it?"

"Not really." She set down her coconut and pulled her knees up to her chest, hugging them close.

Max's heart sank. The sound of the artificial surf filled the silence before he found the courage to break it. "So you went for a swim?"

She gave a mirthless laugh. "Yeah, felt the need to wash the night off of me."

"Oh." Max wasn't sure what else to say; he just sat there with his mouth hanging open as he searched for a way to ask her more. "Is there anything I can do?"

"No." Kira flopped back, spreading her body out in the sand.

Max glanced away on instinct, not wanting to stare at her body on display in the moonlight. "Um, well, I'm here for you. Just saying."

Finally, Kira snorted. "Okay, I get it. You want to know what happened. I was gonna let you wonder a while longer, but I guess we can get it over with now." She took a deep breath before continuing, "I wasn't prepared for how charming Berwyn could be."

"Oh damn."

"Yeah, oh damn is right. That guy knows how to talk to a woman. If I didn't know who he really was, I might have listened to the little voice in my head telling me, hey why not, it might be fun."

Max laughed, getting an annoyed stare. "Sorry, go on."

"Anyway, we walked down here holding hands and the first thing I noticed was that there was no one around. That freaked me out. Made me wonder if he had cleared the place out. Kind of made it clear what he had planned." She closed her eyes. "But the torches set the mood, and he was pretty smooth, so you know…"

"You went along?"

"Yeah, I had made up my mind. There was too much on the line if I chickened out." She rolled to the side to where her coconut sat and took a sip before saying more. "He took off his crown."

"Seriously?"

"Yeah. Said he didn't need it. That he trusted me."

Max scoffed. "That's a dumb line. Of course he trusts you. You're harmless."

"I know." She laughed. "Like, what am I gonna do, assassinate him? I can't even equip a weapon."

"Did he make a move after that?" Max tried to hide the worry in his voice.

"Patience, I'm getting to that," Kira answered, sliding her fingertips down her chest as if remembering something sensual. "He placed his hand on my waist, like he was trying to gauge my reaction. It took everything I had not to slap it away, which apparently meant go for it because he leaned in to kiss me."

Max leaned closer. "What did you do?"

"What do you think I did?" Kira snapped before settling back into the sand. "He caressed my chin with his fingers and drew my face to his, so I closed my eyes and waited." She paused and covered her face with her hands. "Then my cage went up."

"Oh damn."

"Yup, after everything we've gone through and all my mental preparations," she pushed her feet into the sand as if trying to hide, "I just couldn't do it. It didn't feel right, and my cage just responded, just like it's supposed to."

"How'd you explain it?"

"I apologized desperately and started to make up a lie about it being my first time."

"How'd he take it when he couldn't touch you?" Max's mind fell back to the mission.

"He didn't. Eventually, I stopped talking and waited for him to say something."

"And?" Max begged for the answer.

"And nothing. He just sat there frozen in mid-pucker like a fish on a hook." Kira gave Max a wry smile. "Berwyn lagged out."

"Holy shit."

She sprang up and nodded with enthusiasm. "Can you believe it? His connection dropped off. A few seconds later, he vanished."

"Ha! So you got out of it?" Max slapped a hand on his leg.

"How lucky am I? Like, seriously, the internet gods must have been looking out for me."

"Wait a sec." Max shot her a sideways glance. "Did you–"

"Use my godlike powers to screw up his connection?" Kira finished his thought for him. "Nope."

Max let out a low whistle. "So how did you leave things with Berwyn?"

She shrugged. "I waited here for him to log back in, but he was only able to message me. Said he couldn't get back online. Apparently, there was some kind of outage where he lived. I messaged him back, trying to sound as disappointed as possible. We kind of ended up sexting a bit, so he seems like he's in a pretty good mood now." Kira pushed some sand into a mound absentmindedly. "Although, I basically told him he could have his way with me tomorrow night, so we better get things done sooner rather than later."

"I think we can handle that." Max laughed at the thought of his bro sitting in the sand and sexting an international arms dealer.

"Where's everyone else?" The fairy picked up her coconut and sipped.

Max leaned back on his hands. "Kegan and Corvin are getting things ready for tomorrow, and Ginger is back up in the suite. I think Nix is wandering around the palace somewhere. No idea where Aawil is."

"What about Farn?" Kira's eyes darted back and forth before falling back to the beach.

Max couldn't help but notice a hint of worry in her voice that made him question if there might be more to the question. "She logged out."

"Oh."

"Farn was kind of mad at me for letting you go down here," Max gave her a partial truth.

The fairy lowered her head. "Sorry if I messed things up with you two. I still think you have a chance with her."

Max let out a long laugh at how wrong she was. "Don't worry about it. I'm pretty sure Farn and I make better friends."

"Well, as long as you're happy with that, I guess." She picked up her drink and took a sip.

"Oh, I am." Max gave her an exaggerated shrug. "Plus, I kind of just made out pretty hard with Ginger."

An entire mouthful of pina colada sprayed from the fairy in shock. Max started to elaborate, but she cut him off, holding up a finger as she proceeded to empty the rest of her coconut into her mouth. She immediately spat that out as well.

"You done?" Max wiped a bit of pina colada from his pants.

She threw the empty coconut to the side. "I am, and might I add, what the what?"

Max shrugged again, trying to seem modest. "It just

happened. Probably would have gone further if Nix hadn't walked in on us. Man, that was embarrassing."

"Damn it, Nix!" Kira shook her fist in the air before letting it fall back down. "So where does that leave you two? Will something, umm, you know, blossom?"

Max smiled. "I don't know, but it's time that I finally took a risk. So I'm going to see where things go. I like her."

"Aww, I'm so happy for you." She threw her arms around him. "Especially for your penis."

"Dude, don't say it like that." He shoved her away.

She laughed before settling down. "Sorry, but it's about time you put yourself out there." Then suddenly, her eyes widened, and she took a sharp breath. "You should take her out right now. To a tavern or something, just the two of you."

Max smirked. "And leave you here to swim alone?"

"Yes." She pushed at his shoulder. "Get going. I wanted to be alone anyway."

Max resisted her shoving. "Then you should just log out and go to sleep like Farn did." His words hung in the air as she froze.

"Never mind me." Kira looked away, telling Max everything he needed to know.

"Oh, Kira, no." He placed a hand on her shoulder. "You can't, can you?"

She bit her bottom lip. "I tried, and no, I can't right now."

"What the hell, man? How long has it been like this?" He stared down at her.

Kira avoided eye contact. "I haven't used my Somno headset to connect for a few days. But it hasn't been a problem. I've still been able to log out normally. This is the first night that it's failed. I think I just have to wait until I've slept a few more hours before it lets me out."

Max shook his head and sighed. "You know you can't take risks with this stuff. What happened to all that stuff you said the other day about worrying that you might lose yourself?"

"I know, okay," she snapped before sinking back down. "I know, but I can't take a break now. Not in the middle of the mission. You heard the Feds. Berwyn is dangerous, and we're the only ones in a position to stop him. I can't just quit now."

Max released her from his stare, then let out a long sigh. She was right. There wasn't a choice. "One more night. After that, you're going into quarantine again. I don't care if you have to go back to the cabin in the woods you stayed in last year. I don't want you taking any chances."

She nodded. "I know. I'll call Alastair as soon as this job's done."

"Good. Now, how about I call Ginger and we all head to the Frederick for a drink? I'm not letting you out of my sight 'til this thing is done." Max picked her gear up off the beach and tossed it to her. "So get dressed. No one wants to see your sparkling ass anyway."

Kira brushed sand off her dress and let out a huff. "I guess I could be a third wheel for one more night. And I'm sure Kegan and Corvin could use some help getting things ready too."

"That's right." Max pushed himself up from the sand. "I'm sure they'll appreciate some help. So let's get the hell out of here."

"Okay." Kira threw on her gear and followed him away from the beach. "You're gonna buy me some more of those bunny loaves, though. I think they're my favorite food now."

Max waited for her to catch up. "I think I can do that."

Nix watched the pair from where she lurked on the balcony above. The fairy hopped up to Max's side as they walked.

The view made her smile.

They really were fun. If she was honest, which she rarely was, she hadn't enjoyed herself as much as she had in the last week in quite some time. She followed them with her eyes as they disappeared back into the main palace, no doubt to pick up Ginger before heading off to prepare for whatever they had planned for tomorrow.

Nix suppressed a laugh, remembering what she had walked in on earlier. Max and Ginger actually made a good couple. Who would have thought a single mom from New England would work so well with a misfit from Florida?

Then she frowned.

The night was still young, but it was about time she logged out. After all, she had preparations to make as well. She tapped the sign off option on her wrist and took a breath as the countdown ticked to zero.

Noctem fell away, throwing her into her bed in the real world with a sudden jolt. She took a sharp breath as her Somno connection skipped the normal waking process that most users experienced.

It was almost painful.

She closed her eyes and let out an exaggerated yawn to calm her mind after the sudden leap between worlds.

It worked.

It always did.

She sprawled out in the white sheets that had coiled around her during the night. Taking a deep breath, she pulled her fluffy, white comforter close to her face so she could breathe in its freshly laundered scent.

A smile crept across her face, as thoughts of her night drifted back to her. "House Lockheart," she mumbled to herself. Maybe someday they would forgive her.

She shook her head. *Probably not...*

A sigh expressed her feelings as she pushed herself up. "Can't stop now," she said before yanking the magnetic charging cable from the base of her skull that plugged into the Somno unit that was implanted directly into her brain. She had been warned repeatedly by one of her techs to stop pulling the cable by the cord, but she kept doing it anyway. If she had been the type to listen to warnings, she wouldn't have had the thing installed in the first place.

Nix stretched before kicking off the sheets, wearing nothing underneath. There hadn't been time for clothes. There was never enough time.

Obviously, Nix wasn't her real name. She hadn't needed one in a number of years, so as far as names went, it suited her just fine. After all, it suited her; the word Nix was slang for nothing, and officially, she didn't exist.

She had made sure of that.

Blinds that stretched across one wall opened as motion sensors picked up her moments. A view as empty as it was breathtaking filled the horizon—the ocean as far as the eye could see, the moon hanging in the sky. She ignored it and walked over to a row of drawers next to a mirror. She brushed her messy hair back with her hands the same way she did in Noctem.

She missed her fox ears.

They were cute.

Nix ignored the mirror beyond that, having no interest in seeing the rest of her body. Sure, it was slender and athletic, but the scars didn't help. With the chemical burn on her shoulder, the bullet wounds below her breast, and the numerous surgical scars, there was always one too many. At least, too many for a body as young as hers to have.

She riffled through one drawer for a pair of underwear and threw on a loose shirt that hung off her shoulder. A mechanical drawing of the Millennium Falcon adorned the front.

Ignoring the fact that she still lacked pants, Nix stepped out of her room and into the large, connected office where she plopped into a chair behind a sleek, black desk. An identical M9 to her in-game weapon lay to the side unceremoniously next to a smartphone. She threw her feet up and selected a number from her contacts labeled Checkpoint Systems.

The phone connected to a monitor mounted on the wall,

and Nix turned to face it while resting on her armrest and letting out another long yawn.

"Tired?" asked the serious man who appeared on the screen.

Nix finished yawning. "It's been an interesting night, Jeff." She gave a wry smile. "Or should I say, Jeff-with-a-three."

He groaned. "I can't believe that name stuck. Alastair has been using it both online and off ever since that damn fairy started calling me that last year."

"Hey, as long as he doesn't catch on that you don't really work for him, he can call you whatever he wants for all I care. I'm just happy having a man on the inside."

"Thanks."

"You're welcome." She gave Alastair's assistant a smug grin.

He didn't laugh. Actually, he never laughed. "Should I be thanking you for anything else tonight?"

"No, I don't think so." Nix furrowed her brow.

"Oh, so I suppose someone else has a denial of service attack running against our servers right now," he added.

"Ah. That." Nix sunk her cheek into her hand with a satisfied smile. "It was unavoidable. Kira had basically thrown herself at Berwyn. What else could I have done? I couldn't let her go through with that, not with him. That monster doesn't deserve her." Nix shrugged and swiveled in her chair. "And it's not a DoS attack. It just looks like one. I had Carver slip in through a back door and put a temporary block on Berwyn's account as well as a few hundred thousand others to keep it from looking suspicious. Probably can't get away with that a second time. So we better get things resolved as soon as possible before Berwyn gets another chance with her."

Jeff nodded in approval. "Carver's helping out, is he?"

"Yeah. He was happy to when I told him it was to protect his beta test."

"He's full of surprises when Kira's concerned."

"It's the least we could do, considering what we need her to do." Nix looked away from the screen to hide a frown.

Jeff's severe expression softened. "Yes, speaking of the beta, should I send in the retrieval team? I have them standing by in Florida already."

"Yes. If everything goes according to plan, the beta should be ready to harvest." She cringed, not liking the taste of her own words. "I just hope it works this time. We can't afford another failure."

CHAPTER FIFTY-FOUR

NIGHT SIX: THE TAKE

Farn materialized back in Lockheart's suite, logging in after a long day of thinking about who she was and what she wanted.

"Hey," Max greeted as the room came into focus, revealing him sitting alone.

A tension she didn't realize she was carrying faded. "Oh, it's just you."

His face fell. "Thanks, nice to see you too."

She laughed and dropped into the sofa. "Sorry, I thought Kira might be here, and I wasn't sure what I was going to say. Honestly, I've been terrified that I might blurt out a confession the moment I see her, like a bad romance anime."

"Go for it. I'll even be your wingman." Max gave her a smile.

She snorted at the offer, then sat up straight and cringed as she realized something else. "This isn't the couch that you and Ginger fooled around on, is it? I know none of this is real, but still, I'm not sure if I want to touch anything your butts touched. Is that weird?"

"How do you know that?" Max's mouth fell open.

"Kira told me when she messaged me to tell me everything had worked out last night."

"Damn it, Kira." Max slapped his leg. "And yes, that's weird. And yes, that's the same couch."

Farn hopped up like the cushions might bite her just as a teleport shell appeared in the room. Max leaned over the back of his chair to yell at the bubble.

"Damn it, Kira!"

"What I do?" The startled fairy froze as soon as the spell dissipated.

"Who else did you tell about me and Ginger?"

Kira let out an adorable laugh. "Oh, like, everybody. It was big news. I even told Alastair and Jeff-with-a-three. I don't think Jeff cared, though."

Max groaned and rubbed at the bridge of his nose. "Thanks."

"No problem." Kira saluted and threw herself onto the couch only to freeze as soon as she landed. "Wait, is this…?"

Farn nodded. "Yeah, it is."

Kira leaped back up and huddled close at Farn's side. "Okay, what surface in this room is safe to sit on?"

Max grinned. "Oh, well, now I'm not telling. You can just assume Ginger and I rubbed butts everywhere."

The fairy glared at him, then groaned and sat down anyway.

Farn sat down beside her, the need to be close to her overriding whatever might have happened on the sofa. Kira gave her a smile that could have melted the ice that surrounded the city of Rend. It cut right through Farn's armor, straight to her heart. Her mouth moved on its own.

"Kira, I'm in—"

Suddenly, Nix burst through into the room. "Okay! Are you going to fill me in on this plan or what?"

Farn shut her uncooperative mouth and pretended that she wasn't about to blurt out her feelings. Oh well, at least she was close enough to smell Kira's hair. She almost wanted to be caught.

"Okay, Nix, I'll tell you everything." Max held up both hands as if to say, 'slow down'.

Nix dropped into one the chairs and folded her arms. "Spill it."

Max shrugged. "We break into the vault and take out the hard."

Nix narrowed her eyes on him.

"What? I said it was simple," he defended.

"And how do we do that?"

He grinned. "Well, you and I will take care of the vault's guard NPCs, and we'll escort Kira down there to get through the laser grid–"

"Mana fence," Kira and Farn said in unison.

"Yes." He continued without skipping a beat, "Then we just move the hard up here to our suite and teleport it out a little at a time in our inventories. We have a place already picked out to stash it. As long as we move quick, we should get most of it out before Berwyn catches on and disables our home point."

Nix nodded. "And how do we get the hard up here?"

Max held up a finger then gestured to Farn. "Do you want to take it from here?"

"Of course." She stood up and handed a bracelet to both Max and Kira who slipped them on their wrists. "These are called Shift Beads. They're a contract item I got last year, and they allow two players to swap places. You can take everything you're holding with them. The range is limited, so the palace grounds are the furthest we can go. That's why we have to get it all back up here to the suite."

"That's where I come in," Kira took over. "I can't teleport in the vault's entry corridor thanks to its silence field, but the Shift Beads don't count as magic, so they can bypass it. Once I'm through the mana fence, I'll use them to swap you two over to the other side and head back to where I can teleport back up here to the suite." She pointed up. "The rest of our house is hiding back up on the roof and will move to the suite once I'm back. I'll hand off the Shift Beads to someone that can lift more weight. Then all you guys have to do is walk into the vault, pick up as much hard as you can carry, and wait for one of them to switch places with you." Kira slapped her hands together as if brushing them off after a job well done.

Nix sat nodding quietly for a moment. Then she smiled. "I like it. Simple, sneaky, and profitable."

Max snapped his fingers. "That's what we were going for. Berwyn will never even know what hit him."

"Perfect, and Aawil can keep an eye on him to make sure we're not caught with our pants down." She gave Max a wink. "Now when do we start?"

"The last of our house is getting into position now. We should be ready in about twenty minutes." Max threw his arm over the back of his chair, looking as smug as possible. He raised his house ring to his lips. "Time to get what we came here for."

A chorus of voices filled the line.

"Hell yeah!" Kegan cheered.

"For Noctem!" Corvin added.

"And for us!" Ginger chimed in. "Let's take Berwyn for all he's worth. Then you and I are finishing what we started, Max."

"Gross, Mom," Piper added.

"Aww crap, who told my daughter about last night?"

"No one, I understand context."

Nix glowered at Max. "I assume everyone is getting all revved up, but to me, you're all just sitting here in silence. So can we cut this short?"

"Oh, sorry. Forgot you weren't on the house line." He lowered his house ring and held out his hand. "Bring it in then."

Kira hopped closer and placed her hand on his. Farn couldn't help but smile as she added her hand on top and gestured to Nix to join them. Kira let out a victorious laugh as they broke away.

Everything was falling into place.

Almost everything.

"Do you guys hear that?" Nix's ears began to twitch, and she turned to look out the windows.

Farn followed her eyes along with Max and Kira. The room fell silent as a low rumbling grew in the distance, prompting Max to stand and walk out onto the balcony.

Whatever was out there, it was getting closer.

The night sky blanketed Noctem like always, but the foreboding sound drove everyone to squint into the distance.

"Oh my god." Nix's jaw dropped as several dozen small ships emerged from the darkness, each painted black to conceal their approach. The crest of House Winter Moon marked each and every one.

"Oh no. No no no no no." Max shook his head as he spoke as if trying to deny what he saw. "Not now."

"They're attacking." Kira clasped both hands over her mouth.

"This is it." Farn supported herself on the side of the window, trembling. "Oh god, this is what Amelia was planning. Why she attacked the Catacombs. It was just a trial run for tonight!"

Max took three shaky breaths, then spun away from the window. "We have to move now!"

"But what about the others? They're not ready." Kira ran to him.

"There's no time. They'll just have to hurry."

Farn watched as the palace's energy shield switched from standby to active, light shimmering across the sky to hold the Moon's attack ships at bay. She rushed to the others as they made for the door.

"Can we even do this?"

Max spun with an intensity in his eyes that she didn't know he had. "We're going to have to."

CHAPTER FIFTY-FIVE

Chaos filled the hall as the entire House of Serpents practically exploded out of the rooms one after another. Berwyn must have called them back to their home points to defend the palace.

"Watch it." Nix dodged a pair running for the stairs. They paid no attention to her. Why would they? She hadn't done anything to raise suspicion. She was just a mercenary in the employ of the palace lord.

"Lead the way." Max lowered his head to her ear. "No one will stop us if they think we're working with you." There was a tremble in his voice.

Poor guy, Nix thought.

He was just a regular player. Sure, he'd seen some stuff last year, but he wasn't cut out for espionage and theft. Nix, on the other hand, was in her element.

"Good thinking." She gave his stomach a playful slap with the back of her hand.

He turned back to Farn and Kira. "Stay frosty."

Nix rolled her eyes at his words. *Someone has been watching too many movies.* That was when a system chime sounded in her ear. She got moving and checked her journal on the way.

- New Message -
From: Lord Berwyn

Find Kira and get her to the pyramid. I'm going to lock it
down, but I want her safe with me first. The palace shield will
hold for now. Get her!

Nix snapped her journal shut and rolled her eyes again.
Berwyn wasn't taking anything seriously. Here they were with
his palace under siege, and he was still trying to nail a fairy. At
least he was consistent. It wasn't like the palace mattered to him
anyway. Nix had assumed he'd only taken the place so he could
store his dumb book in its vault. As for the whole conquest
thing, that was probably just out of boredom.

Whatever. It didn't matter now. Her plan was almost finished.
All she had to do was get that book before Max.

"Wait!" Kira grabbed the back of Farn's cape, who, in turn,
grabbed the back of Max's vest.

"Hold up." He held up a hand, refraining from grabbing
Nix as well.

She turned back as the fairy swiped open her spellcraft
menu and set up a quick incantation. A puff of glowing feathers
popped into existence above her head and floated down
around her.

Nix checked her stat-sleeve, finding a flight icon next to her
name with a two-minute timer. "Good thinking."

Who needs stairs when we can fly?

Nix hopped the railing and let herself fall between the stairs
and the crystal obelisk at their center. Floors swept past as
members of the Serpents rushed down the steps around her.
Using the flight spell to break her fall, she landed safely in a
crouch. Max and Farn dropped in behind her, followed by Kira,
her wings dematerializing as soon as her bare feet touched the
floor.

They ran for the entrance to the sub-levels. Farn stayed
behind to keep watch as Nix and the others leaped down the

stairs. With Kira's flight spell still active, there was no need to land. Instead, Nix took off down the hall toward the vault. The others followed suit, flying straight to the puzzle lock on the first door.

"I've got this." Max touched down and punched one of the buttons.

The heavy door rolled out of the way, and he flew down the rest of the stairs, stopping just before he reached the guards. Suddenly, he raised his house ring as if hearing something from his team. "What do you mean you're not ready?"

Nix eyed him, wishing she could hear what was being said on the other end of the conversation.

He shook his head. "Damn, the guys aren't gonna make it. We're going to have to take out the guards ourselves."

Nix shrugged. "So this plan fell apart pretty fast."

"Maybe not." Max sounded like he was trying to convince himself as much as he was her. "With all the noise upstairs, I doubt anyone will hear if we use our guns down there."

"Oh good," Kira jumped in. "At least something is going our way."

"Here's to the little things," added Nix with as little enthusiasm as she could. "What's the plan?"

Max rested his chin in his hand for a second then glanced to his wrist and snapped his fingers. "Still thirty seconds of flight left on the spell. We can do this. Just cover me."

Nix furrowed her brow. "Okay, but what—"

"No time. Twenty seconds left." He lifted off the ground and flew straight into the hallway below at top speed.

Nix ran down the stairs after him just as he reached the first pair of guards. She drew her gun, ready to fight. Max rotated in the air, flying upside down and backward as he pulled his pistols from shoulder holsters. The flight spell canceled as soon as he did, and he took aim at both guards.

Crimson light exploded from their heads as they lurched back. Max didn't stop there, using his momentum to carry him to his next target before their combat algorithms could respond.

He fired again and again, streaking halfway through the hall before hitting the floor. He continued to slide as the first six guards fell like dominos.

Finally, he slammed into the opposite door between the guards and the alarm's pull chain. His pistols roared against the remaining enemies until the slides locked back.

Two targets remained, a *Coin* and a *Blade*, each ready to strike. With their focus on him, Nix simply walked up behind them and deposited a round into the back of each of their heads. "Okay, that was pretty damn impressive."

"Well, my name is MaxDamage."

"24." Kira crept into the hallway as if she wasn't sure it was safe yet. "There's a number at the end."

"Thanks." Max pushed himself up and reloaded before hitting the button on the next door. "Okay, Kira, you're up."

The door slid to the side, revealing hundreds of blue beams, crisscrossing through the hallway beyond. The fairy's eyes widened.

"We don't have all day." Nix gave her a light push.

Kira took a deep breath, then slipped out of her dress and tied her hair back with a ribbon. With a shaky first step, she transferred her weight to the pressure sensitive floor.

Nix held her breath and waited.

Max did the same.

The alarm remained silent.

The group let out a collective sigh as Kira crouched down and spread out across the floor, her body being light enough to avoid setting anything off.

Nix had to admit, she was impressed.

The fairy slid her body through the beams with precision, even with the attack going on outside. Her movements were so graceful, a part of her began to understand what Berwyn saw in her as she slipped a slender leg through the space. A moment later, she shifted to an awkward crab walk. It was far less attractive than the movies made avoiding laser grids seem. To make matters worse, each movement looked exhausting.

Kira had to stop and rest every time she got into a position that didn't involve struggling to hold herself up. It was unnerving to watch. Nix found herself wincing each time the fairy passed by a beam. Just a fraction of an inch was the difference between success and blowing the entire operation. Nevertheless, Kira stayed calm, eventually slipping out the other side.

"Oh my god, I never want to do that again." The fairy stretched and stepped off the pressure plate. "You guys ready?" She held out her wrist, shaking the bracelet of black beads back at Max.

"Shall we?" He offered his hand to Nix.

She took it and shrugged. "Sure, why not?"

The world around her winked out, surrounding her in an empty void, only to pop back into being a moment later.

"Woah." She wobbled, leaning on Max's hand for support. "That was weird."

Max ignored her and raised his house ring. "We're in. Everyone, stand by in the suite. Kira will teleport up as soon as she's clear of the vault's silence effect. Be ready to shift on my signal."

Kira snatched her dress off the floor, but before she could get it back on, the sound of an explosion rumbled through the hall.

It was close.

Too close.

Nix twitched her ears. The attack outside grew louder. "I think the palace shield just fell."

"That explosion must have destroyed one of the crystal obelisks." Max slammed his hand against the wall. "Damn, Amelia must have gotten a team inside somehow to take down the shield." He let out a growl and turned to Kira. "Be careful."

"When am I not?" She threw on her dress and took off down the hall.

Once she was gone, Max slapped the button on the final vault door. The mechanism rotated and clicked as if unlocking dozens of tumblers. Then finally, the door opened.

"What the hell?" Max's eyes bulged.

"That's not what I expected," Nix added as she looked down.

There was no floor, just a thousand-foot drop. The space was almost the size of the palace itself with torrents of water pouring down the walls. At the center floated a platform containing several trunks, certainly filled with Checkpoint's freshly replenished hard.

On top of one chest sat a book.

The book.

Nix pretended she didn't see it.

"What the hell?" Max repeated. "There's no bridge. How are we supposed to get over there?"

Nix stared down at the crystal blue water that filled the bottom of the pit. Patterns of reflected light blanketed the walls and refracted through millions of droplets that drifted through the air.

"Well, we can't just stand here." Nix swatted at the globules of water that floated near the door.

"Hey." Max grabbed her hand.

"Not really the time." Nix gave him a sideways look.

"No, the water moved." He let her go and thrust his hand into the space.

As soon as his fingers crossed the threshold, Nix noticed some of the droplets move toward him, stopping when he pulled his hand back. "That's different."

He reached into the vault again, keeping it there as the water moved, collecting in a layer that pooled in front of the door. A thin, translucent surface formed where the floor should have been.

"Oh, I don't like the looks of that." Max took in a sharp breath. "I don't suppose you would consider me a gentleman if I suggested that ladies go first?"

Nix scoffed and gestured for him to get moving.

"Thought so." He held onto the wall and took a step forward to test the surface, then he took another. The water rippled around his foot but held firm, leading him to release his hold on the wall. "I really do not like this."

Nix began inching her way out as well, pressing down with her foot to check how firm the puddle actually was. Once she was satisfied, she hopped twice and splashed around. "I don't know. It's kind of neat."

Max continued on, cautiously moving with his arms outstretched like a tightrope walker. The water shifted and pooled to remain beneath him. The liquid would probably stay with him no matter where he stepped, but still, he seemed uncomfortable with the view below.

Nix shook her head and decided to have some fun as she crouched down into a runner's stance. With a laugh, she took off at a sprint, splashing Max on her way by. His face blanched as he wobbled.

He regained his balance. "Is that necessary?"

Nix gave an answer by skipping through the empty air around the center platform, trying to remind him of Kira so that he might let his guard down.

Finally, he let out a sigh and dropped his hands to his sides before walking the rest of the way to the platform. He must have realized how foolish he looked. There was nothing to be afraid of, or at least, the fall wasn't at the top of the list. No, that list was led by something else.

She eyed the book, trying not to be obvious about it. The contract item was just sitting there on top of a trunk, a gold zero set into its cover. She had to get to it first; everything was riding on it. Nix hopped onto the platform between him and the book, taking a moment to admire her surroundings as water fell all around them. She didn't want to make a break for the book too soon.

"Hey, so I was just doing some math. Are we going to be able to get all of the hard out just by teleporting? With whatever's happening upstairs and all, this might not work."

Max shrugged and took a step towards the book. "Yeah,

well, we thought we'd have more time to work." He took another step. "We'll have to just take what we can."

"I guess you're going to have to move quickly then," she commented, letting a Cheshire grin take over before hopping toward the book.

Max's eyes widened as he made his move as well.

Too slow.

Nix pulled her M9 and snatched up Berwyn's contract.

Max froze for an instant, his eyes darting around the room in panic. Then he reached for his guns.

"Oh, no you don't." She gestured with her pistol.

"Okay, okay." He thrust his arms up.

"I'll be honest," Nix made sure to look as smug as possible. "I really like you guys, so I don't want to ruin your plan. So I'll just take this one little book and let you have all of this hard. Sound good?"

Max let his arms fall back to his sides. "Sorry, but I can't let you do that."

"Ah, so there it is." Nix let out a long breath; it was time to finish things. Time for the fun to end. "You're working with the Feds, huh? I figured Luka and her bland-looking friend Rando had roped you into their little operation. So I guess we're at an impasse then?"

Max didn't make a move. "How did you know Luka was a Fed?"

Nix made a motion with her gun that suggested a shrug. "You would be surprised at how much I know. I have a lot of irons in the fire."

"And what do you want with that book?"

"Wouldn't you like to know?" Nix tucked the stolen contract under her arm and winked.

"What about Kira?" He narrowed his eyes. "You said you'd help her."

She shook her head. "I wasn't lying about that."

"Then do it."

"I don't have to. She can do that on her own."

"What does that mean?" He stepped closer.

"It means that you don't need anything from me anymore."

Max glanced around as if thinking of what to say next. "What about the, ah, pendant? What is it doing to her?"

"You're stalling, why?" Nix raised her gun to aim at his head.

A stupid expression fell across his face. "What? Nothing, I'm not–" Then suddenly, he leaped forward, almost falling until he slammed into the floor at her feet.

"What the?" she sputtered as his hand darted out.

Max smiled back up, his fingers clasped around her ankle and his other hand bringing his house ring up to his mouth. "Now!"

She opened her mouth to speak as the world blinked out around her. She only got out two words.

"Fuck me."

CHAPTER FIFTY-SIX

Pop! Nix appeared, standing with her gun drawn and clutching Berwyn's book against her chest. She was ready for anything.

Then the floor moved.

She wasn't ready for that.

The new room tilted to the side at a sharp angle as noise surrounded her, disorienting her further. It didn't help that Max still held one of her feet anchored in his grip. Her best option was to shoot him, but instead, she fell face first into a small, round window. Her cheek smushed against the glass with an undignified squeak.

The horizon outside passed by in a blur as she looked down on the crystal pyramid. Dozens of transport ships tore through the sky, circling the palace like vultures.

What the hell?

Nix peeled her face off the glass just as the room rocked again, sending her tumbling down to the floor.

"Ow." She rubbed at the back of her head as pieces began falling into place. Obviously, she wasn't back up in the suite where Max had said they were going. The rumble of a transport ship vibrated the floor beneath her.

"Easy now." Kegan appeared from behind her, an arrow drawn and pointed down at her head.

"Don't make any sudden moves." Corvin rested his blade against her shoulder.

Max stood up and drew one of his pistols, gripping a handrail that ran along the ceiling of the cabin for support. "Drop the gun and give us the book."

She did neither. "So I take it Kira didn't teleport back to the suite, huh?"

A smug grin took over Max's face. "No, she did. We still need her to pick up Farn and Ginger before Berwyn figures out anything, but she made a quick detour first."

"She teleported to Reliqua's center, didn't she?" Nix closed her eyes and let her head fall against the metal floor. "That's why you were stalling. You were buying her time to fly to your ship and hand off the Shift Beads."

Then something else occurred to her. "But how did you get your ship ready so fast?" She let out a sudden mirthless laughed as she worked it out. "You already knew about the Winter Moon's assault. The attack didn't disrupt the plan."

"The attack was the plan." Max held his guns out and leaned forward to suggest a bow. "You were right, using Kira to teleport the hard out of the suite was going to take too long. It made more sense to transport it to the Cloudbreaker and run with it all at once. We just needed to cover our escape. Fortunately, Berwyn and his Serpents have made plenty of enemies." He leaned down. "Amelia didn't even need to be convinced when I suggested an alliance over drinks a week ago. All it took was a cut of the hard."

"What about that attack on the Catacombs? Were you in on that too?"

He grinned.

"What better way to gain someone's trust than to save them from assassination? Although, Amelia did take things a little too far by not letting the rest of her house in on the plan. Apparently, she wanted it to seem authentic."

Nix scoffed. "It seemed pretty real to me."

"Yes," Max deflated a little. "Kira getting hit was not part of the plan, but it worked out."

"And the palace shield?" Nix tried to buy time to think. "You couldn't get your ship close enough to use the Shift Beads with the barrier active. So I'm guessing Amelia didn't really get a team inside to take it down? Did she?"

"Nope." Max pulled his half of the Shift Beads and tossed the bracelet to Corvin, who slipped it on and moved to the rear of the cabin where he touched it. Two chests dropped into the space as he vanished. A young reynard girl popped into existence along with them, gripping the handles of each. Even with the fluffy ears and tail, Nix recognized the girl from surveillance footage. Wren—or Piper as she had renamed herself. Ginger's daughter. Nix couldn't help but smile as the young reynard said something into her ring and vanished. Another two chests joined the others with Corvin attached.

Max ignored the operation going on behind him while he continued to gloat, "We're fortunate Ginger has been stealing explosive items from every shop in Noctem for years. All she had to do was drop a bag of bombs down one of the stairwells near one of the crystal obelisks and," he blew out a ridiculous fart noise with his tongue hanging out, "no more palace shield. You really only have to light one fuse; the rest will just go off by being near it."

Nix rolled her eyes as the image of Ginger passed through her mind, walking away in slow motion as the obelisk exploded behind her. Cool women don't look at explosions, after all.

She let her grip on her pistol go slack and closed her eyes. Then she laughed, letting it drag on until she sounded a little crazy. Guffaws reverberated through the cabin, prompting the pilot to turn around to see what was happening.

"What's going on back there?" Luka called back. "Have you secured the book?"

This, of course, drew out even more laughter.

It was all too much. Too perfect. Even Luka was there. Max

had actually roped a member of the F.B.I.'s cybercrime task-force into helping with a heist. Nix had liked House Lockheart before, but now, she practically loved them. She had a good mind to abandon her mission right there and join up. They were her kind of people through and through.

That's what made her job so hard.

She settled down, letting her gun fall from her hand. It clanked to the metal floor. "Fine, you've got me." Nix pushed herself up, unarmed.

"About time." Max held out his hand. "Now, give me the book."

"You know, after all this, I kind of wish I could offer you a job." She let out a sigh, stalling. "But something tells me you wouldn't accept it."

Another two chests hit the metal floor as Piper appeared behind Max. He didn't turn, but his eyes flicked away for an instant. "Why's that?"

"Mostly because of this." She dropped the book and kicked it in his direction, sending it hurtling through the cabin.

"Mother Fisher!" Max yelled as the heavy contract item cracked him in the nose, throwing his head back. With the movement of the cabin, it was enough to knock him over on top of Piper.

"Hold it!" Kegan readied an arrow.

"Too slow!" Nix threw her hand out, clasping his bow as her other darted for his draw hand. She squeezed tight so he couldn't release while keeping tension on the bow. Then pushing him against the wall, she stopped, face to face. "Hi there. We haven't met. I'm Nix." She planted a solid kiss on his mouth in classic *Bugs Bunny* styling.

"What the...?" he uttered as she pulled away.

Before he could recover, she kneed him in the thigh and spun him toward the cockpit, letting go of his hands. The arrow fired with an odd twang.

"Hey, watch ou–" Luka started to say just as the shaft struck her in the eye.

That should do it, Nix thought as the elven agent's body lolled out of her chair, sending the craft lurching to one side. Metal screeched as they sideswiped another ship. Max and Piper tumbled as a chest fell on top of them. Plates of hard spilled across the floor.

Kegan's face went blank.

"Hope you know how to fly." Nix let go of the *Leaf.*

He lunged to the stick and planted himself into the pilot's seat just as the craft began to dive. Berwyn's book slid forward along with Nix's gun, coming to a stop at her feet as the ship leveled out.

"Well, that's convenient." She scooped her weapon up and tucked it back into her holster before shoving the book under her arm. Then without hesitation, she grabbed the handle of the door and slid it open. "I'd love to stay and see how all this," she gestured to Max as he struggled with a chest, "turns out, but I gotta run. So, bye bye."

With that, she jumped. The sound of Max yelling trailed off as she fell toward the pyramid below.

CHAPTER FIFTY-SEVEN

Kira burst into the hall in a cloud of sparkling pixie dust, without bothering to land or even close the door of the suite she had just teleported to. It wasn't like she'd be going back there. The room wouldn't be her home point for much longer anyway. She flipped in the air and streaked toward the stairs, only to plant her feet, skidding to a stop as she ran into Ginger.

The *Coin* caught her with both arms, nearly falling over. "In a hurry?"

Kira hopped back up into the air and hovered. "Sorry. I was looking for Farn. She wasn't in the suite when I teleported in."

"Damn, something must have held her up. We'll have to find her." Ginger spun back to the stairs, her coat fanning out behind her. Then she stopped cold.

"Oh, thank god." Dartmouth appeared from the floor below. "Lord Berwyn has been worried sick. He's waiting to lock down the pyramid until you get there." He beckoned her with a hand, clearly suspecting nothing. "Come along so we can get you to safety."

Kira's chest tightened as Aawil came into view behind him.

The silent faunus didn't skip a beat as she impaled the Serpent's Archmage with her dagger.

"Hurk!" Dartmouth gurgled as she stabbed him four more times. The gloves had come off, and she wasn't taking any chances. He didn't even have time to see who had killed him. The body fell at Aawil's feet just before dissipating into the air around her.

She flicked her eyes up at Kira, blocking her path down. Not even Kegan and Corvin could beat her, and judging from the lethal stare on her face, their alliance wasn't doing so well.

"I've got this," Ginger used one hand to gently push Kira away. "Go find Farn. Make sure you both escape."

"But…" Kira hovered closer as Aawil stalked up the stairs.

"It's okay." Ginger shook her head. "I still have an ace or two up my sleeve. I'll be fine."

"Good luck." Kira nodded, understanding her place. As much as she hated to admit it, there wasn't much she could've done. "You better not die," she added before pulling away and darting back through the hall toward the next stairwell. The sound of daggers clashing echoed behind her as she left the Lady of House Lockheart alone to fight one of the most dangerous players in Noctem.

She better not die, Kira though as she pushed forward.

Racing down one flight of stairs after another, Kira finally found Farn near the first-floor landing. She slowed to a stop a few feet away.

"Come quick, we have to–"

"Thank god we found you," the *Shield* interrupted before Kira had a chance to tell her about Ginger. That was when she noticed the worried expression on Farn's face.

We? Kira question the word. *Who's we?*

That was when Ripper stepped up the stairs behind her friend. "Finally, we need to get back to the pyramid. Berwyn sent me to bring you to him."

"I ran into Ripper on my way to find you." Farn gave a weak smile. She must not have been able to shake him.

Kira froze, not wanting to go with the horrible man. Despite that, she nodded. There wasn't a choice. They couldn't afford to raise anyone's suspicions now. They were too close.

"Come on, Berwyn's going to lock down the pyramid." Ripper beckoned to them both.

"But we'll be trapped in there. We should teleport out of here instead," Kira argued as she swiped open her spell menu.

"No." He reached out and grabbed her arm, almost dragging her down the stairs. "Lord Berwyn was clear. I'm not to return without you."

"Okay, fine. Just let go." She struggled on instinct, not liking how his grip felt.

"The pyramid will be plenty safe once it's locked down. As long as we get there now!" He gave her a firm yank as if making a point before releasing her wrist.

"There's no need to get rough." Farn stepped between them, letting Kira duck behind her.

Ripper said nothing but shot her an irritated stare.

"It's fine." Kira rubbed at her forearm, looking up at him submissively. She hated herself for it. "Lead the way." At least Farn was with her. That was enough.

Ripper gave her a grunt that suggested agreement before turning away. Following him down to the first floor, he led them through the nearest entrance to the pyramid where Berwyn waited. The Lord of Serpents rushed to her as soon as they entered.

"Thank god you're safe," Berwyn breathed the words into Kira's ear during an embrace that went on a little too long. She couldn't help but notice Farn tighten her grip on the handle of her sword. It made her feel a little safer.

Berwyn let her go and took her by the hand, leading her down the stone walkway that cut through the waves to where the throne stood. "Have a seat."

"Is that allowed?" Kira took a step back.

"It is if I say it is." He gave her an encouraging push forward.

"Oh, okay." She hoisted herself up, feeling self-conscious as she sat down. Fortunately, she remembered to keep her legs crossed since her elevated position would give pretty much everyone a free show if she didn't.

That was when Berwyn directed her attention to a small, round button on one of the armrests. It was gold and surrounded with decorative carvings. He smiled up at her.

"Would you mind doing the honors?"

"Sure." Kira shrugged and punched it down without hesitation. Pressing buttons was fun, after all.

Suddenly, the massive doors of the main entrance closed on their own, as did the rest the doors to the other exits. The waterfalls that lined the rear of the space ran dry. Then a low whine came from all around as sheets of polished crystal rose out of the water, sand, and stone on all sides. They stretched all the way to the angled ceiling, cutting off any chance of escape. A tomb of shining glass shared only with Farn, Ripper, and the Lord of Serpents.

Kira swallowed hard as Farn shot her a worried look. A teleport would be the only way out, provided she could cast one without being interrupted.

"That should do it." Berwyn leaned against the throne, sounding quite proud. "The Winter Moons might get in the palace, but they'll never get in here. The crystal around us is much stronger than the obelisks that run the shield. It would take nothing short of a battering ram to get in here. By then our reinforcements will be here to put a stop to this. I've already sent out a mass message to my imperial army." He scratched at the back of his neck. "I'm just glad that we received our yearly budget from Checkpoint tonight. I might not have been able to pay the army without it. They don't exactly take IOUs, you know."

"Yeah, that's lucky." Kira gave an awkward laugh before falling silent and raising her head to the upper floors.

I hope Ginger's okay.

◆ ◆

Aawil leaped forward, kicking off a pillar as her dagger caught the cheek of Lockheart's leader. She dug in, feeling the weapon's edge scrape bone. It was strange how real it felt. How familiar.

The irritating woman leaped back, her hand covering her face. A crimson glow faded underneath. Aawil wasn't sure what Ginger was up to, but her orders were clear. Nix didn't want any interference.

Fortunately, Ginger wasn't much of a fighter. At least, not compared to Aawil. She had studied recordings of each member of House Lockheart, and really, none of them were much to worry about on their own. It was only when they got together that they became more dangerous.

According to the files that Nix's inside man had compiled, Ginger, in particular, was the least dangerous of the group. The only title she'd carried prior to becoming the Lady of her house was 'Purse Taker'. Aawil hadn't bothered getting that one. She didn't even remember what it required. It was something about stealing things.

Whatever. It didn't matter. Aawil would always be stronger.

She pressed forward, striking the wall near Ginger's head. The impact cracked the stone like a pickaxe. Her hand blurred, continuing with a cluster of rapid attacks aimed at whatever parts of the woman were closest. Hand, head, stomach, thigh. Chips of stone flew as she missed.

Hold still, damn it!

Aawil swung through empty air as Ginger seemed to bend out of the way like water. It annoyed her. The woman might not have been much of a fighter, but she was slippery.

Enough of this.

Grabbing the loose fabric that hung from Ginger's coat to cover the woman's bare arm, Aawil yanked her off balance and thrust forward with her dagger. Ginger let out a desperate cry as the blade's edge sought out her throat.

Then she laughed.

What? Aawil thought as the fabric she held firm simply tore away, leaving Ginger free to slip to the side, the dagger catching nothing but a lock of hair. With a quick breath, the slippery *Coin* blew the loose strands in Aawil's face.

She flinched, not expecting something so random, almost leaving herself open. She recovered, blocking the strike she knew was coming. Except it didn't. Instead, Ginger slinked around her somehow, grabbing the fabric that had been torn from her coat and throwing it up. Aawil swung wildly as the small cape covered her face. She ripped it away, finding the irritating woman gone.

Pop.

The sound of a grappling line drew her attention back to the stairs where Ginger winked and held up one hand. She swung her fingers back and forth with a health vial dangling between each.

Aawil screwed up her eyes, not really sure what she was looking at. It dawned on her just as a trail of smoke wafted up from her item bag along with a quiet sizzling. She thrust her hand into her item bag where she kept her health vials, pulling out a small, round bomb. Its wick sparked in her palm.

"Purse Taker," Aawil said under her breath before tossing the explosive item away and diving to the side. It detonated with a wave of heat and an ear-splitting crack. Bracing, her arm lit up with streaks of crimson. She let out a growl as she looked back to the stairs.

Ginger blew her a kiss and downed the vial in her hand. Then she clenched her fist and zipped up the stairwell out of sight.

"Arghhhhh!" Aawil screamed, her cry shifting into a snarl as she lunged up the stairs after the woman. She burst into the hallway an instant later and darted between the pillars before slowing to a stop. Her eyes scanned the empty space, a row of suites lining the wall; Lockheart's door was still open. She stalked toward the room, her vision tunneling in on it.

Reaching the entrance to the suite, she tightened her grip on her dagger and gave a low, intimidating growl. Suddenly, the pop of a wrist launcher echoed down through the hall as a grappling bolt streaked toward her head. Aawil bent back as it sliced through the air, scratching her throat.

Ginger flew out from behind a pillar, propelled by the retracting line. She held her dagger ready to strike.

Aawil couldn't dodge, opting to turn her head to block with her horns. Ginger's blade impacted with a grinding sound that reverberated through her skull. The palace spun as she fell back against the wall, her stat-sleeve erupting with a barrage of status effects.

- 300 HP

- 300 HP

Seconds ticked by like an eternity as some kind of poison drained her health in massive chunks. She tried to get up, but pins and needles filled her legs, paralysis taking over.

Move! she screamed internally as her body flopped to the floor, unable to control her limbs. All she could do was watch Ginger run back toward the stairs from where she came. The woman slowed for a moment, then tossed a cluster of four bombs tied together over her shoulder. It landed off to the side next to one of the massive, potted plants a dozen feet away.

Another -300 HP fell away. Then in an instant, sensation returned to her body, and the debuff icons covering her arm vanished. Only a few hundred points of health remained.

Ginger continued to run for the stairs, leaving the cluster of bombs behind. Aawil pushed herself up and watched the wick sparkle. It was longer than a standard explosive's, like it had been crafted that way intentionally. Not to mention, the woman had dropped it far enough away from where Aawil lay so that it wasn't even a threat.

She was safe.

But why?

Ginger had her dead to rights. So why hadn't she finished her? She might have been trying to cover her escape, but that didn't make sense either.

Then her gaze shifted from the bomb to the potted plant beside it. The potted plant that didn't reset every hour along with the rest of the palace thanks to Dartmouth's customizations. The potted plant that House Lockheart had access to all week. The potted plant that was large enough to hold any number of bombs.

Aawil leaped to the nearest plant and thrust her hand into the soil. Her whole body froze. She didn't even have to dig before feeling the familiar round shapes. There must have been hundreds.

Ginger picked up her pace and raised her house ring to shout, "Get ready for the fireworks!"

Then she dove down the stairwell.

There wasn't a point in pursuing. Aawil just let herself slump back against the wall, her hand still resting in the soil.

"Well, shit—"

CHAPTER FIFTY-EIGHT

The wind whipped through Max's hair as he hung out the door of the Cloudbreaker to search for Nix below. She hit the roof and rolled, landing in an uncoordinated tumble of arms. Berwyn's book skittered a few feet away from her. The mercenary stood back up, rubbing her ass and downing a health vial before scampering over to the book and scooping it back up.

Max shouted to the cockpit, "Kegan! Take us in near the pyramid." He turned back to Piper. "Finish the job and get out of here. I'll get the book."

"Good luck." Piper tossed him a health vial.

He nodded back. Then he jumped.

"Crap, ow, damn, oomphf." Max tumbled down the panels of polished crystal before he lost enough momentum to slide the rest of the way down. He ignored the damage. It didn't matter. It couldn't.

Nix couldn't get away, not with information on whatever Berwyn was trying to sell. If Agent Dawson was right, then thousands of lives could depend on him.

He rolled onto the roof at the bottom and downed the

health vial Piper had tossed him. Transport ships blazed through the sky all around him, dropping explosives and players down on the pyramid's front gates. Spells fired into the sky from the ground in response.

"Nix!" Max pushed himself off the tiles as the mercenary spun and unloaded her M9 in his direction. Max tugged his scarf up over his face and held his breath. Death's blades spun into existence, glinting through the space in front of him. Bullets sparked and clanged against the spectral steel as he kicked off into a run, his health depleting one sliver at a time.

He fired back, grazing the reynard as she sprinted toward one of the gabled windows and dove inside. It was the same space that his housemates had hidden in all week. Max slowed and held his breath, expecting her to fire back from cover.

She didn't.

Probably waiting for me to poke my head in.

No thanks.

Max circled around to the other side rather than following her in. Then he hesitated. She might expect that. She could be watching that side, ready for him. Then again, she might assume that he would expect her to expect that. He was damned if he did and damned if he didn't. He did neither. Instead, he fired blind into the narrow space, hoping to wound her with a ricochet. Then he crept in.

The space was empty except for the book laying on the floor. He resisted the urge to leap for it. It was an obvious trap. Max held his breath to call up his defense.

A sword blurred in at his side, crashing into the wall with a burst of sparks as a bullet streaked down through his arm. He threw himself to the side on instinct, as another few shots came at him from above. Death's blades whirled through the narrow space, only blocking half, unable to move freely in such close quarters. With a grunt, Max hit the wall and pushed off to dodge, pulling down his scarf at the same time. His sub-class wasn't helping, and he didn't need it draining his health. Using his momentum, he spun to find Nix wedged into the ceiling with her feet braced against both walls.

He aimed up as she pushed off the opposite side and dropped down, dodging in a move that was almost a mirror image of his. They both fired in unison while darting to the sides. Both shots missed, hitting the walls and throwing off clouds of dust from the stonework. He slapped her pistol away with the back of his hand. She thanked him with a knee to the kidney as he missed and put two rounds into the wall.

Then his guns locked back empty.

Nix let out a loud, "Ha!" as Max was forced to eject his empty magazines.

He kicked one as it fell, sending it straight into her face, whacking her in the forehead.

"Ha!" he laughed back.

Then she shot him in the leg, because *of course* she still had bullets.

Instead of flinching, he grabbed her M9 and squeezed her hand until he pressed her finger against its magazine release. She kneed him again, this time in the stomach, as her half full mag dropped to the floor with a solid clunk. He ignored it and shoved her arm away, forcing her to fire off the round remaining in the chamber before letting go.

He grabbed a fresh mag and holstered one pistol, unable to reload both at once while fighting. Nix slapped the magazine out of his hand.

He did the same to her.

This left them awkwardly pistol whipping each other with their empty guns, like a couple children having a slap fight. None of their hits did much damage since that wasn't how guns were intended to be used.

Eventually, she caught his arm with her free hand and jumped up, wrapping her legs around him and pulling him off balance. She rotated as they fell, landing on his chest with a knee. His lungs ached as a lungful of air was forced out all at once with a desperate wheeze. She pushed off him, lunging for the book, only to stop short as Max grabbed her tail and yanked.

"Don't be a dick, Max," she growled back before cracking him in the face with the butt of her pistol.

"Son of a!" Max's vision blurred for a second.

It was just the distraction she needed to make a break for it, and make a break she did, grabbing the book and darting out the window back to the roof. She must have reloaded because she let off a few rounds as Max tried to follow her out the window. He snatched his full mag from the floor and slammed it in. Tugging his scarf back up, he called back his *Reaper* sub-class and leaped out sideways, firing.

The chase resumed.

Nix dashed toward the edge of the roof, most likely going for one of the balconies below to escape into the palace. Before she could make it, a beautiful voice rang out over Lockheart's house line.

"Get ready for the fireworks!" Ginger shouted, sounding like she was in a hurry.

"Right on time." Her voice filled Max's heart with joy as he braced for impact.

The world trembled as a blast of heat and flame erupted from the corner of the palace behind him. Nix ducked and stole a glance back at the sound. All color drained from her face.

The windows of each balcony detonated outward in a chain of explosions that rocked the entire palace. One blast after another went off like dominos as the destruction blew away the edge of the roof, leaving only the peak where Max crouched.

He grinned as Nix tried to run. Clearly, the mercenary wasn't expecting the entire top floor of the building to detonate. The best she could do was leap away from the edge before the wave of destruction reached her. It was just enough to keep her alive but not enough to keep her from being launched across the roof.

Max watched her body hit the side of the pyramid like a bug hitting a windshield, releasing the book from her grip as she slid back down. He raced for the stolen contract, Death's swords deflecting bullets as she fired uselessly in his direction.

Dashing past her, he scooped up the book with a victorious, "Ha!" Max ran, excitement carrying him through the clouds of billowing smoke that drifted across what was left of the roof.

He had the book.

He had the hard.

He had it all.

A stupid grin spread across his face, impossible to suppress as he dropped through a hole in the roof and into a bombed-out suite below. With everything going on above and the cover that the smoke provided him, he was confident that Nix hadn't seen where he went. As long as he was quiet and didn't do anything stupid, she'd never find him.

Max dropped to his knees in what was once a sitting area. A broken, stone coffee table was all that remained. He threw open the book and pulled his inspector from his journal to capture images of its contents. Getting out of the palace alive was going to be tricky, so he figured getting the book backed up would be his best bet. He read over a page; dates and addresses covered the paper in dense blocks of handwritten text. Of course, he had no idea what any of it meant, but he hoped that Dawson would. He started snapping pictures.

He didn't get far.

Suddenly, Max's body seized up as a sensation radiated out from his spine. It pulsed and throbbed with every movement that he tried to make. It wasn't painful, but it wasn't comfortable either. He fell limp, catching himself just enough to prop his back against the stone table. His mind raced, trying to figure out what was happening.

Did Nix have another contract? Something like the Death Grip?

He didn't know.

Then he heard her voice, and his heart sank.

"I really didn't want to have to do this, Max." Nix stepped into the room and made her way around the table.

He couldn't believe she had found him. The plan had been good. Hell, it had been perfect. It even had his personal style of being loud and destructive. There was no way she could have gotten to him so quickly.

Then she crouched down, and his blood ran cold.

Her eyes were purple.

CHAPTER FIFTY-NINE

"Holy crap!" Kira ducked as the entire top floor exploded against the walls of polished crystal all around her. Of course, she knew the destruction was coming, but still, it was a big-ass explosion.

Farn moved fast, powering up her gauntlet and stepping in front of her as if she expected the worst.

Kira wondered if they had used too many bombs. At the time, Max's argument of better to use more rather than less had won out. Though now, she was a little worried that they might have overdone it. She glanced around at her surroundings, half expecting it all to come crashing down.

The barrier held, leaving the inside of the pyramid unscathed, save for a few cracks here and there. The lockdown was still in place.

"Ah, yes, well, told you we would be safe inside the pyramid." Berwyn raised his head from where he ducked beside her.

Kira shot Farn a nervous glance combined with an awkward smile. Farn met her eyes, then froze and looked away, a smile of her own spreading across her face.

"What the hell was that?" Ripper scanned the perimeter.

Berwyn shook his head. "Amelia must have gotten a team past our people at the gates, planted some explosives."

"Well, where the hell are Nix and Aawil?" Ripper questioned. "Aren't they supposed to be preventing shit like that?"

Berwyn checked his journal. "They haven't responded to any of my messages. Maybe they got caught in the blast."

Ripper laughed. "One can only hope." Clearly, he wasn't a fan of the two mercenaries.

As Ripper and Berwyn talked, Kira leaned close to Farn. "Get ready for a teleport. I'm gonna try it while they're not paying attention."

"Damn," Ripper clenched his fist, "the blast must have destroyed everyone's home points upstairs. That's going to delay some of our reinforcements."

Berwyn started to sweat a little. "We'll sit tight and wait. The Moons shouldn't be able to get in here anyway."

"What if they go for the vault?" Ripper pointed down.

"They'll never get through the laser grid." Berwyn waved away the concern with a hand.

Kira opened her mouth on reflex, but Farn placed a hand on her leg and squeezed before she had the chance to blurt out a correction. Kira immediately shut her mouth, realizing that it was not the moment to make jokes that could potentially blow their cover.

Berwyn stepped a few feet down the stone walkway. "Amelia doesn't have anyone small enough to slip through the laser beams down there." He laughed, raking one hand through his hair. "I'm pretty sure Kira's the only one that could fit through there anyway."

Suddenly, he froze.

It had obviously been a joke, but there it was.

Kira cringed as she watched the wheels in his head begin to turn. She was the only person he knew with the size, weight, and grace to navigate the vault's entryway. She had also been mysteriously absent when the attack started.

Berwyn turned slowly to face her as she did her best to act

casual, sitting on his throne. His face fell as a half-smile wavered up and down. "Kira, dear? Sorry, but where were you before Ripper found you?"

"Umm…" She gave him her most charming smile without saying more.

His eye began to twitch.

"Aww crap." She winced as the Lord of Serpent's visage contorted with rage.

He stabbed a finger in her direction and glared at Ripper.

"Kill them!"

The cruel *Shield* responded with a grin as he drew his sword and reached out toward Kira with his Death Grip.

Farn threw herself in front of her. "You'll have to go through me!" She glanced back over her shoulder. "Get in the air and stay out of range."

Kira hesitated, not wanting to leave her friend's side.

"Please," Farn added with a thread of desperation in her voice. Her tone made Kira's heart ache, although she wasn't sure why. She nodded and shot into the air.

Farn smiled at Ripper. "I guess it's rematch time."

She didn't bother with her gauntlet, instead pouring its energy into her Feral Edge to unleash its true form. Crimson light climbed the blade.

Ripper's claws glowed as well.

What followed next was a kinetic clash of metal and power that tore through the landscape.

Kira stayed close with a pulse ready to disrupt the Death Grip like she had before. To her surprise, Ripper didn't use the overpowered contract. She furrowed her brow. It made no sense. It was like he was dragging things out, which would have been crazy in the current situation. Thinking practically, he should have gone for a quick kill. The answer struck her like a bolt of lightning.

He can't.

The realization changed everything she knew about the seemingly unstoppable Death Grip.

It did have a weakness.

Of course it did. It had to.

Kira cupped her hands around her mouth and shouted down. "He can't use his instakill!"

Ripper glared up at her, his eyes burning with rage, confirming her suspicion. The Death Grip must only work once per player, meaning that he had wasted his ability to use it on Farn days ago.

Kira smiled and cast a buff on Farn. The fight was as good as over.

In the bombed-out suite above, Max fought against his own body as it refused to obey his mind. He lay on his back against the stone table, his eyes locked with Nix, her violet irises staring back at him. He struggled to speak, his voice coming out thick and jittery.

"You're the same as Kira."

"Not quite." The reynard shook her head. "I was the first test." Suddenly, she winced and clutched her head with both hands, her eyes shut tight. She took a few short breaths and opened them again. "As you can see, it didn't go as planned."

Max looked deeper into her eyes, noticing that they weren't as bright as Kira's. Their violet coloring was blotchy with cracks of blue and red running through her irises.

It looked painful.

"I am what happens if the process fails." Nix rubbed at her temples. "I can't command the system on the level Kira can, but I still have enough power to disrupt the control over your body."

Max choked on his saliva. "Did Carver do that to you too?"

"I ordered him to. I thought I could handle it, but I wasn't flexible enough to form a proper bond with the beta."

"Ordered?" Max wrapped his head around that word. "Carver worked for you?"

"He still does." She smirked. "Who do you think faked the DoS attack on Noctem's servers to kick Berwyn offline last night before he could have his way with Kira?"

"That was Carver?"

She gave a weak smile. "I ordered him to do that as well, though he was happy to do it. It was the least we could do considering the burden that has been pushed on that little fairy."

Max didn't like the sound of that. "What burden? What is she bonded with?"

"The future." Nix stared off into nothing before giving her attention back to him. "Do you have any idea what she's capable of? How powerful she is?"

Max had tried not to dwell on the subject. He knew what the system could do better than anyone. It had access to his mind. A year ago, Carver had used it to recreate his childhood memories. It had reached inside his mind. Kira would never hurt anyone, but with that kind of power, there wasn't much she couldn't do.

"That's right," Nix said as if reading the grave expression on his face as an answer. "A side effect of what has been done to her is that she has an ocean of power within her grasp. All she has to do is give herself to it, to let it take her."

"You're an idiot." Max let out a defiant laugh. "She'll never do it. Do you even know Kira? She has less interest in power than I do in my taxes."

"I know her better than you think. I've watched the both of you for years, believe it or not, and you're right, she's lazy and lacks ambition."

Nix picked up Berwyn's book from the floor where Max had dropped it. "Do you know what Cline, sorry, Berwyn is selling?"

Max didn't answer.

"It's a particularly nasty virus or at least something similar."

She leaned in as if gossiping a secret. "They call it Verschlinger. That's German for devourer."

Max tried to pull away from her.

She flipped through the book. "Do you know how many people this weapon could kill?"

"Thousands," Max said with disgust, repeating what he had been told.

She laughed, pointing up with one thumb. "Guess again?"

He didn't. Instead, he let his expression of horror do the talking for him.

Her smile faded. "Try billions."

The word sent a chill through his heart. "What do you want with it?"

"Me? Nothing." She tilted her head to the side. "Honestly, stopping Berwyn's sale and giving the weapon to the Feds would be the best outcome for me. I just needed a threat."

"A threat?"

She nodded. "Yeah, a crisis, a beast, a villain. Something to stop. As I said, I do know Kira. She might not want power, but if it's to save others, well, she'd pay any price she has to. And really, what's one fairy in exchange for the lives of billions?"

Max felt bile in his throat. Nix was right. He struggled to raise his head, letting out a growl. "Damn it! You said you'd help her!"

"No." She shook her head. "I said I'd do something about that pendant. Calling that help, well, you might not see it that way."

At that, she leaned down to and took his hand in hers, raising his house ring to her lips. It shouldn't have worked, but clearly, the rules didn't apply to her and those painful, violet eyes. She paused as if getting into character, then took a few frantic breaths before speaking. Max's skin crawled as his voice came from her mouth.

"Nix got away with the book, I tried, but I couldn't stop her. Oh god! She said that what he's selling could kill billions! I can't—" She keeled over, pressing her forehead into the floor while bracing her skull with her hands as tears streamed from her eyes. She gritted her teeth and pushed through the pain.

Max forced his hand to his mouth, using the last bit of strength he had left. Before he could speak, his house ring melted off his finger and ran down his vest in a river of silver liquid.

Nix relaxed and raised her head off the floor as a somber expression fell across her face. She had won.

It was too late.

"Will she live?" Max asked in desperation.

Nix looked down at him, her eyes telling him more than he wanted to know. "For what it's worth, I'm sorry. Kira's a good person. Sometimes, I wish Carver had never found her." She stood, leaving the book on the floor beside him. "Your team should have gotten all the hard out of the vault by now. At least there's that." Max fought the numbing control she had over him as she walked out of his field of vision.

"I swear on everything I have ever cared about, I will find you, Nix!" Saliva foamed through his teeth as he screamed. "I will hunt you through both worlds if I have to!" He shouted every threat he could think of, finally seeing her for the monster that she was.

Then suddenly, he was free.

She was gone, and his body was his again. There was nothing he could do from where he was; he couldn't get to Kira with the pyramid locked down. In the end, he did the only thing he could.

He logged out.

CHAPTER SIXTY

"Nix got away with the book, I tried, but I couldn't stop her. Oh god! She said what he's selling could kill billions! I can't—"

Max's voice echoed through the house line, stopping Farn in her tracks as the weight of his words slammed into her.

They had failed.

Agent Dawson responded over the line, his voice angry as he insisted that one of them do something to salvage the op. He clearly didn't realize that he was asking the impossible.

Farn's heart leaped into her throat.

When it came to the impossible, there was really only one option left. She jumped back away from Ripper and shouted up. "Kira, don't!" Farn pleaded up at the little mage. "Don't—"

It was already too late.

The fairy hovered in the air with her hands clasped over her mouth, shaking her head. Then she relaxed and gave herself a determined nod.

Ripper halted his advance for a moment to look up as well, clearly unsure what was happening. Berwyn did the same. No one could have been prepared for what happened next.

A sound rang out from above like a single note plucked from

a harp. It hung in the air as a strange energy filled the chamber. Farn held up one arm, every hair standing on end. The chime echoed back, this time louder and infinitely deeper—so deep she could feel it in her bones.

Then the world changed.

The waves froze and jerked about, losing texture as the throne at the center bent impossibly, folding in on itself. It sunk into the surf like a stone in quicksand. A wave of distorted pixels spread out in all directions from Kira.

The loose sand below Farn's feet went rigid, then vanished, leaving the floor as clean and smooth as the crystal walls that surrounded her. A blank slate. Berwyn's mouth dropped open.

Then came the images.

The walls and ceiling flashed with one picture after another as if searching for something. Some were disjointed and mismatched, while some aligned to make a panorama that made the space appear completely different, like they were being teleported around the world instead of the world changing around them.

For a moment, Farn recognized the red sky of the sphere where they had been a year before, then Alderth Castle in Rend where they had fought Death, then her cubicle where she worked in Checkpoint's headquarters. A gentle caress passed through her mind as images that only she could know filled the walls.

The pictures shifted again, becoming less clear for an instant before returning to focus. The city of Torn under siege appeared across the floor as if Farn was floating in the sky above it. Again it changed, and a view of the ocean at night filled all four walls. A large yacht floated in the distance. Farn didn't recognize it, but from the horror on Berwyn's face, it looked like he did.

Next, the room cut to black, and darkness consumed the world. The only light came from Farn's sword, Ripper's gauntlet, and Kira's wings. A trickle of pixie dust drifted down from her body.

No one moved.

Then came the sun.

Farn shielded her eyes as the light blinded her and sounds reached her ears, sounds from a different world. In the distance, a plane flew overhead. Cars passed by as a city bus stopped, its brakes letting out a familiar screech. Then there were people. Walking, talking people.

They were everywhere.

Farn's head spun as her eyes adjusted to the light. She couldn't wrap her mind around what had happened. The throne room had been there a moment ago, but now, she was standing on a sidewalk while people walked past her in everyday clothing. They paid her no attention, her sword still blazing beside her with power. She reached out and touched a woman's shoulder as she passed, only to pull her hand away an instant later.

It felt real.

Cars drove through the street, honking horns and spewing exhaust. She could even smell it. Farn looked up at Kira as she hovered peacefully. Behind her floated a disk of flawless, black obsidian. It was twice the size of her and hung parallel to her body as if she had created it. Patterns of white streaked across its surface like text on a computer screen, opening in circular windows before closing in rapid succession.

Modern buildings stretched into the sky, bending slightly around where the pyramid's ceiling had been. Farn squinted. It was as if everything beyond a certain point was a projection. She glanced around, noticing the same thing further down the street. The walls were still there, acting as an animated facade to extend the environment. Cars passed through the edge, becoming nothing more than projections as they disappeared down the road. The complexity of it made her head hurt.

Farn returned her gaze to the street, finding Ripper in the crowd. He seemed just as confused.

Berwyn, however, looked utterly terrified.

"This–this isn't possible." He backed up until he nearly fell into a building. His eyes bulged as he clutched his head. "Get out!"

That was when Farn understood what was happening. The city street she stood in was important to him. Kira had somehow used the system to pull the location from his memories. It was just like what Carver had done a year ago in the Sphere when he had recreated her 18ᵗʰ birthday. Her worst memory.

Suddenly, Kira's voice echoed over the house line, despite the fact that she hadn't opened her mouth.

"Dawson, I have the location of where Berwyn is storing his merch. It's in an office building on the corner of..." She trailed off before adding a surprised, "Oh. I can do better." The fairy's back arched, trembling as another loud chime rang out. The circle of black glass behind her erupted with activity. Hundreds of round text windows opened and closed like ripples in a pond during a downpour.

Farn pressed a hand to her chest, her heart aching as she watched from below.

She was helpless.

Down in the hidden field office of the F.B.I.'s cybercrime taskforce, Agent Dawson lunged forward, gripping the edge of a desk. The monitors flooded with information. All he wanted was a location of the sale or the date that it might take place. What he got was like nothing he could have imagined.

It started with an address, then, out of nowhere, came blueprints, floor maps, street views, and public satellite images. It was more than enough.

Then things got scary.

New images came in, this time with far more detail. Too much to come from public systems. The pictures became videos, with timestamps in real time. Next came the number of

Berwyn's men currently occupying the building. Then security footage. Captures of each of their faces shifted from one monitor to another.

Dawson shuddered as a strange sensation swept through his mind. He wasn't sure what to make of it until a new monitor lit up with the Bureau's database already active. His login information populated fields along with a message underneath saying, 'Sorry about this.'

The photos of Berwyn's men ran through facial recognition, each gaining a name along with a laundry list of suspected crimes. Half a second later, hundreds of files appeared, sorting themselves into dozens of folders marked evidence. The photos restructured, becoming a complex network with Berwyn sitting at the top. More faces appeared, with each suspect getting the same treatment. Security footage, documents, and dates populated folder after folder as they sorted into the detailed map.

It was everything.

Everything Dawson could have hoped for. Enough to take down Berwyn's entire organization.

Sweat ran down his forehead as he clenched his teeth, nausea rolling through his stomach. If he had been in the real world, he would have thrown up.

Whatever Kira had become, it wasn't human. It wasn't even possible.

Countless systems had been breached all at once. There wasn't a firewall in existence that could stand up to that kind of power. He hadn't seen the fairy as anything more than a harmless slacker, but now, he couldn't even reconcile what he was seeing. He was out of his depth.

"What are you?" Dawson breathed the words through his shaking fingers.

Text ran across all of the monitors at once, 'I don't know.'

Milo leaped out of bed, nearly scampering across the floor of the small apartment that connected to his office within Checkpoint Systems headquarters. He checked his smartwatch. It had already been six minutes since he'd logged out after receiving an emergency alert from the real world. His heart raced as he grabbed a bathrobe and ran down to the main server room.

Chaos met him as he skidded through the doors.

A continuous beeping sounded as red lights blinked all over the server towers that filled the space. Milo froze for a moment before burying his panic and taking charge.

"What's going on?" he called out to the lead tech on duty.

"We're not sure." The man jumped from one console to another. "Some kind of attack. It's taking over our servers and using them to run an unknown program."

"How did it get through our security?" Milo jumped onto one of the consoles to lend a hand.

"It didn't. It was already inside."

"Can we stop it?"

"It's faster than anything we've ever seen. Just keeps slipping through everything we do to contain it." The tech practically attacked a keyboard, typing in commands at a frantic pace. "Whatever it's doing is well beyond what the system was built for. It's melting servers one after another. We've already lost five percent."

Milo's mouth went dry. "We have to shut it down."

Suddenly, his assistant, Jeff, slid in through the door. A crease ran across his face as if he'd been sleeping on the edge of his pillow.

"What's happening?"

"No time, we're being hacked." Milo ripped a key off a chain around his neck and jammed it into a steel cabinet on the wall. He threw it open, revealing the bright, red button that he hoped he would never need to press.

"Wait!" Jeff held up his hand. "That will kick everyone and force-quit the entire system."

Milo let out a defeated sigh. "We don't have a choice."

"But it will take days to get it back up and running."

"It will hurt the bottom line, but we can recover from that. I learned my lesson last year. I'm not taking chances." Milo reached for the button.

"Please don't," another voice pleaded, stopping Milo cold. It hadn't come from anyone in the room. Milo's eyes welled up as he recognized it. "Kira?"

"Please, don't stop me. I'm so close," she continued, her voice coming from the tiny speaker in his smartwatch.

His hand fell away from the kill switch. "What are you doing?"

She gave a somber laugh. "Would you believe saving the world?"

His heart ached as his mind flowed back to the night one year ago he'd watched Kira's vitals flat-line during Carver's quest. "What about you?"

"It doesn't matter. There's something more important."

Milo let out a sigh. "Okay, what do you need?"

CHAPTER SIXTY-ONE

Farn tore her eyes off of Kira, finding Berwyn on the busy city street.

"No no no no no!" He frantically stabbed at the options woven into his stat-sleeve with a finger. "God damn it! Sign off!"

It was obvious that he'd figured out what was going on. With Kira in his mind, his entire operation was an open book. The only thing he could do was break the connection. Clearly out of options, he ripped the golden crown from his head and threw it to the pavement, taking away his own immortality. It bounced into traffic, disappearing under a car. His empire didn't matter anymore.

The desperate man didn't even hesitate before dashing into the street and stopping in the path of an oncoming truck. He braced for impact.

Brakes screeched and tires squealed.

A few awkward seconds later, Berwyn opened his eyes; the bus had stopped a few inches away. He let out a growl and tried again. This time, a taxi stopped short as another car collided with its rear. Even with that, Berwyn stood unharmed, his face drained of color.

Suddenly, another chime sounded from above, and several pedestrians rushed toward the suicidal man. They grabbed at his arms and forced him to safety. Kira must have had enough with his attempts to end himself. Berwyn struggled to get free, but there were too many, leaving him trapped and unarmed. Finally, he raised his head and yelled to Ripper.

"New plan, kill me!"

The twisted *Shield* gave Berwyn a skeptical glare, then he shrugged and started moving. He shoved pedestrians out of the way, cutting down a few that didn't move fast enough. They cried out and vanished in clouds of shimmering pixels. A sickening grin crept across his face.

"Oh no you don't!" Farn dashed toward him, the crowd parting as she ran.

Ripper spun, catching her Feral Edge with his claws as she swung for his head. Sparks exploded from the clash of contract items as each of their weapons crackled with power. Farn stopped short. He was more prepared than she had expected.

"You think I've just been standing around while you gawked at that fairy?" He tightened his fully charged claws around her blade. "No, I've had plenty of time to get ready for you."

Shit! Farn cursed herself as his sword blurred, just missing her throat and scraping against the dragon scale lining of her cape. He followed with a left hook aimed at her head. Violent energy radiated from the Death Grip, burning her skin without even touching her as she weaved to the side. Farn tried to back away, but she was too slow. He slammed his fist down, cracking the concrete with a blast of power that crashed into her like a tidal wave.

Wind rushed through her hair as her feet were torn from the ground, her body soaring backward into the street. All the air escaped her lungs as she smashed through the side of a parked bus with a roar of shattering glass and tearing metal. She landed in the aisle inside, her health plummeting to the red. Coughing, she reached for a health vial. Only two left. She downed them both, getting close to full. With Kira busy with whatever she was doing, there wouldn't be any heals coming her way. She needed to be more careful.

Farn gripped a handrail and pulled herself to her feet just as a glowing fist slammed into the back of the bus. The vehicle exploded inward, throwing Farn back against the windshield, her body cracking the glass. She glanced at her health. Down ten percent already.

Damn!

Even just being near the Death Grip was dangerous.

"No time to rest!" Ripper climbed through the gaping hole. "Nowhere to run." His voice was cruel, laced with manic excitement. Farn pushed herself off the glass as his wicked gaze drifted to the class emblem on her hand. "Starting to fade already? I didn't even use that much power on that last hit." One of his eyebrows slid up his forehead. "Oh, that sword of yours has a tradeoff, doesn't it?"

Shit! Farn thought as he figured out her weakness. Using the Feral Edge in its true form may have given her more damage and range, but it also cut her defense in half.

Ripper chuckled to himself. "All that extra power has to come from somewhere, doesn't it?"

Farn readied her sword. "We can't all drain the lives of other players to fuel our contracts. Some of us just have to have skill." He narrowed his eyes and clenched his fist, his claws beginning to glow again. "Oh, I'm sorry, did you not like hearing the truth?" Farn taunted, trying to buy time.

She didn't actually have to win. No, all she had to do was keep him occupied. The real fight was going on in the sky above. A sharp pain echoed through her chest at the thought of Kira. She just hoped the girl would be safe when everything was over.

Farn shook off the thought and tightened her grip on her weapon, taking in a breath. Then she charged, her sword held out to the side, its blade of crimson energy roaring. Letting out a growl, Farn tore across the narrow space, carving through the interior of the bus in a storm of sparks and desperation.

Ripper back-stepped and blocked everything until finally, Farn made her move. Confusion washed over his face as she cut off the flow of power to her sword. The shining blade of ferocity shattered just before she darted to the side and slammed her gauntlet into her chest plate. "Sure-Foot," she snarled as she planted a boot on the undamaged wall of the bus and ran past him, using her skill to gain a new angle. She swung back down off a pole behind him and slashed at his rear.

"You're it!" she shouted, imbuing him with a glowing red streak across his ass. Farn spun on her heel and raced for the back of the bus. *Come on, chase me, you idiot!* Farn thought as she did her best to piss the guy off.

A furious scream flooded the vehicle behind her. She cringed. *Okay, that might have worked a little too well.*

A blast of stolen life energy exploded from the space, hitting her from behind and firing her out of the bus like a cannon. She braced as she soared through the air, coming down on the windshield of a taxi cab with a crash. Several cars behind slammed into each other.

Farn rolled off the hood, landing on the pavement as the sound of traffic accidents engulfed her. She checked her health and sighed in relief. Still two-thirds remained. Deactivating her sword's contract was the right choice. She needed all the defense she could get.

"Farnsworth!" Ripper screamed in a wild, unhinged tone.

She ducked, keeping her head down to stay out of sight behind the cars that now littered the street. That was when she heard it.

A small pigeon cooed by her hand.

"Shoo shoo." She swatted at the bird, trying to get it away before it gave away her position. The little thing hopped away but returned a second later, pecking at her gauntlet. "Stop that." Farn pulled her hand away.

That was when the bird held out both wings and hopped around in a circle as if frustrated. It was a strangely human act. Farn froze, debating on if she had lost her mind. Then she remembered that the bird wasn't real. Which meant it could only have been controlled by one person.

"Kira?"

The bird nodded in a way that almost seemed annoyed that it had taken her so long. Then it hopped to her side and pointed under a car with its beak.

Farn dropped to the pavement and peered under to find an item, shiny and gold, glinting in the shadow beneath the car. Her heart skipped a beat as she snatched it off the ground and shoved it in her item bag, hoping to find a use for it later.

Ripper's boots came down on the hood of a sedan as he emerged from the bus and stalked toward her, using the cars as stepping stones. Farn's new pigeon friend flew at his head, exploding in a burst of pixels as his sword cut it in half.

Farn skittered away on her back, trying to get some distance. "How's that new butt crack I gave you treating you?"

He glared down at her. "Just for that, I'm going to take my time with that fairy once I'm done with you. Gonna drain her slow."

"Don't you touch her!" Rage rumbled through Farn's chest at his words.

"Oh, I won't have to." Ripper flexed his claws. "I only have to get in range," he added, flicking his eyes up at Kira then across to the building closest to her. "Actually, I might be able to walk right up there."

"Not if I kill you first," Farn growled, trying not to give in to the anger that spiked through her heart. It was what he wanted. He was taunting her just like she had taunted him a moment before.

"You know," Ripper crouched down, scraping his claws against the car beneath him, "I might just skip dinner and go straight to dessert." Then he leaped away and ran toward the building, Kira floating helplessly nearby.

"No!" Farn stood in a panic, realizing that killing Berwyn wasn't the only way to break the connection. Killing Kira would work just as well.

Ripper slammed his gauntlet into his chest and hurled himself onto the wall, climbing straight for the fairy. Farn pushed off with everything she had, racing forward until her feet hit the wall behind him. Gravity shifted around her to reorient to the new angle as she continued her pursuit.

"Don't you dare hurt her!" Farn ran, being careful to keep at least one foot in contact with the plate glass windows of the high-rise. One wrong move would cancel the skill and send her crashing to the pavement. It hadn't been created to be used like that to begin with. Ripper ignored her, sprinting into the sky toward Kira, toward the woman Farn loved.

"Fight me, you coward," Farn cried, in desperation.

With that, he spun, slashing back at her with his sword. It came at her fast. Too fast to block properly. She raised her arm, feeling his weapon bite into her wrist before the system dulled the pain. Farn ignored it and struck forward, just missing his shoulder. She followed with a solid punch to his face. The blow didn't cause much damage, but it did surprise him. Not to mention, it made her feel better.

He struck back, his sword raging against hers as their reflections clashed across the vertical surface, the sun silhouetting their battle from above. The glass squeaked with every step, threatening to crack under the strain of the fight. Farn didn't stop, forcing herself between him and Kira until she stood face to face with the monster of a man. Farn held him back, their blades creaking in protest as her arms trembled.

"Looks like you can't charge your Death Grip's attack up here." Farn smiled. "Another attack like that would shatter the glass you're standing on. Wouldn't it? I guess it's going to be a fair fight from here."

"I don't need a contract to kill someone weaker." Ripper pushed against her.

Farn spat out a mirthless laugh. "You have no idea what strength is."

"And you do?"

"You don't understand your class. We're both *Shields*. We're only strong when we have something to protect." She pushed back.

"That just means you have more to lose." He flicked his eyes over Farn's shoulder at Kira.

"I won't lose her," Farn ground the sentence through her teeth.

He gave a disdainful laugh in response.

"I love her." Farn's mouth fell open, realizing she had actually said the words out loud. They felt right on her lips. Soft and warm. The corner of her mouth tugged up, unable to suppress a dopey smile, even in the middle of the fight.

"And I thought your house couldn't irritate me more," Ripper groaned.

"Sorry," Farn laughed, "but you don't know how long those words have been on the tip of my tongue. So thank you for making me say them." Farn glanced back at the shining fairy. "I guess I should probably tell her."

"Heh, not if I kill her first. Something tells me that taking her out right now might do more than just disconnect her." He shoved forward against her, almost forcing her feet off the glass. Her smile contorted into a snarl as she back-stepped and reactivated her Feral Edge. She'd had enough of him.

"I will keep her safe." She swiped through the air in a figure eight, her blade blurring around her into a wave of crimson light. Then in a single, fluid motion, she spun and struck the glass by her feet, sending a cascade of sparks up from its surface. An instant later, she cut off the contract's power and slipped her sword back into her sheath.

Ripper froze as the reality of what she had done reached him. He glanced at the window as if to check that he was standing on the same pane of glass. Tiny cracks spiderwebbed from her feet to his. His eyes bulged as she crouched down and prepared to jump.

"Wait, don't—"

She cut off his words with her fist as she leaped toward him, the glass shattering beneath them. Gravity reclaimed its dominance, and the world righted itself.

Farn fell, the wind whipping through her hair as she plummeted toward death in a cloud of broken glass. She thrust her hand into her pouch and grabbed the golden item that Kira's pigeon had pointed out earlier on the street below. She just hoped it wasn't bound to its previous owner.

"You're insane!" Ripper screamed with all the anger of a man who had never lost before.

"I will keep her safe," Farn yelled, ending with a roar that tore through the air. Her heart pounded in her chest as every emotion poured out. The ground reached up to claim her. She raised the golden item in her hand and slipped it on her head.

Glass and metal erupted in all directions, and sounds blurring together with Farn's battle cry as she and Ripper exploded through the roof of a parked van. Her fist made sure every point of fall damage counted.

"How?" Ripper wheezed as the dust settled, the spark in his eyes fading to a dull, lifeless gloss.

Farn pushed herself up, her arms shaking. Fragments of glass trickled off her back as she removed her gauntlet from Ripper's face. She checked her health.

Still two-thirds left.

She reached up and adjusted Berwyn's golden crown so that it sat straight on her head. Its rules were simple; as long as she didn't draw a weapon, she couldn't take damage. Apparently, not even fall damage. Releasing a heavy breath, she clasped a hand over her heart and gave thanks to Kira for getting the contract item to her during the fight.

"You were always there for me."

That was when Ripper's body began to change.

The black coloring of his armor seemed to drip from him like ink, leaving his gear a dull, metallic gray. The Death Grip on his hand shifted, its claws retracting as glowing embers escaped from the overpowered item. The light grew until a torrent of bright red energy flowed from the contract. It was like every life that Ripper had hoarded within it had been set free. Then his body crumbled to ash, Death Grip and all.

Farn smiled, letting the embers dance through the white fingertips of her gauntlet as they drifted around her. It felt warm.

Then it began to burn.

Panic flooded through Farn's mind as she flailed her hand back and forth, her gauntlet's fingertips twisting into claws. Darkness climbed up her arm, staining her white armor black, the color of graveyard dirt.

Finally, the burning subsided as a low system chime sounded on her ear. She didn't need to check her journal to understand what it meant. The Death Grip hadn't been bound to its owner either. Of course it wasn't. Something that overpowered had to have a weakness. No, not a weakness, a purpose. The Death Grip was meant to be passed on. It was meant to be wielded by the strong, and now, it was hers.

Farn shivered, hating how the contract felt. The idea that she would ever use it made her skin crawl. She reached for the crown on her head, wondering how it would react to the second contract item. Any way she thought about it, the Death Grip was a weapon, one that couldn't be sheathed. She removed the crown and watched as the inky darkness attempted to crawl across its surface. Then it crumbled in her hand. Apparently, the two couldn't coexist.

It was just as well. Immortality didn't suit her anyway.

That was when a sound drew her attention. Actually, it wasn't a sound but rather the absence of one. The street had gone silent.

Every car on the road stopped moving.

Farn shoved herself out of the wreckage of the van, stumbling as she hit the ground. The fall from before was still throwing off her balance. Her claws scraped against a nearby car when she tried to steady herself. The sound sent a chill down her spine, and she caught her reflection in a window. A dark figure stared back at her. She ignored it, realizing that the people in the street had vanished, including the ones that were holding Berwyn back.

That was when a loud bang came from the wall of the space where the main entrance had been before Kira had rebuilt it. The banging repeated, causing the image projected on the wall to ripple like water. Now that the street had gone silent, Farn could make out a voice shouting commands from the other side. It was muffled through the thick crystal of the wall, but the words 'battering ram' were in there somewhere.

Berwyn slumped against a wall. "I assume that's Amelia, here to take my head." He let out a sigh. "And from all of this," he gestured at the street around him, "I can assume that the Feds are on their way for me out there in the real." He shook his head. "I never thought this was how things would end for me. How does one fairy have this kind of power?"

Farn looked up as Kira floated back down to the pavement; the circle of black glass behind her drifted away as if she had discarded it. She wobbled as her bare feet touched the ground.

Farn rushed to catch her, throwing her arms around the girl before she toppled over, holding her tight. The fairy felt frail like she might break at any moment. Kira returned her embrace as Farn's eyes welled up.

"Thank god you're alright."

Kira raised up on her toes, pressing her cheek against Farn's neck. "So, what was all that about being in love?"

Farn froze, her nose buried in Kira's hair. "You, ah, heard that?"

Kira let out a quiet but beautiful laugh. "I'm everywhere right now. There isn't much I don't hear."

"Sorry…" Farn stopped herself, then held the girl tighter. "Actually, I'm not sorry." She inhaled, taking in Kira's scent. "I love you. I should have told you months ago."

"I wish you had."

Suddenly, a warm tear fell against Farn's neck.

Her heart nearly stopped as she tried to pull away.

Kira's small hands held tighter as she hid her face against Farn's shoulder. Her entire body trembled. "Damn it, Farn. Why didn't you tell me sooner?"

The obsidian pane of glass that had floated behind Kira drifted through Farn's vision. Its surface was blank, save for one word that kept repeating itself over and over.

Error.

Error.

Error.

Error.

Error.

The battering ram continued to slam against the outside of the space as the projection on the walls distorted and failed. Blank, crystal walls surrounded the pyramid again.

Farn tore herself away from the fairy so she could see her face.

"I'm sorry." Kira wiped at her eyes with both hands, unable to stop herself from crying until finally giving up. She sniffed and looked up. "I'm so sorry."

An ache swelled in Farn's throat as soon as she saw her. "No."

Kira's eyes sparkled through her tears. A bright crimson stared back up at Farn, replacing the purple that had been there before. As if answering the question on Farn's mind, Kira spoke, "You heard Max on the house line. People could die. Someone had to do something."

"Why did that someone have to be you?" Farn clutched her chest.

Kira lowered her eyes to the ground. "Because I could. I was the only one with access to enough power to help."

"But at what price?" Farn didn't want to know the answer.

"I'm sorry." Kira fidgeted with the hem of her dress. "I never wanted you to be sad. I know I wasn't ready to face a lot of things about myself. I didn't even understand how I felt until you said something." Her tears fell to the ground. "Of course I love you. How could I not? I just wish I had more time…" Her voice trailed off, and she stopped crying, her hands falling to her sides.

"No! Stay with me!" Farn grabbed the fairy by the shoulders as the crimson in her eyes faded back to purple. The color continued to change until they returned to the clear blue that Kira originally had back when they'd met a year ago. Back before Carver had altered her.

That was when Farn realize the truth.

Kira's eyes had never been purple, to begin with. No, the crimson had always been there, just hiding behind the blue, the two colors blending together as one. The pendant around her neck also changed, returning to a dull sapphire. Then it cracked.

"No!" Farn's heart shattered as the spark in Kira's eyes faded into the same lifeless gloss that Ripper's had a few moments before. Everything that she was seemed to vanish along with the red spark that no longer brought her to life.

The battering ram outside slammed into the wall again, sending a crack up the crystal barrier.

Kira's voice faded, her mouth still moving without making a sound. Her lips formed the words, "I'm sorry," over and over.

Farn collapsed to her knees and threw her arms around the fairy just as the wall of the chamber gave way. Members of House Winter Moon poured in with Lady Amelia leading the charge. They stopped dead in their tracks at the scene before them.

Silence filled the city street as the buildings towered in the space, the sun above blacking out in sections of triangular darkness. Eventually, the light vanished altogether.

Farn filled the silence, her chest heaving as sobs wracked her body. Her tears soaked the front of Kira's dress. She was gone. All that remained was an avatar.

A lifeless echo.

Back at Checkpoint headquarters, the last server running Kira's program melted.

CHAPTER SIXTY-TWO

Wyatt fell out of bed, still feeling a lingering stiffness from whatever Nix had done to his brain to disrupt the control he had over his body. He ripped off his Somno unit and threw it to the side, not caring where it landed. It wasn't important.

He scrambled over to the glass door where his best friend had greeted him every morning for the last year. He hoped he would make it to Seth before he did something stupid online as Kira. Wyatt had no idea what he could do for his friend, but for now, he just had to get to him.

Sliding the glass door open, Wyatt carefully hoisted himself up onto the railing and stepped across the gap between their balconies. He prayed that Seth had forgotten to lock his door and blew out a sigh of relief a moment later, finding it open a crack. Suddenly, the wood railing beneath his foot creaked, echoing into the night as he straddled the gap between their homes.

That was when he heard voices coming from inside Seth's room.

"You hear that?" asked a man in a gruff but casual tone.

"Yeah, it came from the balcony," answered another voice, this one sounding softer. "Check it out while I pack up this guy's Somno."

Footsteps came toward the door, sending a jolt of panic through Wyatt's body. He pushed back to his balcony and ducked back into his room as quiet as he could. Dropping low, he peeked out just as a large man stepped out of Seth's room.

He was huge.

Not so much tall, but thick, like every inch of him was covered with slabs of solid muscle. A strange mask covered his eyes. All black, save for a diamond over one eye like some kind of court jester. It struck Wyatt as odd when a simple ski-mask would have made more sense.

The large man glanced around, then shrugged. "Nothing out here."

"Okay, get back in here and pick up this guy so we can get out of here," responded the softer voice.

Wyatt got moving as soon as the man went back inside, snatching his phone off his nightstand and dialing 911. He gave his address and explained the situation before hanging up. The operator had asked him to stay on the line, but he couldn't just sit there on the phone while his friend was in trouble next door.

He couldn't wait for help to come.

Wyatt tried to think, knowing that there wasn't much he could do against the two men on his own, especially considering that one was much bigger than him. If he had a gun, things might be different. He hadn't ever tested the theory, but he should have had the same skill with a firearm in the real world as he did in game.

But, that was just it, this wasn't a game.

He could die.

Finally, after pacing his room for a full minute, he shook off his fears and rushed back to the balcony. He wasn't the only one in danger.

Hoisting himself back up on the railing, Wyatt made sure to cross the gap quieter than before. He carefully peeked into

Seth's room from the top corner of the door. Then his heart sank.

They were gone.

He dropped down and stepped inside, stopping at Seth's empty bed. He covered his mouth, struggling not to throw up. His throat burned as he refused to accept what he saw.

Seth was gone.

Just gone.

The sound of an engine starting came from outside, and Wyatt choked down his feelings. He ran for the stairs of Seth's side of the duplex, nearly tripping on the clutter his friend had left in the hall. He leaped down the steps before bursting through the front door that had been left open.

A black, windowless van sped off as Wyatt ran in desperate hope of catching up, his bare feet slapping the pavement. Rocks dug into his skin, leaving a trail of bloody prints behind him as he sprinted faster until his leg muscles burned and his chest ached. The van only got further away. He struggled to read the plate number through the tears in his eyes, only catching the first two digits before tripping over his own feet.

Wyatt slammed into the pavement face first, scraping the skin off his cheek and nose as he tumbled. He felt something crack in his wrist as he tried to stop himself, pain shooting up his arm with no system in place to dull it back down.

Finally, he came to a stop, tasting blood. He coughed and tried to push himself up, feeling one hand collapse under his weight. It lolled at an unnatural angle as he fell back down. He clutched his shattered wrist to his chest as he lay on his side, screaming into the distance.

The van disappeared down the street as the sound of police sirens came from the distance. They were too late. No, worse. Wyatt was too late.

He had waited too long in his room. Wasted too much time calling for help. He should have just gone in. He should have swallowed his fear.

He should have saved his friend.

The heist didn't matter anymore. Berwyn didn't matter anymore. The Feds didn't matter anymore. His best friend was gone, and all he could do was cry on the pavement.

CHAPTER SIXTY-THREE

Milo buried his face in his hands as an agent from the F.B.I.'s cybercrime division stood in his office and went over the events of the last few days. He wasn't listening or, rather, he didn't need to. Milo had heard it all already from Wyatt after rushing down to Florida to see him in the hospital the day after everything had happened.

With several pins sticking out of Wyatt's shattered wrist, he had been in rough shape. Though, even that didn't compare to the loss.

Milo pushed his palms into his eyes, rubbing them before they welled up at the memory. Apparently, he had sent Max and Kira right into the middle of an undercover investigation without knowing it. Christ, he hadn't even known that the Feds had a division operating within Noctem. Well, he probably did know at one point since they rented a space within his world to use as a field office, but he had signed so many papers in the last few years. He simply couldn't stay abreast of everything.

A pang of guilt dug into his chest, only to be replaced by a seething anger at the man in his office.

"Are you listening?" Agent Dawson folded his arms.

"No, I'm not," Milo snapped back. "You put the lives of everyone in House Lockheart in danger by convincing them to take over your failed mission. Not only that, but you forbade them from informing me, and I'll tell you this, if I had known, I would have put a stop to it."

Dawson held his ground. "I assure you, the players in question were well informed of the risks. If there had been another way—"

"They were my friends." Milo slapped a hand on his desk. The words shocked Milo as much as they did the man before him. The guilt returned as a heavy silence fell over the office.

"Is that why you're not fighting their claim to the hard they stole? Because you have a personal relationship with the members of Lockheart?"

Milo scoffed. "I couldn't fight their claim even if I wanted to. They didn't break any rules."

"I'm pretty sure what Kira did to the system would constitute as cheating."

"Yes, well, that all happened after the hard had been removed from the vault. As far as our logs are concerned, everything was on the up and up. There's no reason to look into the heist any further." Milo gave the agent a smug smile to let him know he was right and that there wasn't anything he could do about it.

"Fine." Dawson's mouth curled down into a frown.

"Did you at least catch your man, the player behind Berwyn's account? Obviously, you have bigger problems than a few million in missing hard."

Dawson blanched as if remembering something he'd rather forget. "Yes. We were able to run raids on his entire network. We can't actually use anything Kira gave us in court, but she showed us where to find everything we needed. From here, it's just a matter of getting warrants."

"Good, then that means the rest of Lockheart is safe." Milo blew out a sigh of relief. "They've already lost enough."

"About that." Dawson placed both hand's on Milo's desk. "Kira couldn't have survived, right?"

Milo flinched at the question like it had slapped him across the face. Dawson's wording was clear. Whatever Carver's experiment had done to her had turned her into something dangerous. Something like her couldn't be allowed to exist. Her death was probably the best-case scenario for Dawson. Still, the question hurt as a quiet memory of the fairy's laugh echoed through Milo's mind.

"From what our data shows, probably not. But without access to her real body, there's no way to know for sure. Her brain stopped sending information just before taking over the system. From that point on, all of her activity originated from within our servers, all of which burned out a few minutes later. Apparently, our system wasn't enough to run her program."

"And what was her program?"

"If I knew, I would tell you." Milo held out his hands, empty. "She was a victim of Carver's final experiment back when he was fired last year. He bound her to some kind of evolving artificial intelligence. We thought we had stopped its progress, but apparently, we only slowed things down. As long as she didn't activate the A.I., she could live a normal life. But with your operation in jeopardy and the consequences that were on the table," Milo paused, feeling an ache in his throat, "well, Kira was always one to put others before herself. It seems she let Carver's A.I. have her."

Dawson removed his hands from Milo's desk and stood back up. "If she is truly gone, then what is controlling her avatar back in Noctem?"

"It's an echo." Milo sunk into his office chair. "It's what happens when a player dies while logged in. If the system stops receiving from a user without a logout signal, it tries to fill in the blanks from the memories of other players. Of course, most of the time, the information loses stability within a minute or two, but in Kira's case, she'd left a fairly deep imprint on the players around her. Combined with the abnormalities in how her mind connected to the system, it seems her echo is here to stay."

"A ghost in the machine?"

"No." Milo shook his head. "There's nothing conscious behind it. An echo is just the system showing people what they expect to see. No matter how lifelike it is, it's not. As much as I wish there was more to it, she's nothing more than a dream."

Dawson's shoulders relaxed, like the knowledge that she was gone was a relief. "I expect you to turn over all of the servers that this A.I. inhabited."

Milo rolled his eyes. "Sure, my people couldn't salvage anything off them anyway. They're scrap at this point."

"And I expect to be given every file you have on this Nix character. If she has anything to do with Carver and turning Kira into that thing, then she needs to be stopped." With that, the agent took his leave, ending the conversation and heading for the door.

"One more thing." Milo stood from his chair.

"Yes?" Dawson turned around.

"Whoever Nix is, she has kicked a hornet's nest. House Lockheart is made up of the strongest players in the world, players that have just stolen nine million in hard. Now, I don't know about you, but that much money can go a long way. And if I know Max and Farn, and I think I do, they will literally tear through Noctem until they find the person that took their friend." Milo slapped his hand down on his desk. "And I will do everything in my power to help them."

Dawson's face hardened. "What is that supposed to mean?"

Milo narrowed his eyes. "It means stay out of their way."

LOGS

Checkpoint System's Message Board - One week after the heist

Topic: Looking for information on House Lockheart?

TheNoctemTimes: My website is looking for information on the members of House Lockheart. After everything that happened in Reliqua, this story is going to be huge. However, so far we haven't found much beyond the names, GingerSnaps, MaxDamage24, Kirabell, Farnsworth, Corvin, and Kegan. If anyone has partied with these players before please DM me.

CronicTheHedgehog69: Yeah, you and everyone else.

MandalorianMan: No idea where they came from, but holy crap! They just got away with millions. That's insane.

TheNoctemTimes: From what we've learned, Checkpoint had to rework the storage system for each city's vault so that this doesn't happen again.

HelveticaNue: I'm just glad they put a stop to the House of Serpents conquest that has been screwing up the farming for half the game. I've been struggling to craft for weeks.

BullShifters: I can help here. Okay, so this one time, me and my buddy Keith partied with some of those guys from Lockheart. We had found them through LFG. An' le'me tell ya, they were something else. I reckon there ain't no healer out there better than that fairy. Their *Shield* is pretty much unstoppable, and that *Fury* is a beast.

TheNoctemTimes: Are you on their friend lists? And if so, could you send them my contact information. They seem to have their accounts set to anonymous because I can't find them in search.

BullShifters: Nah, that would seem like, what you might call, poor manners. I messaged them a congrats last week after they got away with the crime of this here century, but it seemed like they wanted to be left well enough alone. Probably getting a veritable horde of messages.

EMPIREriot: That makes sense.

BullShifters: One odd thing tho, the message I sent Kirabell never went through. It just bounced right back.

◆ ◆

Gameplay recording
Title: Late Nite in Lucem - Episode 253
Uploaded by RoyalAssistantFour
Number of Views: 11,265,584

Music plays while a still image of Lucem's cityscape fills the screen, its grand archway reaching across the sky. A logo appears just before the title screen fades to a player's view. They walk into a large room where they join an audience of around fifty other players to sit down in front. A woman occupies an ornate desk beside a chair as an elven man sits down to join her. The woman smiles at the viewers.

"Hey, hey, and welcome to Late Nite. I'm your host and Lady of the Silver Tongues, Leftwitch. Tonight, we've got an interesting guest on to shed a little light on the fall of one of my fellow rulers, Lord Berwyn. So let's give a big hand for Dartmouth, the new Lord of the House of Serpents." She gestures to the elf beside her.

"Thank you so much for having me on the show. I have to say, I don't know where you find the time to run a city and entertain all of us." He gives her a slight bow.

Leftwitch gives an exaggerated shrug. "I have eleven million viewers; I have assistants for the boring stuff. But we're not here to talk about me. What about you? How's the new Lordship treating you now that Lady Amelia has executed your predecessor?"

"Well, I'm not going to lie, many out there would like to see the House of Serpents disbanded after Berwyn's attempt at world domination. But with the fall of our Lord, we're determined to build a new house, one that might help the players rather than just lord over them."

"Ah, speaking of, do you think Berwyn will ever show his face in Noctem again?"

"No idea. He hasn't logged on since losing his throne."

"That's one hell of a rage quit." Leftwitch laughs.

"Truly. Unfortunately, his absence has thrown half of Noctem into chaos now that three cities have suddenly lost their ruler. I think Torn has had six rulers in the last week during the power struggle."

"Ouch."

"Ouch indeed."

She leans closer. "So I take it you won't be throwing your hat in the ring then?"

"Oh, lord no." Dartmouth waves the question away. "We don't have that kind of strength anymore without a city's hard behind us. Not to mention, many of our members have left for greener pastures. I've had to recruit a new Archmage and Knight just to keep the house together."

"Ah right, you no longer have the Death Grip in your ranks. I heard he up and left. What's he up to now, anything interesting or just becoming a standard murder hobo?"

"Ha, yes, I wouldn't put that past him, but seriously, Ripper was Berwyn's right hand. I don't think he felt like he had a place within the Serpents now that his Lord's account has gone offline. Plus, he's no longer the Death Grip." He arches an eyebrow.

"That was certainly unexpected. Who would have thought that the contract would pass onto the player who took him out? And that actually brings me to the meat of why I asked you on tonight. Tell me," she leans on one hand, "what do you know about House Lockheart?"

Dartmouth gave a polite laugh. "Unfortunately, not much. They had me fooled just as much as everybody else. All I know is that they have a Death Grip of their own now and a fairy that knows her way around a dance floor. Oh, that, and they're significantly richer than they were."

Leftwitch gives him a charming smile. "Come on, you gotta know something more? The world is dying to know. Lockheart can't have just gone silent after overthrowing an empire and pulling off the greatest heist of the modern world."

Dartmouth gave her a wink. "Sorry, but all I can say is this —everything you've heard about them… is true."

◆━━━◆ ◆━━━

Gameplay recording
Title: They're Back
Uploaded by Hoover
Number of Views: 89,746,625

The throne room of Torn, as seen through the eyes of a player, fills the view. A large *Blade* class player reclines in the city's seat of power with an intentional swagger.

"Welcome to the reign of the House of the Boar. I am Lord Tusker, and I'm settling into my new throne pretty well. I've got my Knight by my side," he gestures to the player recording before continuing, "so let's see if we can hold our kingdom for more than a day."

Suddenly, a voice speaks over the Boar's house line, "Hey Tusker, I'm done setting up the NPC guards at the front gate, and you're not going to believe who's walking toward us."

Lord Tusker raises his house ring. "Who?"

"It's them, House– Hey! what the hel–" the voice cuts off mid-sentence.

Another speaks up, this time from inside the palace. "Oh shit, that didn't even slow them down."

"Didn't slow who down? Damn it!" Tusker growls into his house ring.

"No no no–" the voice shouts back before going silent.

More reports come in, only to end before getting out more than a couple words.

Tusker steps back and signals to a few *Leaf* players standing by the door. They take up defensive positions on either side just as the sounds of combat reach the viewer from down the hall.

Silence takes the room again.

Tusker looks at the player recording the events as they draw their sword and hold it at the edge of the view.

A man, recognizable from dozens of blurry screenshots, appears in the doorway. A dark scarf covers his face. His name is well known.

MaxDamage.

House Boar's archers let loose, firing arrow after arrow as several translucent swords blur around him. He doesn't even slow down. The pings of metallic impacts echo through the room, arrows falling to the floor at his feet. Max raises a pair of pistols and fires into the archers on both sides, landing head-shots without even looking.

Behind him enters a dark *Shield*, her name now living in infamy, Farnsworth the Death Grip. A small woman sticks close to her side, a hooded cloak hiding her face from the viewer.

Finally, the Lady of House Lockheart, GingerSnaps, strides into the room bracketed by a *Leaf* and a *Blade*, Kegan and

Corvin, respectively. The bodies of the fallen players shimmer as she passes through the cloud of drifting particles.

Tusker readies his sword. "If you think you're taking my city, you have another thing—"

His words cease as Farnsworth raises a clawed hand. The Lord's body lurches forward as if yanked by a cable bound to his heart. The dark *Shield* snaps her fist shut, and all at once, a torrent of red light explodes from the ruler of Torn's body. His health swirls toward the Death Grip's glowing claws.

The player recording the events steps back as if in disbelief. GingerSnaps slinks forward.

"I am sorry for the trouble, but this was… convenient for us. You are recording everything, right?"

The player gives a slow nod before speaking. "Aren't you taking the throne?"

Ginger laughs as if the idea of ruling Torn was a joke. "No thanks." She gives the player a predatory grin, then gestures to the *Fury*. "Give him the message."

MaxDamage stalks closer, ignoring the sword pointed in his direction until he's standing face to face with the player. A painted grin of bright white teeth stretches across his scarf where his mouth would be had it not been covered. He tugs it down, showing his face clearly.

There's no grin underneath.

Max pushes away the player's sword with the muzzle of one pistol before raising his other gun to the man's face. He takes aim, almost as if targeting the audience watching through the player.

"I hope we have your attention, Nix."

He tightens his finger around the trigger.

"Because we're coming for you."

ABOUT D. PETRIE

D. Petrie discovered a love of stories and nerd culture at an early age. From there, life was all about comics, video games, and books. It's not surprising that all that would lead to writing. He currently lives north of Boston with the love of his life and their two adopted cats. He streams on twitch every Thursday night.

Connect with D. Petrie:
TavernToldTales.com
Patreon.com/DavidPetrie
Facebook.com/WordsByDavidPetrie
Facebook.com/groups/TavernToldTales
Twitter.com/TavernToldTales

ABOUT MOUNTAINDALE PRESS

Dakota and Danielle Krout, a husband and wife team, strive to create as well as publish excellent fantasy and science fiction novels. Self-publishing *The Divine Dungeon: Dungeon Born* in 2016 transformed their careers from Dakota's military and programming background and Danielle's Ph.D. in pharmacology to President and CEO, respectively, of a small press. Their goal is to share their success with other authors and provide captivating fiction to readers with the purpose of solidifying Mountaindale Press as the place 'Where Fantasy Transforms Reality.'

Connect with Mountaindale Press:
MountaindalePress.com
Facebook.com/MountaindalePress
Twitter.com/_Mountaindale
Instagram.com/MountaindalePress

MOUNTAINDALE PRESS TITLES
GameLit and LitRPG

The Completionist Chronicles,
Cooking with Disaster,
The Divine Dungeon,
Full Murderhobo, and
Year of the Sword by Dakota Krout

A Touch of Power by Jay Boyce

Red Mage and
Farming Livia by Xander Boyce

Ether Collapse and
Ether Flows by Ryan DeBruyn

Unbound by Nicoli Gonnella

Threads of Fate by Michael Head

Lion's Lineage by Rohan Hublikar and Dakota Krout

Wolfman Warlock by James Hunter and Dakota Krout

Axe Druid,
Mephisto's Magic Online, and
High Table Hijinks by Christopher Johns

Dragon Core Chronicles by Lars Machmüller

Pixel Dust and
Necrotic Apocalypse by D. Petrie

Viceroy's Pride and
Tower of Somnus by Cale Plamann

Henchman by Carl Stubblefield

Artorian's Archives by Dennis Vanderkerken and Dakota Krout

APPENDIX

CHARACTER STATS

MaxDamage24

TITLE: Pale Rider
HOUSE: Lockheart
LEVEL: 147
RACE: Human
TRAIT: Versatile – All stats develop equally.
CLASS: Fury
SUB CLASS: Reaper (-30 HP every 3 seconds while active)

STATS
Hit Points: 3584
Skill Points: 400
CONSTITUTION: 112
STRENGTH: 64

DEXTERITY: 196
DEFENSE: 102
WISDOM: 0
FOCUS: 0
ARCANE: 0
AGILITY: 23
LUCK: 38

ACTIVE SKILLS

SLOT 1: Custom Rounds, level 6 – Convert a magazine to a different type of ammunition. May be used once per magazine.

SLOT 2: Last Stand – Fire an empty pistol by creating bullets from your hit points. Duration lasts until death or reloading.

SLOT 3: Heavy Metal – Drastically decreases range and increases recoil enough to damage the wielder and make firearms difficult to handle but grants +75% damage.

REAPER SLOT 1: Unbreakable Defense – Summon the blades of Death to deflect all incoming physical damage (ranged only). Activate by holding one's breath, lasts as long as breath is held.

PERKS

SLOT 1: Dual Wield – Allows a second pistol to be equipped. -5% damage output for each missed shot with an off-hand weapon for a maximum damage penalty of -40%. Penalty lasts until both weapons have been reloaded.

SLOT 2: Last Chance – The last round fired from a magazine deals +50% damage, increasing the likelihood of finishing an enemy before needing to reload.

SLOT 3: Quick Draw – Any shot fired within two seconds of a weapon being drawn from a holster will gain +25% damage.

Kirabell

TITLE: Archmage
HOUSE: Lockheart
LEVEL: 147
RACE: Fairy
TRAIT: Fragile – Receive a significant bonus to arcane, wisdom and focus, however strength and constitution are soft-capped. Physical capabilities are also limited due to character size.
CLASS: Breath Mage

STATS

Hit Points: 50
Mana Points: 2101 (+1000 in reserve)
CONSTITUTION: 4 (-75% racial penalty = 1 total)
STRENGTH: 0 (-75% racial penalty = 0 total)
DEXTERITY: 0
DEFENSE: 50
WISDOM: 142 (+25% racial bonus = 177 total)
FOCUS: 153 (+25% racial bonus = 191 total)
ARCANE: 0 (+25% racial bonus = 0 total)
AGILITY: 70
LUCK: 41

ACTIVE SKILLS

HOUSE SLOT 1: Overcast – Increase the potency of any spell by increasing mana consumption. May use from 1% to 100%. Can only be used from spellcraft menu.

PERKS

SLOT 1: Dual Cast – Allows a second caster to be equipped. Spells cast with off-hand cost 20% more mana.

SLOT 2: True Flight – Wings are the mark of a true fairy.

SLOT 3: Wellspring – Increase the potency of spells while a fairy's bare feet are in contact with the ground.

Farnsworth

TITLE: First Knight
HOUSE: Lockheart
LEVEL: 144
RACE: Human
TRAIT: Versatile – All stats develop equally.
CLASS: Shield

STATS

Hit Points: 5888
Skill Points: 280
CONSTITUTION: 184
STRENGTH: 128
DEXTERITY: 62
DEFENSE: 196
WISDOM: 0
FOCUS: 0
ARCANE: 0
AGILITY: 11
LUCK: 14

ACTIVE SKILLS

SLOT 1: Death Grip (CONTRACT) – Can't be unslotted.

SLOT 2: Taunt – Gives weight to your words to draw the attention of an enemy. PVE only.

SLOT 3: Feral Edge (CONTRACT) – Unleash your inner beast.

HOUSE SLOT: Sure-Foot – Hold your ground while fighting on any surface, may ignore gravity.

PERKS

SLOT 1: Damage Absorption, level 5 – Your shield blocks 90% of damage taken.

SLOT 2: Annoyance – Increases the likelihood of getting an enemy's attention by attacking it.

SLOT 3: Protector – Increase defense by +15 when standing between an enemy and a party member.

Kegan

TITLE: Deadly Wind
HOUSE: Lockheart
LEVEL: 115
RACE: Elf
TRAIT: Control – At creation, choose one stat to receive a bonus for each upgrade point used and choose two stats to receive a soft-cap.
CLASS: Leaf

STATS

Hit Points: 2848
Skill Points: 250
CONSTITUTION: 89
STRENGTH: 125 (+25% racial bonus = 156)
DEXTERITY: 90
DEFENSE: 80
WISDOM: 0
FOCUS: 0 (-25% racial bonus = 0)
ARCANE: 0 (-25% racial bonus = 0)
AGILITY: 45
LUCK: 21

ACTIVE SKILLS

SLOT 1: Camouflage, level 3 – Temporarily change your skin and equipment's coloring to blend into a variety of terrains. Must be holding still.

SLOT 2: Piercing Strike – The next arrow fired will continue moving through your target to hit another behind it. The arrow will continue until it runs out of momentum or hits an obstacle. Each consecutive hit decreases damage by -10%.

SLOT 3: Light Foot – Remove all sound produced by your movement for five minutes for better stealth.

PERKS

SLOT 1: Speed Chain – Increase damage by 5% for each arrow fired within three seconds of the last.

SLOT 2: Charge Shot – Increase damage by 10% for every second you hold the bowstring back.

SLOT 3: Sticky Quiver – Arrows will not fall out of your quiver.

Corvin

TITLE: Nightmarebane
HOUSE: Lockheart
LEVEL: 77
RACE: Reynard
TRAIT: Nine Tails – All nine attributes gain a bonus equal to half your lowest.
CLASS: Blade

STATS
Hit Points: 2272
Skill Points: 150
CONSTITUTION: 58 (+13 racial bonus = 71)
STRENGTH: 55 (+13 racial bonus = 68)

DEXTERITY: 26 (+13 racial bonus = 39)
DEFENSE: 41 (+13 racial bonus = 54)
WISDOM: 26 (+13 racial bonus = 39)
FOCUS: 26 (+13 racial bonus = 39)
ARCANE: 26 (+13 racial bonus = 39)
AGILITY: 26 (+13 racial bonus = 39)
LUCK: 26 (+13 racial bonus = 39)

ACTIVE SKILLS

SLOT 1: Phantom Blade – Launch a blade of malicious intent at a target. Damage and range dependent on skill level.

SLOT 2: Hone – Temporarily hone the edge of a blade to increase sharpness and damage. Lasts for a number of cuts equal to skill level.

PERKS

SLOT 1: Awareness – Hear better than most.

SLOT 2: Quick Draw – The first cut executed within three seconds of drawing a blade has a chance to deliver double damage.

Ginger Snaps

TITLE: Lady of House Lockheart
HOUSE: Lockheart
LEVEL: 134
RACE: Human
TRAIT: Versatile – All stats develop equally.
CLASS: Coin

STATS

Hit Points: 3168
Skill Points: 310

CONSTITUTION: 99
STRENGTH: 60
DEXTERITY: 136
DEFENSE: 91
WISDOM: 0
FOCUS: 0
ARCANE: 0
AGILITY: 65
LUCK: 61

ACTIVE SKILLS

SLOT 1: Blur – Decrease a target's ability to target you. PVE only.

SLOT 2: Paralyze – Immobilize a target after a successful backstab. Removes critical hit bonus.

SLOT 3: Five Finger Discount – Will cause an NPC to turn around. Common items are fair game.

HOUSE SKILL SLOT: Royalty – You may claim the throne of any city in Noctem. If you can take it, that is.

PERKS

SLOT 1: Grappling Hook – Fire a line from a wrist mounted launcher.

SLOT 2: Sticky Fingers – Any material taken from an enemy can be converted to an item to be used or sold.

SLOT 3: Backstab – Increase damage by 150% when doing it from behind.

BESTIARY

Nonhostile Creatures

LAGOPIN – Being half rabbit and half bird, these mounts are seriously fun to ride. So, saddle up and hang on tight.

JEROBIN – A small kangaroo-like race, these sentient creatures are often seen working in the cities of Noctem.

Basic Monsters

SCALEFANG – A large lizard bearing a mane of bright feathers. They attack with their entire bodies from their tail to their teeth. Their rotating elemental weakness makes them particularly hard to deal with, especially in large groups.

BASILISK – An enormous black snake with a paralyzing stare. Avoid direct eye contact at all costs.

GHOUL – These animated corpses of the dead are known for their physical attacks, but they have been observed using magic as well.

POPLO – A spherical manifestation of elemental energy, capable of a number of spells that match their affinity.

MISFIT – A cave dwelling monster that likes to bite and kick.

SILVER ANGEL – A silent observer who watches those who travel down the spiral.

PLAGUE TOAD – Wet, slimy, and vicious, these creatures exist to eat. They will try to lure you in with their tail and attack from below. They especially like easy targets.

MIND FLAYER – A squid-like creature that inflicts madness on a target by spraying it with ink. Resides in the caverns beneath Rend as well as many other parts of Noctem. Not particularly dangerous in and of themselves, but the madness status can easily kill a target or innocent bystanders, as it alters the perception of the target. Players may look like monsters and vice versa. Environmental hazards may also be manipulated.

MIMIC – A monster disguised as a common treasure chest. Recognizable to any experienced player by a bent handle on one side. Highly lethal ambush predators, mimics give up relatively easily if they have not caught their prey quickly.

MARIONETTES – A low level monster found in the city of Rend. A simple ball-jointed doll with a hostile nature. Appears in groups, usually with a leader.

PORCELAIN BEAST – A conglomerate of Marionettes. If

too many of these weak monsters are brought together, they may combine into one mass of writhing bodies.

Nightmares

RASPUTIN – This mad monk exists to tear and rend all asunder, earning him the title of Destroyer.

SENGETSU – Sometime sacrifices cannot be avoided. It is up to you to fear them or not.

KAFKA – Change is necessary for growth, but will that growth create a monster?

RACKHAM – Not all battles can be won, but that doesn't mean you should accept defeat.

Unique Nightmares (The Horsemen)

FAMINE – The bell of Famine rings a steady rumble in one's stomach. Nothing can be eaten in this Nightmare's dungeon.

PESTILENCE – The horde is coming and it's hungry.

DEATH – Like a force of nature, this nightmare claims everyone in the end.

WAR – The embodiment of war, this Nightmare consists of two dragon kings locked in combat for centuries. There is no stopping them. It's best to just run.

CITIES

Valain

The unofficial capital of commerce, Valain runs like a well-oiled machine. Its citizens work hard and party hard. This city and its territories are the only parts of Noctem that are fully under the control of Checkpoint Systems. (Current Ruler: Alastair Coldblood, Lord of House Checkpoint.)

Lucem

The city of light, Lucem stands as a shining example of what can be done through clever negotiations and diplomacy.

Artists and entertainers have flocked to its peaceful and vibrant streets. If you're looking for a night out, you can't do much better. (Current Ruler: Leftwitch, Lady of the House of Silver Tongues.)

Sierra

Previously lost for generations, the city of Sierra hid below ground where its people, the Deru, thrived and innovated. Now known for its unique architecture, which makes use of the cavern ceiling as much as it does the floor. A complex system of railways connects the city. Its towers are filled with crafting workshops for the diligent, while its streets are lined with games and food reminiscent of a carnival.

Tartarus

While not an official city, Tartarus defies logic by existing in the wilds on the dark continent Gmork. It has been constructed of entirely farmed and crafted materials. Enter at your own risk.

Rend

Once the sister city to Torn, the majestic kingdom of Rend fell to the greed of its ruler, who attempted to offer the city to the Nightmare Rasputin to form a contract. Its palace, Castle Alderth, has become a frozen tomb, home to nothing but death and darkness. Even now, it remains waiting for the day that someone breaks its curse.

Reliqua

The city of rest and relaxation. Its inhabitants walk the streets of this tropical paradise at a leisurely pace. Home of the Jewel of the Sea, a crystal pyramid that towers over the tranquil streets.

Thrift

A city-wide bazaar where cultures of all worlds mingle. All are welcome, none are turned away.

Torn

A winter kingdom not for the faint of heart. Its throne has been in near constant dispute since Carpe Noctem was released.

CLASS LIST

Melee

FURY – Fast, loud, and full of style. In the right hands, this class can dish out an impressive amount of damage. That is, if they can actually hit their targets.

Weapon: pistols

LEAF – At home sniping from the trees, this class will attack from where you least expect it.

Weapon: bows

COIN – Don't take your eyes off this class for a second, lest you find yourself a few items lighter. Coins excel at stealth and mobility.

Special equipment: grappling line

Weapon: daggers

BLADE – You can't argue with a classic. This swordsman class is best suited for attacking.

Weapons: sabers, rapiers, and katanas

SHIELD – Built to last, this class specializes in protecting others.

Special equipment: shield gauntlet

Weapon: straight swords

WHIP – A trainer class capable of keeping a familiar.

Weapon: whips

RAGE – Known for its capability to equip anything as a weapon, this class is built for all-out attacks.

Primary weapons: anything and everything

FIST – This unique class has two different paths. On one hand, the MONK is capable of infusing their hits with mana. On the other, the THUG is a brawler through and through.

Weapons: gloves, brass knuckles, and their bare hands

RAIN – Death from above. This class can use their mana to augment their movement, often launching themselves into the air to attack when least expected.

Weapon: polearms

Magic Users

BREATH MAGE – This frail but kind class can keep their party alive through whatever the world may throw at them.

Special equipment: casters

Weapons: clubs, canes, and additional casters

CAULDRON MAGE – Specializing in destruction, this mage class is slow but dangerous.

Special equipment: casters

Weapons: clubs, canes, and additional casters

VENOM MAGE – This mage class excels at slowing the enemy down, weakening a target, and causing damage over time.

Special equipment: casters

Weapons: clubs, canes, and additional casters